In the Shadow of

Babylon

A novel

John Schwartz

PUBLISHED BY JOSS INTERNATIONAL INC. 1ST EDITION
COPYRIGHT (C) 2011 JOHN M. SCHWARTZ
ALL RIGHTS RESERVED.
ISBN: 146110713X
EAN: 9781461107132

To Jill, the ultimate she-beast.
Without her this book would not exist.

(Prologue)

THE BEYOND (11,000 BCE)

My name is Ayuba. I am the shepherd of Hamood, father of Bynethia, master of the Ben, avenger of the twan, hero of the Gleb, protector of Bensheer, and son of the Beyond. This is my story.

I stood in the middle of our devastated camp, my eyes stinging, suffocating in the smoke of death. Hyenas circled on the edge of night snarling and yelping, the scent of blood exciting their hunger.

I ran through the camp in a futile search for survivors.

My father lay half exposed under the torn tent flap, felled before he could flee. The smoke from his smoldering beard covered his face like a fog. The wild dogs arriving before me had chewed his shoulder. My two uncles and brother lay at the edge of the spring, jagged spear wounds in their bellies and chests. They lay back to back, having died in defense of each other.

Blue-black flies, the scourge of the desert, swarmed over the bodies, lapping at the thickening blood. The snarling hyenas grew bolder, darting in and out of the swirling smoke. Swinging my staff wildly over my head, my grief turned to anger; I chased the cowardly beasts back into the night. Exhausted, I leaned on my staff, sucking in draughts of oily smoke. I retched, my body wracked with uncontrollable spasms. I fell to my knees. The smoke-stained sky pressed down on my small shoulders...they sagged under the unbearable weight of aloneness.

"Mother," I whispered to the charred form lying half in the fire pit. A small foot protruded from her punctured belly. Wiping the blood from the tiny leg, I took the toes in my hand and felt their softness. I wanted to trade places with the baby. To die in the warmth of my mother's womb, our hearts stopping as one, was a better choice than being alone in the pitiless place called the Beyond.

In the midst of the chaos I sat throughout the night holding the small foot, afraid to let this last contact with my family slip away. Everyone was accounted for except my three sisters who, no doubt, had been the target of this destruction. The crackling of smoldering skin and the whining of the hyenas punctured the silence. The crisp night air was fouled by the stench of burning flesh.

The warm rays of the sun fell on my back before I realized the horrible night had fled. Smoke stained the otherwise clear sky. As I sat paralyzed with grief, the dogs crept back into camp to feed on the corpses. Gently releasing the baby's foot, I grabbed my staff and once again vented my anger on the beasts. "We should have moved," I heard myself saying over and over through my sobs as I dragged the bodies of my family to the center of the smoldering ruins. Several days before, my uncles had argued strongly with my father that we had stayed too long at this oasis. There are few sources of water in the Beyond; eventually, they said, another tribe would seek out this place. Mistakes are punished harshly in the desert wilderness.

"We should have moved!" I screamed in anger while struggling to pull Father's charred remains from beneath the tent. Sweat mixed with tears blurred my vision. Without ceremony, I stacked mounds of dried fronds and camel weed atop the carcasses. What stirred my soul to such effort I know not. *We should have left...we should have left,* I thought like a death litany as I watched the flames consume all I had ever known.

As the smoke of my family billowed into the empty sky, I returned to the gorge where the afternoon before I had penned the goats. During the night the frightened animals had trampled the hastily constructed barrier and fled in fear of the howling hyenas. Perhaps because they were my responsibility, I felt their loss even more keenly than the destruction of my family. I stood for a long time looking at the empty pen as though my presence would somehow make my panicked charges return.

For the first time in my life I was alone. Surrounded by the hostile desert, the silent cliffs, and the endless sand. An undeniable weariness consumed me. I lay on the harsh shale and slept.

I do not know how long I lay unconscious. When I awoke, shadows were long and the sun was disappearing in the west. A thin coat of sand, blown by the predictable afternoon breeze, covered me.

Gathering my few belongings I blindly stumbled throughout the night and following day. I did not try to hide from predators or clans. I would have welcomed their violence to vanquish the numbness in my heart. I did not think of my family, although the foulness of their deaths still stained my nose and soiled my tunic. I did not drink or eat. Grief dulled my senses. My eyes were dry but unfocused. I frequently tripped and fell, lying still, aware only of my heart beating against the sand as though pleading with it to admit me to the bliss of death.

An angry slash of light at the edge of a leaden sky announced the arrival of night. The fiery resistance of

v

the sun awakened me from my stupor. Climbing among a wall of boulders, I took shelter beneath a stone shelf safely above the approaching parade of nocturnal predators.

As night suffocated the remainder of the day I squatted beneath the rough stone and cried. Hugging my knees to my chest, my sobs echoed across the vast, empty plain. Tears tracked small rivulets down my dusty legs. Like a dying beast I hurled my pain into the night.

Thirst dragged me from the bliss of unconsciousness. My body cramped, my vision was blurred, and my head throbbed. I found my small goat bladder, which in the confusion of the last two days I had failed to fill. Carefully I drank what little remained of the tepid water.

My small shepherd's kit contained a few nuts and a wedge of honeycomb. Chewing the sweet wax, I looked out over the barren plain. Nothing moved in the morning sun...not a bird or a lizard, not a leaf or blade of grass. It was as though I alone was capable of movement or sound.

How suddenly my life had changed. Three days before the violence, I had left the oasis to find adequate grazing for our small herd of goats. After three days alone with my charges, in happy anticipation of fresh meat and cool water, I turned toward the comfort of our camp. Gradually I noticed the goats begin to act strangely—their velvety noses turned to the sky, eyes darting in fear, bleating incessantly.

I looked skyward to check the weather. It was then I saw a distant smudge of smoke. More than the smoke of a campfire...it was heavy and oily, like blood.

I could not travel any faster than the herd and I dared not leave them to the mercy of predators. As the sun set, I drove the animals into a small, steep-walled canyon. I quickly threw up a screen of camel weed and other deadfall to keep the frightened goats penned while I rushed to see what had become of my family.

I forced my mind away from the horrible memory. The vision was too raw. Like butchered meat, it bled with a sadness I could not bear.

The land of my birth was populated by small nomadic tribes speaking many different languages. On the rare occasion that tribes met, they approached with great care. The only commerce between these extended families was in goats and women—both traded to improve the breeding stock of the tribe. The cold realities of life on the edge of the earth formed our patterns of existence. Each dawn brought the specter of destruction and each evening the relief of survival. Almost from the moment they could conceive, girls became pregnant and remained so until barren, if indeed they lived beyond their own fertility.

By age ten I joined the hard practicality of life as a clan male. I cannot recall ever playing a game. Singing and laughter were rare events. As strange as it sounds, when viewed from the perspective of life in a civilized society, the harshness of our lives forced us into a dependency of trust that defined our manhood. We knew each other's capabilities and weaknesses. We needed each other. The clan could only exist by working together. It was this honest assessment of each other that led to respect, if not love. This closeness of brotherhood nurtured me from childhood to puberty, defining my life.

Now it was gone. I realized that to live, I had to move out into the Beyond. I was alone.

(1)

"They always come in the middle of the night," whispered Amira, clutching the sheet beneath her chin.

"It's nothing, don't be alarmed," said her husband, pulling on his undershirt.

"How can you be so sure? They say it happens all the time."

"What do you mean...*it?*"

"You know exactly what I mean." Her lower lip shivered despite the suffocating heat.

Sitting on the edge of the bed he took her hands in his. "It's okay. It has happened before. You know that. It's always some stupid idea they think I can help with."

"Shhh," she whispered, holding her finger to her lips.

"They can't hear me, they're outside smoking."

"How can you be so calm?"

His voice smiled at her through the darkness. "Listen, my love, I'm just an old retired professor in an arcane specialty most people have never heard of... What possible use am I to these Ba'athist thugs? Go back to sleep. I'll probably be back before the call to morning prayers."

"Will you wake Zahra?"

"No, why disturb her. I'll be back before she's ready for school."

He kissed his wife lightly. The fear sweat on her forehead tasted bitter on his lips.

Slabs of soft muscle turning to fat jiggled as the tired-looking man flipped the cigarette over the wall separating Professor Elman Darshi's house from its neighbor in the middle-class district of Ar Rasafah.

"Ah, Professor, there you are. We were afraid you might have slipped out the back." The younger of the two men waiting on the sidewalk smirked at the thought of the old man trying to slip away. It irked him that the old geezer seemed unafraid. "Sometimes it's smart to try to escape," he sneered as he slipped the blindfold over Elman Darshi's eyes before opening the rear door of the ancient Mercedes.

It's all part of the fear package, thought Darshi. The hammering on the door in the middle of the night; no explanation, just "come with us." No ID, no reason proffered, blind obedience expected. It didn't matter if the minister just wanted someone to play cards with or if the victim was to be tortured for some real or imagined crime. It was always the same—they always came in the middle of the night.

There were no inside handles on the back seat doors. Big Muhammad and Little Muhammad (that's what Darshi named them in his mind) climbed into the front. The air conditioner wheezed as it struggled with the ninety-degree moisture-filled air of the Baghdad night.

Well, at least it's cool, he thought. Like most things under Saddam, cool air was a privilege to be controlled. A tool, a bribe used to hook a person like a narcotic. With electricity only available a few hours a week, air conditioning was a dream, far behind running water, lights, and refrigeration.

He was tired yet wide awake. Music blared from the dash. It was the same song that had played during his last visit...some sort of screeching Hindi movie theme only Bollywood could conceive. *It's all part of the fear package,* he thought. The bitter taste of bile rose in his throat. He'd experienced motion sickness even as a child and the blindfold made it worse. The smell of the urine-stained seat mixed with cigarette smoke made him want to vomit.

"Please," calling toward the front seat, "is it possible to open a window?" No response.

Darshi managed to keep it together until they reached their destination, the Ministry of Cultural Affairs. Climbing out of the back seat, humid air suffused with car exhaust burned his throat as he gave up the struggle to hold back the contents of his stomach.

"Oh shit, now look what you've done!" shouted Little Muhammad. His thin frame shook with anger as he grabbed Darshi by the shirt and pushed him against the car. "Look at the puke on my shoes, you old fart!"

Big Mo let out a laugh. "He can't see your shoes, you dumb fuck, he's blindfolded."

Embarrassed, Little Mo grunted, "He'll see 'em soon enough. When the minister's done with him he can lick them clean."

Darshi felt weak and confused as the two goons shoved him down an echo-filled hall. Yanking the blindfold off, Little Mo whispered, "See what you've done to my sandals?"

"I'm so sorry...the car ride made me sick."

"Yeah, well, not as sick as I'm going to make you before you leave...*If* you leave." Little Mo pushed the old man down onto a concrete bench running the length of the small, unadorned anteroom.

Darshi recognized the dull green walls broken only by the requisite photo of Saddam waving a shotgun while chomping on a cigar. Strangely, he was calmed by the familiarity of the place. He recalled the two other times he'd been yanked from his slumber by the minister. The first time he'd behaved badly, breaking into tears, clutching at their legs as they pulled him from the car, pleading with the guards to tell him why he was being imprisoned. He was embarrassed to think how weak he'd been.

He was especially ashamed when he discovered he'd been dragged from his bed to place a value on a small Sumerian statue. The assistant minister was not the least bit apologetic about the terror he'd caused. His only comment: "This is the personal business of the minister. You are not to say anything to anyone. Do you understand?" That was it. Back into the car, blindfolded, and dumped a couple of blocks from home. It was still dark! All so the minister could sell a priceless six thousand-year-old figurine on the black market. *Minister of culture indeed*, he thought.

The Muhammads sat on the bench across from Darshi. The smoke from their cigarettes filtered through their identical Saddam look-a-like mustaches. Bluish horsetail clouds of smoke layered the air. The professor slumped in his seat trying to find an uncontaminated layer in which to breathe.

The second summons had been even more bizarre. After the usual fear tactics, he was led to a small room with a tiny wooden desk, two chairs, a pressure pot of tea, and some pencils and paper. After waiting alone the remainder of the night he heard the amplified voice of the muezzin calling the faithful to morning prayers.

A stout lady, her head covered with a hijab, entered the room leading a sleepy-looking boy about age ten. "This is Hamid Bin Awase, the minister's eldest son," she said, stiffly pushing the boy toward the desk. "He needs some help with his homework."

The professor was dumbfounded. "Homework?"

"Not just any homework. After all, you are a big shot professor of ancient Iraqi—"

"*Retired* professor," interrupted Darshi.

"No matter. This homework is in your field of expertise."

Darshi looked at the boy staring back at him as though examining a slug. "Homework?" was all he could say.

"Actually it's the final term paper for the boy's graduation from level one to level two. So you see it's very important to the minister. I presume you can develop the paper from memory? We have no books here."

Of course, after all it's only the ministry of culture, thought Darshi.

The door opposite the one he had entered from the parking area opened and a smartly dressed man about thirty-five stepped into the room. "Professor, I'm so glad to meet you." His outstretched hand bore the unmistakable gold ring of the Iraqi Air Force Academy. "I've read many of your works," he said, shaking the professor's hand vigorously.

"You have?"

"That surprises you?" chuckled Colonel Abdullah. "I admit they are a bit obtuse and at times downright dull, but oh, what a light they shed on our glorious past." Guiding Darshi toward the door, the colonel turned to the Muhammads. "That will be all tonight. And oh yes…clean up that mess in the garage before you leave."

Big Mo stared at his feet, his head bobbing obsequiously. Little Mo gave a sharp nod toward the colonel, glaring at the professor.

The conference room was straight out of a Mozart era palace. Twelve cream-colored gilded chairs with velvet cushions graced a table the size of a squash court. No windows. The lower half of the wainscoted walls covered with fake wood grain vinyl paneling. The top half was festooned with photos of Saddam Hussein.

Colonel Abdullah motioned for Darshi to sit. The muted sound of the powerful air conditioner accompanied the sixty-cycle hum of a ceiling full of bare neon bulbs.

"Coffee?" asked the colonel, reaching for an enameled pressure pot.

"Yes, please."

"The minister will join us presently," he said, handing a Styrofoam cup across the table.

"The minister?"

"Yes. This is his private conference room. Surely you didn't think it was mine?" The colonel chuckled.

"No, no, of course not. It's just that the other times I've been here I've…uh…well…I've always dealt with…" His voice trailed off in uncertainty.

"Yes, I know. I've read your file," said Abdullah, picking up a manila folder lying on the table. "Foolish to waste the time of such an exalted academic. I must apologize. It was no doubt the overzealousness of some functionary in response to a request by the minister. Imagine asking you to do homework when a high school teacher would have served just as well."

Darshi could imagine the chain of events leading to his selection for the homework assignment. The minister casually mentions to an aide that his son needs tutoring in history. Seeing an opportunity to ingratiate himself with his boss, the aide orders his aide to find someone to help. Fearful of his boss's displeasure, the aide uses a cannon to kill a sparrow. *It is the way the world works under Saddam*, he thought.

People were not committed to the country or to a project, only to the next man in line—an unbroken fear chain of sycophants leading to the man in the pictures on the wall. *I wonder if it ever occurs to them*, Darshi thought, *that in a real world the kid would be responsible for his own results.*

"Please, Colonel, can you tell me why I'm here?"

"I will leave that to the minister." Smiling, he continued, "I can say for certain it won't be for a homework assignment."

When the minister entered unannounced, both the colonel and Darshi sprang to their feet. Taking a seat at the head of the table, the heavyset master of all things cultural said, "Let's get started."

"This is retired Professor Elman Darshi, the world's leading expert on ancient Sumerian and pre-Sumerian languages and the author of the leading textbooks on Assyrian, Eblaitian, and Akkadian. He is, I believe, uniquely qualified to assist with our project."

Without acknowledging the professor, the minister said, "Have you explained what we need?"

"No, sir. I thought you would want to do that."

For the first time, Minister Awase looked at Darshi. His gray eyes, hooded by immense shaggy brows, were dull—absorbing rather than reflecting the light. A prominent nose veined with cave-like nostrils drooped over a salt and pepper mustache.

"Professor, what I'm about to show you has only been seen by me and one other person…" Pausing for effect, "President Hussein. The president has asked me to personally take charge of this project. Even Colonel Abdullah has not seen these." Opening a red leather pouch marked *Top Secret*, the minister withdrew a sheaf of large black and white photos.

Darshi stared at the films.

"Well?"

"Please, sir…can you tell me what I'm looking at?"

"You cannot read it?"

Darshi felt the unspoken rebuke in the minister's voice. Avoiding the powerful man's stare he ventured, "Some symbols are familiar, but generally they are unlike anything I've seen." The photos were of panels of indeterminate size with the strange script carved into the surface.

"Surely, Professor, you've seen this writing before. You are, after all, the world's leading expert…or so says Colonel Abdullah." The minister's voice was as dull as his eyes.

"Look again…" urged the colonel. "Take your time." Darshi noticed a thin bead of sweat on the colonel's lip.

"Yes…take whatever time you need," said the minister, pushing back his chair. "Colonel, come to my office when you're finished." Before either man could rise, the minister left the room trailing a cloud of disappointment.

As soon as the door shut the colonel said, "Professor, you do understand what just happened?"

"What do you mean?"

"This is an order directly from Saddam."

"Of course, Colonel. I understand the president is interested in the results, but…"

"Interested? Don't be so naïve, Professor. The president," he said, pointing to the picture on the wall, "demands results." The colonel's voice had taken on a theatrical air as though performing before an audience.

"I will of course do my best for the president," offered Darshi weakly.

The two men spent the next twenty minutes examining the photos. Irritated at the colonel's lack of understanding, the professor finally said, "Colonel...this is an entirely new language, at least to me. Unless you want to call in someone else you will have to be more patient. Look," he said, pointing to one of the photos, "some characters appear to be cuneiform, perhaps Eblaite? Yet others are almost Semitic. Without knowing the date of the panels it is impossible to know whether these might be pre-Akkadian."

"It is not *my* patience that should concern you," said the colonel, seeking Darshi's eyes.

His back and neck aching from the tension of the morning, the professor slid his chair back from the table. Flexing his arms and legs he said, "I understand your position, Colonel, but without more information, without context, it is impossible."

"What do you mean by *context?*"

"Come, come, Colonel...the who, what, when, where, and why. Of course I understand the minister may not have this information, but perhaps we can interview those who do. Barring that, can we examine the actual panels?"

"I can tell you one thing for certain, Professor, you will never know the why. Where these panels are located, perhaps...how and when they were found or created maybe...but the why will be known only to Saddam," said the colonel in a whisper.

The great secret society, thought Darshi, *Everything is a secret.* For a time, even his books on the world's oldest languages were reviewed by a special committee to determine if they should be classified as state secrets. It was only after Dr. Gudabi, curator of the Iraq Museum of Ancient History, appeared before the tribunal explaining that Professor Darshi's books were in every university library in the world did the committee of reclassification decide it would be futile to restrict access.

Standing, the colonel said, "I will talk with the minister. In the meantime some food will be sent in."

"Thank you, Colonel...but a toilet would be more helpful."

∾×∾

"Professor...Professor."

Darshi felt a hand shake his shoulder. "Sorry...after eating," he said, gesturing toward the tray at the end of the table, "I waited for some time then I must have..." He paused. "Colonel is something wrong?"

The look of confidence that had so impressed him when they first met was gone. The colonel's eyes were unfocused, his lips pursed, his nostrils flaring with each breath. Sitting heavily on a chair across from Darshi, the colonel stared blankly at the table.

"What's wrong, Colonel? Are you unwell?"

Lifting his head, the colonel stared at the professor. Slowly he brought his index finger to his pale lips, signaling for silence. Drawing a tablet and pencil in front of him he began writing and speaking at the same time, his voice uncharacteristically harsh.

"Professor, I cannot accept any excuses. As the top man in your field we expect you to translate this script no matter how long it takes." Darshi started to object, but once again the colonel motioned for silence while writing furiously.

"If you need books or reference materials I will get them for you. You are assigned to this department until the job is done...do I make myself clear?" Darshi wondered what could have happened to this sophisticated, pleasant young man after leaving the room.

"Have I made it clear what the president expects from you?" the colonel said, sternly pushing the tablet across the table. In bold letters it said, AGREE!

Darshi looked into the colonel's fearful eyes, "Yes, Colonel, I understand."

Tapping his finger on the tablet the colonel said, "Good...now I want you to take a few moments to review the notes we made this morning."

Darshi read the Colonel's hasty scrawl: THERE ARE NO SURVIVORS. LABORERS WHO DISCOVERED THE PANELS AND THE PHOTOGRAPHERS...ALL DEAD. SADDAM PARANOID ABOUT THREATS FROM PAST. AGREE TO TRANSLATE BUT STALL. OUR LIVES ARE IN DANGER...EVEN MINISTER IS AFRAID.

Darshi's mouth tasted like metal as he fought back the fuming bile in his throat. His hand shook as he took the pencil and wrote: WHERE CAN WE TALK?

"Here are the rules, Professor," said the colonel, drawing the tablet across the table. "All work is to be done in this building. I will assign you an office and provide anything you need. You are not to bring anything into or remove anything from this building. Is that clear?" The colonel again scribbled on the pad.

"Yes."

Turning the pad toward Darshi, he continued, "You are not to mention this project to anyone...not your family, friends, colleagues. The minister and I are the only people you can discuss this with. Is that absolutely clear?" DO AS I SAY. I WILL CONTACT YOU.

Glancing up from the pad, the professor replied, "I will speak to no one."

"Go now. A car will pick you up each morning after Azhan and deliver you home at sunset until the project is successfully completed. *Assalamu alaikum.*"

"Peace be upon you also," whispered Darshi, watching the colonel stuff the tablet into his briefcase while leaving the room.

❧

In a spacious apartment on the edge of the University of California Berkeley campus, an impish Iraqi grad student named Jamilah gestured toward the TV and cried out, "Allah be praised!"

"What are you praising?" said a girl slouched on the couch with a notebook computer on her lap. Tom Wait's unmistakable voice leaked from the headphones as she pulled them away from her ears.

"What a hunk! Alexandria, come here…I just found you a man!" Jammy called without taking her eyes from the screen.

"I don't need any…wow, who's that?" Coming from the kitchen, Alexandria wiped her hands with a dishtowel. Perching with one leg on the edge of the sofa she said, "Turn it up."

A man of Middle Eastern descent who appeared to be in his early thirties was being interviewed by a well-known newswoman from Fox News.

Smiling, he answered a question, his dark eyes sparkling with intelligence. "Yes, of course I'm surprised. Not just because you're interviewing me, but by your very presence." His chiseled lips parted, revealing perfectly white teeth. "It's not often we attract national coverage in our obtuse field."

"That may have been true in the past, Professor, but after 9/11, Afghanistan, and now Iraq, the history of the Middle East has become increasingly relevant."

"Did you hear that?" squealed Noora, the stunning Kuwaiti roommate of the two Iraqi students. Peeling off her earphones she said, "Middle Eastern history…my major!"

"Shush!" the other girls said in unison.

"The purpose of the American Middle East Society is to bring together academics from throughout the U.S. for a frank exchange of information about current events in the region."

"What does a professor of Middle Eastern history at the prestigious School of Oriental Studies at the University of Chicago have to contribute regarding current events? Seems a little out of your field," the pretty blond interviewer asked.

The professor smiled. "Look, Marilyn, you're going to get me in trouble with my boss. I'm an *associate* professor."

"Sorry." She smiled.

"Oh god, she's going to gush all over him," cried Jammy, pulling off her jogging shoes.

The professor continued, "There are current events even in history, although I admit that's a bit of an oxymoron. I've just returned from my first trip to Iraq following the invasion. At the conference I presented a paper on the decline of Babylon under Saddam's rule."

"He has no accent…he must be second-generation American," mused Alexandria.

"Who cares? He's gorgeous!" Noora said, moving her feet to make room for Alex as she slid down onto the couch.

"Will you return to Iraq anytime soon?"

"I hope so. It is, after all, the birthplace of civilization. There are so many unexplored treasures to investigate. In fact, the day before I returned to the States, the Iraq Museum of Ancient History announced that the U.S. military had discovered a tomb. Of course it's not that unusual to find a new tomb in this region, but evidently this one contained panels inscribed with a language never seen before."

Alexandria's eyes widened. Her hand covered her mouth. She didn't hear Jammy say, "Too bad he's so far away...it's a long way from Berkeley to Chicago."

✧

Returning from church by bus on a Sunday morning, Professor Darshi was surprised when a woman in an Afghani-style burka carrying a large shopping bag wheezed herself into the seat next to him. Although this extreme Islamic dress was not unprecedented in Iraq, it was unusual. Completely covered by the heavy black robe, the woman's hands were hidden by black cotton gloves and her eyes shielded behind the garment's woven grill. Darshi thought how he often joked with his wife that if she misbehaved he'd convert from Christianity to Islam just to get even with her.

"Doctor." The voice was so faint Darshi wasn't sure he'd actually heard someone speak. "Professor, don't look at me and don't speak." The colonel's muffled voice was softened by the thick fabric of the burka. Darshi looked through the grimy bus window. Visibility was limited by an early spring storm blowing swirls of sand down the side streets.

As if reading the professor's mind, the colonel whispered, "We are being watched."

Darshi quickly glanced over his shoulder.

"Don't do that! Keep looking out the window and just listen. You may think I'm being too cautious…" *He's reading my mind,* thought Darshi. "Well, I'm not. Think of the worst rumor you've heard about Saddam…random killings, rape rooms, torture…it's all true. He lives in constant fear. His paranoia is legendary. In the palace he's building in Babylon he's installed a huge portrait of himself and Nebuchadnezzar at the entrance to the ruins. On the bricks being used to rebuild the temple he's inscribed *Built by Saddam Hussein, son of Nebuchadnezzar.*"

The professor let out a sigh. Having spent most of his life trudging through the dusty annals of history, he'd read about this sort of megalomania many times.

"Before being assigned to the cultural ministry I served as an aide to Saddam's son, Uday. Even he claims his father is crazy. I once overheard him talking with his brother about Saddam visiting some sort of oracle who told him the past would destroy him, not the West. Saddam had this shaman, or whatever he was, crushed beneath the wheels of his jeep. He kept driving over the man until he was nothing more than a stain. All the while yelling 'I am the son of Nebuchadnezzar!'"

The professor hunched his shoulders, quietly asking, "Why are you telling me this?"

"You are an academic…you have been sheltered from the realities of life under this monster, but now you have been sucked into his maw. I want to scare you. I want you to begin using that fine mind of yours to think of ways to delay the final translation of the panels.

As long as we are needed, we are safe. More importantly, once the translation is finished, you must read it with paranoia and try to fathom if it could in anyway be taken as a curse or threat to this butcher." Darshi shuddered at the epithet only whispered in private.

"Everyone connected with this project has been murdered. He will not hesitate to kill us. You must do all you can to shelter your family. If possible, get them out of the country."

The burka-clad figure reached over Darshi, pulling the signal cord to stop the bus. "Take this same bus every Sunday," whispered the colonel. Gathering up his shopping bag, he moved toward the exit.

Darshi rested his forehead against the glass, staring out the window. *The colonel's right,* he thought, *I have lived a sheltered life.* Like most academics at the university he had heard rumors…only distant fears easily ignored. Until now.

(2)

HAMRABI (11,000 BCE)

For two cycles of the seasons after the slaughter of my family, I wandered aimlessly in the Beyond, living like the creatures of the desert. I licked dew from stones and ate what I could find...lizards, grass, grubs, and the occasional stolen goat. Carefully avoiding all humans I moved constantly in search of food and water. As a lone male, my life represented nothing more than an unwanted mouth to feed to the clans of the Beyond. Even on the coldest nights, I built no fire. My goatskin tunic became shredded and was eventually discarded, leaving me a naked, furless animal.

Water was my greatest need. The Beyond has few oases, and the nomadic bands that populate the barren vastness visit these frequently. The sun bore down on me like a great weight, pressing my body dry. Rain was a distant dream, teasing the land like a ghost...disappearing as quickly as it came.

On nights when the sun's track was far to the north, the desert grew bitterly cold. In place of fire, I often dug a pit and covered myself with warm sand. Only my head was exposed, covered with scraps from my shredded tunic.

One morning, cosseted in my burrow as the first rays of the winter sun began to find the earth, I was stunned by a sharp blow to my head. I let out a yelp. Struggling to free myself from my sandy coffin I was struck again, this time by a tremendous weight on my stomach. The sounds of men shouting penetrated the fog of my fear.

As suddenly as it came, the weight was removed. Gasping for air, I saw a huge camel standing over me snorting and stomping. Strong hands grabbed me by the hair and yanked me to my feet. Two men shouted at me in an unfamiliar language while the camel continued to hiss and spit. Another blow struck me behind the ear. Blackness again seeped over my eyes.

It was late afternoon when I awoke. All I could see was the desert floor slowly passing by. Goat hair ropes tightly bound me. There was no feeling in my arms or legs. Trussed like a bundle of reeds, I was strapped to the camel's harness. My eyes were crusted and my mouth sealed with dried blood. Dust clogged my nose. Struggling to breathe, I slipped back into unconsciousness.

I was jarred awake in the early evening as I was unstrapped from my disagreeable host. When my captors—two nomadic reed gatherers—loosened my bonds I tried to stand but the pain of a thousand burs made it impossible to put weight on my feet.

The older of the two men had a withered arm. He began collecting camel dung and twigs for a fire. The other man, not much older than me, had a foggy eye. He made a noose and roughly forced it over my head, tying the other end around my ankles. I lay face down in the sand with my legs bent at the knees. If I tried to straighten my legs, the noose tightened, choking me.

As night pushed its way into the remnants of the scalding sun, a young girl with straggly hair and sad eyes laid a gourd of soup near my head and scampered back to the safety of the fire. Rolling on my side, I grasped the gourd. The broth soothed my swollen lips and tongue, filling me with hope.

At dawn, the one-eyed man rolled me onto my stomach and unfastened the rope around my ankles.

I screamed when I straightened my legs. He made a grunting sound, pulling me to my feet. I stood hunched like an old man. He then tied the loose end of the rope to the kneeling camel's cinch. When the camel stood, the place where my tether was fastened was far above my head. The man tightened the noose, prodded the camel, and we started across the fractured plain.

Our small caravan consisted of four camels—a young male, an old shaggy bull, and the she-beast, all laden with bundles of reeds. The fourth camel was an unburdened calf still dependent on its mother's teat. Two donkeys carrying tents and camp gear followed behind.

Nightly, with only a gourd of broth to nourish me, I lay naked on the sand unprotected from the bitter cold. All day I trotted alongside the angry she-beast. Trying to protect her offspring, she kept me at the end of my tether, causing the noose to blister and burn my skin. I grew weak. The nightly broth was not enough to keep me alive for long.

The she-beast's offspring also found the pace of our march difficult. Trying to suckle while on the move, it whined and groaned while its mother plodded across the splintered trail.

Watching this tragic comedy several times each day, it slowly occurred to me that a source of sustenance was at hand. Even people of the Beyond knew camel milk to be richer than goat milk. Unfortunately, the she-beast protected its source vigorously and would not let me near it or her calf.

My captors seemed not to notice or care that I was slowly wasting away under the blistering sun and freezing nights. The wound on my neck festered, oozing a foul-smelling sap onto my chest.

On the morning of the eighth day of my captivity our caravan paused while the men adjusted the bundles. The calf urinated noisily while suckling. Stupidly, I stared at the foaming puddle. It sparkled with golden bubbles in the harsh light. Slowly, I recalled a trick my father taught me when I was first learning to care for our goats. When a she-goat with young died we rubbed the orphaned kid with the urine of a nursing calf so the kid's mother would accept the orphan at her teat.

Quickly, before the urine evaporated, I scooped up the wet sand and rubbed it on my body and hair. Once the caravan began to move, I inched closer to the grumpy female. She started to snap but stopped suddenly. She looked confused, her large nostrils working vigorously to sort out the difference between what her eyes saw and her nose smelled. Twice more during the day I was able to capture the calf's discharge to strengthen my scent.

That night after drinking my soup, I inched closer to the dozing camel. Soon I lay against her heaving side. Her large, soft nostrils brushed against me several times as she gradually accepted me, and for the first time since my capture, I slept warmly against the great creature's belly.

The following day I continued to stumble along although now closer to my adopted mother. The calf too seemed to accept me, nudging me playfully. In the late afternoon we had an unexpected halt in our march to wait for the herd of goats. My adopted sibling used this pause to take her fill. As soon as she finished, I slipped beneath the giant beast and took the warm, wet nipple in my mouth.

The rich milk flowed faster than I could swallow. I slurped nosily, relishing the life-giving liquid. The sticky fluid ran down my chest and across my groin. Soon my stomach was ready to burst. I crept from under the innocent creature, confident I could now survive whatever lay ahead.

I had been a prisoner of the reed gatherers for a moon's cycle when one morning the young goat herder scurried into camp, screaming and gesturing toward the eastern horizon. The men hid their meager possessions between the resting camels. With only slings for weapons, the girl gathered fist-sized stones from a nearby gully and piled the ammunition at the men's feet. The older of my captors quickly bound my hands.

Straining my eyes toward the east, I could see nothing but the low morning shadows as the orb of life rose from the edge of night. Suddenly, like the flicker of a bird's wing, I saw a shadow on the horizon. Over the next hour the apparition grew recognizable—it was a lone rider on a camel, heading straight for our camp.

When the stranger was within hailing distance, he dismounted. He wore a garment like none I'd seen before, more of a robe than a tunic, made from some sort of animal skin finer and more flexible than the skins worn by my family or captors. It billowed about him even in the slight breeze. Its deep blue color reminded me of my mother's eyes.

Standing on a small dune, the stranger lifted his garment over his head and slowly turned around, displaying his naked body. Silhouetted by the sun with his robe above his head, he looked like a huge bird preparing for flight. I had never seen such an odd greeting, but my captors were evidently pleased by his strange dance. They began shouting while they too lifted their tunics, laughing and dancing in evident joy. I later learned this was the common way civilized peoples demonstrated to strangers that they carried no weapons and approached with peaceful intent.

As the man led his mount toward our camp, I began to see his features more clearly. Although similar to my captors—dark complexion, black hair and blacker eyes, prominent nose, jutting jaw—he was at the same time different from them or any other I had seen. His hair and beard were carefully trimmed and flecked with gray. The hair was plaited in the back and must have been oiled, for it glimmered in the morning light.

His demeanor too was different. Although he wore a loose-fitting robe, his shoulders bulged at their margins. His posture was upright and proud. My captors, by comparison, were stooped and worn.

The reed gatherers were obviously delighted at the prospect of the visitor. They quickly killed and spitted a kid, and the girl drew fresh milk. Skins were placed around the fire…clean sides up. The stranger's mount was settled with a gourd of grain near our small herd. It too was different. Its coat was a cream color and had a fine texture. It strutted with the same sureness and mystery as its master. As the sun rose in the blank desert sky, crude shelters were quickly raised. It became obvious this would become a much-welcomed day of rest.

When the she-beast stood to nurse her calf, I followed and drank my fill. With a full belly and no prospect of travel, I hollowed out a bed in the sand as best I could with my bound hands and went to sleep in the shade of the camel's hump.

A hard kick to my ribs woke me. The man with the withered arm tugged on the rope around my neck, leading me away from the she-beast. On the far side of the old bull, he forced me to lie on my face, tying the bitter end of my noose to my ankles. I could barely move without strangling. As soon as I was alone, I rolled to one side and peered beneath the bull's neck. The she-beast was no longer kneeling.

I heard, but could not see, the stranger's mount rise. Loud voices mingled with his soft but firm voice in what I assumed were farewells. The forelocks of the white camel came into view as it plodded past.

To my horror, the she-beast, with calf in tow, turned and followed the stranger. She struggled at her confinement, looking back toward camp.

Without meaning to I cried out, "No!" Desperately trying to stand, I gagged, the noose strangling me. Through tear-filled eyes I watched the source of my survival turn toward the horizon. "Mother," I whispered.

My captors chatted happily around the fire, sucking at the bones left from the feast. I lay with my head on the sand. Night fell as my tears watered the desert's uncaring heart.

Deep in the starless night on the edge of sleep, a soft breeze tickled and caressed me. Images of my mother fogged my dream. In the Beyond, we called these night-time entertainments "visitations." We never questioned the reality of dreams or their source and often sought them out as an escape from the desperateness of our lives.

I heard my mother's laughter and felt the gentleness of her cheek against mine. The sweet smell of roasting goat filled me with hunger. I groaned at the unfamiliar sense of well-being, a feeling I had never before experienced so completely. Now all the small pleasures scattered over time came together in one great balm washing over me, healing the lonesome wounds in my heart.

The dream breeze grew louder, tugging at my ear. The laughter of my family transformed into the amused chuckle of the bearded stranger who had stolen my security. I tried to force myself back into the bliss of sleep, but the voices grew louder and the sound of the desert wind blew away my dream.

I opened my eyes. At first I thought I had slipped from one visitation to another as I looked into the huge brown eye of the she-beast. She nuzzled me with a mother's tenderness. Her breath roared in my ear as she gently nibbled at my lobe.

Momentarily forgetting the noose around my neck, I threw my arms around the great camel and held her huge head close to my chest. The beast turned toward the noisy confusion nearby where my two captors were trying to subdue the calf trampling through bundles of reeds and camp gear. The bearded stranger sat atop his beautiful mount and roared with laughter.

In the excitement, my noose tightened and I blacked out. When I regained my senses the stranger was leaning over me, gently patting my face. Then he cut my bonds. I gasped, sucking in as much of the morning desert air as I could while retching and coughing.

The smiling stranger who slashed the primitive goat hair noose unknowingly severed the bonds of ignorance and fear that had dominated my life since birth. It was the first unselfish human act I had experienced since the slaughter of my family. It is only now, recounting these events of my youth, I realize how vital this small act was to my future. It was so unexpected that had not the she-beast taken charge by pushing me toward her teat, I would not have moved although unbound for the first time since my captivity.

Sated, I stepped back from the great beast and watched as the stranger took command of the chaos within the camp. In short order he calmed the calf, loosely strapping it to its mother. The bundles were restored and mounted to the camels and the camp was put to order. An animated conversation took place between the stranger and the elder reed gatherer. As the sun breached the horizon the men embraced, having settled their differences amicably. The stranger said something to me as he mounted his majestic beast festooned with colorful tassels and an elaborate riding carpet. The tassels were the color of the night jay's throat and the carpet was dazzling in its variety of hues and patterns. The great she-beast, reloaded with reeds, was roped to the stranger's mount. The man headed west out of camp with the calf scampering behind. Untethered, I stood watching as once again the source of my salvation was led away. The reed gatherers interrupted my despair by roughly pushing me toward the departing caravan. I did not understand what they intended, until turning in his saddle, the stranger motioned for me to follow.

Joy and fear attended me instantly. No longer bound, I could flee to the vastness surrounding me. I knew how to survive in the hostile desert. Being fleet of foot, given half a step I could outrun my captors.

What stayed this natural instinct? What force wobbled on the edge of my mind and whispered, *Don't run toward the past. Follow the stranger. It is the way of hope.*

Frozen with indecision, my heart pounding, a groan rose from my throat. Glancing at the stranger, I turned toward the Beyond.

There was amusement and sadness in the stranger's gaze. *I have set you free,* said his eyes. *Will you follow me or flee to your empty past?* I hesitated. My heart calmed and tears blurred my vision as I turned toward him—and the unknown.

Shortly before dark we came to a small oasis. It was a poor affair, more like a puddle than a true desert spring. There were a few shrubs with many animal and human tracks baked into the brittle clay of the receding shore.

The man sat motionless, his black eyes surveying the area. From high upon his mount he could see a great distance. Tracks of hyena, camel, wild dog, and goat led toward the small pond. On the far side, where the water edged close to an embankment formed by an ancient river, day-old tracks of a herd of ibex confused the shore. Sniffing the air, I searched for telltale scents.

The man dismounted. After drinking his fill, he removed the goatskin bag from his mount and carefully filled it. He indicated that I should drink from the pond. The sight of the water was so inviting (even though muddied by the calf we'd been unable to contain) I dropped all caution and ran to the pool. Kneeling on the wet foreshore, dipping my hands in the cool water, I drank with unfettered joy.

The man showed no intention of building a fire. Normally I would never sleep near an oasis as it drew many night predators. I was relieved when the man mounted his camel and began to lead our small party up the embankment into the moonless night.

What joy to walk freely under a sky punctuated by countless stars! Streaks of light flamed across the speckled dome. As a shepherd, the great formations in the night sky often entertained me...I was comforted to find they followed me like constant companions.

The man seemed entranced by the glittering bowl as well. He pointed to formations and called out their names in his strange language. Presently he began to sing. Although I could not understand the words, his song pushed back the darkness and wove its melody among the stars. My exhaustion vanished and tears welled in my eyes as my heart filled with a long-forgotten emotion—the joy of simple human contact.

We walked throughout the night and next morning with only brief breaks. The sun neared its zenith as we approached a vast stand of trees. In my entire life I had never seen more than a dozen trees at one oasis. To see so many at one time was exciting and a bit frightening.

This was an unusual oasis; the trees were standing in rows instead of the random clumps found at most watering holes. The transition from bright sun to the dark, cool shade of the grove caused me to shiver.

The man whistled sharply. This confused me as one usually approaches an oasis as quietly as possible. In the distance I heard a reply to the man's whistle like an echo.

Peering down the row of trees I saw a boy running toward us, laughing and waving his arms. The man dismounted and shouted something to the boy.

Just before the boy reached us he stopped suddenly, having caught sight of me, his brow knitting with fear. Pointing at me, he asked the man something and the man apparently assured him I meant no harm.

The boy hesitantly approached, keeping one eye on me as if I might attack. The man scooped him up in his arms and the two of them laughed and hugged. The warmth of their reunion filled me with an intense feeling of aloneness. I had never been greeted as the man greeted the boy. To my knowledge a human being had never missed or desired me. I wanted to be that boy.

Tears came unbidden to my eyes. I stood in the grove naked, my body wizened from the harshness of the Beyond, my stomach distended from constant hunger. My hair fell in tangles across my scarred and burnt shoulders. My desperate hunger, burning thirst, and crushing exhaustion paled compared to my need for affection.

The man put the boy down and motioned for me to come forward. My feet felt heavy, my legs weak. Approaching these two mysterious beings, my heart thumped. Pointing at the boy (who was slightly younger than me) the man said, "Frion." I must have looked confused as the boy then pointed to himself and repeated in a strong, sure voice, "Frion."

Thus it was I learned my first word in the language common to all peoples outside the Beyond. It was the name of the boy who would become my friend and brother.

The man spoke to Frion who immediately removed his robe and handed it to me. Having only worn the skins of animals, the cloth was surprisingly light. I held the robe to my face, feeling its softness. Now wearing only a breechclout, Frion slipped the robe over my head. I shivered as it caressed my sunscorched body.

Frion again pointed at himself, saying "Frion." Then he pointed at me with a questioning look on his face. I stood staring into his eyes. Furiously I searched my memory for a name I must have had but could no longer remember. Overwhelmed and confused, my tongue was dry as sand and would not move.

Stepping forward, the man gently placed his hand on my shoulder saying, "Ayuba." Smiling on the edge of a laugh, Frion repeated, "Ayuba."

And so it was that I became Ayuba...camel boy.

Leading the camels, the man started down the path between the palms. Shortly we came to a substantial clearing with a large center structure. I had never seen a house before, having dwelt only in tents and caves.

Several people ran to embrace the man. There was much laughter and cheerfulness. The women were tall with light-colored hair and dark eyes. A boy named Pitoon, who appeared older than Frion led the camels to a small pond at the far side of the house. The rest of the family—a woman I assumed was the man's wife and Frion's mother, a comely girl about my age called Linta, al Summers only daughter, and an ancient woman who exuded great dignity despite her age, greeted me as an honored guest rather than a wild foundling from the Beyond.

Looking back through a tunnel of shade toward the desert of my past, I could see the noonday heat shimmering in the distance. Stepping from the harshness of the Beyond into the coolness of an unknown future, my fear of these remarkable humans abated in the warmth of their generosity.

The village was called Hamrabi and the country, Hamood. It was my good fortune to be rescued by Aroon al Sumer, the western gatekeeper of the Hamoodian government. In his official capacity he was charged with patrolling a large section of the border separating Hamood from the Beyond.

On the edge of the date grove was a small herd of exquisite camels. Since time beyond the songs of Hamrabi, the al Sumer family bred these remarkable beasts. Traders from all over Hamood and Bynethia came to buy or trade for al Sumer camels. The she-beast was now stabled with this small but elegant herd.

The elite pedigreed camels shunned her and her calf. Her shaggy appearance belied her beauty—even among beasts there is arrogance and prejudice.

The camels of Hamrabi are well fed. Fronds and stems left from the date harvest are chopped and mixed with the leaves, roots, and stalks from vegetable gardens. The camels maintain a great love for bitterbrush, that wild and thorny king of empty spaces, more commonly called camel weed. This strange plant survives where nothing else can. When the wind blows, its tenuous roots easily detach from the sandy soil. Free, it sails and tumbles over the desert, its seeds drifting to new life on the wind.

Hamrabians have a unique method of harvesting substantial amounts of this noxious weed. Beyond the oasis in a depression formed by an ancient river, the wind funnels in constant fury. Strung across this barren and gravelly wash is a single goatskin rope with the hair still attached. Suspended waist high, this hairy vine snags one of the flying bitterbrush balls, then another, and another, and within a short time, thousands of these interlocking weeds form a great wall across the old streambed.

I had lived in Hamrabi for more than four years. Almost from the beginning it was my job to haul this thorny feast to the camel herd after the midday break. This day, however, was different.

The ground groaned when touched by the first rays of the day. The harsh edge of sunrise pressed against my back as I headed toward the catchment. Small stones cast long shadows ahead of me.

Although I carried only my sheaving knife, my step was labored as though carrying a great weight. The burden fogging my vision and pressing upon my chest was the death of my adopted grandmother, Marun.

She was the oldest person I had ever known. People in the Beyond rarely lived past two score cycles of the sun—Marun lived almost five times longer. I had seen older members of my previous tribe die in battle...in the agony of starvation...but never anyone who died in their sleep. To be perfectly healthy one day and then, without warning, die during the night was new to me. I felt a strange sense of abandonment at her passing. Reaching the camel weed barrier I sat on the edge of the windy defile. With sightless eyes I stared out over the trap and thought of Marun.

As matriarch, it had fallen to her to educate me in the history and customs of clan and country. Although she lived her entire life in Hamrabi, hard on the edge of the Beyond, I was the first person she'd met who came from that mysterious land. Each morning from first cockcrow until the sun drove everyone into the shade for a midday rest I worked with and learned from Marun.

She taught me the names of fruits, vegetables, and animals. If a name for the item existed in my limited "Beyond" vocabulary, she would repeat it carefully—learning my language so she could teach me hers. I had little to offer, but her love of knowledge was so great she treated each grain of information as though it was a rare gem to be safely stored in the vault of her mind. In a short time, Grandmother knew my entire vocabulary whereas it took me a long time to feel comfortable speaking her native tongue.

I recalled how she once questioned me in detail about the different colors of shale strata forming a great bench that ran as far as the eye could see across the heart of the Beyond. I described the black soft bands layered with turquoise stripes and ocher-colored seams. She wanted to know in what order the colors appeared…was the black on top, followed by the turquoise?

I laughed, saying, "Grandmother, what possible use is that knowledge to you? Even if I could remember, why is it important?"

She looked at me for a long time with a thoughtful smile on her leathery face. I knew this look meant she was trying to put a thought into words I could understand—a thought with a meaning beyond the physical, some bit of understanding she had come to fathom over time that could help me make the great leap from simply surviving to thriving.

"When wandering the Beyond how did you spend your days?" she asked softly, squinting through her wrinkled brown eyes as she tied a bunch of herbs for drying.

"Looking for food and water."

"What kind of food did you look for most often?"

"Lizards were my favorite because they were the most filling, but I would take anything."

"On days you found ample food, did you stop hunting until you became hungry again?"

"No, Grandmother. I was always looking for food."

"Even when you weren't hungry?" she asked, pushing back her thick white hair.

"Yes, even then," I replied, wondering where she was going with this line of questioning.

"Knowledge is like food, Ayuba. Even when you think you are full you continue to gather it. Harvesting knowledge is what separates us from the beasts," she said, patting the old donkey we were loading with herbs and vegetables.

"But why gather knowledge that has no use, Grandmother? The banding of the great bench has no use to you that I can see. So why carry that information in your head?"

"When searching for food did you ever pick up a seed or nut you were not sure was edible?" she asked.

"Oh yes, many times. There was no one to tell me what was edible."

"And did you eventually taste the unknown seed or the nut?"

"Of course! I was always hungry."

"Before you tasted the new food, did you look closely at it so you would recognize it in the future?" she prodded carefully, her gnarled fingers twisting the stems from a bunch of radishes.

"Yes, Grandmother, I needed to know what to look for or avoid in the future." I wondered if I had missed some nuance in her speech. Her interest in what I ate while wandering in the desert was a mystery.

The wizened old woman took my hand as we started toward the clay storage well where we dried and kept the vegetables.

"Just like food, one can never gather too much knowledge, and just like food, one must carefully examine what one puts in one's mind so it can be recognized in the future. I am an old woman and I know not if I will ever again meet someone from the Beyond...but if I do before I die or perhaps in the afterlife, I will tell them of my grandson, Ayuba, and describe how you ran from the hyenas beneath the great turquoise and ocher bench, and they will know that you are real."

I thought about this for some time. The chances of her meeting someone else from the Beyond in her lifetime were small...but who knows what happens after death?

"Grandmother, are you saying all knowledge should be stored, regardless of its usefulness?"

"All knowledge is useful even though we may not perceive its use when we gather it," she said, pausing to tighten the strap on the donkey, a warm smile wrinkling the skin around her eyes. "You act as though you are afraid your brain will get stuffed if you don't carefully choose what and how much you feed it!"

I laughed at her insight. "You're the one who keeps comparing knowledge to food! Are you saying I cannot fill my mind like I fill my stomach?"

"Exactly. The mind is like the desert and knowledge like the streams that flow from the springs and the rain that falls from the sky. No matter how much the desert drinks, it is never full."

It was the moaning of the great bundle of camel weed straining against its bond that tugged me back from the sweet thoughts of Marun. Unknowingly, I had been sitting next to the dry riverbed for most of the day. I was startled to see the goat hair rope was about to break. Normally I untied the rope at both ends and dragged the prickly ball (which was very light despite its size) to wherever the herd was grazing. This ball, however, was a snarling beast taller than a palm tree and angrily pushing at the confining banks.

Quickly I withdrew my sheaving sickle to slash the rope where it was anchored to a boulder. The rope was so taught I barely nicked it when it snapped and flew toward the far bank, releasing its hold on the vast wall of weeds.

The wind gusted with its customary afternoon vigor. The mass of weeds began to roll down the dry channel. A million tiny thorns and branches gouged the sandy floor of the ancient waterway, displacing fine grains of sand that joined the great tumbling ball as the wind pushed it faster and faster.

A short distance downstream, the wash made a sudden turn to the south. The rumbling mass hit the far bank at the bend, launching it into the air like an angry cloud. A fierce gust of wind caught it, pushing it higher and higher toward the Beyond. I laughed as I thought of what some clan in the wastes of the far desert would think seeing this snarling mass of camel weed sailing across the sky!

The shadows were long by the time I located the camel herd. I walked through the drowsy beasts talking softly to them. I told them of Marun's passing and whispered her name so it would be carried with them wherever they went. I sang the songs Marun had taught me—songs of the desert and sky, of far-off lands filled with gods and wonders only dreamed of in Hamrabi.

The she-beast lay slightly apart from the other animals. She snorted as I drew near. Holding her shaggy head in my hands I rested my forehead against hers. I looked into her baleful brown eyes, her lashes tickling my cheek. Sensing my despair, her sandy tongue licked my tears.

I lay all night curled against the familiar warmth and rhythmic breathing of the great beast. Watching the stars rotate through the heavens I thought of the many things I learned from Marun. I thought of the great weed ball sailing across the Beyond and how differently I would have reacted to its sight if I had not been succored and schooled by the al Sumer family.

Marun was right...it is knowledge that nurtures the soul, setting us apart from all other creatures. As the pre-dawn teased the eastern sky, I fell into a deep, undisturbed sleep.

(3)

Pushing through the revolving door, Assistant Professor Ibrahim al Feroz checked his watch...10:45. He was fifteen minutes early. The restaurant she had selected—Kitty O'Shea's—was at the far end of the Hilton lobby. Sitting in a booth with a clear view of the entrance he ordered coffee. Pulling a folded sheet of delicate stationery from his pocket, he read the handwritten note once again...

Dear Dr. Feroz,

My name is Alexandria Darshi. I am a doctoral student at the University of California at Berkeley. I am the sole surviving member of Professor Elman Darshi's family. My father, mother, and sister all disappeared on the same day over two years ago. Although never confirmed, I believe they were abducted and murdered by Saddam.

Two weeks prior to their disappearance I received a large packet of information from my father. You may recognize his name as the author of the widely used text on ancient Sumerian languages.

In the cover letter he spoke of an archeological discovery on which he was working. He said it was of such magnitude that, when confirmed, would substantially change our understanding of human history. Although excited about the discovery, he hated working for Saddam and was afraid once the president understood the import of the find, he would either withhold the information or use it for self-aggrandizement.

My father had a premonition his work might result in harm to him; however, I don't think he anticipated any risk to his

37

family or he would have taken steps to protect them...or perhaps events simply overtook any plans he was making.

Father instructed me to safeguard the material until Iraq was free from the Ba'athist tyranny. The appointment of the interim government last month by the coalition authority appears to be what he had in mind.

I have been away from Iraq for many years and do not know whom to trust. When I saw your interview on Fox, I decided to contact you and ask for your advice. I will be in Chicago for a nuclear imaging conference on the 11th. Is this convenient for you?

Convenient? he thought, refolding the letter. *Wild horses couldn't keep me from meeting this woman.*

Looking up, he saw a tall young woman with olive skin wearing a black sweater and pants waiting for the hostess. Long black hair fell in soft waves over a wine-colored scarf covering her shoulders. A convention badge hanging on a neck strap nestled between her breasts. In one hand she carried a shopping bag filled with brochures and program guides. In the other, a black suede designer briefcase. Dark eyes veiled in thick Semitic lashes scanned the room. When she saw him, she gave a brief smile of recognition.

"Miss Darshi, I presume," he said, standing.

"Dr. Livingstone?" she asked, laughing.

"Oh, I can't tell you how relieved I am," said Feroz. "I was afraid you'd turn out to be a traditionalist in full hijab."

Sliding into the booth she said, "I'll take that as a compliment."

Unlike the women Mother's constantly pushing at me, this elegant woman looks straight into my eyes, he thought. "I like your confidence."

"An acquired trait...an American survival skill," she smiled.

"How long have you been here?"

"You mean America? Just under five years."

"Your English is flawless."

"As is yours," she quipped.

"No contest. I was born here. A product of American public schools," he drawled in his best John Wayne imitation. Declining menus, they ordered espressos. The restaurant was empty with the exception of two sales types at the bar.

"Did you hear from Baghdad?" she asked, stirring a generous spoonful of sugar into her cup.

"Yes, I have it with me. But first, may I ask why so cautious?"

"You obviously were not raised in Iraq," she said. For the first time since entering the restaurant she diverted her eyes.

"I apologize. I understand. With what happened to your family and all..." He awkwardly reached across the table to squeeze her arm. She let his hand linger for a moment and then withdrew her arm.

"When I was a child I attended a private Chaldo Assyrian Christian school. The daughter of Tariq Aziz, the foreign minister under Hussein, was my classmate. Telal and I were very close, but our relationship made my parents nervous. They constantly reminded me to be careful of what I said in her presence. Each time I returned from Telal's home they would grill me about what was said, by whom, to whom...they were very afraid."

"Were you also afraid?"

"Not at first. You know what kids are like. You're afraid of what's under the bed, not of politicians."

"And later?"

"Later, I too became wary."

"How did your leaving come about? That couldn't have been easy."

"Actually it proved easier than my parents thought... mostly because of our relationship with Aziz. Although suspicious and fearful, my father worked closely with Aziz on school committees and various church functions. When you are a Christian in a Muslim sea, you grow close to each other despite political differences. Of course, the fact that my father had all his royalty checks banked in America helped. He told the government that a distant cousin had agreed to pay my tuition and living expenses. All the government cares about is that you're not going to say anything bad about Saddam and you're not planning to send money overseas."

"Hard for an American to comprehend such restrictions."

"It's what I love about America," she said. "Yet even after five years the caution I learned from my parents is still a part of my daily life."

She paused. The waitress refilled their water glasses.

"Shall we get started?" she asked once they were alone.

Reaching into his coat pocket Feroz withdrew a neatly folded fax. "This is a photocopy of one of the panels in the tomb discovered by the marines," he said, sliding it across the table. "It was sent to me and every other expert around the world several months ago to see if anyone could decipher it."

Her hand shivered as she reached for the paper. "I'm nervous. I didn't think I would be. It's a connection to my father—or at least I hope it is." She stared at the paper for a long time. The tip of her tongue moistened her lips.

Feroz leaned forward in his seat, unconsciously shuffling the empty demitasse cups. Alex suddenly felt warm. Squinting, she tried to hold back her tears.

Feroz took her hand. "You recognize the writing on the panel!" It was a statement, not a question.

She picked up the paper with the strange symbols. Closing her eyes, she whispered...

Sleep, and in the veil of night
Dream of valor in the light
When comes the awakening dawn
It is your dreams you act upon

Stunned, Feroz said, "What did you say?"

She repeated the verse. "It's the first stanza of a poem by someone named Ayuba...the poem my father, mother, and sister died for."

"My god!" At a loss for words, he picked up the fax and peered at the mysterious runes. "Is there more?" he asked.

"Where is the tomb located?" she asked, changing the subject.

"Don't you know? Your father didn't tell you?"

"He never saw it. He worked from photos—and not very good photos at that. He became apprehensive about the project after learning the photographer had disappeared shortly after filming the panels. I gather from his notes everyone associated with the find disappeared... probably killed because of Saddam's paranoia."

"Did he send you copies of the photos?"

"No. Only handwritten notes he created from memory. He wasn't allowed to take anything from the ministry and was threatened should he talk about the project to anyone...even my mother."

"Shortly after I returned from Iraq I had a call from Dr. Gudabi curator of the Iraq Museum of Ancient History, he told me the tomb was discovered by engineers from the Fifth Marine Expeditionary Force while securing Azzohour Palace."

"Azzohour Palace, in the heart of Baghdad? I passed by there every day as a child on my way to school! It's the only palace that predates Saddam's rule. All the rest were built after he came to power. How was the tomb discovered...before the marines?"

"No one knows for sure. Dr. Gudabi speculates a pneumatic hammer shattered the tomb's ceiling during Saddam's remodeling program in the early nineties. When engineers repaired the tomb's ceiling, a narrow opening in the roof was constructed. A steel stairway leading to a false electrical panel in the palace utility room was the only access. The marines would never have found it without the help of the palace engineer."

The sadness in her eyes changing to anger, Alex said, "God, it's so typical of that suspicious monster to keep something like this a secret! I mean was he afraid...of a poem?"

"I suppose it depends on what the poem says. As you're the only person in the world who knows, only you can say for sure. Unless of course you'd like to share it with me?"

"Please, Professor—"

"Alexandria," Feroz interrupted with a smile, "I suspect we'll be spending a lot of time together in the coming months, so how about we adopt the American style. Please call me Bryan."

She liked this man. He was smart but unaffected, much like her father. Perhaps that's what appealed to her.

"Okay, but only if you call me Alex."

"You're on. Okay, now that we've got that settled, how about sharing the rest of the poem?" he laughed.

"Sorry, Bryan, I can't do that yet."

"Why in the world not?"

"The translation of this poem and the decoding of what appears to be an entirely new language is all I have with which to honor my father. Until I'm sure he'll get official recognition I can't hand over the rest of the translation. Please understand."

Bryan looked away. He could understand her caution. Intellectual theft was common in his field, but especially so in the Middle East. The fact that Dr. Darshi was deceased would make honoring his work doubly difficult.

Bryan focused on the beautiful woman across the booth but was suddenly distracted by the sound of dishes rattling, people talking, the guys on Sports Center babbling on the TV over the bar. He looked up. The lunch crowd had arrived in force. All the tables were now full.

"Are you free this afternoon?"

Surprised by this sudden change in the direction of the conversation, Alex nodded her head.

"Great," he said, sliding out of the booth. "I'm starved, how about you?"

"Yes, but why are we leaving? This is a restaurant."

"Yeah, but a noisy one. I know a place across the street that has great food, wonderful views, and is a lot quieter." On the way out, he slipped the hostess a twenty-dollar bill. Winking, he said, "This is for the coffee." The daggers she'd been aiming in their direction while they monopolized one of her tables turned into a smile. "I'll take care of it," she said, slipping the bill into her pocket.

The breeze off Lake Michigan was surprisingly warm for April. Bryan, carrying her convention bag, guided Alex by the arm across the street into Centennial Park. The trees were in full bud, some showing early color. Stopping at a small food stand, Alex read the faded sign on the side of the cart—*Chicago Hot Dogs...you'll bark for more.* Bryan ordered two dogs with all the trimmings and two cream sodas.

"This is the way I've celebrated every milestone in my life...graduation from high school, college, grad school...you name it. For some reason Chicago d–a–w–g–s," he drawled, "have become my celebratory feast!"

"Did you serve them at your wedding too?" she asked nonchalantly.

"Clever, very clever. Never been married," he said, leading her to a bench with a view of the lake. They ate in silence while looking out over the sparkling waters of Lake Michigan.

"That was indeed a gourmet meal," Alex sighed. "Certainly something I would never have experienced on my first trip to the Windy City without such an experienced guide." Her dark eyes smiled at Bryan.

"Midwestern hospitality," Bryan said with a fake bow. "In O'Shea's you asked me to be patient. I understand how important this is to you. I want you to know I'll do everything I can to ensure your father gets the recognition he deserves."

Sometimes it seemed she'd been alone all her life. When she left Iraq she couldn't possibly have known she would not return, much less never see her mother, father, and sister again. The pain of separation was, at times, almost too great to bear. To save herself from the sadness that seeped from the empty place in her heart, she had buried herself in her studies. If she did not raise her head from her books she would not see what she did not have.

She looked at Bryan. She wanted to cry but forced her eyes to stay focused. In little less than an hour this perfect man in his gray suit, black knit tie, and shiny shoes had destroyed the defenses she had so carefully erected to keep the emptiness at bay. She felt the warmth of his hand on her back.

"Are you okay?"

"Yes, I'm fine. I was just trying to find the words to adequately thank you."

❧

Professor Darshi stood in a soft drizzle waiting for the car from the ministry. The sky lightened as the faithful poured from a nearby mosque after morning prayers.

Six days a week for the past nine months he'd worked on the new language in a small office in the ministry. The colonel was his only contact, except for the Muhammads, who picked him up each morning.

He had only met with the colonel dressed as the burka-clad woman twice since the charade began. Shortly after their second meeting, the colonel announced in the official voice he used for the hidden microphones in the office, "Professor, from now on I will be your transport home in the evening. This will give us time to discuss your progress."

Shocked, the professor said, "Yes, of course, Colonel, whatever you wish."

Later, the colonel told Darshi the minister suspected the professor was delaying the translation. The colonel had suggested that since no one but Darshi had the slightest idea how to interpret the language on the panels, perhaps he should befriend the professor and earn his trust. The minister had readily agreed. Darshi was delighted at the prospect of sharing his progress (and his fears) with someone. He had been true to his word—he'd not spoken to anyone about the project.

He was disappointed when the colonel, afraid his automobile was bugged, insisted they communicate by exchanging notes. Instead of the conversational release he had hoped for, he and the colonel scribbled notes while entertaining the unseen listeners with drivel about the weather and other inconsequential tidbits. It made the drive more stressful than listening to the burka woman on the bus.

But the ride home last night had been different. The colonel—claiming he had to pick up some fruit—pulled the car to the side of the road near a small market.

"Come, Professor, perhaps your wife would also like something fresh. I hear there is a new shipment of avocadoes and oranges." Unaware it was a ruse, Darshi followed the colonel. But instead of entering the market, they walked down a sparsely inhabited side street.

"Professor, we need to talk," started the colonel. "We can stall no longer. I assume you've completed your translation?"

"Yes, some time ago actually. I thought you didn't want to know so you couldn't be forced to admit we've been stalling?"

"Yes, but that time has passed. What does it say?"

"I can't recite the whole thing. I have no notes."

"I don't mean verbatim…in general. Is it threatening in any way to the regime?"

"You mean to Saddam?"

The colonel nodded, sidestepping two small boys kicking a soccer ball against a wall.

"I can't speak for him...I mean, who knows what goes on in his mind."

The colonel took hold of Darshi's arm. "Softly, Professor...softly."

My god, thought Darshi, *does he really think those little boys are part of the Mukhabarat?*

"Colonel, 'The Song of Ayuba' is a poem about dreams...not nightmares. It is inconceivable that anyone could interpret it to be threatening in any way."

The two men walked on in silence. An old woman gave them a fearful look before disappearing behind a gate.

"The minister is very worried," said the colonel. "Last night during a poker game Uday asked about the tomb project. When the minister said it was progressing slowly, Uday offered to send over some of his experts to expedite the process."

"What kind of experts?"

"The kind you never want to meet...experts at getting people to say and do whatever the president wants."

Darshi felt sick.

"Unless we divulge the translation soon..." Pausing, the colonel pulled out a handkerchief and blew his nose loudly, "the minister will have no choice but to accept Uday's offer."

"Why? I mean, why can't he simply say we are making progress?"

"You are a nice man, Professor, but you are also a fool. It was not an offer from Uday. It was a demand from the president." Having circled the block, they again stood in front of the market.

"Look, Colonel, I know I'm naive about these things, but I am confident there is absolutely nothing in this poem to threaten anyone, no matter how paranoid. If you're prepared, then so am I. Let's reveal it to the minister tomorrow and get this painful sham behind us."

Now, waiting for the Mos in the gray light of dawn, Darshi yawned. He'd had little sleep. Banning his wife from his study, he had spent much of the night preparing a package for Alexandria. Throughout this nightmarish adventure he had followed the colonel's instructions—in every way but two.

The diary he kept hidden in a plastic bag suspended by a wire in the cistern on the roof detailed the steps he'd taken to decipher the new language. He recalled how the answer to the ancient puzzle had been revealed. He had been sitting on a worn carpet in the small courtyard of his mother-in-law's house just over a month ago. He was exhausted from trying to pries the message on the panels from the complicated and mysterious runes. He had made a pledge that today he would set aside his work and focus on his family. The fear the colonel had instilled in him slowly evaporated in the warmth of his loved ones. His daughter, Zahra, Amira, his wife, and her mother, Fatima, sat across from him as he blessed the elaborate luncheon spread out on the carpet between them. *If Alexandria was here it would be perfect,* he thought

As they ate and chatted about friends and family he was struck by the similarities between the three women—alike in many ways, yet distinctly different in others. Amira had Fatima's eyes, but Zahra's were less angular and lighter in color. Zahra's chin was much like her grandmother's and completely different than her mother's or Alexandria's. Dappled sunlight winked through the leaves of the fig tree shading the courtyard. It played across the features of the women, confusing their similarities and differences.

He recalled the startling sensation of the moment when it occurred to him that, like the genetic variations in a family, the ancient characters on the panels were the roots of all subsequent languages! For months he had been trying to extract characters from the new script that were similar to Akkadian or any of the other ancient languages. Now, with certainty, he knew that the new script was the "genetic" wellspring of all later languages. Once he reversed his approach, the meaning and beauty of the mother language became clear. It was the Rosetta Stone of Ayuba.

His joy at making the discovery was tempered by the fact that the paranoid fear of one man would determine whether or not the world would ever hear of his find.

Disobeying the colonel a second time, he had not tried to get his wife and daughter Zahra out of Iraq. It was probably impossible now that Alexandria was in the States. The government liked to keep families of students studying abroad close at hand...virtual hostages ensuring good behavior. In addition, he had been unable to find anything in the poem the least bit threatening to the existing cabal.

Hopefully this will be the last day of this farce, he thought now. Today he would give the translation to the minister, having done all he could to protect his family and his work. Earlier that morning he'd met with Abbasid Khayzuran, a childhood friend now serving on Tariq Aziz's staff, and for a fee, he had agreed to carry the small parcel to the United States and post it to Alexandria.

The ancient Mercedes wheezed to a stop. Greeting the Mos, Darshi slipped the blindfold over his head, slavishly following the foolish protocol, hoping this would be the last time he started his day blindfolded in the confines of a back seat smelling like a fetid swamp.

❧❧

"My god…I had no idea it would be like this," said Noora. The three roommates, dressed in elegant evening gowns, peered through the darkened windows of the limo as it crept between satellite TV trucks and news vans lining the street leading to Mandell Hall on the University of Chicago campus. Banks of lights illuminated the red carpet stretching from the curb into the venerable building.

"Can you believe it? A red carpet," squealed Jammy. "All we need now is a glass slipper."

"Or a tranquilizer," whispered Alex. The black Cadillac slipped alongside the curb as the hall's gothic windows faded into the early evening dimness.

"Okay, girls…here we go," said Alex.

Dr. Farrell Watson, president of the National Geographic Media Group, stepped forward to greet them. National Geographic was now a full partner with the university and Iraqi museum and was financing much of the research and all of the TV production and promotion. Watson was famous for his ability to excite the common viewer about esoteric subjects that would otherwise have received little attention in the mass media.

His promotion of Ayuba had been brilliant. Ayuba had been billed as "A voice before God," disturbing the Christian Right bloggers and ensuring a large, if skeptical, audience for tonight's documentary.

"You look lovely, Alex," he said in his rich southern accent.

Turning toward Noora and Jammy he said, "As do you ladies," as he handed them from the limo. "Please follow Alex and me. After we enter the hall there will be someone to escort you to your seats." Temporarily blinded by camera flashes, Alex clutched Farrell's arm.

"I suppose it would be foolish to suggest that you not be nervous," Farrell drawled. "I wish I could take that advice too. Just remember none of us have done anything like this before. In fact no living person has ever been in this situation."

"Thanks, Dr. Watson, but I'm not at all sure that's comforting," Alex said, smiling into the glare of a half-dozen banks of TV lights.

"What I meant, my dear, is that we cannot err as there is no precedent." He laughed.

A voice speaking Arabic with a Kuwaiti accent yelled through the glare, "Miss Darshi, Al Jazeera TV here. Please, a moment to speak to the Arabic community."

"Al Jazeera?" she whispered to Farrell.

"Sorry, no interviews until the press conference following the formal announcement," Farrell said to the blinding light. Turning to Alex he said, "Oh yes. They're all here...Japan's NHK, Beijing TV, German, French... virtually all the Europeans. Plus our networks and several cable news outlets too."

A tuxedo-clad usher met Jammy and Noora at the entrance to guide them to their seats. Alex and Dr. Watson climbed the stairs to the stage.

Seated on the dais, Alex was stunned by the number of people involved in staging the program. Sound and lighting technicians scurried around making last minute adjustments. Three flat panel screens formed a semi-circle across the back of the stage. She watched the director advise technicians in the tomb in Baghdad how to handle problems with glare off the ancient gold panels. As Alex stared intently, Bryan moved into the shot.

"Okay, Baghdad. Bryan, let's do a sound check."

"Good evening, or should I say good morning from Baghdad," said Bryan, smiling into the camera. A technician moved into the picture adjusting his microphone.

"Now, Miss Darshi, may we hear from you."

Alex felt a slight wave of nausea…her palms damp. "Good morning, Bryan. You look very nice in your tux and matching bulletproof vest," she quipped.

"Hello, Alex." Bryan's eyes lit up at the sound of her voice. "You have an unfair advantage…I can't see you. There's not enough room in here for monitors. My guess is you look stunning."

It was true. Alex was magnificent in a floor-length charcoal gown, her raven-black hair shimmering in the light. The rise and fall of her breasts a tantalizing hint above a modest décolleté. An elegant strand of black pearls radiated against the richness of her complexion.

"Okay, Bryan and Alex," the director interrupted, "sounds good. We're starting the countdown."

The screens flickered. Bryan's image was replaced by the National Geographic Society logo and—*"The Song of Ayuba," a Global Television Event.*

The doors to the hall opened, admitting the tuxedoed and gowned elite of academia. Once everyone was seated, Dr. Watson approached the podium, his elegant tuxedo barely confining his vast bulk. The folds of his neck seeped over his collar. Salt and pepper hair smoothed straight back from a receding brow revealed a large, intelligent forehead above pale blue eyes.

"Good morning, Dr. Gudabi, Dr. Feroz. Greetings to you and your guests from Mandell Hall at the University of Chicago."

For the next half hour Dr. Gudabi, the curator of the Iraqi Museum of Ancient History, and Bryan, America's leading expert on middle eastern history at the renown

School of Oriental Studies at the University of Chicago, explained how the panels were discovered—first by Saddam's workmen, then rediscovered by the U.S. Marines. Arabic subtitles flowed beneath the images on the screen. Viewers were transported down a long, dark hall leading to the palace utility room and the false electrical panel. Bryan demonstrated how the narrow metal ladder had been inserted into the tomb following reconstruction of the shattered roof. One of the screens held snapshot photos of the workmen and photographer who had been killed by Saddam following their work on the ancient tomb.

"Of course," said Bryan, gesturing toward the panels, "what makes this find so rare is its antiquity. We have dated the panels using the signature block at the base of the ancient inscription that states that the song was written when the constellation Leo appeared in the eastern sky on the vernal equinox. Specifically, it says…"

Bryan knelt next to a panel, and the camera zoomed in tight on his finger tracing the strange runes carved into the solid gold, "'…the Lion greets the dawn when day equals night heralding winter.' This esoteric measurement of time, based on the earth's processional movement, places the vault somewhere between 9,000 and 11,000 BCE. To put that in perspective, these panels have been hidden from view throughout all of recorded history. They were already five thousand years old when the Egyptian civilization was formed and nine thousand years old when Alexander rode through the valley of the Tigris." A collective murmur ran through the hall as the ancient date was revealed publicly for the first time.

Bryan continued, "The fact that the author was aware of stellar time based on the movement of the zodiac indicates a profound knowledge of the universe that could only have been learned by careful observation over countless millennia. This makes 'The Song of Ayuba' the oldest writing ever discovered and will require archeologists and historians to completely rethink the roots of civilization."

The focus then turned again to Dr. Gudabi. His English was excellent; however, he spoke again in Arabic with English subtitles.

"This secular poem, or 'song' as it is referred to by the author, predates both the Code of Hammurabi (1500–1600 BC) and the Laws of Urnammu (2300 BC) by approximately eight thousand years." His dark eyes peered into the camera. Repeating himself he said, "'The Song of Ayuba' being heard for the first time this evening, pre-dates any known writing by eight thousand years. It is remarkable not only for its great age, but for its secularity in a period that must have been ruled by superstition and spiritual mysticism. 'The Song of Ayuba,' however, appears to be a complex philosophical guide embracing no particular faith."

Alex recalled the Iraqis' concern during the planning of tonight's program about the importance of addressing the relationship of the song to current day religion…namely Islam. Dr. Gudabi had insisted the secularity of the song be stressed to mitigate any violent resistance by fundamentalists. As with many things in the Middle East, the shadow of religious dogma dimmed the brilliance of the moment.

The three screens faded to black then slowly resolved into three new images: On the left, a live image of Dr. Watson at the podium; in the center, a photo of Dr. Elman Darshi; on the right, a close-up of Alexandria.

Dr. Watson spoke of her father's prominence in the academic community and revealed for the first time that, except for Alexandria, he and his family had died for his efforts. Alex felt a great sense of pride, not only in her father but her country and people.

Her breathing grew calm and her hands steadied as she heard Dr. Watson say, "And now Dr. Darshi's daughter Alexandria will read 'The Song of Ayuba.'"

Alex looked out over the hall. Behind her, the left screen morphed into a photo of her mother and her sister on the right.

"It may be impossible for a civilized mind to understand the brain of a tyrant. It is akin to an ant comprehending the universe. When I first learned of the death of my family I couldn't imagine how a few lines written in the ancient past could excite a paranoid mind to such destruction. I'm not sure if my mother, Amira," turning to the images behind her, "or my sister, Zahra, knew the reason behind their torture and death. After reading the poem my father translated, I am convinced he misunderstood the fear this ancient voice might create in the unstable minds ruling Iraq at that time. 'The Song of Ayuba' asks us all to dream a different dream for ourselves, our country, and our world."

Without further comment she began to recite the world's oldest written words...

The Song of Ayuba

Sleep, and in the veil of night
Dream of valor in the light
When comes the awakening dawn
It is your dreams you act upon

❧

In the Shadow of Babylon

Daylight dreams
Are the guides of life
Not the dark visitations of sleep

Masters of dreams
Dream the distant shore
Beyond a shoaless sea
They dream of a destination
That dreams of a path
And the path of a destiny

When I wrote these lines
I dreamed of you
When your eyes traced these lines
Did you not dream of me?

The voice within
Is the midwife
Of your feelings
Words of hate, feelings of anger
Words of love, feelings of joy

The mind is the desert
Dreaming of rain
The desert drinks
But is never full

Death too is a dream
Dreamed by the dying
We leave naught in passing
But the joy of our dreams
Trusting the inheritors
Will not taint them with tears

Chicago (2004 CE)

The dreamless ones
Question not the beating heart
Or the air we breathe
Dreamers wonder where
Or if, what, or when
In awe of it all

God is a dream
An individual dream
A thousand people
Dream of a thousand gods
Their prayers
Define their dreams

We control only our dreams
They are the music of our lives
The one-stringed lute upon which
The song of our attitude is played

It matters not to me a wit,
What lies at the end of the road
For it is the journey that counts most
Not where my pack is finally stowed

Ayuba
Shepherd of Hamood
Father of Bynethia
Master of the Ben

Avenger of the Twan
Hero of the Gleb
Protector of Bensheer
Son of the Beyond

As Alex read the English translation, a prerecorded video of her reading it in Arabic was broadcast throughout the Middle East.

(4)

Returning to the compound about midday following the day of Marun's death and expecting to see a crowd of villagers gathered to mourn her, I was surprised to find three camels resting in the otherwise empty courtyard. Each was festooned with a brightly colored halter and saddle. I recognized the colors and silver trappings as the same riding gear Father's camel wore when we first met. In addition to the finely tooled leather saddles, each camel sported two large spear cases, one mounted on either side just behind the saddle. The bronze spear tips glinted in the morning light. Frion was feeding the mounts as I approached.

"Oh, Ayuba, I'm so glad you're back in time."

"In time for what?" I said, picking up an empty gourd from one of the sated camels.

"There was a raid several nights ago at Bensheer. Two people were killed and fifteen camels stolen. The twan of Hamood is here. Father and Pitoon are preparing to go with him and his men to track down the killers."

Just then Father, Pitoon, and three strangers emerged from the house. The guests were large men dressed in light gray tunics made of finely woven cloth. They wore beautiful sandals of polished leather with thongs crisscrossing their calves secured with silver buckles just short of their knees. Their tunics were cinched with wide belts inlaid with turquoise and silver. Each man wore a scabbard decorated with precious stones and seamed with silver thread. Although each dagger was

59

the same in size and shape, the scabbards were unique to the wearer's rank.

I recognized the twan of Hamood by the symbol on his scabbard. His dark complexion and forceful demeanor radiated power and authority. His hair, although oiled like Father's, was long and hung unadorned to his shoulders. The other men, including Pitoon, wore their hair pulled tightly back terminating in a single braid.

The twan stopped in front of me, his dark eyes looking me up and down with the amused interest of one examining a new foal or some freak of nature blown in on the wind.

"So this is the foundling," he said matter-of-factly. "How do you communicate with him?" he asked. His eyes locked on mine to see if I understood the question he directed to Father.

Although the twan was of superior rank, only al Sumer had the stature and reputation to address him as an equal. Putting his arm around my shoulder Father answered, "Yes, this was the foundling, but now he is my son." Looking directly into the glowering eyes of the twan he continued, "You may call him Ayuba."

The twan glared at Father. It was clear he was not used to being spoken to so directly. It was also clear Father would brook no insult to his family. Trying to diffuse the situation, I made a deep bow to the twan.

"Does your son speak?"

"I do indeed, Your Highness," I replied, in the formal Hamoodian dialect I learned from Marun. "How may I be of service?"

From the corner of my eye I caught the ghost of a smile cross Pitoon's otherwise somber face. The twan and his two bodyguards were clearly taken aback, as though a tree had spoken. Such was the ignorance of even the highest-bred officials in Hamood—raised to believe creatures from the Beyond were void of any recognizable intelligence.

Still not deigning to speak directly to me, the twan turned to Father. "Does he still speak the language of the Beyond?"

Parrying the indirect insult, Father said, "Ayuba, we need your advice and help." The twan flinched at the thought of asking for help from someone he perceived as sub-human.

"We have reason to believe the bandits who raided Bensheer have fled into the Beyond. The twan and his men tracked them as far as the Shale Sea but lost their tracks where the sea enters the Beyond. Are you familiar with the area?"

A shiver ran through my body at the mention of the Shale Sea. Shortly after my family was butchered I followed the tracks of a goat onto the sea and became lost in its vastness. When dawn came, I could see no landmarks. The sea of ocher-colored stone flowed in all directions without interruption. Not a plant or dune or outcropping of any kind broke the horizon. I wandered three days without water or food. The rocks radiated heat of such intensity that, if I closed my eyes, it was impossible to tell which way was up. It felt as though I was standing in the center of the sun.

Setting aside this unwelcome memory, I responded, "Yes, Father, I have been across the Shale Sea. It is trackless and without water. I doubt the bandits will survive unless well equipped."

The twan interrupted, "The thieves are from the Beyond and must know the area well."

"Pardon, Your Highness," I blurted out, "I doubt the men you seek are from the Beyond."

"Why do you say that?" he scowled, addressing me directly for the first time. Father shot me an encouraging look.

"Because, sir, the peoples of the Beyond are more afraid of what they call the 'tribes' than people here are of Beyonders. Children are taught from an early age that if caught by the tribes they will be roasted alive."

The twan and his men laughed.

"This may be so," he said, "but it only shows their ignorance. It does not mean they would not kill and steal."

"What you say may be true, Your Highness, but none in the Beyond are ignorant of the dangers that lie on the Shale Sea."

Sensing the direction this exchange was taking, Father stepped in. "We will learn the identity of these killers soon enough. The fact is they have headed onto the sea. Ayuba, fetch your mount and be ready to ride within the hour."

Just before departing, Father told Pitoon he would not be riding with us. His disappointed eyes pleaded with Father but to no avail. Father explained the band we sought might circle back and attack Hamrabi. Pitoon was to organize the villagers to stand watch in Father's absence.

There was polite laughter when I brought out the she-beast. Compared to Father's elegant war mount and the excellent breeding of the twan's camels, my old friend looked out of place, her shaggy coat and droopy ears in stark contrast to the sleek, royal demeanor of the others.

We left the compound just after the sun reached its zenith. Cresting the ridge where the day before I had mourned Marun, I saw Pitoon and Frion standing in the shade of the grove. Knowing what awaited me, I envied their cool redoubt.

We arrived at the sea by nightfall the following day, making camp at a small oasis. It was clear man and beast used this spot frequently (it was the only water within a day's journey) but our presence would deter any less heavily armed band from using the spring that night.

"Ayuba, is it possible to track the thieves on the Shale Sea?" asked Fairtoo, the second in command, as we sat around a large fire of animal dung and dried fronds. The night was bitterly cold despite the day's scorching heat.

"The sea is made of solid rock with a crumbling skin of shale. It will be difficult to track them, sir."

"But you have crossed it before?" he asked.

"Sir, I was but a boy when I was last here. To say I crossed it would be untrue. To say I *survived* it would be more accurate."

"Fortunately we are better prepared," he said smugly. "Besides, I'm sure the creatures we seek from the Beyond will grow careless."

I started to reply that I was convinced the thieves we sought were not from the Beyond, but Father said quickly, "Come, Ayuba. Let's circle the camp before we sleep."

"We leave at false dawn," grunted the twan, lying back on his saddle.

Father and I walked into the empty desert. The sky was blazing with stars. A sliver of a moon peeked over the horizon. A slight breeze carried the scent of camel weed and sage. The silver clouds of our breath quickly evaporated in the dry, cold air. We did not speak until well beyond the camp.

Finally Father said, "What's troubling you, son?"

I did not know how to answer. Uncomfortable ever since meeting the twan and his men, I had shrugged off the feeling believing I was simply unsure how to behave in their presence. Now, however, I knew it was something more.

We slowly worked our way around camp, looking for any danger lurking beyond the edge of the fire's light. I was comfortable walking through the night with Father's great strength nearby. I thought of the countless nights I had crept through the dark alone, shivering from fear and cold. Suddenly it came to me how to answer Father's question.

"I'm afraid of what tomorrow will bring," I said softly, wondering how that would sound to a man who seemed fearless. I hurried on, justifying my fear. "Father, the closest I have come to dying was on the Shale Sea. Crazy with thirst and hunger, I felt I was being roasted alive. It was only by chance I survived."

Sitting on an outcropping, Father motioned for me to sit beside him. We stared out over the vast emptiness of the desert.

"When wandering alone in the Beyond, did you ever savor a night like this? Did you sit as we are now and let your eyes wander through the stars, your lungs drinking in the fragrance of the night?"

"I was afraid of the night."

"What were you afraid of?"

"Everything!" I blurted out. "I mean…hyenas and lions, the clans, starvation, thirst, being…alone."

Father turned toward me, his dark eyes shining in the starlight. "And did any of the things you feared actually happen?"

"You mean, did I ever starve or get eaten by a lion?" I asked, not understanding what he was trying to tell me.

"Exactly," he smiled. I looked at him as though he was telling a joke, but I could see by his eyes he was sincere.

"Of course not."

"I think you're wrong, my son," he said, putting his hand on my shoulder. "Every time you feared being eaten or attacked, every time the specter of death grasped your mind and shook you with fear, it was as though you actually died."

"But I—"

"No, let me finish." I felt the comfort of his nearness. "The death you imagined was far worse than actual death. Do you know why?"

"I'm not sure what you mean, Father. How can something I imagine be worse than the real thing?"

As he often did, he answered my question with a question. "If you had not shivered in fear night after night when you wandered in this vast place, would you have been eaten by a lion or would any of the other things you worried about have happened?"

"You mean if I took all precautions but just didn't worry about it?"

"Yes."

"Well, uh...no. I guess it would not have changed things. But—"

"No but, Ayuba," he said gently.

"Yes, I would have survived. But Father," I said, ignoring his instructions, "I don't have your courage. I was alone and I was afraid."

The guardian of the western border of Hamood let out a laugh, startling me. "So you think courage is something only others have? What is courage?" he asked.

"Not being afraid," I answered quickly, unsure of why he found this subject so humorous.

"But that's only half the answer. Fear is the unseen partner that rides with us all…you, me, even the twan. The difference between those with courage and cowards," he said, looking deep into my eyes, "is simply a feat of imagination. When faced with a charging lion or a screaming warrior with a spear, we all feel fear. It's what gives us strength to overcome the threat. So at the moment of…" he hesitated, "…finality, the coward and the hero feel the same fear."

"Why then do the two react so differently?"

"Because the coward has experienced that fear many times…and in his imagined fear he has seen his death." Father's smile was gone now. A look of sadness crossed his wide brow.

"And the hero?"

"He too responds as he has imagined that moment—with valor and certitude. He has lived the victory many times in the dreams of his heart and with each dreaming, he has been victorious."

A lone cloud raced across the sky, blocking out the slivered moon. I wrapped my robe tightly around me thinking about what Father said. Sensing my confusion, he placed his arm over my shoulders. We sat listening to the wind and the far-off cry of a hyena. Father began to hum softly and then began to sing. It was more like a whisper than a song…it was a Hamrabian dream song in which the singer makes up the words so it is different each time it is sung with only the chorus in common.

This night, Father's dream song was about the Shale Sea. He sang of fearless warriors challenging the steaming vastness with certainty. He sang of the beauty of the stone and the heat from the sun. He sang of the crispness of the nights and of victory won.

Then he sang the chorus I first learned from Marun but until this night never fully understood…

Sleep, and in the veil of night
Dream of valor in the light
When comes the awakening dawn
It is your dreams you act upon

Father wove beautiful images. He sang about me leading our band through a trackless waste and of my cunning and bravery. He painted a picture for me that was different than I would have created on my own. On that cold, star-riddled night he showed me how to dream a different dream.

❧

By first light we were on the edge of the Shale Sea—a bold line as though carved by a dagger slicing through the desert brownness. Radiating heat from a thousand days of searing sunlight, mirages danced and skidded across its blood-red surface. It would be easy to follow the path of the bandits as a trail of dried camel droppings headed toward the horizon.

The great war camels ridden by Father, the twan, and his men were nervous at the prospect of stepping onto this barren slab of heat. The she-beast, however, showed no emotion, accepting her fate and the comfort of my presence. A scorching breeze blew directly into our faces as I led our group westward with the sun blazing against our backs.

In mid-afternoon, the dung trail disappeared. Leading the group in a constant direction well beyond the last droppings, expecting another pile to appear at any moment, it was some time before I realized we were no longer on the trail. We were simply trudging blindly toward the constant mirage that marked the horizon. Turning around, I rode back toward the rest of the party.

"The trail has disappeared. The bandits must have made a sudden turn. In any case, we must backtrack to the last dung heap or we could become hopelessly lost," I said through the muffle covering my face.

"That makes no sense," grunted the twan. "The Beyond is due west of where we entered the sea and thus far the bandits have headed directly toward it. Why would they change direction?"

"I do not know, Your Highness, but I do know we must locate the trail or..." I fumbled my words as a faint whiff of my wanderings on the sea, like a bitter smell, drifted across my mind, "We may not find our way back."

The twan was not a man familiar with retreat. It was obvious he did not like covering ground already traveled. "Al Sumer, what do you think? Has our prey suddenly turned away from their homeland? Is it possible they sense we are trailing them?"

Turning in his saddle while shielding his eyes from the glare of the sun, Father looked back in the direction from which we'd come and then in the direction we were heading. "If these fools are indeed from the Beyond, I doubt they would shift their direction unless they had a marker to tell them where to turn. If they are not from the Beyond, they could simply have turned looking for a way off these coals. If that's the case then, like them, we could wander until we fry or come across their charred remains. Your Highness, I agree with Ayuba. Before night falls we should retrace our steps until we find the last droppings."

The twan grunted acknowledgment. "I'm not prepared to turn back yet. I'm sure these murderers are from the Beyond," he said, scowling at me as though I had some connection to the men we sought. "However," he continued, "I agree we must not lose the trail. Fairtoo!"

"Sir?"

"I want you to backtrack until you find the end of the dung trail. It should be due east so keep your shadow directly in front of you. The dung heaps should stand out clearly against the slanting rays of the sun. We will remain here as a guidepost. When you have traveled to the point where we appear to be standing on the horizon, lay a spear on the stone pointing in the direction you are heading. When you reach the trail, make camp and wait for us. If we do not arrive by dawn retrace your steps, as it will mean we have picked up the trail westward. We will mark our path with spears and our own mounts' droppings as well."

The twan's instructions were clear and thorough. I was impressed with his instant mastery of the options available in the otherwise optionless land. Fairtoo immediately turned his camel away from the sun.

"Ayuba," the twan barked, "I want you to dismount and run straight east for one thousand paces." He paused, "You can count, can't you?" he growled.

"He is my son, Your Highness. He can count," Father answered, saving me the embarrassment of replying to the twan's unconscious insult.

"Good," the twan mumbled. "At one thousand paces make a half circle in an arc from north through west to the south and see if you can pick up their trail."

As I dismounted, Father handed me two small bags made of camel hide with the hair still attached and a goat water bladder. "Put these over your sandals. The hair will protect your feet from the heat."

Until dismounted, I was unaware how much cooler it was when perched high above the ocher stone. As I began to trot away from our group, the heat rose under me like a physical force. It felt as though I was moving through soft sand, even though I was on hard, fractured rock.

Between the time I dismounted and sunset, I made four complete arcs from north to south. When I completed an arc, I drank from Father's bag and moved forward two thousand paces, repeating my search pattern.

Tracking on the blistering shale was mostly luck. The only place a print might be found was in the small grooves cut into the stone by the unrelenting wind where tiny deposits of sand hid. My hope was that one of the bandits' camels had stepped in one of these depressions.

Although my face was muffled with a fine cloth, the searing wind dried my eyes so much that after the first hour of tracking I had to kneel on the insufferable stone and squint at each depression. In the four arcs I made I found only one faint print... the unmistakable talon of a vulture.

The sun does not set on the Shale Sea...it slams shut. One minute it is light and boiling hot; then suddenly, as if a candle is blown out, it is dark. Instantly the wind turns cold and the temperature plummets. It is this sudden change in temperature that creates the shale surface of the stone.

Returning from my fourth arc, I found Father, the twan, and Dalnt dismounted and struggling with the camels that would not stay couched; the heat from the stone so intense that they felt commanded to lie on fire. The beasts were moaning and spitting, shaking their great heads and pulling at their tethers. It was at this moment the sun plunged behind the horizon, chased by the searing heat.

Suddenly there came a great crackling sound—like a dry camel weed fire. Everyone stood still. The very air sparked as though the falling temperature was being driven by a thousand devils with snapping whips.

"Grab the camels!" I shouted over the deafening sound, but my warning came too late. The sudden nightfall, combined with the plummeting temperature, was so unexpected even seasoned desert travelers like Father and the twan were momentarily distracted. The sound of splintering stone frightened the beasts. Shaking with fear, they reared, dislodging their packs while bolting into the crackling night.

As quickly as it had begun, the noise from the fracturing stone ceased. There was fear in the twan's eyes as he surveyed the confusion of packsaddles, spears, and water bags strewn on the now quiet shale. The sound of the retreating camels came on the cold wind that blew from the east. It was this bitter wind that brought us to our senses. We were stranded on the Shale Sea days from the nearest oasis.

Father was the first to react. "Check the water bags for leaks."

Two of the four bags had burst. The twan's was undamaged and mine was missing...presumably still attached to my saddle on the she-beast.

At the twan's command we spent the next hour making packs for each man to carry. Dalnt, the strongest, carried the water skin. Father, the twan, and I carried packs of blankets, dried fruits, and three spears each.

Although the night was moonless, we could see clearly by the light of the stars. The wind was crisp and cold, but the stone still radiated heat. Our faces and hands were freezing, yet our feet and legs were warm. After assembling our packs, Father suggested we rest until the guide star circled into view. Without it to follow, we could become hopelessly lost. The twan agreed. Exhausted from tracking in the sweltering heat, I promptly fell into a deep sleep.

"Wake up, Ayuba, wake up. I have a surprise." It was Father's voice, but I wasn't sure if it was a dream.

I remembered another time when Father surprised me with my own set of spears in a finely tooled goatskin quiver. What fun Pitoon and I shared as he taught me to hurl the fine beech shafts tipped with bronze points at a stuffed sheepskin swinging from the limb of a pomegranate tree.

"Ayuba, wake up."

The persistent voice drew me from this happy dream within a dream. I felt the warm rock beneath me as Father's strong hands gently shook me awake.

I opened my eyes. Staring down at me were the smiling faces of the twan, Dalnt, and Father.

"What's wrong? Why do you all look so happy?" I asked, somewhat alarmed by this strange vision.

"You'll be smiling too once you stand up," Father replied, the smile growing larger on his handsome face.

I let out a whoop of joy. Standing not ten paces from me was the great mother camel. As I ran to her I noticed she was already loaded with our packs, water, and extra spears. With her shaggy head in my arms I hugged her and ruffled her floppy ears.

"She came back shortly after you fell asleep," said Father. "She wouldn't let any of us near her until she sniffed you to make certain you were safe. Since then, she's been as docile as a kitten."

"Why didn't you wake me sooner?"

"None of us could sleep in this horrible place but you had walked so much in the heat we felt you needed to rest," said the twan with newfound respect in his voice. I was not sure if it was for the camel or me, but his next comment made it clear.

"At first I thought Ayuba a strange and somewhat funny name. I had never heard of anyone named 'camel boy.' But now I know why al Sumer chose that name for you. You and this dilapidated beast may have saved our lives. If indeed we do survive, I intend to appoint you an honorary captain of my personal guard, and I'll buy that loyal friend of yours a cart full of the best Bensheerie barley!"

The mistrust that had shaded his eyes since we met was gone.

We plodded through the night. Father kept the guide star on our right to keep an easterly course. By predawn the wind abated. The heat, stored in the rock over countless eons, lay like a fog around us. The sun rose, a fire blazing across the uninterrupted stone.

Father suddenly trotted ahead. He turned and yelled, "We've found it!"

We quickened our pace to see what he was pointing at. Not five hundred paces ahead and slightly off to our right was a stone cairn holding a spear pointing in a northeasterly direction. As we approached the pile of neatly stacked pieces of shale, the Twan said, "Had we begun our walk an hour earlier, we'd have passed it in the dark. Fate is on our side."

"It may be fate, Your Highness," replied Dalnt, "but I'll reserve my thanks for Fairtoo." He laughed, praising his companion.

"Look," Father said, pointing in the direction of the spear, "camel droppings."

I never thought I'd be so happy to see a pile of camel dung drying in the morning sun, but this was a sign that Fairtoo had found the trail off the Shale Sea and toward the oasis. Surely his camp was just beyond the horizon. After refreshing ourselves with sips of water and a few dates, we started again, this time with joy in our hearts and confidence in our step.

With the sun directly overhead we came in sight of Fairtoo's camp. Two of our missing camels were standing over a third that was lying on the stone. Out of caution Father and I mounted the she-beast and rode ahead to inspect the camp, concerned that Fairtoo had yet to acknowledge our presence.

About a hundred paces from the camels, Father drew a spear from the quiver at his knee. He put two fingers in his mouth and let out a whistle. The unfettered camels started to move about, shaking their heads and grunting loudly.

"Look," I said, pointing toward the fallen beast. "What do you think is wrong with the camel on the ground?"

Father did not respond for some time. Finally he said, "Flies. It's covered with flies."

Although nothing seemed to live on the vast rock desert, as soon as blood or sweat-soaked skin was exposed, great blue-black flies appeared out of nowhere to bite and suck on the host.

The stench was overwhelming. The dead camel had been gutted. The stone was carpeted with steaming offal covered with hungry flies. Their eager buzzing made a low droning sound. There was no sign of Fairtoo.

We dismounted, covering our faces to keep the flies from our mouths. Father approached the dead beast while I gathered up the confused and frightened war mounts. As I struggled to bring the twan's camel under control it tugged me behind the fly-infested carcass.

"Father!" I cried out. "There's a man's body behind the camel."

Father ran to where I stood.

"It's an Effrifrian soldier!" he exclaimed.

Nothing about the naked corpse indicated his rank, but the shaved band running across the crown of his head and his long black hair pulled straight back and tied with a dark blue thong was the unmistakable sign of an Effrifrian warrior.

"But where's Fairtoo? Do you think he was captured?" I asked, finally getting the errant camels under control.

"I don't know. Go get the others," Father commanded.

When Dalnt, the twan, and I returned, Father stood several paces from the fly-covered corpse. He was vomiting.

"What's the matter?" said the twan, leaping from his mount before it had time to couch.

While the twan and I were focused on Father's distress, Dalnt approached the dead beast. One of Father's spears was protruding from a slit in its belly. Prying open the split, Dalnt screamed, "Oh no! Oh god!" Dropping the spear, he backed away from the carcass, holding his hands to his face and sobbing, "Poor Fairtoo, oh Fairtoo!"

His stomach empty, Father wiped his nose and mouth on his sleeve. The twan moved toward the steaming corpse. Father took the twan by the shoulder and led him to where he could see the Effrifrian bandit.

"The thugs must have surprised Fairtoo. He killed this one, but they must have killed Fairtoo and then fled."

"How can you be certain they killed Fairtoo and didn't take him prisoner?" asked the twan, bending down to examine the Effrifrian more closely.

Father glanced at Dalnt. "Because..." Father faltered, his dark, sun-scorched face whitened, "because Fairtoo's headless body is inside the camel."

It was the ultimate insult to a warrior, an act of terror peculiar to the hated Effrifrians. All peoples believed that if a person's head were removed while still alive, it would forever end their life cycle. Most religions, then and now, believe that life continues after a normal human death, just in another place. It is widely believed that sleep dreams are proof of worlds beyond the present. Removing the head is life's finality.

The twan's face reddened in anger. Hate filled his eyes as he glared at the prostrate Effrifrian at his feet. The flies buzzed and swirled around the cadavers like an evil wind.

There was no place to bury Fairtoo. The flies, maggots, and circling vultures would make short work of his remains. Gathering the camels and what was left of Fairtoo's possessions, we moved away from the gory scene. Dalnt and I were mounted on the she-beast. Father and the twan were on the war camels recovered at Fairtoo's camp.

Well away from the steaming mass of rotting flesh, the twan signaled for us to pause. With a new determination in his voice, he asked, "How far do you think we are from the oasis where we slept before entering this god-forsaken sea?"

"If we ride hard we should arrive by the middle of the night," I answered.

"Al Sumer," said the twan, turning in his saddle to face Father, "how many Effrifrians do you think are in this band?"

"I'm not certain, my lord, the tracks are confusing."

After some thought, the twan said, "It's clear from the fresh dung they are heading for the oasis. The question is, how long will they linger. Surely by now they must know Fairtoo was not alone."

"But sir," said Dalnt, "if al Sumer's mount and yours arrived at Fairtoo's camp *after* they attacked him, how would they know he was not alone?"

"They may have tortured the information from him," I ventured.

"Never!" barked the twan. "Fairtoo was a captain of my guard. He would never break under torture, no matter how extreme."

The twan was quiet for a moment. "I'm sure they must suspect. No captain of the guard would be camped on these embers alone. However, it makes no difference what they suspect. We need to stop wasting time." With that he whacked his mount with his crop and headed toward the oasis.

"Your honor," I blurted out, urging the she-beast forward. The twan kept riding, but slowed slightly for Dalnt and me to catch up.

"Sir..." I hesitated.

"What is it, Ayuba? Speak up."

"I was thinking, sir, the bandits have a considerable lead on us. If they suspect they are being followed they won't stay long at the oasis."

"All the more reason to hurry," said the twan impatiently.

"But sir, if they simply stop to water their mounts, they will have left the oasis long before we get there. With such a lead they will reach the Effrifrian border in only two days. Then we will never catch them."

Father, riding on the far side of the twan, leaned forward. "Are you suggesting we give up?"

"Oh no, Father. I want to make these animals pay for what they did to Fairtoo as much as the rest of you. What I'm saying is unless the bandits are stupid, and thus far they have proven pretty clever, and spend too much time at the spring we will never catch them by following them."

The twan thought for a moment. "Are you saying we need to cut them off?"

"Exactly, sir," I said, now committed to explaining my thoughts. "I believe there is only one oasis between the pool where we camped and the Effrifrian border—"

"The Gleb Spring," Father interrupted. "The bandits will have to stop at the Gleb if they are pushing their mounts hard, otherwise they'll give out before reaching their homeland. If we head east we could intercept them."

Unfamiliar with the terrain, the twan looked at Father. "Is this possible?"

"Yes, but it will double the distance we will have to travel on this scorching plateau. We have little water and the animals are weakening. It will be very difficult," he said, calculating the distance as he spoke.

"It seems our only chance," said the twan. "We owe it to Fairtoo." With that he pulled hard on the reins of his mount and headed directly away from the mid-afternoon sun.

❧

Later that day we came across evidence the bandits knew they were being followed, but it took us some time to figure out what we had found—pieces of cloth filled with steaming camel dung spread across the shale floor.

"These are savvy thieves," Father said, a mixture of disgust and admiration in his voice as he walked among the smelly piles. "No wonder we lost their trail. They must have suspected they would be followed. They purposefully led us onto this barren rock knowing we could only follow them by tracking the dung piles. Once they led us far onto the sea they tied these slings under the camels to capture the droppings then turned abruptly away from their original direction."

"So that's why the trail turned cold," exclaimed the twan.

"Exactly, and their ruse would have worked perfectly had you not sent Fairtoo back to find the trail," mused Father. "They must have waited here for a day and then backtracked to the oasis."

"Fairtoo stumbled right into their plan," said Dalnt.

We were silent as Dalnt's comment raised the gruesome vision of Fairtoo's headless body rotting in the bloated carcass.

"These killers may be smart," grumbled the twan, "but this trickery will at least tell us how many there are."

We counted twenty-two slings. Fifteen camels were stolen from Bensheer, so there were seven additional beasts. Fairtoo had killed one, so Father's original estimate of six remaining killers seemed accurate.

As Father predicted, it was a difficult ride. Even though we rationed what little water we had, we ran out long before reaching the spring. The intense heat sucked the moisture from our skin so that it cracked and peeled like bark. Our tongues swelled and rasped against splintered lips. Wavering mirages beckoned with pregnant clouds seeping moisture just beyond our touch. Despite abandoning everything except our spears, a small bag of dried fruit, and the empty goat bladder, all the camels were lame by the time we reached the sandy desert shore.

The Gleb Spring lies hard against the Shale Sea. It takes its name from the Gleb Gorge, a rocky defile forming a natural border between Effrifria and the kingdom of Hamood. No caravan trails run through the remote land and it is never visited from the direction from which we came. Unless lost, no one would venture from west to east across the fiery rock. Only Father had visited the Gleb many years before while tracking a missing herd of camels.

We had grown accustomed to Father's ability to navigate by the stars. Once again his instincts and skills proved superior. We stepped off the sea at mid-morning just north of the spring. Even before leaving the searing rock the camels' great noses began to twitch. The poor beasts quickened their pace as much as the pain in their charred pads would allow. Dalnt and the twan dismounted several hundred paces from the spring to reconnoiter on foot.

"Al Sumer, how far do you estimate we are ahead of the Effrifrians?" asked the twan, returning from scouting the area.

"There's no guarantee," said Father, looking at the sun, "but my guess is they will arrive by sunset."

Small, flightless birds skittered across the stony plateau chirping warnings of our presence. Although the air was still and hot, it felt refreshing after our recent suffering. Smelling water, the camels tossed their great heads.

Dalnt reported what he and the twan had found. "This gully is the only way in or out of the oasis. There's a ledge about the height of a man encircling the spring... it's like a bowl with water in the bottom. Once in, there is no place to hide our mounts. We dare not approach on foot. The Effrifrians have a large number of beasts that will panic when the attack starts. So even if the thugs have dismounted, a stampede will allow some of them to escape in the confusion. There's a grassy area about a hundred paces deep that starts just as you enter."

"I recall it now," said Father. "One must ride across the foreshore after entering the depression to reach the water."

"Exactly," said the twan. "We must find a hiding place so the bandits will enter without being aware of our presence. Once they're inside we will block the entrance." He paused a moment. "For now, let's get some water before these ornery beasts throw us off...but pay attention. Don't dismount until the camels are in the water. Don't step on the shore."

Although we'd only been on the Shale Sea for a little more than three days, it seemed a lifetime. The cool air and sweet smell of this wild garden soothed our parched senses. Like children, we leapt into the deep, cool water. Even the twan dropped his great dignity (along with his sandals and robe), splashing and diving like some giant fish. Although still saddled, the camels plunged into the water, scooping up huge gulps of the desert nectar with their parched, split tongues. The mud oozed over their padded hooves like a balm.

Dozens of ancient palms lined the banks. In most oases dead fronds are harvested by wandering clans for firewood, but here in isolation, the skirts of dead fronds hung down the length of the trunks undisturbed. Flowering bushes and lush grasses spread out from the shore. The fragrance of the foliage lay on the water's surface like sweet honey.

I drank until I thought my stomach would burst. I could see the skin around Father's eyes relax as the cool water relieved the desiccated wrinkles the sun had seared on his face.

Wringing the water from his hair as he stood, the twan said, "We need to leave now before we get trapped in this beautiful prison."

Fetching the reluctant camels, we led them deeper into the pond so we could wade up to their backs, leaving no sign of our visit except for camel tracks in the sand. These were mixed with hundreds of tracks of wild camels, lions, hyenas, goats, and countless other desert dwellers. The water dripping from the beasts would evaporate soon after leaving. Four smiling, naked men mounted three dripping beasts and headed back to the stony desert waste.

Backtracking a considerable distance, we found a dry streambed heading due east. We expected the Effrifrians to approach from the north, so we headed up the narrow defile until it bore north and dismounted out of sight of the main path. We dressed, ate the few remaining dates and figs we had saved, and settled down to wait. Dalnt walked down the streambed to watch the main trail while the camels dozed.

Our plan was simple: once the Effrifrians passed by we would follow, out of sight. When they dismounted to frolic in the pool, we would ride in and catch them unaware. The twan had no intention of capturing them—we were there to exact vengeance for Fairtoo.

Once we entered the main part of the oasis, my job was to position the she-beast across the exit. We wanted the thieves' camels to stay in the enclosure and create as much confusion as possible. In the unlikely event that any of the bandits should get past Father, Dalnt, and the twan, it would be my job to stop them. Although not a warrior, I was more than capable with a spear. However, I suspected throwing one at a human would be far more difficult than hitting a sheepskin in a pomegranate tree.

As we waited for our prey, the twan slept noisily. Father and I joked that his snoring might give away our location. We sat lost in our own thoughts, until Father asked, "What are you thinking about?"

I was embarrassed to admit I was worrying about the upcoming battle with the Effrifrians.

"It's normal," said Father. "What clouds your mind?"

"I was trying to do as you told me," I said sheepishly. "I was imagining myself successfully stopping one of these murderers by thrusting my spear into him as he tries to get past me, but...sometimes I can't control what I see and I'm afraid I will run away."

Father chuckled softly. "It's normal to have dark thoughts. The important thing is that when they start to enter your mind, you are aware of them and force them away so you can picture the outcome you prefer." Father smiled at me. "In my mind, I see you proudly entering Hamrabi and all the girls squealing when they hear of your bravery."

I blushed at the thought of being a hero.

The Effrifrians arrived shortly before sunset. Dalnt reported there were indeed six well-armed soldiers with fifteen camels in tow. They appeared to have ridden hard; the camels were agitated and frothy with sweat. Dalnt went ahead on foot to make sure we would not accidentally ride up on our prey as they examined the oasis.

While we waited, the twan made a small change to our plan. Dalnt would now ride Father's mount during the attack and Father would ride the she-beast. I would be stationed at the entrance to the spring with three spears to keep any camels or men attempting to flee within the confines of the spring.

"The bandits are too well armed for us to assault them with two of our fighters on the same mount," the twan reasoned. He was concerned the she-beast would bolt and come searching for me once she realized I was not with her when the fighting began.

Maintaining a safe distance, we left our hiding spot and headed toward the main path into the Gleb.

The bandits let out great hoots of joy as they entered the oases. As we waited for them to become fully distracted by the charms of the ancient spring, I had the she-beast couch. Removing my breechclout I tied it around her nose so my scent would be intense. Then I remounted behind Father.

With the twan in the lead, we started down the draw into the Gleb. As we reached the foreshore I gave the she-beast a great kick and yelled, urging her to charge. As I felt her legs dig in, I slid off her back onto the sandy approach to the spring. Father and my great shaggy protector charged into the fray.

From my elevated position at the entrance to the oasis my view of the battle was unobstructed. Charging through the narrow defile, Father, the twan, and Dalnt took the bandits by surprise. Although the enemy was only a hundred paces from where the charge began, the three screaming warriors managed to spread the angle of attack so each approached from a slightly different direction, making it difficult for the startled thugs to focus their response.

We expected to catch the murderers unarmed while splashing about in the pond but we misjudged our timing. Instead we found the string of stolen and unburdened camels knee-deep in the water. The war mounts were couched on the foreshore, the bandits removing their saddles and gear, thus putting the Effrifrians within easy reach of their weapons.

Father was first to let loose a spear. It was a deadly bolt that found its mark in the chest of a large, bearded warrior, pitching him backward into the water.

Dalnt's first spear would have been true, except the camel his intended target was unloading swung its head at that exact moment, taking the spear through its left eye. The beast let out an awful roar, struggling to stand. In its rage, it stumbled and crashed against the thug Dalnt was aiming for, causing both man and beast to lose balance. Frantically the man clung to the packsaddle, his legs flailing as he tried to mount. The camel lurched, blood gushing from its eye, Dalnt's spear swinging wildly. The camel slipped on the bloody sand and pitched sideways into the pond. The Effrifrian frantically tried to climb onto the beast but was trapped by its great weight. He shouted out a plea I could not hear. It faded into a gargling sound as the injured bull rolled over, crushing him beneath the shallow water.

In the time it took Father and Dalnt to loosen their salvos, the twan hurled two spears. One passed through the throat of a young Effrifrian with such force the entire spear came out the back of his neck, lodging in the hip of the camel Dalnt had wounded.

There was great panic in the oasis. Camels, bolting in all directions, began that strange rumbling noise they make when alarmed. Some went deeper into the pond until their dread of deep water overcame their fear of the commotion on the shore. Others charged up the foreshore toward Father and the twan. This gave the remaining Effrifrians precious time to grab their weapons.

With several enraged camels charging me, I lost my view of the fighting. Standing in the middle of the only exit from the Gleb, I quickly removed my robe and waved it frantically over my head and screamed at the beasts. Briefly their charge slackened. Their dark eyes widened—it only took these wise desert animals a moment to understand that this skinny, naked boy waving a robe was the lesser of the threats in the oasis.

The three young males in the lead were in full panic. As they came closer I was forced to back up quickly without turning away. Suddenly there was a great crashing and skidding sound as all three beasts entered the narrow defile side by side. The stone walls forced the camels on either side to lunge for the center causing the lead camel to lose its balance…it went sprawling in front of the other two. All three came crashing down, grunting and bellowing, as legs snapped and heads cracked against the unyielding stone.

Laying in painful confusion, the injured beasts blocked the exit more securely than the she-beast and I could have done under the original plan. The rest of the terrified beasts swiveled away from the bellowing barricade, circling back toward the pond.

While trying to block the panicked beasts, I had dropped my spears and the lead camel had fallen on them. As I bent to retrieve them, I saw an Effrifrian warrior running directly for me through the retreating herd. His shaved head was bloodied, his hair billowing in his wake.

My spears were wedged tightly beneath the camel's vast bulk. The wounded beast snarled and bit me on the shoulder when I pulled on the shafts. The bandit was getting closer but had yet to see me crouching behind the mass of fallen animals. I pulled as hard as I could on the spears, but they wouldn't budge. I looked for a stone or stick…anything I might use to defend myself. Still hiding and frantically searching the area, my heart beat wildly, thudding against my throat as though try-ing to escape my body. I felt the blood pounding in my temples, my legs weak, fear sweat stinging my eyes.

The fleeing killer leapt onto the fallen beasts and was in mid-air when he saw me. His blue tunic was torn, his chest smeared with blood, his eyes radiating fear. He held a bronze sickle-shaped blade in his right hand, now extended over his head for balance. Distracted by the sight of me, he landed with one foot between two of the struggling beasts. The other smacked into the head of the camel that had just taken a bite out of my shoul-der. The blow caused the suffering beast to make a great effort to stand, freeing my spears.

In that instant I grabbed a spear and lunged at the Effrifrian. The experienced warrior twisted his body sideways to narrow my target area while swinging his blade down toward the shaft of my spear, but his feint was too late. I felt the tip of my spear split his skin, slid-ing along his ribs seeking the unprotected entrance to his gut.

I heard him scream. Lunging forward I felt a spray of blood on my face. I dug in my toes and leaned against my spear until my hands pressed against the slime of his belly. I heard his blade rattle against the stone as he fell forward onto my shoulder.

I lay entangled with the dying warrior. Sucking in huge draughts of fetid air I felt the dying man's final breaths, weak and hesitant on my back. The sudden strength I felt defending myself from certain death drained away like water on sand. I slid from under the dead warrior on a slimy coat of blood and sweat in time to see Father running toward me.

"Are you alright?" he shouted, leaping onto the groaning beasts. His tunic was gone and his breechclout was stained with blood. There was a deep, oozing slash across his stomach. His eyes were burning with incredible clarity. He was breathing hard, his chest heaving. The sweat on his body shimmered in the starlight.

Father grabbed me by the shoulders. "Sit down… rest," he commanded, fear in his voice.

"I'm alright Father. I'm not harmed."

"Yes, you are…look at the blood on your chest!"

Looking down I saw my chest covered with blood. Cautiously I ran my hand across the stain. I couldn't help myself as I started to laugh. "It's not my blood, Father, it's his," I said, pointing to the slain warrior who lay between the camels and the wall.

"My god…you got him! That's the devil that wounded me," Father exclaimed, pointing at the gash that ran the entire width of his belly.

"Is it deep? Does it hurt?" I asked. It was hard to imagine Father in pain or, worse yet, dying in battle.

"I'm fine…it's only a surface wound."

The oasis was eerily calm. The camels were grouped at the far end beneath the palms like chastened children.

The twan was dead.

The hero of Hamood lay face down in the bloody foam at the edge of the once pristine shore. The man known as the greatest warrior of his time had turned white, his blood draining onto the fetid beach. He had taken a spear in the back from the warrior I had slain.

"It is a sad victory," said Dalnt, his blood-smeared hands shaking as he removed the twan's scabbard and sign of rank. "The death of sixty of these devils would not atone for the deaths of the twan and Fairtoo."

There was nothing more to say. Yes, we had defeated these horrible raiders, but at a high cost. The twan and Fairtoo had been in many great battles. Songs were sung of their bravery, strength, and honor. Now they had fallen in the desert waste at the hands of a few camel thieves. It was a death neither man would have wanted.

The camel that had been hit in the eye by Dalnt's first spear was lying on the shore, thrashing and moaning. Using his obsidian knife Dalnt gently slit its throat. The great beast's head dropped to the shore with a sigh, its heavily lashed eyes closed forever.

Turning to me Dalnt said, "Can you take care of the others at the gate?" Faint images of circling vultures passing in front of the moon reflected in his eyes.

Father and Dalnt went about the grisly business of beheading the Effrifrians to fulfill the twan's vow. We dragged the headless bodies onto the sand where the circling jackals were sure to feast on them.

Going through the dead men's belongings I found a large amount of dried fruit and goat meat, two fine water bags, and Fairtoo's scabbard and dagger. We expected to find Fairtoo's head, but it was not there.

"It doesn't surprise me," said Dalnt bitterly. "These heathens are without honor."

Mother camel performed perfectly during the battle and was now saddled and ready to leave the garden we had turned into a gory swamp. The smell of blood was heavy in the cold night air. Images of my mother and the little bloodstained foot haunted my mind.

I attached a rope to the hindquarters of one of the fallen camels blocking the exit, and the she-beast used her great strength to open a path through the destruction and out of the Gleb.

Exhausted, our small caravan plodded away from the sadness of the Gleb. Watching Father's broad back as he dozed on the lead camel, I realized that if not for people like him, who were willing to risk their lives to ensure peace, the world I had so recently discovered outside the Beyond would not exist. I wondered how many men perished unheralded in the empty places of the earth defending the rights of people they'd never met. How many stone graves roasted in the desert sand, unremembered and unhonored?

As the sky began to lighten, I vowed from that moment on to begin each day singing a song of tribute in my heart to the lonely graves of fallen heroes.

We were five days from Hamrabi. We had plenty of food and water and our beasts well provisioned. Father led a string of nine camels and I three Bensheerie beasts and five Effrifrian mounts. Dalnt led a camel with the twan's body wrapped in a camp carpet.

The route home would be much easier than our trek across the Shale Sea. Unlike the harsh rock, the sand absorbed the rising sun. Sitting high on our mounts a constant breeze attended us. Father's camel, and indeed my trusted friend, seemed to sense which direction led to Hamrabi as they plodded on unerringly. Exhausted from the work at the Gleb and from the days of peril leading up to the battle with the Effrifrians, we slept to the gentle rocking motion of their gait.

We rode all day. When the sun was low on the western horizon we came upon a large embankment. We unloaded the camels and gathered a pile of twigs and dried dung. That night as the cold desert wind howled above our heads, we were safe and well fed for the first time since stepping onto the Shale Sea.

By the firelight Father and Dalnt talked of the twan's many feats. They took turns singing songs of his valor, praising his intelligence and devotion to duty. I stared into the fire listening to the deep melodies drifting on the desert wind. I was confused by the cheerfulness of the songs. There was no hint of sadness in either the timbre of their voices or the meaning of their words.

Dalnt sang a dream song about Fairtoo. It was filled with brave deeds and ribald tales of Dalnt and Fairtoo roaming the land in the service of Hamood.

Father's dream song was about Marun. It was the first acknowledgement of her death I'd heard from him. His rich voice told of her warmth and humor. He sang as though he was speaking with her—thanking her for giving him life and honoring her as a mother.

I unrolled my blanket by the fire's edge. My body ached from the violence at the Gleb. The pains fed on the turmoil in my heart as I replayed in my mind the horror of the last few days.

Somewhere in Hamood, I pictured Fairtoo's wife and children going to bed unaware that the hero of their lives was moldering in a stinking morass on a scalding slab of ancient stone. For now they slept in the sweet bliss of ignorance, unaware of the approaching storm of sadness that would shatter their lives.

I wondered also about the slain Effrifrians...were they not human? Didn't their children also sleep peacefully and unaware they were now orphaned? Would their pain be any less than that of Fairtoo's children? The sorrow of death has no nationality... knows no borders...confined only by the heart's love of another.

And the twan...a nation slept feeling protected by his ever-present courage and valor. The keystone of their security now cold and bloodless lying on the edge of night rolled in a carpet. Hamood would soon howl with grief, fear, and anger, but for now it seemed I alone grieved.

Father and Dalnt continued to talk about the twan and sing praises to him while, confused by what I perceived as their heartlessness, I sought the relief of a fractured sleep.

The following day as the sun approached its zenith, we came across a faint path intersecting the trail we followed—the path leading to the capital city of Hamood... Hamleed.

"Dear comrades, I must leave you now," said Dalnt, somewhat formally. "When I return to Hamleed I will be appointed twan. It would have been Fairtoo's honor to succeed the great twan, but the responsibility now falls to me."

Opening his pack, he pulled out the twan's inlaid scabbard and knife. "Ayuba, the twan grew to have great respect for you. Indeed he vowed to make you an honorary captain of the guard, so I know he would approve the action I now take in his name."

Dalnt buckled the beautifully inlaid belt around me. The belt was heavy on my waist, its brilliant jewels sparkling in the sun.

"Ayuba, you must come to Hamleed where I will prepare an honorary captain's dagger and belt to replace this one. Until then this symbol of the twan will keep you safe. If any soldiers attempt to detain you, show them the belt and they will render any assistance you might need."

I was dumbstruck. I stammered, "Dalnt, I mean... Your Highness...it is too grand a gift. I cannot accept it."

Dalnt laughed. "You have no choice, my friend from the Beyond. One of the great pleasures of being twan is that my orders must be obeyed!"

Both Father and Dalnt laughed. Father took Dalnt by the shoulders and looked into his eyes.

"This will be the last time I address you as Dalnt. It is a great honor you do my son. It will be reflected on my family and on Hamrabi. You can count on our friendship and support in your new role as twan."

The two warriors embraced. Dalnt placed his arm around my shoulders and said, "We are bound by a shared experience, by blood, and by courage. We meet next in Hamleed." Mounting his beast he turned east with the camel following behind carrying the lifeless body of the twan.

Father and I headed north toward home, riding the remainder of the day in silence, each captive to his thoughts.

As night fell we made camp in a small wadi whose banks shielded us from the cold wind. The sky was clear, a quarter moon sitting coldly on the horizon. We ate the remainder of the goat meat from the Effrifrians' baggage. Then contented, we sat staring into the fire.

"You've been quiet since the Gleb," Father said. "Are you feeling well?"

I was unsure of how to answer. I did feel sad, but also confused and resentful of Father's lack of emotion. It was as though Father and Dalnt knew a secret they were unwilling to share—a secret that allowed them to accept the unacceptable despair of death.

"I feel terrible about the loss of Grandmother and the others," I said, avoiding his eyes. "I can't…" I paused, choking back tears. "It's…well, it's what everyone feels when someone they love dies. It's normal," I blurted out.

Father stirred the coals, a shower of sparks rising into the black sky. "Tell me, Ayuba, what will the grief you're feeling do for my mother or Fairtoo or the twan?"

"Do? What do you mean *do*?"

"Exactly what I said. Will it bring them back to life?"

"Of course not," I said angrily, "I'm not trying to *do* anything for them. I simply feel sad at their leaving."

"Do you believe they would want you to feel sad?" he continued in the same gentle voice despite my harsh response, "or would they want you to sing of their life and celebrate their memory?"

"It's not something I can control," I mumbled. We sat in silence. The wind moaned overhead. Our small fire valiantly held back the vast blackness of the desert. A fox barked nearby.

"Did Marun ever tell you the story of Griefere?" Father asked.

"No."

"It is from this ancient myth handed down through countless generations that we learn the destructiveness of grief. Would you like to hear it?"

I really didn't want to hear a myth. I just wanted to be alone with my pain. Nevertheless I nodded, staring at the dying fire. The glow of the embers lighted Father's black eyes, glinting off his oiled hair and beard.

"Long before men learned to plant crops and live in villages, they worshiped many gods different from those we worship today. It is said there were 'good' gods and 'evil' gods. The problem was evil gods would sometimes act like good gods to trick people into honoring them. Because they were evil, those who followed them also became evil. This led to much confusion and was considered to be the source of all bad things…starvation, disease, floods, murder, and thievery.

"The greatest and most powerful of the 'good' gods was the Sun God Adree. The growing evilness and pain alarmed Adree, so in secret he gathered all the good gods and formed a mighty army. On the summer solstice he led his army down to earth and a great battle took place between good and evil. It raged through a thousand cycles of the seasons and wrought much destruction. Mountains were leveled, rivers loosed from their banks, great winds sucked trees, animals, and humans into the sky in tremendous screeching funnels."

Father was standing now waving his arms over his head, his brow furrowed, his voice shouting above the howling wind. He looked like some ancient desert god with his robe flapping, legs spread wide. He was a powerful speaker—indeed, his voice sounded divinely inspired. Then he dropped it so low I had to lean forward to hear him.

"Finally, with the earth shuddering in fear, Adree and his army trapped all the evil gods in the Valley of Griefere. There the final battle between good and evil was fought. On the day of the final battle Adree and his forces caused the earth to heave up in a great cataclysm. The walls surrounding Griefere collapsed, trapping the evil gods in a prison of immovable pillars of stone."

Father stopped for a moment, the image he painted of the great battle hanging in the air. The silence was punctuated by the snapping of the fresh camel weed I added to the fire.

Then sitting, he continued. "The world rejoiced at this great victory. All evilness, all pain and suffering, starvation, disease, war, and pestilence vanished...forever. This blissfulness, this peace, this blessed world without suffering, lasted for thousands of generations."

Father was then silent as though gathering strength to finish the story. I wanted to urge him to continue but held my tongue as I savored the thought of living in a world without the evilness that had caused me so much pain and suffering—the story I had so reluctantly agreed to hear diverting me from my sorrow.

"Although ancient gods had many powers, they were not immortal. The myth does not tell us what caused his death; it simply says that on the rising of the crab on the date of the autumnal equinox, Adree lay down and died in the fortress of Griefere. At the news of Adree's death a great sadness spread over the world like a dense fog. The god army of Adree shredded their gowns, beat their chests, and shaved their heads. The female gods sobbed great oceans of tears. Indeed their pain was so great they ignored their duties. Hearths became cold. Crops were left to rot in the fields, but worst of all, they failed to man the stone battlements imprisoning the evil gods. Seeing the good gods and people of the earth were immobilized by their pain and sorrow, the evil gods crept from their prison and once again were free to bring chaos to the world."

When Father paused I asked, "Is Griefere where the word 'grief' comes from?"

"Yes. Like so many things we learn through myths, there is a lesson in the story of Griefere. Here the lesson is that grief left unchecked can immobilize us. We all miss people when they disappear...we miss their joy, their knowledge, and their love. We struggle to fill the space in our lives they once held."

"You said it so clearly," I replied. "It's what I'm feeling about Marun and the twan. I can't just stop feeling bad and start singing like you and Dalnt did last night. It just seems wrong not to be sad!"

"Of course you can stop grieving," said Father gently. "Did you grieve for your family after you found them slaughtered in the Beyond?"

"Yes."

"Do you still grieve for them?"

I thought a moment then said, "No. I think of them, but I don't grieve."

"What caused you to stop grieving?"

"I don't know. I suppose I just got so busy trying to stay alive I didn't have time to think about them," I said, wondering when I actually had surrendered my grief and accepted the fact they all had perished.

Father smiled.

"Why are you smiling?" I asked, irritated that I must have missed something.

"You said you were too busy surviving to grieve. That's the point and the message of the myth. Everyone eventually gives up grieving. They just get busy with life and have less and less time to grieve."

"Well, that's not much of a revelation," I said, somewhat sarcastically.

"Oh, my son, it is greater than you might suspect. When we sing, we are choosing to end paralyzing grief now, instead of in the future. We are casting off the heavy stone of grief from our hearts; a stone that, if not removed, will weigh us down so we cannot act, cannot think, cannot plan. We are saying grief ends here and we choose to replace it with the joy of memories."

The wind ceased. The cold desert air closed in on the dying coals. Father rolled himself in his cloak. I moved closer to the embers. That night I dreamt of the twan and Marun. I sang of them. Strange, iridescent birds filled the sky, carrying away the seeds of my grief.

Men like Dalnt, Father, and the twan were more than warriors. They were men who thought deeply about life because they knew how fragile it was.

❧

We arrived at Hamrabi three days later. Pitoon intercepted us about an hour outside the oasis. When we reached the edge of the compound, Father's warning whistle brought Frion running through the grove. The four of us walked into the compound. I was surprised how worried the family had been during our absence, but relief now radiated from their faces. Pitoon and Frion kept hugging me and slapping me on the back, laughing and joking.

Our return was cause for a feast. Released from the fear and tension that had permeated Hamrabi since the raid on Bensheer, the villagers were in a cheerful mood. Copious amounts of sweet date wine, peculiar to Hamood, helped relax and enhance the celebrants. Great quantities of fruits, vegetables, and sweets were spread by a bonfire blazing in the middle of the compound. Children scampered about and young men like Pitoon, Frion, and I joked and laughed, while keeping a close eye on the unwed girls chatting and preening on the other side of the fire.

This was the first oasis-wide gathering I had attended. In fact, it was the largest group of people I had ever seen. I couldn't recall ever being happier. Not just happy… comfortable. I was a part of this. Granted, my story was different and unusual, but the people of Hamrabi had accepted me. And that meant everything.

Once everyone was sated, Father rose to speak. The crowd grew silent—this is what they had come for, to hear him recount our experience chasing the Effrifrian bandits. With fire in his voice he made the attentive audience feel the heat of the Shale Sea. They cried when he described Fairtoo's fly-covered coffin. Then, to my surprise, he exaggerated my minor role during the battle at the Gleb relating how I killed the twan's murderer. The crowd cheered.

Father raised his hands, gesturing for quiet. He asked me to join him. Once again the crowd hollered their appreciation. My face reddened. My hands were sweaty. The comfortable feeling I had relished just moments before retreated like a coward under the gaze of so many people. Father put his arm around me as the audience grew quiet.

"You have already heard me describe the valiant deeds Ayuba performed on the Shale Sea and at the Gleb," Father said, "but there is something I have not told you. Dalnt, the new twan, has honored Ayuba for his valor by confirming he is to become an honorary captain of the guard." The crowd murmured its delight at this news. "As a sign of his sincerity, the twan bestowed the great twan's scabbard and blade on Ayuba until his official induction in Hamleed."

As Father spoke, Mother worked her way through the crowd carrying the twan's scabbard in her outstretched arms. The distinctive weapon and scabbard were recognized and honored by all. Father took the scabbard and buckled it around my waist. Mother took my arm, squeezing it tightly.

I recalled Father's words to Dalnt as we separated on the trail. The twan's scabbard and my honor was indeed an accolade for our family and for Hamrabi, and the people sensed this. Their cheers were for Father and me, but on a deeper level, they were applauding themselves.

"Although Ayuba is indeed valiant in battle and fearless when faced with the terrible Shale Sea, he is not so courageous when it comes to speaking to you all." The crowd laughed. I blushed, my eyes drilling holes into the sand at my feet. "I won't embarrass him further," Father said, squeezing my shoulder tightly, "but I do have one other announcement to make. If you wish to congratulate Ayuba, you must do so within the next two days as he will then leave for Bensheer. After returning the stolen camels, he will travel to Hamleed to receive his honor from the twan."

The people of Hamrabi whistled and clapped. Standing now, they crowded around Father, Mother, and me. Their love and admiration were sincere. Many hugged me and wished me godspeed in my upcoming travels.

I mumbled my way through the heartfelt wishes. Being the center of attention was new to me. I found it exciting while at the same time uncomfortable in its intimacy. I was concerned by what Father had said about Bensheer and Hamleed. To travel as a guide for great warriors like the twan and Father was one thing; to be alone facing new cultures, peoples, and customs was another.

Well-wishers began stopping by our compound shortly after the morning meal the following day. I was in a constant state of embarrassment at being the center of so much attention. Frion and Pitoon teased me about being so shy.

"All an enemy will have to do to defeat you," teased Frion, "is send a pretty girl with a bag of dates and you will forget to draw your weapon!"

Each visitor brought some small gift to ease my journey. There were, however, two gifts of rare value. One, a polished piece of crystal in a soft leather wallet that was so finely honed objects became much larger when seen through its surface. Using it to focus the sun's rays I could start a fire almost instantly. The second gift was a stunning hooded black robe. It was not dyed; rather, it was made from those bastard black sheep—the unexpected product of a white ram and white ewe. Marun had gathered the wool for it over several season cycles and Mother and Linta had woven and sewn it.

The night before departing for Bensheer I lay awake, relishing the familiar smells of my home. I imprinted on my heart the soft breathing and rustling sounds of my sleeping family. The snoring of the camels and distant howling of the hyenas crept through the unshuttered windows. It was the music of my life in Hamrabi. Music that would warm and accompany me wherever my journey led.

By noon the following day I was ready to depart. Mother and Linta finished packing my baggage. The camels were tethered in a line. Pitoon and Frion loaded the baggage camel and put my saddle and spear case on the she-beast. Surveying the caravan while waiting patiently in the shade, Father said, "Walk with me, Ayuba."

We walked through the date grove away from the compound and toward the Beyond. The cool shade contrasted with the bright band of intense sunlight peeking beneath the western edge of the grove. We sat on a fallen date trunk. Father peered at the fiery slash of light.

"I never come this direction in the grove without recalling the day you first came to Hamrabi."

I remained silent, not trusting myself to speak.

"You had no clothes, no family, friends, religion, or culture…you were poor indeed. What joy you have brought to our family. At first it was like having adopted a wild animal, never sure if it would flee or bite." He and I both laughed at this veiled reference to the time I bit Frion on the nose during a brotherly altercation.

Father now voiced a feeling I had long harbored but refused to accept. "Although this will always be your home and we will always be your family, Hamrabi is not your destiny."

Something in my soul had always been agitated by the prospect of wandering. Born a nomad, perhaps it was in my blood. The thought frightened me because it meant eventually leaving Hamrabi and my family.

"But why, Father?" I pleaded. "Is it because I was not born here?"

He looked at me for a long time. A small kid goat wandered up. Father petted its speckled head.

"I cannot give you an answer. It is what you must discover for yourself. All I can tell you is I'm as sure of this as I am that the wind will blow on the desert and that all living things die. You are my son, no more or no less than Frion or Pitoon. This will always be your home, but I suspect the road from Hamleed will take you to places unknown to either of us and adventures beyond our dreaming."

The entire family gathered around the she-beast as I mounted—the boys and Father showing bravado smiles while Mother and Linta softly sobbed and waved good-bye.

As I led the caravan from the compound I felt an overwhelming sense of joy. The joy of traveling alone, of adventure, but most of all the joy of knowing that no matter how far I traveled, I would always be connected by an unbreakable bond to this place and these people.

(5)

"There is more than one kind of crusade," said the wizened old cleric. He stood on a wooden box so the faithful in the rear of the mosque could see him. "There are crusades against property, crusades against morals, and, worst of all, crusades against faith."

Dark eyes peered from beneath his black turban. Slowly he scanned the more than two hundred men kneeling on the concrete floor. A faint asphalt smell scudded through the open windows of the concrete block structure. The constant hum of the nearby refinery at Iran's Abadan complex on the Persian Gulf accompanied his Friday sermon.

"The Prophet (peace be upon him) tells us the infidel uses many ways to attack Allah. The most insidious is the sneak attack where enemies of Islam mislead our children, distracting them from their study of the holy Qur'an." Somewhere in the distance a raven squawked.

"Satan is cunning. He does not shout epithets at the Prophet (peace be upon him). He knows we would overwhelm him with a million martyrs should he blaspheme within our hearing." The old preacher's voice crackled as he tried to shout his anger. It was hot inside the flat-roofed structure sitting on the edge of a fetid salt marsh near the main entrance to the giant oil facility.

"No, the devil is too clever. Instead he hides gold panels in Iraq thousands of years ago among our Shi'ite brothers for the Americans to find. The Americans are the devil's instruments. The Americans use their TV to tempt the weak among us calling Allah a DREAM! Can you imagine? Allah, the knower of all things, a DREAM? Not only do they insult Allah, the false prophet of the Americans—Ayuba—says there are many gods and all prayers are DREAMS!"

One of the worshippers shouted, "No crusade... death to America!"

∽◊∾

ASSOCIATED PRESS: LONDON: FIVE THOUSAND MUSLIMS GATHERED OUTSIDE BBC HEADQUARTERS IN THE CITY PROTESTING THE NETWORK'S AIRING LAST WEEK OF 'THE SONG OF AYUBA,' THE OLDEST WRITTEN DOCUMENT EVER DISCOVERED. THE PROTESTORS OBJECT TO A SECTION IN THE SONG (POEM) IN WHICH THE AUTHOR, A MAN NAMED AYUBA, CLAIMS GOD AND PRAYER ARE NOTHING MORE THAN DREAMS. THE POEM IS THOUGHT TO BE OVER 15,000 YEARS OLD.

∽◊∾

Dust swirled in the morning sunbeams coming through the clerestory windows of the museum. The wooden floor creaked beneath Bryan's feet as he made his way to the rear of the building. *This place is as old as the artifacts it contains,* he thought as he skirted a huge glass case filled with priceless Assyrian pottery.

"Good morning, Dr. Feroz," said Gudabi, rising from his chair and taking Bryan's hand. There were two other men in the room. "Bryan, this is Amhal. He is a graduate student who works as a museum photographer." The young man with a scraggly beard and thin as a cadaver nodded in Bryan's direction.

"And this is Colonel David Thomas of the coalition authority."

"Pleased to meet you," said the athletic-looking man, taking Bryan's hand. "Dr. Gudabi has told us many good things about you."

"Your timing is perfect, Dr. Feroz…I've been trying to call your hotel all morning, but…" throwing his hands in the air in frustration, "ever since the invasion, the phones are impossible."

"Dr. Gudabi, we prefer to say *liberation*," said Colonel Thomas with a polite but weak smile.

"Yes, yes, of course…an unfortunate choice of words." Amhal shifted against the wall.

"Actually I just dropped in to say good-bye. As you know I'll be leaving this evening." Bryan had stayed on in Baghdad for a week following the TV documentary as an advisor to the coalition's cultural reconstruction division and was anxious to return home.

"Any chance we could get you to hang around another couple days?" asked Colonel Thomas.

"What's this about?"

"Amhal…the photos please," said Dr. Gudabi. Without comment, the sour-looking student pulled a manila folder from his backpack and withdrew a black and white photo of Ayuba's tomb.

"You see here," said the student, his breath thick with the smell of tobacco and coffee, "at the base in stone. You see?"

Bryan raised the photo, peering closely where Amhal had indicated. "Sorry, Amhal, it just looks like stone to me."

Withdrawing another photo from the folder Amhal said, "Okay, now close up. Now you see...small cracks?" Bryan could see faint fracture lines in the stone at the base of the tomb wall.

"Are these new?"

"We think so," said Dr. Gudabi.

"When I photograph tomb for museum, big bomb go off outside. I can't hear it but feel tomb move, like..." Amhal shook his body as though he was shivering. "Then I see these," he said, pointing at the photo in Bryan's hand.

"It's a shame," said Colonel Thomas. "This thing has rested undisturbed for fifteen thousand years. Now all of a sudden it's in danger."

"The coalition authority suggested we move the panels to the museum for safekeeping," said Gudabi, "but I think they'll be safer under the military headquarters in Azzohour. Here, any Taliban fanatic that decides the panels are a threat to Islam could blow them up—just like the giant Buddhas in Afghanistan."

"I can't say I disagree," said the colonel. "On the other hand, we have a lot of folks who depend on the Green Zone for their safety and we've noticed an increase in attacks since 'The Song' was made known to the world. The safety of my people must come first. That's why we've come up with a compromise we'd like to run by you."

"Fire away," said Bryan.

"Beneath Al Asad Airbase in Al Anbar Province... you know, out toward Jordan," said the colonel, pointing to the west, "Saddam built a huge nuclear facility. It's the dandiest thing you've ever seen—smack dab under the main runway. When I say *under* I mean about a hundred feet under. Anyhow, it's got all the trimmings...

clean room, air filtration, and security up the wazoo. It's the perfect place to store the panels until things settle down."

"Sounds perfect," said Bryan. "Any problem detaching and transporting the panels?"

"We have a lot of experience moving relics," said Gudabi. "As our partner in this venture, we want to make certain the institute and National Geographic agree with the plan. And, of course, we would like you to be on hand to monitor the actual transfer of the panels."

"Uh...hello."

"Alex, it's Bryan. Seems I'm always waking you up... sorry."

"Oh no...I'm so happy to hear your voice." Alex tried to sound awake as she sat up in bed and reached for the light on her nightstand.

"Are you okay? You sound, uh...different?"

"Yes, I'm fine. Just worn out from all the excitement."

"I know what you mean; it's been hectic here too."

Alex thought how difficult it must be for Bryan. In addition to the constant threat of violence, there was the physical discomfort of the heat, lack of electricity, uncertain accommodations, and iffy transportation. Compared to what he was going through, the stress she was dealing with concerning post-program publicity seemed trite.

"Are you still planning to come home next week?" she asked.

"Well, that was the plan...until today. Now I'm not sure."

"Why? What's happened?"

"You know I've been monitoring the transfer of the panels," he said, careful not to mention over an open phone line exactly where they were housed.

"Yes. In your last e-mail you said you hoped to transfer two panels yesterday...uh, tonight," she said, trying to calculate the time in Iraq.

"That's right. We transferred the first panel with no problem. But when we detached the second panel we found a large ceramic urn hidden behind it. Can you believe it?"

"My god, Bryan...is it intact?"

"Yeah, it's in perfect condition. In fact, there appears to be a copper cap sealing the mouth that, unbelievably, is still in place."

"Have you opened it yet? What do you think it contains?"

"Who knows? As heavy as it is I suspect it's some sort of offering, but we won't know for sure until we open it. That's why I called. I'll be delayed here indefinitely, until...you know...until I can examine the contents of the urn."

Trying to hide her disappointment, Alex said, "I understand. I'm so excited for you."

The irony is almost overwhelming, Bryan thought as he pulled on a white clean room suit. *Here we are about to open an ancient relic using some of the world's newest technology.*

As he opened the airlock deep in the bowels of Al Asad Air Base and entered the ISO Category 4 clean room, Bryan noticed the hum of the air circulation system filtering the air every three minutes. Shadowless light from a translucent ceiling flooded the room.

Dr. Gudabi and Colonel Thomas had followed Bryan into the facility and the three men stood looking at the urn. It sat on a white table near the center of the space in a sterile stainless steel tray held in place by foam-cushioned clamps.

"When I brought it here I did some preliminary measurements. It's sixty cm tall and thirty cm at its widest part," Bryan said, pointing at the vase. "The mouth appears to be approximately twenty-four cm in diameter, but we can't say for sure until we remove the lid. It weighs 15.9 kilos."

"That's heavy for a vessel that size. What were the results of the x-rays?" asked Dr. Gudabi.

"Inconclusive. There appears to be a filler of some sort, possibly ashes, with a hollow core, but the medical people who looked at it couldn't agree on the substance."

"Well then," said Dr. Gudabi, "let's find out." His hands perspired inside the latex gloves as he tightened the circular clamps steadying the vase. With a pair of stainless steel dental forceps he slowly pried the lip of the copper lid away from the neck of the urn.

Bryan felt a rivulet of sweat drip down his neck. The room seemed warmer. He realized he was holding his breath. Colonel Thomas circled the table taking close-up digital pictures.

When Dr. Gudabi had loosened about a third of the cap, there was a crunching sound as the top two inches of the ancient container with the cap still attached shattered and dropped into the metal tray. Gudabi froze—his hand with the forceps rigid above the now fractured urn.

"Oh shit!" cried the colonel.

"What happened?" asked Bryan.

"I don't know. I was being as gentle as possible," Gudabi said, looking at his trembling hand.

"Okay...everybody settle down and take a deep breath." Peering into the tray holding the urn Bryan said, "Well, at least we know what the filler is...it looks like sand."

Pulling a bio-cart up to the table, Colonel Thomas said, "I assume you'll want to culture it."

"Absolutely," said Bryan. He used a sterile sampling kit to bag some of the sand.

"How long will it take?"

"We'll probably phase it. First reading in twenty-four hours, then three more readings twelve hours apart."

Still stunned, Dr. Gudabi ventured, "Shall we empty the rest of the container?"

"I don't think we should handle the urn itself without reinforcing the inside of the container. Maybe we could vacuum out more sand without disturbing it."

"We have a peristaltic vacuum, but I'm not sure we should use it. If there are any unusual micro-organisms it could destroy them. Plus we have no idea what may be mixed in with the sand; there could be human ashes. I mean, it seems pretty odd to store an urn with just sand inside," said Colonel Thomas.

Having decided to remove the sand manually, the two scientists waited while Colonel Thomas appropriated a long-handled teaspoon from the chow hall and had it sterilized. The irony was not lost on Dr. Gudabi. "So much for high-tech wizardry," he commented as he gently began scooping out the filler.

At eight cm, the spoon struck something solid. All three men peered into the container.

"It looks like another container," said Bryan.

"Do you have a fiber optic video lens?" asked Dr. Gudabi of Colonel Thomas.

Within minutes, a magnified image of the inside of the container came up on the monitor. The obstruction they had uncovered was clearly defined—the top edge of a tightly wound scroll.

⟪⟫

He's tired, thought Alex, looking at Bryan across the broad mahogany table. She thought about his last few days isolated in the bunker beneath the air base—very little sleep, MREs for food, and the unrelenting responsibility of caring for and handling the fragile scroll. As if that wasn't enough, there was the dangerous midnight convoy from Al Asad to Amman, Jordan...the flight to Rome...ten hours to Chicago...the limo from O'Hare to the university campus...and now this meeting with Dr. Anthos Baradacchi, dean of the Oriental Institute, Dr. Watson, and herself.

Dr. Baradacchi, formerly the dean of the University of Bologna's Ravenna campus, was the founder of that prestigious institution's department of conservation of cultural heritage. His continental insouciance, small frame, stylish wardrobe, and richly accented English set him apart from most American academics. The fact that he had been selected following a global search to chair one of the University of Chicago's most renowned branches had silenced those within academia put off by his flamboyance.

"I agree with Bryan," he said. "It is critical we keep the scroll's existence confined to as few people as necessary...at least until it is translated."

111

"I'm sorry, but I don't quite understand the reason for the secrecy," queried Dr. Watson.

Referring to recent marches in Pakistan where several people had died while demonstrating over the stanza in "The Song" that referred to god as a dream, Dr. Baradacchi said, "Farrell, think how many people senselessly died when we revealed the 'Song' on live TV. And before that, the turmoil and violence in the Muslim world over the Danish cartoons. Until we know what's in the scroll, keeping it secret will prevent unfounded speculation by the extremists."

"There will always be extremists. We shouldn't make decisions based on their reactions. The vast majority of Muslims view Ayuba as we do…an ancient secular voice unconnected with Islam in any way…and are as interested and excited about this as we are. I could argue just the opposite—that by issuing a press release now we could blunt future extreme reactions. Besides, it might turn out to be a shipping document or a laundry list and we'll have missed the opportunity to capitalize on the interest and excitement generated by the 'Song.'"

"It's a moot point, Farrell. We have already agreed with Gudabi that we will not reveal anything before we have the scroll translated. The museum has the final say and we are bound to honor their wishes. Besides, it could take years to translate the scroll. Sadly, the one person who could expedite the process is no longer with us." Baradacchi nodded toward Alex, acknowledging the loss of her father.

Bryan had insisted Alex attend the meeting despite doubts expressed by the two renowned scientists. She was there simply as an observer representing her father's claim to the new language. No one expected her to take part in the discussions.

"I don't believe it will take long to translate the scroll," said Alex. The men looked at her as though she had blasphemed some academic icon. Her cheeks flushed.

"We appreciate your optimism, my dear," Dr. Baradacchi said condescendingly, "but Dr. Gudabi informs me that for the past thirty years under Saddam there has not been one graduate student in the ancient Sumerian languages. And little has been accomplished outside of Iraq...much to our shame."

Oh god, thought Alex, *now you've done it. How do you explain to these famous and powerful academics that as a girl, your father delighted in playing word games with you using Akkadian and Eblaitian characters? Would these men whose measurement of academic success is based on articles published and the number of letters one can attach to one's name understand that you chose not to formally study ancient languages because, to you, it was indeed child's play?*

"I know this will seem, um, unbelievable, but I can read, write, and speak both Akkadian and Eblaite."

The room went silent. Somewhere in the distance a car alarm went off.

"Really, my dear? I didn't know anyone could actually speak these ancient languages," said Dr. Watson, breaking the silence with his skepticism.

"You're correct, of course. No one knows for certain how those languages were spoken, but my father and I created a phonetic glossary for both languages as a game when I was a girl. Not only did it allow us to communicate without worrying about the dreaded security department, the Mukhabarat, it was Father's way to get me interested in history and language." Alex looked at Bryan. She wanted to laugh. His mouth was actually hanging open as though he'd just witnessed the second coming. The other two men looked confused and doubtful.

"Look, Alex, I'm sure you're very bright, but this project will take more than childhood games to do it right," said Baradacchi gently.

Smiling, Alex replied, "I understand your concerns and expected you to be doubtful. After all, you are scientists."

Pulling four sheets of paper from her briefcase and passing one to each of the men she said, "I've prepared a cross reference table between Ayubian, Akkadian, Eblaite, Arabic, and English based on my father's original work. As far as I can tell from his notes in the cuneiform orthography of Eblaite, several proto-Semitic phonemes are lost in the comparative with Ayubian. Proto-Semitic glottal and pharyngeal stops and fricatives are lost as consonants either by sound change or orthographically, but they give rise to a diphthong— *oo*—not known in proto-Semitic. The interdental and the voiceless lateral fricatives seem to be merged with sibilants as in Canaanite, leaving nineteen consonantal phonemes. When these anomalies are delineated phonetically with—"

"Enough! I give up," cried Baradacchi, throwing up his hands in mock surrender.

"Me too," said Watson, letting out a satisfied chuckle.

Bryan just smiled, the tiredness in his eyes momentarily replaced with pride and delight.

Alex, her dark eyes radiating intelligence, said, "I wasn't trying to show off. I just wanted to make the point that I'm capable of carrying on the work for which my father gave his life. I understand the ancient structures, but more importantly I know how my father analyzed and thought about languages." She hesitated, fighting back tears. She continued, "I'd like to be the translator of the scroll."

Translating the scroll proved easier than Alex anticipated. Daily she thought of her father as she applied the matrices he had created to convert the unusual Ayubian script into Arabic. She felt a closeness to him, as though his spirit lived in the vitality of his work. Although all the characters in the scroll were not used in the limited verses of the "Song," their meanings were easily determined by the unfolding content of the text. Within six months, more than half the scroll was done. Within nine months, the translation was complete.

Alex was living with Bryan's widowed mother, Salawa, in her elegant home in the upscale, gated community of Fox Glen in the Chicago suburbs. Bryan's mother was delighted to have a companion, and the two women had grown close over the preceding months, each finding in the other the fulfillment of unacknowledged needs.

Salawa had grown increasing lonely after the death of her husband. A year before the Ayuba discovery, Bryan had taken an apartment in the city to be closer to his work. Although proud of Bryan's many accolades, on another level she resented his accomplishments because each promotion laid claim to him in ways she could not. Alex's presence had softened the scar that had formed over her heart to protect her from the pain of aloneness.

For Alex's part, Salawa reminded her of the mother she no longer had; the way she raised one eyebrow when unsure of a comment; her penchant for stylish yet clunky shoes. But most of all, the respectful way she spoke of her marriage. Her very movements at times were so like her mother's that Alex felt transported to a happier time in Baghdad.

A small group of friends and colleagues had been invited to Salawa's spacious home to view the screening of the first half of the two-part documentary on the scroll. Peering over the edge of his champagne flute, Bryan admired Alex as she moved through the gathering. A lapis necklace glowed against her dark complexion, its pendant drawing his eye to her elegant cleavage. The midnight blue satin of her knee-length dress was the perfect counterfoil to her cascading ebony hair.

"It's impolite to stare," his mother whispered from behind. "Although I can't blame you...she is stunning."

"I didn't think I was so obvious."

"Perhaps not to others, but I am your mother after all."

"Why do I get the feeling you two were talking about me?" asked Alex, approaching Bryan and his mother.

"Can you blame us?" replied Bryan with a smile. "You look radiant."

"Thank you very much, Professor," Alex replied with an abbreviated curtsy.

Leading the way from the living room to the family room where a large flat panel screen had been installed earlier in the day, Alex and Bryan encouraged the guests to find their seats.

Promptly at eight, the National Geographic Society logo filled the screen..."The Scroll of Ayuba...changing world history!" Dr. Watson, as he had done with the original program about Ayuba's song, gave a brief history of how the song and scroll were discovered. He explained that this evening's presentation was the first of two three-hour specials to be aired two weeks apart.

Combined, they would cover the entire contents of the scroll.

The screen slowly morphed from Dr. Watson into a wide-angle view of a dune-strewn desert with the sun just breaching the horizon. The haunting music of Rahim Alhaj's "Iraq Music in a Time of War," like a soft breath seemed to emanate from a distant mirage barely visible on the screen. The unmistakable voice of Sharrif al Bardan, the exiled actor who for many in Iraq had been the voice of hope over the banned Radio Free Iraq, began to read "The Scroll of Ayuba."

(6)

I traveled two days due east. On the morning of the third day, a long gash of bushes and trees announced the presence of the river Ben. It ran from horizon to horizon, north to south, dissecting my path. As instructed by Father, I turned north, following the river toward Bensheer.

Never having seen anything but intermittent desert streams, I was anxious to see the river. Tales were told of epic battles fought in the Ben River valley between nomadic tribes, whose lives depended on hunting wild beasts and gathering plants, and the more recent stationary villagers who raised crops and animals for a living.

It was said the river Ben ran red with blood more often than brown with silt. From the songs and poems sung by the fires of Hamrabi I expected to find a churning torrent. I was disappointed.

The river was shallow and sluggish. Although the riverbed was wide, with sandy tree-lined banks, the stream itself was so narrow I could leap across it in several places.

I made camp on a wide beach. The hobbled camels were free to roam, drinking their fill of the tepid water while grazing on the succulent foliage. I spent the day exploring the river.

As the sun neared the horizon, I checked on the camels. Gathering a large pile of deadfall, I used the polished crystal lens to capture the sun's remaining rays and quickly started a fire.

That night lying by the fire on the edge of sleep I felt a deep satisfaction. I was literally wrapped in the love of my family as my black cloak warmed and comforted me. Although unsure of my future, I put any concerns aside and reveled in the present. As my lids began to sag I counted my fortune in the stars.

When sleeping in the Beyond, there was always a part of me that was vigilant. The snap of a twig, the rustle of a bird, a distant growl, and I would awaken instantly. My only weapon was flight; a step or two's advantage meant the difference between life and death. However, living in a village would prove to have dulled my sleep awareness...

"Move at all and my spear will rip out your throat," said the high-pitched, nervous voice.

I opened my eyes slowly. The gray light of dawn silhouetted a boy about fifteen standing over me. His hands, grasping his spear, shook slightly. I could feel the spear point shiver on my throat.

"You Effrifrian bastard. I should kill you at once," he spat.

I shifted my body slightly, my hand inching closer to my dagger.

"Don't move!" I felt the spear break the skin on my throat.

"I'm not what you think," I whispered, afraid to startle the boy.

"Don't talk, you lazy fool. I know exactly what you are. I've seen the camels you stole from our village and those inferior Effrifrian mounts. And your blue robe certainly damns you." The anger rose in his voice. His hands steadied as his confidence grew.

"It's not blue, it's black. I'm from Hamrabi."

"Silence!" he shouted. "Roll over slowly. If you make a move I will gladly end your life."

I had no choice. Carefully I rolled onto my stomach. It was the last thing I remember.

On hearing children shouting and laughing, I tried to open my eyes. My head throbbed, my back felt as though I had been trampled by a herd of camels.

For the second time in my life I woke peering through blood-soaked lids as the ground passed beneath me. The shrill sound of women screeching came from nearby. I tried to raise my head, but the rope around my neck held me firmly in place. When I tried to lift my legs, the rope pulled tight around my throat. Memories of my capture in the Beyond flashed through my mind.

"Come quickly," a voice shouted, "Tarley's captured one of the killers! Look, he got our camels back!"

"No! No!" I tried to shout. "I'm not Effrifrian." I no sooner had spoken than I felt a burning lash across my back. I screamed in pain. Another followed, and then another.

"You bastard! This is nothing compared to what you are about to suffer," a voice growled in my ear.

I was strapped across one of the Effrifrian mounts. My robe was gone. I wore only my breechclout. My hair and eyes were caked with blood from the gash on my head. My sunburned back was being flayed with willow switches wielded by angry villagers.

"Look, look…he also killed the twan! See, here's the twan's scabbard!"

I recognized the boy's voice, now much bolder than before. A roar went up from the crowd. Women wailed and children shouted, "Stone him. Stone him. Stone the killer!"

Something solid slammed into my exposed back. I jerked instinctively and the rope tightened around my throat. I lost consciousness.

A fly crawling up my nose caused me to sneeze. I wanted to swat it away, but couldn't move my arms. I forced myself toward consciousness…more flies buzzed around my ears and mouth. Sneezing again, I felt a searing pain rip through my chest and arms. People shouted, "He's awake!" Another voice responded, "Not for long." Then laughter.

Forcing my eyes open, I wanted to vomit. Everything was swaying. I closed my eyes. The pain in my arms and chest was suffocating me. I puked. I felt the warm vomit run down my chest and across my groin.

Opening my eyes again, I saw a blurry crowd of angry villagers fade in and out. I was hanging by my arms from the limb of a tree. Both shoulders dislocated. To breathe, I had to pull up on my arms to relieve the dead weight of my body. I was drowning in pain. I could feel the flies feasting on the vomit on my chest.

A deep voice called, "Stay awake, you murderer, we want you to feel your life seep away just as my brother's did on the end of your spear!" Something soft and wet plowed into my chest.

"Here's some fruit for the flies. It will sweeten your vile skin."

More laughter. I couldn't breathe.

I don't know whether it was the cold water thrown in my face or my feet touching the ground that pulled me from the edge of death. My arms were still above my head, stabbing pain lancing through my shoulders. I sucked in huge gulps of air. I was not fully conscious… voices and dreams mixed like a soup in my mind.

"Grandmother, you are wrong. He stole our camels!"

"He's not an Effrifrian, I tell you!" came Marun's voice.

Marun? How could she be here? I must be dead. Again, Marun's voice.

"You'll have plenty of time to kill him if I'm wrong."

Another splash of water brought me fully awake. I could see the hem of a robe and many sandaled feet surrounding me. I tried to raise my head, but my dislocated shoulders wedged it firmly onto my chest. Vomit, blood, and fruit slime covered my body. Flies were everywhere. Again Marun's voice.

"Let his arms down. Are you afraid he will run off? He's practically dead."

I felt my bonds loosen. Screaming in pain as my arms fell forward, the muscles in my shoulders failing to respond. Falling, I slammed into the ground in a great swirl of dust and flies.

"Turn him over," said Marun.

"Marun," I cried, "help me!"

"What did he say?" a man's voice said.

Someone kicked me hard in the side. I lurched onto my back. The midday sun lanced my eyes, forcing them shut. Again the male voice.

"Alright, Grandmother, here's the coward. Ask him whatever you want."

I felt a robe against my skin. Someone was kneeling beside me, shading the sun from my face. Opening my eyes I looked into the familiar face of my grandmother... Marun.

"Oh, Marun," I choked.

"Hear that? Did you hear that?" Marun shouted.

"Hear what, Grandmother? It sounded like the grunt of a pig."

"Come down here where you can hear," Marun ordered. "He won't bite."

I could feel people crowding around.

Gently now, Marun spoke, "Say it again, boy...what did you call me?"

My eyes locked onto hers. "Marun...Grandmother," I pleaded, "it's me, Ayuba."

Laughter.

"Camel Boy...is that what you wanted us to hear?"

Again chants of "Stone him, stone him!"

"Shut up, you fools! Don't be so anxious for revenge. He said Marun. My sister's name!"

The old woman pushed the hair from my forehead, saying, "How do you know my sister Marun?"

"Probably killed her," grunted the man.

Through the confusion I looked more closely at the old woman. Her face was more wrinkled than Marun's. The eyes and mouth were similar, but her nose was veined and crooked, unlike Marun's.

"My name is Ayuba. I'm from Hamrabi, and Marun al Sumer was my grandmother," I grunted. At the mention of the name al Sumer a low murmur came from the crowd.

"Was? What do you mean *was* your grandmother?" the old woman asked.

"Marun is dead."

Once again the man's voice, still angry but less certain, "He probably killed her."

Ignoring the man, the old woman asked sadly, "How did she die?"

The pain in my arms was so great I could barely speak. "In her sleep," I groaned.

A dark veil of sadness shaded the woman's eyes.

"It proves nothing," I heard the boy who captured me say. "He had our camels and the twan's scabbard." This caused the crowd to once again call for my death.

Ignoring the angry villagers and her grief, Marun's sister said, "If you expect to survive, you need to explain how it is you have our camels and the twan's scabbard."

"Please, Grandmother. The pain in my shoulders…I can barely speak. Please help me sit," I pleaded.

The old woman looked hesitantly at me for a moment before slipping her bony arm under my neck. "Give me a hand," she said to a man standing near my head.

The man jerked me upright. The force of his effort caused both my shoulders to snap into place. It felt as though someone stabbed a spear in my back. I clenched my jaw so hard one of my teeth shattered. I convulsed in pain, spitting broken pieces of tooth in a stream of fresh blood.

"More! More!" shouted the crowd.

The old woman knelt directly in front of me and said, "Boy, you better talk quickly or these people who have suffered much will rip you apart."

Pushing the dreadful pain from my mind I spoke. "My name is Ayuba. I am the son of Aroon al Sumer, protector of the western border from the oasis Hamrabi."

"Liar!" came a shout from the crowd.

A large man with a dark gray beard stepped forward. "I served with Aroon al Sumer in the war against the apostate general Barnkoo. I have visited his home. He has only two sons, Pitoon, the eldest, and Frion, the second. It is impossible for this boy to be his son."

"Liar! Liar!" the crowd shouted.

"Please!" I shouted, "let me explain. You are correct…I am the *adopted* son of al Sumer."

The former soldier who knew Father laughed. "Al Sumer adopt an Effrifrian bastard? Never!"

"I'm not an Effrifrian," I cried before the crowd could start chanting again. "Look at my hair. Is it shaved like an Effrifrian warrior"? I tried to point at my head but the pain paralyzed my arms. "Have you ever seen an Effrifrian without a shaved head?"

"He has a point," the old lady said. "I've lived longer than anyone here and have seen hundreds of Effrifrians."

"What about the blue robe and the twan's scabbard?" shouted someone I could not see.

"My robe is black, not blue," I responded as forcefully as my pain would allow. "If you'll bring it here you will see. It was made for me by al Sumer's wife, my adopted mother, and my sister Linta."

The familiar voice of the boy who captured me rang out, "He's lying. It's blue. I saw it."

Marun's sister stood and faced the boy. "If it is indeed an Effrifrian robe, then let's settle this man's fate once and for all. Tarley, fetch the robe," she commanded.

"Why should I?" cried Tarley. "He's a lying Effrifrian. Are you taking his word over mine?"

The old woman looked down at me. "He knows far more about the al Sumer family than any marauding bandit could know. He knows the name of my sister." She paused, choking back her tears as the reality of Marun's death flashed across her mind. "Settle this now, Tarley. Unless you have something to hide, bring the robe."

"Why don't you tell us how you happen to have the twan's scabbard? The twan was here only days ago and was in excellent health. I suppose he met you on the road and adopted you too," said the ex-soldier. The crowd laughed at the jest.

Bensheer (11,000 BCE)

Sitting naked in the dust of Bensheer, with my own vomit and blood caking my fly-covered body, I told the story of the Shale Sea and the battle of the Gleb. The crowd leaned forward to hear. My voice was faint and raspy. I finished by explaining that Father instructed me to return the Bensheerie camels on my way to Hamleed to be honored by the new twan.

The boy Tarley pushed his way through the crowd holding my robe.

"It is black!" shouted someone in the crowd.

The boy knelt in front of me. "I was wrong...it was barely light and I was sure your robe was blue and the hood covered your head. I'm sorry."

Tears filled the old woman's eyes. "I'm afraid we've made a terrible mistake."

The people of Bensheer were as generous in their repentance as they were violent in their revenge. I was carried to Marun's sister's house.

Her name was Ventie. She bathed me and rubbed my wounds with palm oil. She brewed tea made from dried flower pods, the brew relieving the pain in my shoulders and soothing the pain from the lacerations on my back. She made a thick pile of sheepskins on the floor in front of the hearth for me to lie on.

I closed my eyes. Strange images floated in my mind. I talked with Marun and told her of the great weed ball, but when she laughed, her voice sounded like the twan cursing the Effrifrians. Images of Mother drifted through rich colors brighter than the Shale Sea. Linta rode the she-beast, waving good-bye through deep shadows punctured with vibrant crimson sunlight. Tarley

127

floated in and out of my mind. He cried and laughed. He knelt in front of me with a candle in his hand. I forgave him. He cried some more.

Warm hands massaged my limbs. Someone fed me sweet broth. I slept, dreaming of Hamleed and a vast throng of people shouting my name. The she-beast was festooned with marigold chains, the other camels kneeling when she passed by. I walked through an unfamiliar city where the path, glittering with silver, rose to meet my feet. The severed heads of the Effrifrians bounced down the lane in front of me. Garish green foliage streaked with gold separated, revealing a brightly robed choir singing praises to Father.

It was the sound of singing that finally awakened me. It wasn't singing like Father's or the twan's, but a low chant. I struggled to pull myself out of my deep slumber. They were calling...my name.

"Ayuba. Ayuba...forgive us."

I started to sit up, shaking the mysterious images and music from my mind.

"Welcome back," said Ventie softly.

Strong hands helped me sit up. It was Tarley. His eyes were red, and fear and confusion dulled his boyish face.

"How long have I been asleep?" I asked, stretching carefully.

"More than two days," said Ventie. "Did you enjoy the flower dreams?"

I closed my eyes, recalling the vividness of the strange sleep journey. I gingerly flexed my shoulders, surprised there was little pain. "Is that what they're called? Two days? It can't be."

"Actually almost three," said Tarley, as though afraid to speak.

I looked at the sad-faced boy. "You were in my dreams. You were crying and holding a candle."

"That was not a dream. Tarley has been with you the entire time. Even when I slept, he stayed awake in case you might need attending," explained Ventie.

"Strange," I said bitterly, "I thought you wanted to kill me."

The boy knelt and bowed so his head touched the floor. Sobbing, he cried, "Your Highness, forgive me. I am young and mistook you for the killers of my uncle and cousin. Please forgive me."

I looked at the boy's back as he sobbed, tears welling in my eyes. How many times as a boy his age had I lived in fear and felt alone? The reed gatherers' harsh treatment came to mind. I lifted his head; his streaming eyes sought my forgiveness.

"Tarley, you were very brave. Your fear clouded your judgment."

"Oh, thank you, Your Highness," he sobbed, wiping his eyes on the back of his hand.

"Tarley, please stop calling me Your Highness. I'm barely a man and not worthy of such a title." I tousled his hair, giving him a smile.

"I told you an al Sumer would forgive you, Tarley. Now please go outside and tell everyone to go home and be at peace," Ventie said. Seeing the confusion on my face, she continued, "After everyone was convinced you were an al Sumer from Hamrabi, they were afraid you would demand the boy's life. All the time you slept they have prayed for your forgiveness."

Thanking me with every step, Tarley backed out the door. The chanting stopped. Soon a loud cheer went up from the crowd.

To build my strength, Ventie and I walked in the evenings along the banks of the river. The setting sun glancing off the sky reflected in the torpid stream. A deep orange slashed across the west. The sky turned from powder blue to dark violet then to black. Small birds skimmed the surface of the river, snatching water creepers and other insects from the cooling air. Bats darted about with sharp jerks and turns, decimating the night bugs.

Sitting on a grassy bank near the house we watched the stars break out of the blackness. She knew many of them by name. I told her how al Sumer could navigate using the stars as a guide. She responded that some stars were not stars at all, but worlds and moons. She taught me the different stellar formations and said this was an ancient method known to all civilized peoples. Even though she knew many things about the moon and stars, when she spoke of them she whispered in awe, as though her voice might shatter the crystal light.

"Grandmother," I asked, "you are so familiar with the heavens, why do you act as though you are in awe of them as one would who is ignorant?"

She thought for a moment, the sound of the river gurgling in the background.

"I am in awe of many things," she finally said. "I am in awe of the sun rising each day. Of plants sprouting and the birth of a baby. I wonder at the rain that comes just when needed. Why does water boil? I am in awe of my heart beating, stopping only once and then forever. I'm in awe of the fact that the river never runs dry and the air...where does it come from? More importantly, why does it exist?" she said with wonder in her voice. "Are you not in awe of many things, Ayuba?"

The stars were fully out now, although dimmed somewhat by a full moon rising at our backs. A sudden quacking sound came from the shore as a fox disturbed a flock of ducks. I felt the air against my face as the birds skimmed in front of us. Ventie and I laughed.

"I guess I'm in awe of the fact that we didn't get hit in the face by those ducks!"

Trying to answer Ventie's questions I said, "Most of my life has been spent simply surviving. Until the al Sumer family adopted me, I was steeped in the ignorance of the Beyond. I did not speak to another soul as I wandered the desert. I was afraid of the night and the day. At night I could not see, unlike the animals I most feared. During the day, I could be seen by hostile bands who would think nothing of killing me. After coming to live in Hamrabi, it took me a long time, even with the patient coaching of your sister, to understand those things that lie beyond the basics of survival."

"What things?" asked Ventie.

I thought a moment. "I did not know any of the Hamoodian language. I had to learn like a child. After several season cycles of patience on her part, I could finally understand when Marun told me tales of courage, loyalty, love, and friendship. It's only recently I've been able to appreciate these..." I stumbled, trying to find the right word.

Ventie helped finish my thought, "Feelings?" The moon was almost overhead. We sat in the shadow of trees overhanging the river's bank. The moonlight a sheen on the water, like slow-moving quicksilver. The birds had nested. It was as silent as sleep.

"Yes…feelings. I guess you could say I am in awe of these ideas or feelings."

Then I told her what Father had taught me about courage and cowardice to demonstrate how recently I had learned of things children usually learned at an early age.

"You are a rare mixture of ignorance and perception. Be careful in your quest for knowledge that you don't lose your ability to be inspired by the simple things in life."

The night grew cold. We walked back to the house and prepared to sleep. As my eyes grew heavy, I asked Ventie what she meant by the simple things.

"Be in awe of all things…for all things are connected in ways we can never know. We sleep now so other animals may roam. The sun sets so the moon can rise. The coolness of the night relieves the burning of the sun. It is an awe-inspiring harmony."

The day before my departure, a delegation of notables visited me stating that the people of Bensheer wanted to officially apologize for the treatment accorded me upon my arrival. They also asked if I would address the people about how the Effrifrian raiders were tracked and killed. Although nervous about speaking to such a large crowd, I agreed to their request.

Ventie urged me to tell my life's story in addition to the story of the twan's death and the execution of the camel thieves. She said I was the first—and more than likely the only—person from the Beyond the villagers would ever meet and this was an opportunity to dispel many myths about the land of my birth.

On the morning of my departure, Ventie gave me a deep red tunic made from tanned lambskin. She had made it for her husband, but he had died before having a chance to wear it. Tarley delivered my sandals that had been damaged during my capture. The new leather thongs and silver buckles reminded me of the twan's beautiful sandals. I was humbled by these rare gifts. I felt proud in my new tunic with the twan's scabbard at my side. As we left the house, Ventie put my black robe over my shoulders.

The entire population gathered in the center of the village. Shops and granaries backed three sides of the area with the fourth open to the river. A small platform stood on the riverbank near the tree from which I had so recently hung. As I entered the square, accompanied by Ventie and Tarley, the crowd cheered. The sun, just breaching the horizon, shone directly on the east-facing platform. The village elders greeted Ventie and me as we mounted the dais. Tarley took a place seated on the ground with the rest of the throng.

An ancient man named Barlek addressed me. With tears in his eyes he apologized for the cruelty of my capture. When he finished, the entire population bowed their heads and asked forgiveness. Having received such generosity after the initial horror of my capture, the apology seemed unnecessary.

With relief in his voice, Barlek continued, "Now we would like to honor and thank you for avenging the murder of two of our most respected citizens and for the return of our stock."

My protest was interrupted by a commotion in the audience. People began to shout and whistle as a man carrying an elegant camel saddle worked his way through the villagers. The saddle was entirely covered in leather with black sheepskin padding. The richly tanned leather bridle and harness were festooned with brightly colored balls of yellow yarn. The pommel was capped in hammered silver. The backrest was tooled with intricate glyphs that read *Protector of Bensheer.*

Placing this rare gift at my feet he stood back, grinning. The crowd cheered loudly. I was overwhelmed. Barlek quieted the crowd.

"Ayuba, we present this small token of our appreciation for all you have done for Bensheer and as a tangible form of apology. We ask only two things of you... that you remember Bensheer in your dreams as a place where you will always be an honored guest, and..." he paused for effect, "that you speak to us now about the Effrifrian adventure."

Happily, the villagers hooted and clapped in support of this request. And so it was that I began my career as a storyteller.

I took Ventie's advice and spoke of my life in the Beyond. It was clear most of my audience knew only myths and rumors about this mysterious land. I tried to dispel their fears and misconceptions. The longer I spoke, the more comfortable I became. I was no longer a naked orphaned boy from the Beyond. Looking into the eyes of my listeners I realized that although I spoke of my past, their image of me was much different.

They saw a man dressed in fine garments, bringing news of places and events they could only imagine. My body had filled out, my shoulders and arms strong from working in Hamrabi. Much to my embarrassment, Ventie said I was handsome. She claimed all the village girls were talking about the deep gray color of my eyes and my wavy black hair.

Whether through ignorance or simple enthusiasm, I incorporated the important lessons learned during my stay in Hamrabi. I was pleasantly surprised to see neighbors nodding to neighbors, mothers prodding children, in effect saying…this is important, listen carefully. With few amusements, small villages like Bensheer are receptive and thankful when a storyteller arrives. It is doubly so when the teller of tales has information about a person or event directly affecting their tribe or family.

When I finished, women kissed my hands, babies were proffered for me to touch, and men, some with tears in their eyes, vigorously shook my hand. With my arm around Ventie, I followed Tarley, carrying my new saddle, to where the camels grazed with most of the villagers following.

Tarley strapped on the saddle and transferred my spear case. My other effects were already bundled on one of the Effrifrian mounts. Several other camels were saddled and loaded with travel packs. When I asked where this caravan was headed, a tough-looking lad named Lasheed said it was my escort to Hamleed. I protested, assuring them I was capable of finding my way to the capital.

"Indeed," said Lasheed with an ironic smile on his face. "You found Bensheer even though you'd never been here before, but in what condition?"

Tarley looked embarrassed at this reference to my capture and torture. Ventie squeezed my arm.

"Ayuba, Bensheerie men are hardheaded…they want to make certain you arrive safely in Hamleed; it would reflect badly on our village if tragedy should befall you."

In truth I welcomed the company. Hamleed was six days' ride from Bensheer through unfamiliar country. Affable companions who knew the way would certainly lessen my burden.

I climbed onto my magnificent saddle, and my great beast rose. The crowd cheered as our caravan of six Bensheerie guards and sixteen camels found its way through the village, down the bank, and across the river Ben.

(7)

At a late night supper following the first National Geographic scroll documentary, Alex and Bryan bathed in compliments from the assembled academics. Dr. Watson was honored with toasts for the artistic yet culturally sensitive way the story was revealed. Candlelight softened the hard edges of the older women while enriching Alex's youthful radiance.

Before the meal was served, Salawa stood, saying, "Please join me in a toast to the two people most instrumental in bringing this wonderful find to the attention of the world." Everyone stood. "Dr. Elman Darshi, who not only found the key to this new language but raised a remarkable daughter, and Ayuba from the Beyond."

After the guests had departed, Salawa, claiming exhaustion, retired to her room. Alex walked Bryan to his car. A full moon softened the chill of the autumn night.

"What a fitting sky to highlight such a magical evening," said Alex, breathing in the crisp night air.

"Indeed, a perfect night graced by a perfect woman," Bryan said, turning to Alex. Lifting her chin he leaned in to kiss her. Alex drew closer. Their lips almost touching, she turned her head away gently, Bryan's lips softly caressing her cheek.

"What's the matter?" he whispered.

"Nothing. It's just...the timing's not right." Her head rested on his shoulder.

"I'm sorry," he said, pulling back to look into her eyes. "I thought...you know...you had the same feelings."

"Oh, I do," she said, squeezing his hands tightly. "I just think until we've finished this project we need to stay focused. Believe me, almost since the moment we met I've dreamed of this. But don't you see if we give in to our emotions now, the intensity of both the project and whatever develops between us will be less than if we wait just a few more weeks."

"Oh, how I hate logic," Bryan said, his voice trailing a frosty mist.

"Me too," she sighed, brushing her lips across his ear.

"And when we've finally launched Ayuba?"

Looking up at him with a radiant smile, Alex said, "You will know the pain of too much tenderness," she giggled, quoting from *The Prophet.*

Placing his lips on her forehead Bryan breathed in the perfume of her hair. "And you will know the joy of unbridled passion."

⚮

Most newspapers and networks led the following morning with reviews of the program. The *New York Times* featured a pessimistic review on the front page (above the fold). The headline read: *Ayuba more and less than anticipated?* followed by a discussion of the incredible global ratings for what amounted to a "rather common" story about an orphaned boy.

Other outlets offered a more balanced view, many gushing praise and amazement that the history of the world was being rewritten in front of hundreds of millions of viewers.

Throughout the world, hospitals reported hundreds of newborn baby boys were named Ayuba.

The classy Palm Springs Club on Tokyo's fabled Ginza announced a new cocktail, called the She-Beast, made from real camel's milk, Cointreau, Triplesec, and a dash of bitters. Price: $175. Customers complained when, due to unexpected demand, the bar ran out of milk.

Universities reported increased student interest in archeology, ancient history, and anthropology.

The Baghdad fire department restricted the number of visitors to the museum of ancient history citing fire safety concerns. It was the first time in the venerable institution's history that, despite frequent suicide bombers in the area, there were more visitors than space allowed.

Capitalizing on renewed interest in all things ancient, travel agents were swamped with reservations for tours to Greece, Egypt, and Rome, although Baghdad was still considered too dangerous as a destination. The *Wall*

Street Journal ran an article entitled *Ayuba revitalizes travel industry.*

✦

The Italian tenor Luciano Pavarotti announced a starlight concert of composer Bohuslav Martin's *The Epic of Gilgamesh* in front of the ancient ruins at Pella in Jordan. Asked why he selected such an arcane piece, he answered, "Gilgamesh until now was the oldest known written story. It too is from Iraq. Hopefully someday an opera or libretto will be written about the shepherd boy Ayuba."

✦

"Don't you see the parallels? It's so clear," exclaimed the older man, squinting through dusty glasses.

The two men had not bothered to turn on the lights after watching the National Geographic special. The neon from the busy street below cast harsh shadows across their faces.

Lighting a new cigarette from the stub of another, the young chain smoker said, "It's just an ancient story. Why make something out of nothing?"

"Have you been too long among these infidels... these American devils? Have you forgotten your scripture?" The older man closed his eyes. Swaying from side to side he began to recite...

Now when thou seest them, their outward appearance may please thee; and when they speak, thou art inclined to lend ear to what they say. But though they may seem as sure of themselves as if they were timbers firmly propped up, they think that every shout is directed against them. They are the real enemies of all faith, so beware of them. They deserve the imprecation, "May God destroy them!" How perverted are their minds!

Automatically matching the elder's gentle sway, the younger man listened to the lilting voice quoting the Qur'an in Urdu. Closing his eyes, he pictured the madrasah in Lahore. The lectures, the mind numbing rote memorization of the sacred text filling the void left when his mother died and his father abandoned him for the mujahadeen in Afghanistan. He recalled wanting to become a hafiz like the man across from him. To memorize the Qur'an's entire 114 surah (chapters) and their 6,000 verses was a dream shared by many boys left in the care of radical imams in Pakistan.

The smell of the old man's robe reminded Amin of the human smell that permeated the school in the gritty slum of Lahore.

"Do you remember what you learned at school?" asked the man once he finished his recitation. "Or have you drowned in the fast food of the West?"

"I remember."

"Good, then you must understand this Ayuba fable is a perversion of belief."

"But my friend," said Amin, "what purpose does it serve? Perhaps it is simply a story like many old stories that lie under the sands of our homes."

"Can you not see? Nowhere does Ayuba or his family praise Allah. Is not Allah eternal and infinite? Would not Allah in one of his many names have been known to this falsifier, even in ancient times?"

"Perhaps," said Amin, tiring of the conversation.

"Do you know what brothers of the true faith call this blasphemy?" An arrogant smirk crossed his face as he answered his own question, "Ayubush!"

Amin burst out laughing at the predictable epithet. "What would we do without George Bush to hate?" he sputtered.

The old man looked sad. *Youth today, especially those exposed to the satanic ways of the West, are growing weaker and weaker,* he thought.

"You may laugh, but it is only through ignorance that you have been blinded. It is so apparent to the true believers that this fabrication was created by the enemies of Islam to further alienate the weak among us... like you."

"You may be right. I admit to being weak, but from hunger not spirit. I have no money and no food. Soon they will disconnect my electricity. Chicago is colder even than Pakistan in the winter. For now, I'll leave Ayuba or Ayubush to the imams to debate. I must find work."

After his father died in Afghanistan, Amin's aunt in Toronto sent for him. For three years he worked in his uncle's small garage changing oil and lubing cars. The dislike between the uncle, Amhal, and the boy was reciprocal. The day after his aunt's funeral, Amhal told the boy to pack his bags. The next day they drove to Chicago. After driving all night they arrived in the early morning outside the mosque on the edge of Blue Island, a seedy Chicago suburb. Amhal handed the boy five hundred dollars.

"This is from your aunt," he said, indicating Amin should get out of the car. Standing on the empty sidewalk clutching the five one hundred-dollar bills, he watched the taillights disappear up the on ramp to the freeway north to Canada.

The day after the Ayuba program, the hafiz with the dirty glasses approached the boy after prayers.

"I have found work for you," he said, taking the skinny eighteen-year-old by the arm. Together they went to the imam's office, a small, ugly room behind the stairway leading from the prayer room to the street.

"Cleaning the mosque doesn't pay much," the imam told him, "but it does include a place to sleep and three meals a day."

Delighted, Amin accepted.

Surrounded by the faithful praying five times a day and reading the Qur'an nightly, Amin slowly shed the scant dusting of western culture he'd accumulated in Canada. He never spoke English in the mosque, only Urdu and Arabic, and he rarely left the building. Like the madrasah in Lahore, the dingy mosque was his refuge. When he thought about his life in Canada he realized that in three years he had not made a single friend. For two years he attended a local middle school even though he was of high school age. He was the only Muslim in his class. He was not treated badly...worse yet, he was ignored.

The imam told him Christians did not follow their own faith, that Christian charity was a myth. "Amin, we must live among them here in the U.S. but we cannot become like them. They are infidels. Look at you...did the Christians take you in when your father became a martyr? Did the Christians welcome you into their homes? Did they offer you food and shelter? Did the Christians take care of you like a brother as instructed by the Prophet (peace be upon him)? No. It was those of the true faith that offered you hospitality."

An all female topless band called The She-Beasts opened at a new jazz club in Greenwich Village to a sold-out crowd.

⌒⋎⌒

In Paris, the disaffected North African Muslim community took the opportunity to further their own agenda. Burning cars and hurling molotovs at police, they screamed, "Allah is not a dream...jobs and equality are dreams!"

⌒⋎⌒

Militants in Pakistan called for continuous marches in Islamabad, Lahore, and Peshawar. Four people were trampled to death on the first day, stimulating more aggression on the part of the radicals. Twelve people died from riot police gunfire on the second day when radicals tried to storm the U.S. embassy.

⌒⋎⌒

Salman Rushdie, author of the proscribed *Satanic Verses,* under a fatwa from the Ayatollah Khomeini that included a six million-dollar bounty on his life, quipped in a phone interview with the BBC that he'd be happy to have Ayuba for company while in hiding.

⌒⋎⌒

I wonder how many black limos there are in this city, thought Alex, looking out her window at the long line of Cadillacs and Lincolns waiting in front of the Kennedy

Center. Most tickets were reserved for the glitterati of D.C. The few that reached the public were being scalped on eBay for over a thousand dollars each.

Sitting between his mother and Alex, Bryan could see the long row of gleaming taillights. "I'll bet the president won't have to wait in this line."

"Is it definite he's coming?" asked Alex.

"In his news conference this morning he said he wouldn't miss it."

Alex was startled by the size of the grand foyer. Bryan, who'd been to the Kennedy before, enjoyed playing tour guide. "This hall alone is one of the largest buildings in the world. They say you could lay the Washington Monument on its side and still have room for a seven-story building."

"I wish I'd worn my comfortable shoes," quipped Salawa, looking down the length of the foyer.

Giant Orrefors crystal chandeliers lighted the huge space with a soft glow. An usher greeted the threesome, leading them past the lines of tuxedo-clad gentlemen and elegant ladies and through a richly decorated side hall to one of the six onstage boxes unique to the Kennedy. Leaning over the railing, Alex could see that the 2,400-seat concert hall—the largest of the Kennedy's six performance venues—was filling quickly. The Washington Philharmonic Orchestra was seated just below. The four thousand brass pipes of one of the world's largest pipe organs glowed softly as a backdrop to the stage.

After the customary formalities associated with the arrival of the presidential party, Dr. Watson escorted Sharrif al Bardan to the stage. His dark complexion, salt and pepper hair, and regal demeanor made more than one lady swoon as he gracefully took his seat.

Dr. Watson greeted the audience, both in the theater and on TV, on behalf of the National Geographic Society. He explained a special musical score entitled *New Bynethia,* composed and directed by Fatima Sistanni, Iraq's only classical music composer, would accompany the final reading of "The Song of Ayuba."

The orchestra stood as the genteel artist in a black gown assumed the podium. The lights dimmed. A giant screen was lowered, covering the organ pipes at the back of the stage. The first Arabic woman to lead an American symphony orchestra raised a petite hand holding a white ivory wand.

The haunting prelude was accompanied by an on-screen summary of the preceding chapters of the scroll. When the prelude concluded, the narrator stood and in a richly accented voice began to read...

(8)

HAMLEED (11,000 BCE)

By sunset, we arrived at a high bank of sand dunes running as far as the eye could see. Hamleed lay due east. My companions assured me that by starting before dawn we would cross these undulating waves of sand before nightfall the following day.

The Bensheeries were a cheerful group. Each was heavily armed and experienced in warfare and desert travel. Around the campfire they described feats of bravery but mostly fantasized about girls. They sang ancient songs and danced under a star-filled, moonless sky.

In the pre-dawn we headed east across the dunes and were quickly surrounded by waves of sand. When we breached the crest of a dune and starting down the other side, the sand cascaded down the steep slope, filling our tracks. It was odd to look back at a dune we had just descended and see no evidence of having been there.

With the sun overhead, we paused briefly in a valley to eat and adjust packs. Cresting the next dune, Lasheed called a halt. Pointing to the north where the sky darkened he said, "We must make camp quickly," nudging his mount down into the next valley.

As soon as we reached the bottom, Lasheed directed us to couch our mounts in a staggered formation across the valley floor.

"Ayuba, have you ever been in a worley?" he shouted over the increasingly noisy wind.

"What's a worley?"

"This will make the Beyond look like paradise," he yelled, pushing me down behind the she-beast. "Stay in the lee of your camel no matter what happens…don't go to sleep or you might suffocate." With those meager instructions he ran to the shelter of his mount.

Camels, unlike horses and donkeys, have what is called a third eye. It's really not an eye, but a second eye-lid used as a shield from dust and sand. The she-beast's eyes looked milky white, barely visible behind the fil-ter of her thick lashes. Her nostrils were closed tightly, another unique defense of camels. She squirmed back and forth, pressing her calloused belly skin deep in the sand. Throwing my robe over my head I pulled it tightly around me, burrowing against the faithful animal's side. I waited, expecting the wind to rise. Instead it grew calm. Heat from the sand radiated from beneath me. Then I felt the she-beast shudder, bracing herself. The worley hit.

I felt the camel lean toward me as though she might topple over. Sheltered somewhat from the brunt of this raging wall of stones I was assailed by ear-shattering thunder. Sand in solid sheets swirled around the groan-ing beast. I clung to the saddle cinch with both hands. The wind filled my robe, lifting me until I was streaming behind the camel.

Suddenly the wind shifted, slamming my body to the ground. I scrambled to regain the lee of the beast without taking my hands from the cinch. Twice more the wind picked me up, held me horizontal, then dash me hard on the sand. I pressed myself as tightly as I could against the stolid body of my protector. I knew if the force hurled me again into the stream of sand I wouldn't have the strength to maintain my hold.

The painful roar in my ears suddenly changed. Although the force of the wind had not abated, its cry was higher now—more like a screech than a howl. Instead of swirling from one side of the camel to the other, it was blowing directly at the side of the beast. Sand cascaded over the camel's hump.

The air was sand and the sand was air. I had no sense of the grains entering my mouth; it was as though it had always been there. Sand packed my ears, deafening me. The grit passed through my fleece robe unchecked, filling my groin and armpits. There was no defense. I panicked, feeling myself drift toward a suffocating drowsiness.

It was the ground moving under me that aroused me from my torpor. At first I thought the she-beast was trying to stand. Wedging my arm under the cinch to hold myself in place I knelt with my face pressed against the beast's side using the fine hairs of her coat as a filter.

The sand under my knees moved. The violent force was digging away at the very ground, determined to reach me. The memory of lying in the river Ben feeling the water flowing over me came to mind. I was floating on a sea of sand.

The she-beast sensed our peril. Letting out an anguished bellow, she splayed her legs, trying desperately to hang on to the shifting surface. Something hard slammed against my head. From somewhere came a distant cry that faded fast, snatched away by the wind.

I wasn't sure when the wind actually calmed. I was still sucking air through the camel's coat when it dawned on me I could no longer hear the wind—it was gone as quickly as it had come.

The great beast's sides heaved in relief. When I moved my head, a cascade of sand spilled over me and buried me up to my chest. Had the wind continued much longer, I'm sure the worley would have drowned me.

Overall our group weathered the worley well. One of the pack animals had panicked and tried to stand during the most violent part of the storm. The wind ripped its packsaddle off, knocking the animal on its side. It was the debris from the saddle that hit me on the head. The unfortunate animal was now wedged against the she-beast, covered in sand, its neck broken.

The hair on the flanks of the camels facing the wind had been shaved clean. Their bare skin oozed blood, scabbing quickly in the dry air.

Most of the day was spent gathering what was left of the packs. It was late afternoon by the time we were ready to travel. We decided to keep going rather than camp on the dunes—no one wanted to risk another storm.

The dunes cut like a knife blade through the western third of Hamood. West of the dunes was high desert with few inhabitants who lived in small settlements like Bensheer and Hamrabi. The villages were separated by great tracks of arid space. Where there was water, there were people, except in the farthest reaches near the Beyond.

East of the dunes is where the majority of Hamood lay, where life was very different. Water was abundant as two great rivers formed its borders. Over many centuries the industrious Hamoodians dug irrigation canals that now crisscrossed the country, turning the arid land into fertile farmland.

Just before dawn we rode down the last dune into this fertile world. We camped in a copse of trees planted in neat parallel rows. The crisp smell of greenness filled the air. The trees held the dunes in check to the west, bordering rich farmland to the east.

Walking to the edge of the wood, I gazed out over a landscape unlike any I had seen. It was early autumn and as far as the eye could see were fields of golden grain. Elevated paths and ditches separated the fields. The canals were dry now, the crops ready for harvest. In the distance was a small walled compound, its ocher walls glowing in the morning sun.

We stepped out of the trees where we had sheltered onto a raised path separating two large fields. It ran directly toward the village. As we approached the compound we could see what appeared to be the entire population assembled outside the wall. Lasheed dismounted when we were within earshot and announced that we were from Bensheer and on our way to Hamleed to return the scabbard of the twan. He referred to me as the "Hero of the Gleb," explaining I was to be feted by the king. He finished by telling the assembled villagers we had survived a worley and would much appreciate the opportunity to wash and refresh ourselves at their well.

It was hard to determine which impressed these simple farmers most…that I possessed the twan's scabbard or that we lived through a worley.

Young boys took our mounts to a duck pond on the edge of the village. Women drew crocks of water for us from the well in the center of the village square. We stripped naked and poured the cool water over each other, rinsing away the last vestiges of the worley. Young girls took our breechclouts for washing and then laid them on the wall to dry in the sun. The older women prepared a feast of wheat cakes, nuts, and honey.

As we readied for our departure, an old man named Richlood warmly thanked us for our efforts in returning the twan's scabbard. Then, speaking directly to me, he went on to say that it would be terribly impolite for us to have taken advantage of their hospitality without offering something in return—a violation of all norms of politeness. Lasheed wore an amused grin.

"Grandfather, what is it you would like?" I asked.

The old man squinted through rheumy eyes. "Why, a story of course. We get few visitors, but when we do we always request a story."

Lasheed responded quickly, "Ah, Grandfather, you have asked the right person. Only two days ago Ayuba told all of Bensheer a story that made women cry and men cheer."

I shot a warning glance at Lasheed, but he ignored me.

"We are in no hurry and would love to hear it once again."

And so, for the second time in as many days, I told the story of my humble life. It was a bit longer this time as I added the details of the worley and our journey across the dunes. When I finished, there were tears in many eyes.

The villagers applauded, gathering around to thank and touch me. I was embarrassed as before, but not surprised by their reaction. It was becoming clear to me that people felt a connection to storytellers—as though in the telling of a tale there was a shared experience.

The weather was much less harsh on the eastern side of the dunes. Although the sun shone brightly, it did not burn. Lasheed told me that the four-day journey to Hamleed would be through similar terrain…a pleasing prospect.

The sun lowered in the west as we sought a place to camp. For most of the afternoon we had passed through an enormous date grove. The path was like a tunnel with no end in sight, so we decided to make camp in the trees.

As we guided our mounts off the path into the grove, a shepherd boy with a small herd of goats came toward us. When he saw us he ran off through the tightly packed trees.

Lasheed dismounted and ran after him shouting, "We are friends...we are friends!" Lasheed returned, out of breath. We laughed at the thought of this athletic warrior unable to catch a young shepherd boy.

It was a most pleasant camp. Locating an opening in the trees, we built a fire. The grove floor was covered in sweet grasses for the camels. I took out a bundle one of the village girls had given me and was surprised to find several dozen wheat cakes and a large pot of honey. The food, fire, rustling palms, and smell of fresh grass were in stark contrast to the deserts of my birth. An orange moon crested the trees.

Lasheed laughed. "If things get any better, beautiful virgins will come dancing out of the trees."

This led to teasing about my encounter with the girl who had given me the honey and cakes. One of my companions, a young man about my age named Fairtee, said, "Ayuba, I envy you."

I laughed. "Why? Because a village girl, no doubt at the behest of the village elders, gave me some very nice wheat cakes?"

"The cakes are very nice indeed, but I was thinking more about the freedom you have." The rest of the group mumbled their agreement. I seemed to be the only one who didn't understand.

"Ayuba, you're as dumb as a tree trunk about some things and smarter than a raven about others." Everyone laughed at Lasheed's remark.

"Can't you see that with your story, and I might add your ability to tell it so well, you can travel anywhere?

Every village will feed and house you, give you wheat cakes, and..." He paused, the fire dancing against his white teeth as he grinned, "Probably their daughters too, just to hear of the Beyond and your other adventures."

"You envy me because I come from the Beyond?" This startled me. Ever since Father rescued me and I came to Hamrabi I felt that, outside of my adopted family, I was looked on as a curiosity. By some with pity, others with disgust, but none with envy.

"It's not just that you come from the Beyond," Lasheed's brother joined the conversation. "I'm sure living in that wild place was difficult and dangerous. It's what has happened to you since. Think of it...you are on your way to meet the king of Hamood! None of us will ever meet the king...the tax collector definitely, but not the king. From living like an animal eating grubs and lizards to dining with the king in what..." he paused, "just a few season cycles?"

Fairtee added some fronds to the fire. The sparks followed the smoke through the trees into the moonlight.

"I understand that meeting the king is unusual, but it's only because I was included at the last minute in the hunt for the Effrifrians. Not because I earned it. It's... it's..." I stammered, "sort of a mistake really."

"I don't agree," Lasheed responded. "Any of us could say this or that event was a mistake or a gift from one of the gods. A few days ago I was leading the group that wanted to kill you for revenge. Now that would have been a mistake, but no one would have ever known. We would all have felt we'd meted out a bit of justice and you would be dead."

"So what are you saying?" I asked.

"Life is a series of events, and though we may head in one direction or another, it's what happens along the way that counts." He paused, licking honey from his fingers. "To say a single event was a mistake or a lucky experience is pure camel dung."

The fire dimmed with just enough glow from the embers to light our faces like miniature moons circling the sun.

"All young lads seem to think the destination is what is important," continued Lasheed. "Well, there are plenty of dead soldiers buried across this land who would, if they could, rise up and say you are wrong! Look at what has happened to us since we left Bensheer. Do you think it was more important to that poor beast with its broken neck that we were on our way to Hamleed or that we got caught in a worley? Usually, wherever you're going is less exciting than the trail that got you there."

The moon, now directly overhead, cast shadows of lacy palms over the grassy floor of the grove. Except for the occasional snapping of the fire, the earth was silent.

It is tradition in Hamood for travelers to entertain themselves with song contests. It began as a way to glorify or honor a battle or a fallen compatriot. I first experienced this when Father and Dalnt sang of the twan's greatness after the battle at the Gleb.

Lasheed began to sing...

The road winds on beyond my view,
No hint of where the end might be.
I step onto the gentle path,
Will it end at fence, field, or sea?

Lasheed pointed at Fairtee, indicating it was his turn to add a stanza. He rose to the occasion with...

It matters not to me a wit,
What lies at the end of the road.
For it is the journey that counts the most,
Not where my pack is finally stowed.

Joklee followed...

Here's a hill that's mighty steep,
Forward...dig in my toes.
Confident that beyond the grade,
A downward trail flows.

With a broad grin, Joklee nodded at me. I had little experience singing and much less at rhyming. I closed my eyes and thought about our journey, then hesitantly offered...

Sometimes the view is black indeed,
As clouds wrestle with the sun.
The winds buffet and push at me,
And it seems my trip is done.

Everyone clapped and cheered at my reference to our horrible experience on the dunes.

The song continued as each of us tried to outdo the other. I forget now who was responsible for the remaining verses, but the song is clear in my memory, having sung it many times since that night...

No! I scream, shoulders squared,
The road will not end here.
I lean against the evil force,

Hamleed (11,000 BCE)

Setting aside my fear.

I crest the hill, leaving behind
The blackened, noisy sky.
I see my road, smooth and wide,
And hear its whispered cry.

Follow me, be stout and true,
There is nothing else to explore.
The road knows not where it ends,
The trip is all, there's nothing more!

So friend, when the road narrows
To a foggy, single path.
You leave a road well traveled
With a cheerful wave and laugh.

What a grand adventure
Offers each and every road.
When willingly explored
With a light and gentle load.

Having slept late the next morning, a tickling on my face awakened me. Opening my eyes I stared into the dark brown eyes of a goat. The small herd had found its way into our camp seeking safety during the night. While the others packed and loaded the camels, I milked the does, and we breakfasted on fresh goat milk. I was surprised the shepherd boy had not returned to rescue his flock.

Lasheed believed the next village was nearby so I volunteered to herd the animals. It was a delightful morning and I welcomed the opportunity to stretch my legs. The morning sun cast long shadows across the path. My companions led with the camels and I followed with my cheerful band of bleating goats.

About mid-morning, the date grove ended at the edge of a field of mixed vegetables on one side and freshly harvested wheat on the other. Sheaves stood in perfect rows drying in the crisp morning sun. The village lay on the west side of the path. Joklee was sent ahead to announce our arrival.

Shortly after entering the walled compound, he came back through the gate accompanied by several villagers and beckoned us to enter. When we reached the village walls, a young man in an ill-fitting peasant tunic welcomed us. I was the last to enter, herding my charges in front of me. As the last goat cleared the gates, two young boys swung them shut.

After dismounting, Lasheed began to explain our mission, when out of the surrounding huts soldiers appeared with drawn bows and spears.

The man who greeted us yelled, "Stay where you are if you value your lives!"

Everyone froze. Pulling off his disguise, he exposed his leather soldier's tunic and scabbard emblazoned with a sergeant's rank.

"Now very slowly, you gentlemen sit on the ground."

"Gentlemen? The hell you say!" said an old crone, too ancient or too stupid to hide. "More like goat thieves."

"Now, Grandmother," said the sergeant, "suppose you let me determine that."

I noticed Joklee's hands were tied behind his back. A burly soldier stood behind him.

"Which of you is called Ayuba?"

"I am…I believe there is some confusion here, sir," I said, my voice quivering. I had never before been at the mercy of the king's soldiers.

"No confusion, just precaution," said the sergeant. "Your messenger here," he said, pointing at the hapless Joklee, "claims you are a man of some importance and that you are on your way to meet the king. I find it hard to believe that a goat herder, or goat *thief*, could make such a claim."

"Indeed, Sergeant, I understand your confusion. My name is Ayuba and I am on my way to Hamleed at the invitation of the new twan. I bear the scabbard of the slain twan. Whether I am to meet the king I know not. It will be up to Dal...the twan," I replied, more forcefully than before. Before he could interrupt, I continued. "As for the goats, we are simply returning them to the village as there was no shepherd to protect them."

Glancing at his men, the sergeant said, "Show me the scabbard."

I retrieved the scabbard and held it out for all to see. This symbol, this talisman, was so powerful, I saw several soldiers visibly sag in its presence.

"Lay down your arms!" the sergeant commanded. "Your Highness, please forgive me for detaining you," he said, bowing deeply. "When the messenger from this village came to our camp, he claimed a large group of bandits was nearby. I could take no chances, not knowing your strength." He bowed again. "I was alerted by the twan himself to be on the lookout for you and to extend any assistance." With that he bowed a third time, as did his soldiers. All this bowing made me uncomfortable; I was not used to courtly formalities.

"I understand, Sergeant. I will report your attention to duty and your courtesy to the twan. In the meantime, please release my friend," I said, pointing to Joklee who, despite being bound, had a broad grin on his face.

"Of course. Please, the rest of you rise and accept my apology for this inconvenience," he said, bowing in the general direction of my escort.

"Apology accepted," said Lasheed in a booming voice as he rose to his feet. "It was worth the inconvenience and more to see the look on your face when our goat herder brought out the scabbard." With that, the Bensheeries laughed and hooted, embarrassing the soldiers.

"Pay them no mind, Sergeant, they are from Bensheer and known to wrongly accuse and torture innocent goat herders without a thought," I said.

The sergeant smiled, relieved I had come to his defense.

"Now that we've all said our piece, let's see what sort of hospitality these villagers have to offer."

The people of Bahrim swamped us with kindness fostered by relief. As if by magic, all manner of fruits and meats appeared. Wheat cakes and honey were accompanied by a sweet wine.

During the feast, I asked the sergeant about Dalnt. He said he had been appointed the new twan but could not officially take the position until he had possession of the scabbard. He also told of the twan's lavish funeral in which Father and I were honored with a sacrifice for our role at the Gleb. I was being called "Avenger of the Twan" for killing his murderer.

Sunshine bore down on the courtyard from directly overhead as we finished the feast. The wine and bountiful meal made us all sleepy.

"It's time to depart," I said to my escort. "We've a long way to go, and important people await our arrival."

At this there was much groaning and pleading. The villagers too inquired if we might not spend the night. I rose, motioning to the others to follow.

"People of Bahrim," I called out in a loud voice, "you have treated us graciously despite the fear our presence caused. We wish you much prosperity. Your generosity will be heralded in the court of Hamleed, but alas, we must depart."

Turning to fetch my mount, I heard Lasheed say in a loud voice, "Dear friends, how can we repay your excellent hospitality? We have no gold, we have no sheep, alas, we have nothing to give; like you we are simple farmers thrust into this honorable journey." He paused for effect. I knew where he was heading and began to interrupt, but he was faster with his tongue.

"What?" he said in mock surprise. "Did I hear someone say...give us a story?"

Several villagers shouted, "Yes, a story!"

"Oh, people of Bahrim, you are so clever for you have found us out...indeed we are rich in stories."

The villagers and some of the soldiers shouted, "Yes, a story. Give us a story!"

Lasheed held up his hands to quiet the crowd. "We not only have one of the most remarkable stories you've ever heard, but one of the best storytellers in Hamood!"

While my escorts slept in the loving arm of the wine goddess, I told the story of my life to the people of Bahrim and the soldiers. With each telling I was becoming more proficient, remembering more details. Instead of simply telling them Fairtoo was stuffed in a camel, I made the buzzing sound of the flies to help them smell the stench of decay. This time the story ended in Bahrim, with a description of how my escort got drunk and stuffed with overwhelming hospitality. The crowd hooted and clapped knowing their generosity would be spread from village to village as part of the story told by the man from the Beyond.

161

It was mid-afternoon when we departed. The sergeant detailed two men to ride with us, sending a third ahead to notify the twan of our progress. The remainder of the guard resumed their patrol.

We were now two days from Hamleed. The warm sun and sweet wine, combined with the gentle swaying motion of our mounts, made sleep impossible to escape. Our beasts plodded on throughout the afternoon without guidance or encouragement. The sun set beyond a jagged silhouette of purple mountains to the west. Palm trees, like great black birds, pierced the gloaming.

We made camp at the base of some ancient ruins in a charming grove of thorn trees. Camels from previous occupants had trimmed the limbs higher than a man could reach, leaving a soft green canopy over the camp. The two thick walls of the ruins were barely recognizable, neighboring villagers having plundered many of the ancient stones. The soldiers said the ruins were from a time long past before Hamood consolidated the tribes. I was enchanted by these stone memories. There were no traces of past peoples or lives in the Beyond. I thought of the camp where my family died knowing without question that there was no marker honoring their existence.

Mid-morning the following day a large village appeared in the distance. Although some way off, I could see it straddled our path. As our party came in view, the gates swung open and a sizeable contingent of local officials and villagers came out to meet us. Three soldiers on beautiful roan horses followed.

At some distance from the greeters, Lasheed yelled out to our group, "You see…you see what honor these villagers pay to Bensheeries! See, they not only call out the elders at our approach, I'll bet they are bathing their daughters in anticipation of capturing our seed."

There was much guffawing and teasing at Lasheed's bawdy wit. The two soldiers escorting us feigned disgust at the bragging and bantering. The ranking corporal responded, "More than likely the villagers don't fear for their daughters as much as their sheep!"

Drawing closer, the soldiers pushed their mounts through the crowd and rode out to greet us. I recognized one of the riders as the scout from Bahrim. Our camels grew restless at the proximity of the horses. Spitting and bleating, they made their feelings known.

The soldiers dismounted gracefully before their mounts were fully stopped. In unison they bowed, and the ranking member cried out, "Avenger of the Twan, we bring greetings from Twan Dalnt. He apologizes for not coming himself. His presence is required by the king. He begs you godspeed and asks that you make haste to Hamleed where he will greet and honor you and your father, Aroon al Sumer, protector of the western border."

"Thank you for coming to escort us," I responded in what I hoped sounded like a formal voice. "On behalf of my father, protector of the western border, I accept Twan Dalnt's greeting and will make haste to Hamleed as requested."

Lasheed, in a false whisper, said, "Too bad for the local girls. They will surely be disappointed by our brief visit."

The soldier in charge, a lieutenant named Glardoo, squinted at Lasheed, then at each of the other members of my escort. "I see Your Highness has acquired an escort from the famous village of Bensheer. I hope your health, as well as your purse, is intact." Although the Bensheeries accepted this jibe as a compliment, I was embarrassed for my friends.

"On the contrary, Lieutenant, both my health and my purse have been enhanced by the brave men of Bensheer and I am honored to ride with them." At this, the Bensheeries hooted and whistled at the lieutenant's discomfort.

Remounting, the soldiers led our small caravan into Alat. Young girls appeared with garlands and placed them around my neck as a tribute to the "Avenger of the Twan." An elder gave a flowery speech about how honored they were at my visit. I felt my face flush. I thanked them for their courtesy. Explaining the urgency of our mission, I begged their forgiveness for our haste.

Dalnt's soldiers were restless as all soldiers are when unable to carry out their orders. The Bensheeries were teasing the young village girls and I knew they would create some pretext for us to stay if we did not leave immediately. Bowing to the elders, I mounted the she-beast. My escort followed, reluctantly.

Riding through the southern gate, we found the path we'd been following expanded to twice its previous width. The uneven, packed surface was now level, covered with carefully fitted stones—the first road I'd ever seen.

After riding on the remarkable structure for some time, I dismounted and walked beside my mount in wonder at such a feat. Lieutenant Glardoo walked with me.

"Does this road continue all the way to Hamleed?" I asked.

"Indeed, Your Highness, this is but one of four roads leading toward the cardinal points of the compass from Hamleed. The king built these at great expense to accommodate carts hauling produce to Hamleed and supplies for the military."

"Excuse my ignorance, Lieutenant, but I am from Hamrabi and prior to that from the Beyond and am ignorant of many things," I said by way of introduction to the torrent of questions I was preparing to ask.

"Please, Your Highness, there is no need to apologize. The twan has told us of your remarkable life. He said there would be much in Hamleed that is new to you, but your ignorance of our way of life pales in comparison to your knowledge of the vast deserts beyond the dunes."

"I fear that by his courtesy the twan has overstated my simple life, but I am honored by his kindness." Once again I was perplexed and embarrassed at the thought of people unknown to me talking about my life.

"Please, Your Highness, I would be happy to answer any questions you have."

And so it was that my introduction to modern civilization began. The gates of Alat closed on the path leading from my past and opened onto the road of my future. I was unsure of where this road might lead but was comforted in the knowledge that the gates of Alat swung both ways.

Glardoo and I walked together the remainder of the day while the rest of our escort snoozed on their mounts in the warm afternoon sun. I heard for the first time about carts and wheels, lodestones and some of the remarkable history of Hamood. My patient guide told me of many gods...for women...warriors...animals... weather. Gods and more gods.

As evening approached, I saw a large group of buildings hard against the purple-silhouetted mountains. Glardoo instructed his men to find a place to make camp. When I suggested we press on to Hamleed, Glardoo looked surprised.

"You see now, Lieutenant, why Ayuba needs an escort?" laughed Lasheed. "He still has not accepted that he is an honored visitor to Hamleed. Instead he wants to sneak into the city under the cover of night." With this, there was much laughter from the Bensheeries. They, more than I, were delighted to bask in the reflected light of my supposed glory.

"It's true, Your Highness. I would be severely punished should I fail to notify the king of your approach so a proper welcome can be arranged," Glardoo said, as though addressing a child, and with that, he sent one of his men on a fast horse ahead to Hamleed.

We made camp in a freshly harvested wheat field. The smell of toasted grain reminded me of fresh bread baking on the hearth in Hamrabi. The waxing moon rose shortly after we finished our evening meal, its silver light casting deep shadows across the fields of stubble. Perfectly spaced sheaves stood like sentries around our camp. The evening star was so bright it eclipsed the moon in intensity. I walked away from the camp and its fire, so I could see the sky more clearly.

The past few days, I had felt myself turning inward as though trying to hide from the constant attention. Walking through the moon-washed fields, I tried to isolate my feelings.

Prior to leaving Hamrabi, my life had been spent in isolation. Each day was defined by necessity…find food, weed a garden, collect camel weed, avoid being seen by others who might kill me. Why was it I never felt this gnawing unease when given those simple tasks? Since leaving Hamrabi I was constantly trying to peer over the horizon.

A small, lonely cloud skirting the edge of the moon reminded me of the night Father and I spent together before entering the Shale Sea. The night he taught me about courage and how some men see victory and others see failure.

Was that it? Was I simply being cowardly? No, it was not fear I was feeling, it was something less palpable, something more insidious, like a fine veil of smoke blurring the edges of reality.

I was distracted from my thoughts by a soft rustling sound from a nearby sheave. I stopped instantly. The rustling continued.

From the corner of my eye I caught a glint of silver off of something lying still and smooth in the stubble. Although fainter, the rustling continued, moving deeper into the sheave. The silver shadow moved like slow water flowing without effort.

The snake paused; its tongue licked the air. Whatever was in the sheaves continued to rustle, unaware each movement it made, each breath or subtle twitch, was tasted and savored by a flickering tongue.

Normally I would have killed this silent hunter, devouring its bony meat. Tonight, however, my hands began to sweat. I felt my heart quicken and my leg muscles tighten.

I stared at the shining back of the serpent. The moon lay softly on the fine pattern of its scales; its sides rhythmically moving, its tongue sucking in the scent of its prey. I wondered if I could remain as still as the reptile and if its heart was beating with anticipation. I was not afraid of this simple rat snake. It was the life or death drama playing out on this lonely and unobserved stage that captivated me.

The movement was so fast, I'm not sure I actually saw the snake launch itself into the forest of straw. I heard a faint squeal. Was it surprise, pain, or simply the little creature's lungs collapsing under the crushing jaws in the moonlight? Exhaling, my body relaxed. I drew in a deep draught of cool night air. The snake vanished into the thicket.

Looking back toward camp, I felt as though I'd been far away, and yet the campfire was no more than a hundred paces. Turning back toward the sheaves where the snake disappeared, I recalled what I had just witnessed with incredible clarity. Yes, that was it, clarity.

I had been feeling distracted, and yet when I watched the snake hunt, I became aware of the purity in its effort. The snake was focused on its prey. The mouse focused on storing seeds. The snake was living in the present with no thought of tomorrow while the mouse was distracted by the future—only to die in the present.

I walked parallel to the camp to where the hobbled camels were resting in the moonlight. The she-beast sensed my presence long before I reached her. She nuzzled me as I scratched her ears and leaned against her wooly flank.

Thinking about the many things distracting me I chuckled, wondering why some snake hadn't eaten me! I wouldn't have survived in the Beyond for a moment had I become so distracted from the present.

There was nothing I could do; no amount of thought or worry would affect how people perceived me. If they found my name strange, nothing I could do here in this field under this moon would change that. If people believed creatures from the Beyond were less than human, no amount of worry on my part could alter their ignorance.

Instead of living in the present, I had been worrying about the future. I had let the present...subtle portents of danger, the laughter of the village children, the beauty of girls who brought us water...pass by while I was busy trying to fathom a future that might never happen. What futility!

Wrapping my robe around me I closed my eyes. Drifting toward sleep I vowed to live every moment in the present. The mouse would never see the sunrise because it had lost sight of the night. The future is only a dream that may never happen.

We broke camp at midday, having spent the morning bathing in a nearby pond. We dressed our hair with oil and cleaned our packs and clothes. Today we would enter Hamleed.

Although pretending to be nonplussed, the Bensheeries too donned their best robes, polished their saddles, and festooned their mounts. We made a fine-looking caravan as we set out on the final leg of our journey.

In the distance a line of trees cut across our path from east to west shielding our view of the river Leb that bordered and protected Hamleed. Beyond the trees the city rose in a gradual incline toward the mountain's base. This terracing allowed the approaching traveler to view the city street by street as it rose toward the largest building in the world.

When we were halfway to Hamleed a group of riders emerged from the tree line trotting briskly forward, silver bridles and spears glittering in the morning sun. A light cloud of dust rose behind them, raising a gossamer veil between Hamleed and us. With the sun at their backs, the horses raced into their shadows.

Unsure of the protocol, I dismounted...content to let events unfold. The Bensheeries dismounted and immediately knelt. I almost broke out laughing at the sight of Bensheerie rumps in the air.

Dismounting with ease, Dalnt hurried to embrace me. There was a murmur from his escort. It was unprecedented for a twan to treat a subject with such affection and respect. After embracing, I started to bow, but Dalnt put his great arms around me, vigorously slapping me on the back.

"I'm so glad to see you, my dear friend. Have you traveled well?"

"Yes, Your Highness, I have indeed. My escort is from Bensheer; however, that would be hard to tell simply by looking at their backsides."

Dalnt laughed. "Enough of this, you Bensheerie rascals. Rise up and let me have a look at the men who tried to kill my friend."

As usual, Lasheed was the first to speak. "Your Highness, it was a—"

I interrupted before he made a fool of himself, "It was an honest mistake and one that has been atoned for many times over."

Dalnt feigned gruffness. "I should hope so. You know the Bensheeries have a bit of a reputation for mischief."

"So I've been told by everyone this side of the great dune."

"I see you've stayed loyal to your old friend," Dalnt said, rubbing the she-beast's nose. "She is certainly better equipped than when I last saw you. Come to think of it, so are you," he chuckled.

I told him how I came to have such an elegant saddle and kit and about all of the other adventures I had experienced since we separated after leaving the Gleb.

The fields bordering the road to Hamleed extended to the very edge of the break lining the river. The road gradually widened as we came closer to the city. The arching trees formed a shady tunnel dappled with sunlight.

Exiting the woods, the blazing sun and roaring river made the camels skittish. Dalnt suggested we dismount and lead the animals across the bridge rather than run the risk of getting thrown into the roiling river.

The bridge is one of the world's most famous engineering feats. More than two hundred paces long, it is wide enough for six riders to pass side by side. Six stone arches rest on solid bedrock deep beneath the river. Waist high stone walls line the roadbed. Halfway across, two stone columns, each the height of three houses, rise up on either side. The tower bases are beneath the bridge and angle outward, making them impossible for invaders to climb.

Suspended between the towers is a massive bronze gate fitted into tracks chiseled into the columns. The gate is hoisted aloft by a series of pulleys and ropes drawn by twelve holy white oxen housed in a temple on the far side of the bridge—the Hammer of Hamleed.

Once the Hammer of Hamleed was devised, it had a remarkable effect on the culture of the Hamoodian people and their rulers. Although their fields and stock covered vast areas beyond the city, there was enough space and sufficient resources within the natural barriers guarding the city for the extended tribe to shelter in times of danger. This ultimate safety tempered the hearts of the fierce Hamoodians. Over time, they redirected the creativity that made them successful as warriors into less violent forms of expression.

Stepping onto the ancient road, I knew I was entering the most advanced city in the world. A city of philosophers, teachers, poets, and scientists. A city of unimaginable wealth.

Beyond the bridge and the small strand bordering the river lay building upon building of the city proper—some two stories tall, others walled with beautiful gates. Each house had flowers in boxes beneath its windows. The smell of jasmine and gardenia sweetened the air. Many shops and houses were covered with flowering vines.

We rode from deep shade into bright sunlight, and then plunged back into the dark as the road to the castle wound its way up the mountain.

Eventually we entered a handsome square bordered on three sides by shops and the fourth by the gates to the castle. Apartments above the shops were reserved for official visitors. This is where the Bensheeries would be housed.

After dismounting and bidding farewell to Lasheed and the others, Dalnt and I approached the castle on foot. The massive wooden gates, banded by great bronze straps, stood open. A guard in full battle dress bowed as we entered the courtyard.

A distinguished old man stepped from the shadows. With a deep bow to Dalnt and a respectful nod to me, the wizened old man dressed in a green-trimmed yellow tunic, said, "His Royal Highness, king of Hamood, protector of all who reside within and without Hamleed and creator of eternal peace, welcomes the avenger of the twan."

Dalnt took the old fellow by the arm. Turning to me he said, "This is Sanree, chamberlain to the Court of Hamood. This old fellow has been caring for royal guests since my father was a boy. He will see you to your suite. We will meet for dinner."

The long shadows of the late afternoon gave the courtyard an abandoned feeling. It was unadorned except for a small gatekeeper's house and two external stairways leading to the ramparts on either side of the gate.

I followed the chamberlain through an arched portico and entered a long hallway lined with torches. We had climbed three flights of steps when, slightly out of breath, Sanree swung back a heavy wooden door carved with scenes of an oasis that looked very much like the Gleb.

The opulent room was littered with expensive divans and cushions. Exotic tapestries adorned the walls, each depicting a scene from Hamoodian history. Colorful carpets brightened the room. From the corner of my eye I spotted my saddle and traveling pack in an adjacent room.

"Yes, Your Highness...you have a question?" Sanree asked, circumspectly.

"Ah...is this where I'm to stay?" I asked, pointing to the door leading to the adjacent room.

"Yes, Your Highness, that is your sleeping room. This is your lounge," he said with a hint of a smile in his voice.

I walked into the sleeping room. A large pallet covered with pillows and robes made from the finest fleece occupied one corner of the room. Across from the sleeping area was a large stone trough full of water. Turning to the chamberlain I said, "I didn't think animals were allowed in the castle."

His leathery forehead wrinkled in puzzlement. "Animals...I'm sorry, I don't understand."

"The trough," I said, pointing to the water.

"Oh," said Sanree, his face flushing. He thought for a minute, drawing a hand across his face to hide a smile. "It would indeed make an excellent trough, Your Highness, but as animals are not allowed in the castle, we use it as a bathing pool." An experienced diplomat, he lowered his eyes, not wishing to compound my embarrassment.

I blushed, and a picture of the snake and the mouse flashed through my mind. I laughed. In fact, I could not stop laughing.

"Sir, are you unwell?" Sanree inquired gently.

"No, no, I'm fine," I sputtered, wiping tears from my eyes. "Excuse me, it's just that I've been exposed to so many new things since the sun last rose I'm a bit overwhelmed."

"I completely understand, Your High—"

"Sanree," I interrupted, "please call me Ayuba. I know it is a strange name and most of your guests expect to be addressed differently, but Ayuba will do just fine."

At first the ancient chamberlain looked alarmed. Then, as if tasting a strange new food, said, "As you wish…Ayoooba."

"Please, my friend," I implored the old man, "give me a tour of my rooms and explain each item lest I mistake one of the king's pillows for a haystack!"

And so it was that I learned of mirrors, divans, bathing tubs, and sponges. Sanree demonstrated a small bell that summoned two lovely young female servants. He explained the maids would fetch whatever I needed…I wondered if my Bensheerie escort had such a bell in their quarters.

The chamberlain told the girls to fetch hot water to warm the trough in preparation for my bath. He further instructed them to freshen my clothes in preparation for my presentation to the king. Then he excused himself, promising to return shortly to escort me to dinner.

I thought of asking him what was to follow, but caught myself... *Live in the present Ayuba; the future will arrive soon enough.*

The girls proved delightful companions. Like everyone else in Hamleed, they seemed to know that I came from the Beyond. Jute, the younger girl, brought pitchers of hot water, while Neeno, her older sister, undid my hair and combed it. The girls chatted incessantly, peppering me with questions. Their misconceptions and outright fantasies about the Beyond made me laugh.

When the bath was ready, Jute began to unlace my tunic. I knew both girls were interested to see if, indeed, Beyonders were different from normal men, so I boldly disrobed. They pretended to avert their eyes, but I heard a sigh of relief from Neeno and a giggle from Jute signaling that I had passed inspection.

To my surprise the girls joined me in the bath. Using wonderfully soft sponges from the sea of Oxyeon, they scrubbed away the travel grime. Neeno used a type of root that when rubbed vigorously against a sponge, bubbled and gave off the scent of wild berries. She applied this to my hair. The long black strands squeaked as she rinsed away the rich foam.

I couldn't stop grinning. Resting my head on the edge of the tub, I closed my eyes. I felt the softness of the girls' bodies caress me. Tender hands stroked and massaged my arms and shoulders, while others kneaded my legs and feet. I felt Jute's breath against my ear, followed by the flick of her tongue. A sense of joy swept over me. Tears flowed from my eyes.

For most of my life I had been surrounded by danger and uncertainty. A part of me, like a half-drawn dagger, was always ready to flee or fight. But now, oh blessed present, I sheathed my sword, closed my eyes, and drifted on the fragrant breath and silken touch of angels.

I was dried with soft fleece, my skin and hair oiled. Ventie's red leather tunic had been cleaned and polished with beeswax and my black robe freshened. The twan's scabbard was strapped around my waist. Jute and Neeno smiled proudly as the chamberlain fetched me for dinner.

As Sanree and I descended the stairs to the royal hall, my mind was at peace. I felt an overwhelming sense of lightness. And so it was, with this sense of confidence, this immersion in the present, that Ayuba, a savage from the Beyond, walked through the great bronze-clad doors to meet the king of Hamood.

The room glowed. Silver chandeliers studded with hundreds of candles hung from a ceiling so high it disappeared in a smoky haze. On either side of the ornate carpet stretching before me, scores of dignitaries were assembled. The men wore elegant robes and tunics fastened with inlaid belts denoting their rank. The women glittered in jeweled gowns that shimmered in the candlelight.

In a reedy voice, the chamberlain announced, "Your Royal Highness, king of Hamood, protector of Hamleed; royal twan, mighty arm of the king; lords and ladies, it is my honor to introduce Ayuba from the Beyond, avenger of the twan, son of Aroon al Sumer, protector of the western border, and bearer of the scabbard of the twan."

The comforting lightness abandoned me under the gaze of the nobles. My hands grew sweaty, my heart raced, and my mouth grew dry. Sanree took me by the arm and guided me through the murmuring crowd.

The far wall of the hall was unlike the rest of the castle. Not a wall at all, really, but the smooth face of a granite cliff. Carved into the ancient stone was an elaborate arch, inset with turquoise and lapis and festooned with giant candles. An elevated throne carved from bone and draped with the soft pelts of unborn ibex occupied the center of the blazing arch. On the throne sat the King of Hamood.

Dressed in a bright yellow robe with scarlet piping, Dalnt stepped forward. Taking me by the arm, he whispered in my ear, "Be calm, my friend, and follow my lead."

His voice, edged with amusement, calmed my jittery nerves. Together we approached the throne. As Dalnt addressed the court I took the opportunity to observe the king more closely. Expecting to see a man of advanced age, instead I found a young man only slightly older than me. His face was smooth with a strong jaw. His black eyes, wide set beneath heavy brows, sparkled in the candlelight. His hair, oiled and pulled tightly against his skull, framed a wide, intelligent forehead.

As Dalnt finished relating how I came to be the bearer of the twan's scabbard, he motioned for me to remove it from my waist. I fumbled with the clasp, my fingers suddenly thumbs.

The king spoke, "Dalnt, we honor Ayuba as an avenger, not a tailor. Perhaps you can assist him." Although said in jest, it was a generous act of kindness putting me at ease.

Once freed from the heavy scabbard and belt, I approached the king. Kneeling, I handed him the scabbard. As he took it from my shaking hands, the assembly let out a rousing cheer.

This sudden change from somber ceremony to wild yelling and cheering so startled me I almost fell over. Fortunately the king, seeing my predicament, reached out to steady me. Rising from the throne while assisting me to my feet, he put his arm around me. With the scabbard held high in one hand and the other on my shoulder, he joined the jubilation of the court. When the cheering stopped, the king addressed the gathering without releasing me from his embrace.

"Our history is sung by grandmothers to our children. In the oldest of these songs is the story of the twan's scabbard. In hymns from beyond the memories of the singers and countless singers before them, songs first sung when we wandered a nameless land, comes the story of the first Hamoodian—the 'Great Guide.'

"Some say he was a god; a giant among starving savages. He taught us to plant crops and domesticate beasts, freeing us from the bondage of survival and the desperation of war. It is for this giant ancestor, from whom our kingdom issues, that the scabbard of the twan was made. Each twan has held it in trust since the beginning of our time. And although this symbol has been remade over countless centuries, each time a small part of the original is sewn into the new, like father into son. It is this continuum, so the songs say, that if broken signals the end of Hamood. When our boys become men, they vow to die for the twan to protect this history and the future of the kingdom. They vow to avenge the slaying of a twan, no matter the sacrifice.

"If this young man," he said, releasing his grip on my shoulder and bowing toward me, "had not avenged the twan, had not risked his life and found the courage to stay the heart of the twan's killer in accordance with our history, Hamood would have been compelled to wage war on the soulless Effrifrians. Thousands on both sides would have died. Widows and orphans would abound and the smoke of death would linger over the world until we were victorious or ceased to exist."

Once again the crowd cheered. The king's dark eyes smiled at me as he joined in the celebration. Finally I understood why my small part in the battle at the Gleb was honored with such significance. Had the slayer of the twan escaped, the consequences would have affected all mankind.

Raising his arms to quiet the crowd, the king stepped forward and summoned Dalnt to kneel before him.

"Dalnt, son of Harim and royal cousin of the second tier, do you pledge to protect Hamood, to dedicate your life to the honor of the twan, to become the continuation of the unbroken line of servants of the Hamoodian people, and to put the welfare of the people and the king of Hamood before all?"

"I do, Your Highness."

"Do you agree to carry this scabbard and sword in trust for the return of the 'Great Guide?'"

Dalnt, the fearless warrior, shivered at the king's knee as he assumed the second most powerful office in Hamood. "I do, Your Highness."

Tears welled in my eyes. The pageantry and the joy mixed with solemnity pulled at my heart. The assembled nobles cheered wildly, for at last, all was well within the kingdom. Dalnt quieted the crowd.

"I am humbled by this honor. To assume the role that has been occupied by giants is an honor beyond all others." Tears streamed down his cheeks. He bowed once again to the king.

Then a soldier stepped forward, handing Dalnt a black leather scabbard. Dalnt held it over his head for all to see; the leather, burnished to onyx sheen, was outlined with silver brads glowing in the candlelight. On the face of the scabbard was the chevron of a captain's rank. The handle of the dagger was pure silver, capped with a large, uncut turquoise cabochon.

"As his last official act, the great twan awarded Ayuba the rank of honorary captain of the guard for his courage on the Shale Sea. And alive today, he would surely add to this tribute his fearless action at the Gleb."

Dalnt strapped the scabbard around my waist. Stepping back, he bowed and said, "Nobles and ladies of Hamood, I present Ayuba, son of Aroon al Sumer, protector of the western border, avenger of the twan, honorary captain of the guard of Hamleed." With that, everyone in the room, including the king, made a deep bow.

Interrupting this solemn moment, a voice bellowed from the rear of the hall, "And protector of Bensheer!"

It was the fearless voice of Lasheed breaking the somber mood. The crowd, long familiar with the reputation of Bensheeries, broke into laughter. The king pretended to be upset by this ill-considered disruption and shouted, "Guards, arrest that man!"

Lasheed, escorted by two burly guards, was hustled through the audience.

"Ayuba," said the king sternly, "do you know this man, and if so, what shall we do with him for interrupting this hallowed moment?"

I looked at my uncomfortable companion who sheepishly averted his eyes.

"I do indeed know this scoundrel," I responded, relieved that the focus of the moment was now transferred to Lasheed. "He is but one of six uncivilized creatures from the village of Bensheer who once tried to murder me!"

I paused, letting my charge hang in the air. Dalnt winked at me. Continuing, I said, "Although they captured me and were armed with spears and swords, they were conquered by an ancient crone named Ventie, who, with wizened arms and a fearsome voice, chased them away like kittens."

The crowd laughed at Lasheed's predicament and began to boo and whistle. The king called for silence.

"It is good then that we have captured these villains. Obviously my nobles feel we should execute them before we retire for dinner. What say you, Ayuba? As the wronged party, the decision is yours."

Pausing a moment to let the suspense build, I continued, "Your Honor, everything I have said is true, but I must admit, incomplete. I failed to add that my capture and subsequent imprisonment was an honest mistake. To their credit, once the truth was known, these kittens became lions. They have since protected me from a worley on the great dune and led me safely to Hamleed. They have proven brave and considerate companions, if somewhat ill-mannered. Thus my sentence is that they be treated as honored guests while in Hamleed and feted the same as you have done for me."

Now fully aware of the farce, the crowd applauded and cried, "Hail Bensheer!" Lasheed pushed away his guards and with exaggerated dignity dusted off his tunic.

"So be it," said the king, grandly.

The king and Dalnt led the procession through a long, damp hallway to the dining hall. Using all their strength, two servants opened the polished and banded cedar doors, each large enough for a camel to pass through. We were assailed by a wave of warm, scented air, as though approaching an oasis.

The palace dining hall was the most celebrated room in the world. Round in shape, with a domed ceiling, the walls were covered in faintly colored tiles of turquoise, ocher, and cloudy black. Enclosing the space were twelve beautifully carved limestone arches, half of which looked out over the kingdom, the other half over gardens of flowers planted in terraced beds carved into the cliff. The arches facing the cardinal points were inset with precious stones. Between each arch, bronze statues of ancient warriors held giant torches. The blazing lanterns reflected off the highly polished copper dome arching over the entire room.

An elegant round carpet made from the wool of Bynethian sheep covered the entire floor. In the center of the room a large bronze brazier glowed with fragrant cedar charcoal. The dark blue border on the carpet was wide enough for a person to sit cross-legged. The carpet's center, the color of a spring sky, was divided into twelve sections, each displaying a different zodiac formation. Surrounding the brazier (symbolizing the sun) was an elaborate calendar with the solstices and equinoxes in bold yellow.

I was seated in the inner circle with the king, Dalnt, and other leading nobles. Lesser nobles and other guests were seated in the outer circle against the wall. The nobles chatted while a deep red wine was served in alabaster goblets. The goblets were so highly polished and thinly worked that the ruby-colored wine glowed through the stone's milky veneer.

Servants in pure white tunics served endless platters of delicacies—roasted peacock stuffed with dates, baked fish with lemon and olives, whole lambs roasted in a kneeling position with crispy skin oozing rich, fragrant drippings.

Three guests, served by a kneeling servant wielding an obsidian knife, shared each platter. The carvers were adept at their trade; I needed only to stretch my hand toward the desired dish and, as if by magic, a perfect bite-sized morsel appeared. The meal was followed with platters of dates, figs, oranges, grapes, and pomegranates, accompanied by a sweet white wine from the village of Bahrim.

When the dining concluded, Dalnt said to the king, "Your Highness, I have learned from the Bensheeries that our guest has become an accomplished storyteller. Perhaps you could impose on him to tell his story tonight; I'm sure everyone here would welcome the entertainment."

And so once again, Lasheed had thrust me center stage, although this time my audience consisted of the most exalted and educated people of the world. My voice quivered as, at the king's behest, I rose to address the nobles of the ancient kingdom of Hamood.

I lingered over my ceaseless wandering in the stony reaches of the western kingdom. Moving on to my life in Hamrabi, I sensed a subtle disappointment, as though my audience wanted to spend more time in the inhospitable land. This desire to pause was soon replaced by an intense interest in my adventures with the twan, Father, Fairtoo, and Dalnt.

If I'd known the attractive middle-aged woman in a diaphanous gown sitting directly opposite me was the widow of the great twan or that the pregnant lady with elegant eyes was Fairtoo's wife, I would have tempered my description of their deaths and the tragedy at the Gleb. As it was, I spoke in great detail about these events, stimulated by the intensity of the nobles' groans and the encouragement in their eyes. The two women wept softly. The twan and his successor, Fairtoo, were beloved by many and related to all.

I walked slowly around the ancient room in the space between the inner group and the outer ring. This allowed me to look closely into the eyes of each person. I timed the end of my story so I finished standing between the king and Dalnt. Silence hung like a leaden sky over the elegant room.

The king broke the silence. "All honors to Ayuba!" he shouted, raising his goblet. Soon the entire room broke into a strange syncopated clapping.

The crowd shouted, "Ayuba, avenger of the twan," (clap, clap, clap) "Ayuba, avenger from the Beyond," (clap, clap). This continued through several earned or made-up honorifics, ending in unstructured clapping and cheering. I was delighted by the response.

As I resumed my place in the circle, a man with a vulpine face said in a loud voice, "Ayuba, you have spoken of many events and lifted from our eyes the scales that have long hidden the reality of the Beyond. Our hearts have been torn by your description of the vileness of the Effrifrians and the disdainful death of our beloved compatriots. Please, I implore you, speak to us of what you have learned from these experiences. All of us here live in this cosseted realm where laws and customs were established long ago by the ghosts of antiquity. Please speak freely that we might see our land and customs with a purity that can only come from one who was raised by the wind and blown, unsullied, into our midst."

I was dumbfounded. Relating a battle or talking about wandering alone, half starved, was one thing, but being asked for my opinion...my observations... was something I never considered. Dalnt sensed my frustration.

"Ayuba," Dalnt interjected, "although Barnlo is known to be somewhat loquacious (the ladies and nobles laughed) he is the high priest of Hamood and our most learned teacher. His days are spent in the quest for knowledge. He freely shares his findings with all of us, his eternal students. Perhaps now is not the time, but surely you could tease us with an observation or two."

Many voices concurred. The king squeezed my arm saying, "It would honor us greatly."

Sweat trickled from my brow and down my neck. My faced flushed. Joklee, seated in the outer ring just behind me, said in a loud whisper, "Go ahead, Ayuba, tell them why it's better to be a snake than a mouse."

The crowd, thinking this was an insult, tried to hush Joklee. The twan's widow said, "Perhaps we impose too much on Ayuba's good graces."

"No, no, please," I stumbled. "The question was unexpected. I am so honored by your attention and so humbled by your kindness, I was simply thinking how I could express the many things I have learned in such a short time. Joklee's suggestion is a good place to start." I then addressed myself to Barnlo.

"Revered teacher, I do not know if this is what you seek, and I suspect it may be a somewhat mundane observation to you and your students, but nevertheless it was a revealing experience to me." With that, I spoke about the snake catching the mouse in the wheat field.

"I learned from that experience that living in a modern world like Hamood, there are many distractions that tug at the mind, dragging it into the maw of worry and fear, devouring the only thing that exists…the present. And if one lives in the uncertainty of the future, life can indeed be consumed by the snake called time."

The room was filled with the hum of subdued conversations as my observation was discussed among the royals. I was relieved to have the attention lifted from me and started to resume my seat when an old man stood.

"Honored guest, my name is Qualnten and I am the oldest member of this extended family. One of the few pleasures of being the eldest is that I can ask questions that others, who may be bound by the fear of social retribution, hesitate to mention."

"Oh, Grandfather," a beautiful young woman interrupted, "it's not your age that frees your tongue, but the wine."

"Here, here!" cried the king, raising his cup. Everyone followed with a loud round of cheers for the crusty old man. Qualnten emptied his cup in acknowledgement.

"Whether it's the wine or age, I do have a question for the new honorary captain." He paused, waiting for the banter to subside. "Ayuba, in the songs of the ancients it is told that Hamood will be visited by a shepherd who will be able to dream the future. My question to you, dear guest is…" He paused, licking his dry lips. "Are you that shepherd?"

Except for a breeze whispering through the open arches that ruffled the torches, the room was silent. I stood alone in the center of a room that was the center of the world. No one moved…no eye was distracted by the flickering light…no ear wandered to the soft sigh of the wind…no voice uttered a whisper.

The old man had posed the question everyone wanted to ask. The silence pressed down on me like the weight of a thousand nights. An image of Father on the edge of the Shale Sea drifted through my mind. I closed

my eyes to see him better but instead heard him singing. Opening my eyes I looked into expectant stares.

"I wish I could, if only for an instant, be the shepherd in your song, if in that moment I could share with
you a thought or a dream to repay the generosity and
honor you have given me. Unfortunately, I come from
the Beyond and not from the bosom of your past. A lesson learned on the edge of the Shale Sea is all that I
have to offer in gratitude for your many kindnesses:

> "Sleep, and in the veil of night
> Dream of valor in the light
> When comes the awakening dawn
> It is your dreams you act upon."

❦

Several days following the banquet, Lasheed and my
Bensheerie escort left for home. I intended to travel
with them as far as Bensheer and then on to Hamrabi,
but the king and others implored me to stay. I was easily
persuaded...the capital city was full of wonders as yet
unexplored.

On a gloomy autumn morning, I walked with my valiant escort down through the city as far as the bridge.
The great Hammer faded in and out of the mist.

The Bensheeries were in a glum mood, whether from
the sadness they felt about leaving or simply lethargy
from days of constant drinking and whoring, I could
not tell. I embraced each of these stalwart, simple men
with sincere affection and promised to visit them soon.

Lasheed, squinting through bloodshot eyes, said,
"Although you have been honored as few before you,
Ayuba, at times your head is as hollow as a gourd. Even

simple fellows like us know you will never return beyond the great dune."

I was surprised at his certainty.

Mounting his camel, he looked down. "Ayuba, your friendship has brought great honor to us and to Bensheer, but I fear your destiny lies in the east. Your story will live on for eternity...our small part dwindling as the tale increases. But I fear we will hear it from others, not from you."

Walking back up the hill I reflected on what Lasheed said. It wasn't the first time I'd heard it. Father seemed to sense this before I left home. Ventie too was sure Hamleed would not be my final destination. In my heart, I yearned for Hamrabi and my family, but in my mind I saw visions of unknown places filled with adventure.

The atmosphere in Hamleed was so agreeable and the hospitality of the royal family so insistent, I remained for almost a year. The days flew by, each filled with some new experience. Marun's voice encouraged me as I stuffed my head with knowledge.

Frequently I accompanied Twan Dalnt throughout the kingdom inspecting military posts. Hamood's extensive northern border with Effrifria was of the most concern as, over the centuries, many brutal wars had been fought between the two giants.

The border to the east with Bynethia presented fewer problems. It consisted mostly of large tribes who spent their energies fighting each other. The Beyond in the west and the vast swamps to the south were patrolled, but not garrisoned.

As an honorary captain of the guard, I was feted by each military unit we visited. I experienced the pleasure of training with them and attended their councils. I learned to shoot as well as fashion bows and arrows, becoming quite proficient with this new weapon.

I spent most of my days in Hamleed with the venerable Barnlo and the king and most nights with Jute and Neeno. It was an intense education in science and the senses, both of which have served me well.

Barnlo and his considerable staff were the keepers of the knowledge gleaned from countless generations since the founding of the original tribe of Hamood. They were adept at reading the stars and ascribed certain portents to various celestial events. They could predict when an eclipse would occur. Although they knew the moon passing in front of the sun caused this strange event, they also believed it made women more fertile.

It was a discussion about this juxtaposition of science and myth that led to the most startling revelation of my life.

The king, Barnlo, and I had just witnessed a rare eclipse on a cold, clear autumn afternoon. Chilled from standing atop Barnlo's observatory, we hurried down the stairs to the warmth of his study. Servants brought warm cups of sweet wine. Shedding our outer garments, we relaxed by a small fire laid in a brazier.

After Barnlo described the ancient belief connected with the eclipse, I laughed, saying, "In the Beyond, people believe an eclipse means spirits are trying to bring an end to the world. Anyone of breeding age fornicates as often as they can. Whether to create survivors or simply to end their days in enjoyment, I'm not certain. I was too young to participate."

The king smiled. "It is often used as an excuse for abandonment in Hamood as well. I suspect half the soldiers and civil servants are, at this very moment, absent from their posts."

Barnlo replied more thoughtfully, "Since you have been with us, Ayuba, I have learned many strange similarities between customs in the Beyond and Hamood."

"Surely you jest!" I quickly replied, "The barren desert of my birth has no culture or ceremony, no language as you understand it. There is no subtlety or theoretical thinking. The peoples of my memory behave more like wild beasts than humans."

Barnlo looked at the king, then at me. "Ayuba, often when a person finds himself in a situation that is pleasing and perhaps more...advanced...yes, that's it...that person tends to disparage the place from which he came."

Laughing, I responded, "I don't mean to be impolite, but you must disabuse yourself of any notion that the peoples of the Beyond are some sort of wayward civilization trapped in ignorance by their situation. It's simply not true."

Both learned and powerful men looked disappointed at my remarks. I was about to apologize when the king rose to his feet.

"I think it's time we showed Ayuba why we are so interested in the Beyond."

Armed with torches, we traversed the entire width of the castle until we came to a door guarded by two soldiers that opened onto a stone staircase. We descended several floors into the depths of the granite massif.

Presently we came to an archway crested with unfamiliar glyphs. The door was carved entirely of bone. I imagined I could feel the heart of the mountain beating through the soles of my sandals. A profound silence enveloped us.

When Barnlo spoke, his whisper bounced against the stone. "Ayuba, this is the most hallowed place in all of Hamood."

I reached out to touch the stone...it was cool and dry. My mouth was parched and my tongue rasped against my lips.

Whispering, the king asked, "Can you read the inscription?"

Not trusting myself to speak, I shook my head.

The king touched each glyph as he solemnly pronounced them, "Who knows this stone is the shepherd of our dreams."

Finally finding my voice, I whispered, "What does it mean?"

Our guttering torches cast wavering beams of light across Barnlo's wrinkled brow. His eyes wept with sadness as deep as the crushing silence.

"Legend says the stone inside was the last place the 'Great Guide' sat before disappearing. The glyphs are his last words. Our ancestors, from the land of our origin, transported the stone within. It was placed within this mountain, and the stronghold of Hamleed was built to protect it forever. Not even our most ancient songs or myths are old enough to record the trails followed to this place."

The silence, screaming from stone as old as the earth, filled me with a sense of dread.

"Ayuba, custom dictates that only the king and high priest of Hamood can visit this place. Indeed, the stone is believed by most to be a legend."

"My lord..." I started to ask why they had brought me here.

Placing his hand on my shoulder, the king's black orbs stared into mine. "We believe you are the one who will know this stone."

Before I could protest, he and Barnlo handed me their torches. Grasping the bone handle in the shape of a gazelle's horn they struggled to swing the ancient barrier open. The smell of time came from the black, gaping entrance. Dust motes swirled in the torchlight. I was afraid to look within.

"Don't be afraid, Ayuba. Although it is a hallowed symbol to the people of Hamood, it is only a stone." Taking his torch in one hand, Barnlo gently pressed me forward with the other.

Pushing my torch into the maw I lowered my head to clear the massive lintel. Looking up, I was surprised how bright the cavern had become. Three walls and the ceiling were completely covered with tiny crystals. Each crystal magnified the torchlight and shimmered, producing a glow that seemed to emanate from the very core of the earth. The cavern had been hollowed out of a pocket of crystal formed at the beginning of time. A heavy tapestry made from gold and silver threads was directly in front of me; it was completely covered with unfamiliar glyphs.

"This is the original alphabet taught to the Hamoodians by the 'Great Guide' during his last visit. It was woven by prepubescent girls, so the legend goes. Although we no longer use these complicated runes, we have carried on the custom of weaving. The carpet in the great hall was woven in the same manner. All females of the family of Hamood are required to spend their final year of childhood in this endeavor. Males serve in defense of the realm—females in defense of our heritage."

The king handed Barnlo his torch and, without ceremony, drew back the heavy curtain.

I felt dizzy. My torch slipped from my hand, rattling across the floor. The great rock's turquoise bands shimmered in the light. The barely visible ocher layers were marbled with black veins that seemed to throb in the crystalline glow.

The king and Barnlo stepped back, as though suddenly afraid. "You know this stone, Ayuba," Barnlo whispered. It was a statement not a question.

My eyes were stinging from the smoke of the torches. In front of me stood a section of the great, multihued bench that runs deep in the Beyond. There was no mistaking it. I had spent my youth in its shadow, herding goats and playing. I not only recognized the strata, I knew exactly where it came from in the long span of the bench's reach.

The king began to cough, the smoke growing denser. "Look closely, Ayuba, before we leave," he sputtered, still holding back the heavy drape.

"I've seen enough," I said.

We did not speak again until reaching Barnlo's study. Servants brought wet towels to wipe away the soot and cool drinks for our parched throats. Now I would have to tell the others what I knew of the stone. If indeed the myth of the stone were true, my revelations would profoundly impact the people of Hamood. It would confirm that their roots lay in the land of their fears.

I began, "Running farther than anyone has traveled, deep in the Beyond, there is a stone bench. I spent much of my childhood in its lee, playing and hunting. When I grew older, I tended goats along its never-ending spine. I slept in its hollows and banked fires against its face. There is no doubt the Stone of Hamood comes from the Beyond."

The two royals were silent, the import of my claim struggling its way into their minds.

"But how can you be sure, Ayuba? There must be other benches in the world as richly veined and colored as the Stone of Hamood," said the king with a lack of conviction.

"Oh, how I wish that were true, honored friend, but..."

"There's more?" asked Barnlo.

"When I was only eight or nine, my family raided another band and captured a wife for my brother who was thirteen at the time. The girl's name was Let. She had been with us for only a year when we wandered near a section of the bench that caused her to become very agitated. She pointed at the bench, screaming and stamping her feet. She pulled at my brother to get him to run away. As she knew few words of our language, we could only guess at her strange behavior. My mother finally slapped her and tied her to a rock until she regained her composure.

"Although much of the time Let lived with us was spent near the bench, there was something about this particular area that caused her great fear. The only unusual feature in this section was a perfectly shaped depression in the wall's face... in the shape of a rectangle. While Let lay sobbing in her bonds, my father, brother, and I examined this feature.

"Father lifted me up onto the depression. It was as high as a man and an arm's length deep. The walls were perfectly smooth, as though sliced with a sharp knife. Although Father did not understand Let's fear, its intensity fueled his superstition, so we quickly moved on. It was the last time I ever saw the bench."

"You...you believe you actually stood in the place where the Stone of Hamood was quarried?" stammered the king.

"It was the exact size of your relic, Your Highness, and the sides were as smooth as tile, just like the stone cherished by Hamood."

The sun was setting and the air had cooled. Servants brought candles and robes. Others stoked the brazier. Long in the service of these two powerful men, the servants did not tarry sensing matters of great import were being discussed.

Once we were alone again, I continued, "Over time, Let became more proficient in our language and was able to explain her fears. We learned her people called the smooth geometrical depression in the stone the Moon's Tooth. In a time beyond all memory, they believed the moon came to the earth and plucked the great stone from the bench to use as a tooth. The legend said that when it brushed against the land, a tribe camping nearby was plucked up with the stone and never returned. It was her fear of being captured by the moon that so agitated her."

I was concerned that Barnlo and the king would laugh at this superstition even though both were familiar with strange and often bizarre lore handed down through time. No one knew how distorted these tales had become in their frequent retelling, but one had to believe that within the tale lay a truth, no matter how twisted by time and tongue—a truth so unusual and profound it either created its own myth to survive or those who witnessed the event conveyed the tale over eons to preserve it.

The dull light of eventide slowly disappeared as the sun set. With our robes around us we huddled close to the brazier—autumn was turning to winter. Heavy drapes covering the windows muffled the moaning wind blowing down the face of the great stone façade.

Barnlo was the first to speak. "We should compare Let's tribal superstition with Hamood's myth. We Hamoodians have been taught that a great guide has appeared throughout the history of our people. We know not from where he comes; only that he is larger than us physically and has a long beard. Our songs claim he is not a god, but an emissary from an advanced place. In the story, this prophet is sent to help us become civilized."

"It is far more believable than Let's odd story," I quipped, automatically disparaging anything from the Beyond, as was my custom.

"Not necessarily," replied Barnlo quickly. "Over my long life I have learned to never doubt a belief strongly held, no matter how strange it may seem. Beliefs are the glue of the soul and who am I to question what makes you *you*, and me *me*? It is not our age or the color of our hair or skin…it is what we believe. It is our faith in our beliefs that enables our dreams."

Unwilling to concede so easily, I said, "Surely, wise counselor, you do not mean to say you think it possible the moon swept down to get a tooth?" I laughed, looking to the king for support.

"Is it any more farfetched to believe in a bearded giant roaming the earth with powers so advanced he can cut a stone as smooth as a woman's breast? Or a giant who claims he will come again and visit the keeper of the stone, even though a thousand cycles of the seasons may have passed? Faith, my young friends," Barnlo looked at both the king and me, "makes beliefs come true in the hearts of believers."

The wind picked up. The heavy drapes billowed into the room. Servants appeared quickly tying them to brackets on the walls. A pretty young woman brought more fuel for the fire. Hot tea in stone mugs appeared, carried by servants who again promptly disappeared.

"It is possible that the myths are one and the same," Barnlo replied. "The tale of the Stone of Hamood claims that when the 'Great Guide' carved the stone he used magical powers. It is said he spoke to the tribe telling them to face away from the stone. When they complied, there was an intense light and a sudden crashing noise. Dust filled the air, clogging lungs and eyes. It is said many of the tribe were knocked down by this strange event.

"When the guide told them to turn around, they beheld the stone cut from its womb. There was, again according to legend, an intense glow surrounding the stone and the cavity from which it was cut. Could not the glow from our legend be the moon from Let's? It is further written that the guide told the tribe to abandon their nomadic ways and search for more fertile ground where they could plant seeds and provide for their sustenance using the knowledge he had given them. The tribe kidnapped by the moon in Let's fable could have simply been the Hamoodians' departure after the tooth was *extracted*," the king quipped.

We all laughed, dispelling the tension of the moment. Barnlo drew us back to the two remaining issues.

"In all my study and contemplation, I never considered Hamoodians originated from the Beyond. It is truly a revelation!"

"Why was that not a possibility?" I asked, thinking he would say the peoples of the Beyond were too ignorant and stunted to have spawned such a great clan.

He surprised me, saying, "It is written that in order to move the Stone of Hamood the tribe harnessed two hundred camels to drag the great weight. Tribesmen preceded this vast caravan, removing stones and other impediments to smooth the path. Although unfamiliar with the geography of the Beyond, I have crossed the great dune many times. It was inconceivable to me that our ancestors could have traversed the soft sand dunes while dragging such immense weight. No wonder the legend claims the journey took two complete cycles of the seasons!"

I recalled it took me less than ten traveling days from Hamrabi, on the edge of the Beyond, to Hamleed.

"This revelation may come as a shock to many in the kingdom," mused the king. "Among civilized peoples, imaginings of the Beyond are uncomplimentary at best. A favorite insult is *You are as stupid as a Beyonder* or *You must have been born in the Beyond.* These are only two of the more gentle epithets excoriating the land of your birth."

"Yes, I've heard many such remarks during my travels," I said sadly.

"Ha!" exclaimed Barnlo. "It will teach a lesson to those who disparage out of ignorance."

"Maybe so, honored one," the king said, "but nevertheless, finding that we come from a place of universal disparagement will be a bitter tonic to many."

"Hmm," mumbled Barnlo. "The truth will prevail."

⚬⚬⚬

We sat in the silence of Barnlo's elegant study, each attending his own thoughts. The kingdom of Hamood was the most advanced in the world, and soon the world would know it was created in the land of my birth. What a strange journey I'd traveled. In many ways it paralleled the history of Hamood...a comforting, if confusing, thought.

The king rose, stretching his legs. "Yes, the truth will prevail...there is no doubt that our friend with the strange name is indeed the shepherd of Hamood." The king smiled, directing a deep bow in my direction.

Barnlo and the king looked expectantly at me. What could I say? How should I respond? Breathing became difficult. My face flushed. Finally, with great effort, I exclaimed, "I don't know how to be the shepherd!"

The two men looked startled, then began to chuckle. Thinking how this sounded to my exalted companions, I grinned. Soon the three of us were laughing and slapping our knees in uncontrolled mirth. We laughed so loudly the servants peeked in to make certain we'd not upset the fire. The king was bent over trying to catch his breath. Barnlo fell on his side slapping his hand on the carpet. Tears flowed from my eyes...I started to hiccup loudly.

"Listen," sputtered the king, "the shepherd speaks!"

Several moments passed before we regained our composure. The servants brought platters of fruit and cold meats, accompanied by a rich, red wine. Barnlo's daughter, who was in charge of the king's personal staff, joked, "I'm not sure I should serve the wine. The three of you act as though you've already had enough!"

After talking for most of the evening, the food and wine were welcomed diversions.

With a soft belch, Barnlo spoke, "I have not laughed that hard in a long time. Now let me see if I can help Ayuba with his concern without breaking into laughter again..." He paused. "First of all, Ayuba, neither of us knows how to be the shepherd either..." He smiled benignly at me. "In fact, I doubt there is anyone in Hamood, Effrifria, or anywhere who can help you."

Feeling buoyant from the laughter, I quipped, "That was not what I wanted to hear."

"Perhaps this will help," he continued. "Because no one has ever *been* the shepherd...indeed never even *met* the shepherd...no matter how you act, it will be the behavior of the shepherd. Our ancient traditions and the glyphs over the stone decree it!"

This was a comforting thought. I recalled the carving over the door deep in the castle below—*Who knows this stone is the shepherd of our dreams.*

I asked Barnlo how he interpreted this enigmatic scripture. He thought it meant I'd been sent, or ordained, by the "Great Guide" to visit the tribe of Hamood as his emissary.

"No offense to the guide," I said, "but it would have been nice if he'd consulted me...or at least given me some training."

"Perhaps he has," said the king, plucking a great purple grape from the last remaining bunch on the decimated platter before him. "Perhaps everything you have experienced has been training for this moment, and..." he continued, warming to the subject, "perhaps shepherding dreams means you are to understand the deeper meaning of these experiences and share them with the people of Hamood."

"Excellent, excellent!" cried Barnlo, "It is my interpretation exactly...the only change I would make is that Hamood too is part of your experience. Being the shepherd of the guide's dreams can only mean that, just as the giant of our faith set us on the path to civilization, it is now our turn to teach others. You are not a shepherd *to* Hamood, Ayuba, but *of* Hamood!"

Although the cocks were greeting the dawn when I returned to my quarters, I wasn't sleepy. I crept into the room, careful not to wake Jute and Neeno. Fetching my travel robe and saddle, I slipped quietly into the waning night. It took me some time to locate my shaggy friend in the stables. She nuzzled me joyfully. She was eager to be back on the trail where we had shared so many adventures.

"Soon, dear friend," I whispered as we plodded beneath the Hammer and beyond the manicured fields of the kingdom. Within the hour, we reached a barren knoll west of the city known as the Camel's Hump.

A cold morning breeze blew the first rays of sun in from the east. Dismounting, I led the she-beast along the path to the crest, savoring the frosty air as we climbed.

I was assailed by strange and fearful emotions. Who am I? Ayuba, the camel boy? Ayuba, the adopted son of Aroon al Sumer? Ayuba, the shepherd of Hamood? Even the thought of it seemed absurd! But I did recognize the stone. I was perhaps the only human alive to have actually been in the cleft from which the stone was hewn. The king was right in one respect; I had experienced many strange and diverse things in my short life.

The bitterness of the morning wind was tempered by the caress of the rising sun. Struggling with conflicting emotions, my stomach churned with fear and excitement. What if it was all a coincidence? What if it was simply a mistake? What if I could not fulfill the promise of the stone?

"Stop it!" I screamed. "It's these thoughts that create your fears. Remember what Father said, it's what you think about that determines your success in battle. Was this not just another form of battle? If the difference between a coward and a hero is how one has dreamed the outcome, is that not also true for other less violent but no less important struggles?"

I turned with the great orb to my back. My shadow stretched across the knoll in the image of a giant. Turning back to the sun, I closed my eyes, letting its brilliance glow through my shuttered lids. I pictured myself addressing throngs of people...speaking plainly and clearly. My listeners received simple homilies long known but rarely applied with gratitude and joy. The person in my vision was not a god, but a teller of stories.

"I will make the vision of the legend my vision," I cried to the dawn. "I am in control of what I think...of what I see. I choose the demons or deities in my mind. Are we not all someone's legend? Are we not all the result of someone's vision? Is the vision passed through legend any more remarkable than the vision passed from parent to child for thousands of generations?"

As I did each morning, I thought of the great twan lying in the shallows of the Gleb's fetid pool and the countless others who died so I might live. Was my lot a greater sacrifice than theirs? I thought of the starving Hamoodians, dragging the great stone through the desert to its final resting place in the heart of the brooding granite mountain. Did they, even for an instant, deny their destiny? Was I a part of that driving vision? Was the carver of the stone the carver of my destiny?

Like a balm, the sun washed over my heart. Holding the present in my mind, I knew it was the future.

I remained in Hamleed until spring. Nights were spent with Barnlo in his observatory. I learned the names of the stars and how to identify planets. He taught me how to predict eclipses. I studied the rotation of the earth around the sun and the moon's constant dance with the orb on which we lived.

I awoke late spending my mornings bathing and playing with Neeno and Jute. I learned the art of idleness from these lovely companions. They cared not whether I was the shepherd or a camel herder. They lived entirely in the present, relishing the sensations of touch and taste. Their brightness of spirit infused me with a relaxed happiness. They taught me how to savor the hidden flavors of life. I learned by their example the unfettered joy of human touch; seeing not with my eyes alone, but with my tongue, lips, and skin. Like little birds they sang to me of the lightness of life.

Although the king and Barnlo agreed to hold secret our discovery at the Stone of Hamleed, the story leaked from Barnlo's private study into the castle...then, like a small stream, to the city of Hamleed. From the safety of the great stone redoubt it crossed the river Leb and soon covered the kingdom.

Afternoons were often spent with the king in the great hall meeting with various delegations and citizens. As more and more people heard my story, attendance at the king's afternoon sessions grew far beyond normal. The natural temerity and politeness of the Hamoodians when in the presence of royalty checked their overt interest in me, but their eyes sought me out as soon as they entered the hall. I was, in their minds, living confirmation of their beliefs. My existence turned the faith of countless generations to fact.

Two days before the spring equinox, at one of these afternoon assemblies, Lady Dalope, the widow of the great twan, approached the king to request permission to take their eight-year-old grandson to her home village of Swanrab on the western border of the realm. The king and Lady Dalope spoke briefly about the journey and when the king asked who would accompany her, Qualnten, in a voice diminished by age, replied, "Your Highness, perhaps Ayuba should accompany the Lady Dalope."

"And your reasoning?" questioned the king.

Protected by respect for his advanced age, Qualnten often voiced the unspoken thoughts of those more vulnerable. "Well, Great Prince," his reedy voice barely capable of carrying the great hall, "a secret, once common knowledge, must be affirmed to prevent gross distortion in the minds of its holders."

"Please, Qualnten, speak clearly. Your homily sheds little light on your reasoning," the king spoke politely.

"As you wish, sire. It is widely believed that Ayuba is he who knows the origin of the stone and walks in the shadow of the guide." The crowd murmured at this bold confirmation of the rumor.

"Already it is said Ayuba has great magical powers. That he can heal the sick, make the desert bloom, and turn sand into gold."

"Preposterous!" cried Barnlo, standing at the king's side.

Not easily cowed, Qualnten continued, "Preposterous to you, learned one, but a possibility to those who have only rumor and gossip as the brick and mortar of their opinion. To quell these unreasonable imaginings, let them come to know Ayuba as we know him. Let them sit at his feet and hear his story instead of the whispers of old women gathered at the well of suspicion and hope."

The court was silent, as though holding its collective breath. Qualnten's eyes held the king's gaze. Surprisingly, it was Lady Dalope who broke the silence.

"What our most venerable and wise brother says is true, Your Grace. The people of Hamood are excited and at the same time filled with fear by the rumors. They expect great change because of this revelation, and this agitation will only increase without exposure to the truth."

The king and Barnlo looked at me. I had known this time would come. For many moons, secure in the city of Hamleed, I had nurtured the vision I created on the Camel's Hump. I was unafraid.

"Your Highness, I welcome the opportunity to accompany the Lady Dalope to Swanrab."

In the month it took for Lady Dalope to prepare for our journey, I was a guest in the homes of many leading nobles. Nightly I attended banquets and entertainments in my honor. I ate so many delicacies my tunic soon grew tight. Neeno teased that if I continued expanding, soon there would be two of me—one for her and the other for Jute!

The evening before my departure, I was asked to speak to the entire population of Hamleed. As their number exceeded ten thousand souls, a clever device was used to reach so many ears at once.

The castle's parapets overlooked hundreds of buildings, stretching from the base of the castle walls to the river Leb. Mounting the watchtower jutting out from the main wall, the king and I were assailed by thousands of voices, cheering and clapping.

Looking over the city, I was surprised to see the rooftops covered with people. Every building squirmed with waving hands and singing mouths. Their joy flew like a great flock of birds, ascending the castle walls. The chorus of praise echoed off the brooding stone massif behind the castle. The echo collided with fresh cheers from below, creating a continuous roar—a human worley.

I was in awe. Since accepting my fate I had visualized how I would respond to my new role. This tableau far exceeded anything my imagination could create. Waving and smiling, the young king and the unsure shepherd bathed in the love emanating from the joyous throng.

The king quieted the crowd. Their cheers and whistles slowly abated. It was not until he spoke that I noticed soldiers standing on wooden platforms on several of the rooftops. When the king spoke, the translators on the nearest roof shouted out his remarks. The next level picked these up, and so on, until even the most remote listeners clearly heard the message. It was a waterfall of words.

After the king's remarks, he introduced me. For the first time, I was officially referred to as the "Shepherd of Hamood." Like a thunderstorm, the crowd exploded. Women cried tears of joy. Men shouted, waving their arms. I let their love wash over me. Breathing deeply I closed my eyes, retreating within myself.

As if by magic, when I raised my hands the crowd instantly fell silent. Except for the crying of a baby far off to my left and the barking of a dog beyond the Leb, Hamood was as silent as water.

What the crowd wanted to hear more than anything was the story of the stone. The people of Hamood had literally moved mountains with their faith. They were asked to suffer and toil based on a promise so old it could not be placed in time. Their faith became like the air they breathed; it sustained them without thought. But in the dark reaches of the believers' minds, in a place so deep they denied its existence lay a tiny seed of doubt. After all, had anyone ever seen the "Great Guide?" Was he simply a myth?

A soft breeze laced with the fragrance of tilled earth blew in from the vast fields beyond the river. The warm spring sun was dying in the west, casting long shadows over the upturned faces of the crowd. I could feel the beating of thousands of hearts as I told them the mystery of the stone. It was as though the breeze carrying my voice washed away their doubts. I was not a man, but a message from a past they had followed without question for a thousand generations.

"People of Hamood," I confessed in closing, "I know not why I have been given this honor. I am but a vision created long ago in the mind of the 'Great Guide' when Hamood was a tribe wandering the land of my birth. Hamood too is a vision, created by your faith in his lessons. It exists because each of you has pictured it in your mind's eye. You are who you are because you have seen yourself in your dreams. If I am a messenger of the guide, the message is—Hamood's destiny lives in your dreams."

The farewell banquet held in my honor ended just before daybreak. Jute and Neeno consumed the remainder of the night and much of the morning. With passion and tears, they were determined to make my last moments in Hamleed unforgettable.

The birthplace of Lady Dalope lay six day's ride from Hamleed and a day east of the Hamood-Bynethia border. Nestled in a broad valley, surrounded by gentle hills, Swanrab is the largest city in eastern Hamood and a major trading entrepôt.

The festivities held in our honor were elaborate and opulent. The center of the city is home to one of the most colorful and extensive bazaars in the country. Traders from all the tribes of Bynethia haggle with merchants from throughout the world. Dark-skinned traders with aquiline noses and coal black eyes barter rare stones with short, ocher-colored buyers who, it is said, come from far beyond the Sea of Oxyeon. Tanned animal skins, carpets, pottery, spices, slaves, robes, cloth, balms, potions, swords, armor, sandals, wine, fruit, vegetables, smoked meats, precious stones, gold and silver, along with animals of all sorts, are hawked and sold from early morning until sunset. Camel traders on the outskirts of the walled city assemble great trading caravans destined for Bynethia and Effrifria.

Visiting traders live in colorful tents on the plain outside the walls of Swanrab. Non-residents are banned from the city at sunset, a prudent policy that allows the citizens of Swanrab to sleep with both eyes closed. The smell of roasting meat and exotic spices wafts over the city. A polyglot cacophony of voices rumble late into the night as traders argue, bargain, sing, and dance by the light of blazing fires. Wine stalls and teashops scattered throughout the village host prostitutes, fortune-tellers, and musicians hawking their wares to the canny merchants.

Once my official duties as shepherd and escort to Lady Dalope abated, I found myself drawn to this vibrant, ever-changing tent city. Having spent more than a year in the safe and structured towns of Hamood, the raucous exuberance of the trader camp beckoned me.

My story was now known by almost everyone I came in contact with, including traders from countries far beyond Hamood. This fame often made it difficult to carry on normal discourse as any utterance of mine was looked on as bordering the divine. In the traders' camp, however, things were different. Each night I was invited to a different compound not as the shepherd, but as Ayuba. Mine was but one of countless stories.

A black-skinned merchant from a place fifty days beyond the crystal shore of Oxyeon told of triple-decked slavers chasing their trading vessel, forcing it to seek refuge in a great swamp on the shore of a place called Veronite. The swamps were the dread of all sailors, but less of a threat than life as a slave to the king of Sweb. It was said he owned more than a thousand slaves. Each had his right ear cut off as a sign of ownership. The ears were dried and sewn into a ceremonial robe for the king. No wonder the sulphurous miasma of the Veronitian swamps was a feared but welcomed alternative. The story of an orphaned boy wandering alone in the Beyond paled in comparison to this and many other tales of horror and sacrifice whispered beneath the stars outside the walls of Swanrab.

Although the traders' histories were captivating and profound, most nights were spent in lighter fare. Each tribe performed its own dance and music. Competitions arose between the different sects. Whirling, soft-gowned men with flashing swords leapt high into the night, accompanied by the shrill vibration of tambourines. Colorful women in flowing skirts with revealing bodices vibrated their hips and swayed to the ethereal sounds of flutes made from the shinbones of camels.

Every other night, after fires were banked and the traders turned to their rest, I made my way through a date grove between the tent village and the camel pens. Here I checked on my beloved she-beast before rousing the keeper of the gates to allow me to re-enter Swanrab and my elegant quarters in Lady Dalope's family compound.

One starlit but moonless night—having consumed a bit too much Effrifrian wine—I unsteadily felt my way through the palms. The occasional crackle from dying campfires punctured the deep silence, but it was the crackling of another sort that jostled me from my stupor.

Because of my experiences in the Beyond, the cracking of a twig, although similar to the popping of an ember, was unmistakable. My hearing became so acute I heard the blood course through my veins. My heart leapt into my mouth. The sound was near, but far enough away that I had time to react. Pretending to stumble, I swore loudly while staggering behind a large palm. I drew my blade; it felt heavy in my shaking hand.

My ruse worked. I heard footsteps quickly move toward me. Out of the blackness an image appeared. It was a man crouching as if ready to attack. As he passed me, I grabbed his hair, thrusting my knife tight against his throat. I whispered, "If you do more than breathe, you will die." I felt the thief go limp, surrendering his aggression. Pressing harder against his throat, I whispered, "How many others are with you?"

The trembling captive's voice was a soft screech, "None, master, I am alone."

I felt the muscles in my back relax. "Be still and you might yet see the dawn." I released the pressure on his throat. The man whimpered.

"Hush," I spat into his ear. Still holding my blade against his throat, I searched him with my free hand. "What's this? You have no weapon? Do I look so weak you thought you could simply overpower me?"

"No, my lord, I had no intention of robbing you," he gasped. "I simply wanted to talk with you."

"You could have talked with me at the camp."

"Too many Effrifrian spies," he stammered.

It was true. In addition to traders, whores, and dancers, the tent city also accommodated thieves, spies, and beggars.

I could tell from the timbre of the man's voice and the weakness of his frame that he was not a threat. He was either very old or very sick. Removing my blade, I said, "Walk toward the camel pen where I can see you better."

We stepped from the darkness of the grove into the starlight where the crouching attacker was revealed to be a stooped and frail old man. When he turned toward me, I gasped. The left side of his face had been seared by fire. In place of his left eye, there was a festering gash. His left ear was stunted and charred.

"I'm sorry to shock you, Your Highness. I'm sure it is a frightful sight, although I have not seen it myself." The poor creature skewed his head to the right to look at me with his remaining eye, the hunch in his back constraining his ability to look up.

"I recognize you from the camp. In fact, I've seen you each night staring at me from the edge of the fire. Are you a beggar? Is that what this is about?"

The night had grown cold. The man, dressed in the thinnest of rags, shivered. "I did not follow you for money. I followed..." His voice choked, a tear leaked from his eye. "I don't know why I followed you. I guess

I believed somehow the 'Shepherd of Hamood' could help."

The poor creature's eye rolled back in his head as he crumpled like an empty sack at my feet. I gently slapped his cheek and rubbed his withered arms, but there was no response. His cold skin was dry to the touch. Picking him up, I walked toward Swanrab. I was surprised at how little he weighed.

The disfigured old man lay unconscious for three days. Although gracious and supportive, Lady Dalope's family was quietly alarmed at the thought of having a beggar in their home. The servants, efficient and thoughtful, were likewise disturbed by the appearance of the frail creature.

His pallet lay in an unused storeroom next to the servants' quarters. Were I not the shepherd of Hamood, avenger of the twan, this poor heap of human dust would lie in a pauper's grave unremarked by all but buzzards and hyenas. Why had I brought him here? It was the same question the guard at the shuttered gate of Swanrab asked.

"But my lord, why do you want to bring that wretch into Swanrab? I fear he is not a resident, and... well...only residents may sleep within the walls of the city."

Had I not been a captain of the guard, I doubt the fearful gatekeeper would have admitted my charge and me.

On the afternoon of the third day, the one-eyed skeleton sat up with such force he startled me from my drowsy reflections. "Where am I?" he screeched, his one eye frantically searching for an exit.

I knelt beside him, taking his hand. "You are safe here."

He looked at me as though he'd never seen me before. "Where am I?" he again shouted, jerking his hand from mine.

"You're in Swanrab," I said quietly. "In the home of Lady Dalope and under my protection."

"In your protection?" His good eye squinted at me, "And who are you?"

"I am Ayuba, shepherd of Hamood. You sought me out in the date grove."

The old man lay back with a groan of recognition. It took several days of constant attention before the old beggar regained his strength and was able to speak again. Two servant girls helped me move him to the shaded courtyard. A soft breeze rattled the spines of elegantly trimmed palms. The soothing sound of water trickling from a pond helped the old fellow's spirit. Having been bathed and oiled by the servants, his brittle skin looked like worn leather. A new white robe completed his transformation.

The old man's words at first barely escaped his burned lips. Soon his voice became accustomed to its own sound and grew stronger, his thoughts tumbling into the fragrant garden air.

"My name is Rantel al Darem. I did not always look as pitiful as you see me now. I was once quite handsome and powerful. I am a metal worker from the village of Tab. In my small foundry I made everything from ornate cups and jewelry to swords and spears. By the standards of the tribe of Tablem, I was prosperous. I was blessed with a lovely, hard-working wife who treated me with respect. The only cloud in my life was that I was without sons; instead, I cherished the love and adoration of three beautiful daughters. I speak of this life as though it has long past as everything disappeared in less than an hour a little over a year ago. My family, my business, and my village were swept away by an evil wind. My tale is not unique for those who live within the long reach of the cursed Effrifrians.

"The tribe of Tablem is known for its metalworking and pottery skills. Our lands are rich in deposits of tin, as well as veins of gold and silver, turquoise, and lapis. Traders from beyond the Sea of Oxyeon bring us copper. We smelt the tin and copper together in a secret process to make the hardest of metals, which is far superior to the bronze made in Hamood or Effrifria," he said with a professional sniff. "I would guess, Honored One, the sword you so carefully held to my throat is made from Tablemite bronze." He paused, breathing deeply.

"Are you tired?" I asked. "Would you like to rest?"

"No, no. I'm not tired," he said with some urgency. "I'm trying to decide how to proceed. So far, it is but a traveler's tale I've spoken. Now I must tell of things no man has seen and lived to describe." He scratched at the socket where his left eye once lived.

"Perhaps fourteen moons ago," he continued, in a voice so reluctant it was painful to my ears, "Effrifrians raided our small village. It was not a raid on our treasure, although it too was stolen, but a raid of obliteration. Without warning the ugly, shaved-headed killers surrounded us. We knew instantly what was to come... Effrifrians are the evil of our history. From beyond time, the villages of the Tablemites endured periodic slaughter and kidnapping by these wicked neighbors. No one knew the purpose of the infestations because no one ever returned after marching down the slopes of Erite and crossing the border into Effrifria."

I helped the wretched old man take a sip of sweetened water before he resumed his tale of sadness.

"Women screaming, children running in all directions, men seeking their weapons, fire pots hurled into homes. With undulating war cries, their faces blackened with soot, came the heartless beasts. The flat of a sword slammed against my head, plunging me into insensibility. I saw a spear thrust at my wife's stomach as she tried to defend my daughters." His voice became dispassionate, resigned to the terrible pain of his loss.

"When I awakened," he continued stoically, "I was lying on my stomach, hands bound behind my back. Each time I exhaled, dirt and sand billowed into my eyes. I sensed great confusion around me. Not three paces away lay my wife. Eyes that so often praised and warmed me, great brown orbs that saw in me safety and joy, now stared at me with the coldness of stone and disappointment."

The old man closed his eye. Shaking his head as if to clear it of this painful vision, he said, "Master, since the raid on Tab I have experienced many depredations. I have lost my family, my home, and my health. But no beating or torture, no deprivation visited upon me, has wounded my soul as much as the cold accusation of failure in my beloved wife's unseeing stare."

I reached out and held the old man in my arms. His frail body shook. Shudders of pain ran through him.

"Frequently, we misread experiences during times of great emotion. Perhaps your vision of condemnation was distorted by the passion of the moment," I offered weakly. I felt inadequate that I could offer nothing more than the comfort of my arms.

Rantel al Darem lay against my chest like a child. Only the trickling of the water in the pond attended the garden's silence. Reliving this painful memory had caused the old fellow to once again escape into

unconsciousness. He dozed briefly, then without preamble, his voice, now a whisper, resumed.

"What I'm about to tell you no man beyond Effrifria
knows. When I heard of you and the blessings bestowed
on you by the great guide of Hamoodian lore, I was
determined to speak with you."

"But why me?" I asked, "I cannot regain your wife
or family. I have little to offer you but comfort and an
eager ear."

Wiping pus from his weeping eye socket the old beggar peered at me as if contemplating whether to continue. A weak smile cracked his face. "Master, I know
not why I have stumbled and starved to find you. It is
beyond my understanding why within the soul a voice
louder than the wind yet softer than a breath compels
one to seek another."

His voice strengthened. "For two days, hands bound,
leather collars around our necks, tethered to a common rope, the men of Tab were driven down the cliffs
of Erite into Effrifria. We stumbled along steep, narrow
goat trails crisscrossing the face of the great escarpment.
Upon reaching the base of the cliff, we trudged on for
another three days to the fabled mines of Effrifria."

While pausing to gather his strength and refresh
his voice with honey-flavored water, I thought about
all I knew of the Effrifrian mines. It was rumored King
Sognet's vast wealth lay in mines rich in gold and lapis.
Never seen by outsiders, stories of their incredible
wealth had grown into legend.

As if reading my thoughts, the disfigured old man
continued. "The mines lay at the base of the cliffs of Erite
where the river Ben flows down from the Bynethian plateau. The shafts of these ancient mines are in the stone
embankments formed long ago by the river. As far as

being accessible from Bynethia, the source of Sognet's wealth might as well be on the moon."

Long shadows graced the garden as the sun sloped westward. "For countless generations the Effrifrians have raided and looted the villages of Bynethia with no apparent reason or pattern. Often the raiders bypassed more prosperous villages to raid one less lucrative, their reasoning a mystery and the bane of our existence."

"But why didn't the Bynethians raise an army and defend themselves?" I asked.

"The answer is complex. Many generations ago the tribes banded together in an attempt to defeat the Effrifrians. Although superior in number, the Bynethians were soundly defeated because they failed to work together as required for success in battle. Because Effrifrians only raid infrequently and mysteriously pick a single village to devastate, the people of Bynethia have grown accustomed to this menace, much as the peoples who live on the edge of the great dune have learned to live with the random destruction of a worley."

"Your analogy is a poor one...worlies are random acts of nature. Raids by scurrilous neighbors are man-made and can be repulsed," I insisted.

His face sagged with despair. "Rationality is a poor substitute for hope. As my wife lay dying in front of our house and my daughters were ravaged by heartless men with shaved heads, the rest of Bynethia breathed a sigh of relief knowing the evil wind had passed them by."

Worn down from reliving the great sadness of his life, the storyteller again drifted into sleep. I moved his wispy frame onto his pallet inside the house and sat with him throughout the night. His sleep was turbulent, his dreams incapable of quelling the dread that was his life. He awoke at mid-morning and immediately launched into the remainder of his story, as though racing against time.

"Sognet's mines are rich in gold and despair. Upon our arrival the overseers divided us into pairs. Leather collars were replaced with bronze bands hammered shut with hot rivets. Partners were chained together through loops in the collar. The chain dragged on the ground, giving each man enough space to work but making it all but impossible to flee. We were immediately marched into the airless shaft, passing a constant stream of worn and haggard creatures carrying ore in baskets strapped to their bleeding backs.

"My partner, a tanner from Tab, whispered despairingly that we would soon look like that. His observation came true more quickly than I thought possible.

"From sunrise until after dark each day we labored in the mines. One day as a picker and the next, a carrier. Working in almost total darkness, breathing putrid air, each shift as a picker promised to be my last. At the end of each shift we marched out of the mines and were fed gruel in wooden bowls. We slept where we ate, without cover or clothes...we huddled together for warmth, soon losing all modesty." The old man's face reddened in anger.

I noticed the bowl of rice gruel that sat untouched at his elbow. I quietly removed it from his sight, replacing it with fresh fruit and cheese from my tray. The old man attacked the food with relish.

"There is no punishment in the mines, only execution. Any infraction of the rules means swift and brutal death. We could not speak among ourselves. We could not defecate or urinate while working. To fall down meant an instant sword in the throat. We were not allowed to ask our guards for anything...speaking to a guard resulted in death by whatever method the guard chose to employ.

"Once, I overheard new guards being trained. The man in charge instructed his recruits thusly...

"'These,' he said, pointing at the prisoners, 'are oxen. Do oxen talk among themselves?'

"'NO!' shouted the newcomers.

"'Do oxen talk to their masters?'

"Once again, 'NO!'

"'If an ox falls down while plowing, what do you do?'

"'Kill it!' shouted the recruits."

"With such harsh treatment and so little food or rest, it's a wonder anyone lived very long," I said, recalling how weary I became under the harsh treatment of the reed gatherers.

"Many die," he said with a distant look in his eye. "But many survive. Although I felt my life seep from my body, like a pool evaporating in the harsh desert sun, I found a way to survive."

"But how? The temptation to strike out or to simply sit down and die must have been great."

The old man placed the pith of a plum on the tray with great gentleness, as though it might break. "The tanner of whom I spoke yesterday died within a month. He did not yell or scream epithets at the guards; he simply lay down and let them kill him. I will never forget the look in his eyes as the guard raised his spear. He didn't flinch. He didn't pray or moan. When the spear pierced his heart he didn't even blink. It was as though he had already died...the spear was but a detail."

There was nothing I could say. Although in my life I had seen much cruelty and felt deep despair, nothing in my experience approached the destitution of spirit that sobbed in the memory of this gentle soul.

I helped him sit up. Leaning against a cushion, he continued, "In a way, it was the tanner's death that helped me survive. When I saw how cheaply he surrendered his life, a small spark was lit in my soul. The steam from the fire in my heart had no place to go as it grew and grew. To release the pressure I began to dream… while chipping away at the wealth of Sognet." The man was sweating now, even though the breeze coming from the window was cool.

"What kind of dreams could you possibly have in that horrible place?" I queried gently.

He squinted at me as if I was a fool. "Why, of this moment, of course."

With a nervous laugh, I said, "Surely, old man, you are not telling me you are a soothsayer. That you actually dreamed of sitting here with me at this time, in this place."

As if speaking with a child, he said, "I know not if I am a soothsayer. All I know is that when I dreamed of escape, I became frustrated and confused for I could see no way of breaking my bonds. When I dreamed of the past, of my lovely wife, my daughters, and my former life, I became so distraught the tanner's eyes beckoned. The dream that gave me stamina, that dampened the fire in my heart and relieved the pain of my existence, was of this moment."

Perhaps he has gently slipped beyond reason, I thought. It would be no discredit to him. Having suffered more than most it would not be unusual to take refuge in a fantasy that would explain to his fevered mind why he was, at last, safe.

"I see you cannot believe it. No matter. It is a far gentler insult than others I have borne," he whispered.

220

His comment pierced me deeply. "Please, Father, please tell me of your dream and how it led you here."

Softly, he began. "Because true escape seemed all but impossible, I dreamt instead of what I would do should I escape. At first I dreamed of walking across Bynethia. I created the smell of spring flowers on a gentle breeze as I hobbled my way along the edge of the brooding cedar forest of my homeland. These forests were barely visible from the mines, lining the edge of the nearby cliffs of Erite.

"Daily I added a new detail to my dream: An old woman taking pity on me and letting me rest at her gate. Finding me naked and half dead, a shepherd sheltering and feeding me. Each detail made my dream more of a reality.

"My dream consumed me. I no longer lived in the painful mines of Effrifria, breathing the breath of a thousand dying men. The balmy air of Bynethian pastures filled my lungs. I spoke with people as I begged my way toward Hamood. The pain in my shoulders from the harsh cords of the ore baskets became the warmth of the summer sun on my back as I trudged in freedom across the land."

Slowly, the old man drew me into his fantasy. Why else did we have this ability, if not to use it when life slammed the door shut, locking us in a cell with no escape? I thought of being strapped like a bundle of reeds to the angry she-beast and remembered dreaming of fleeing like the wind into the Beyond. Was this not the same?

Sensing my empathy, the old fellow reached out and patted my knee. "I know this sounds like the ranting of one who has been in the sun too long, and perhaps it is. Nevertheless, it is the truth. I no longer created

221

my dreams. Soon my dreams began to have dreams. My dreams became my reality. Eventually I came to Bynot, and it was there while begging in a teashop that I heard of a mythical wise man in Hamood. I immediately set out in search of you. The rest of the story you already know." He finished expectantly, as though it was my turn to respond.

"But wait, dear friend," I implored, "you have told me of your dream, now tell me what actually happened."

Rising slowly from his pallet and with the last shred of his strength, the old fellow hobbled to the window. Gazing at the garden, he said softly, "My dream became my reality."

"Exactly," I said doubtfully.

Turning now, his good eye boring into mine, "Exactly."

I was stunned. Father taught me that we influence our destiny by controlling what we think about. This was, however, the most powerful example I could imagine.

The old man scratched distractedly at the window-sill. He looked at the sky. "May we sit in the garden?"

Once settled on an arbor bench next to the pond, I was eager for him to continue his tale. "You have yet to tell me how you escaped," I prodded.

A half smile split his charred face. "When the time came, it proved easier than I thought possible. As I said, we were chained in pairs. My second partner was a childhood friend from Tab, a weaver who weakened quickly in the mines. One minute we were picking deep within the main shaft, working side by side, and the next he was lying on the ground. In the time it took to take a breath, a guard had slit his throat. My friend coughed and gurgled at the other end of our common chain. I felt his blood ooze between my toes but did

222

not look up from my task. Like a beast I kept my head down continuing to chip away, as though nothing had happened.

"Wiping his blade on the weaver's chest, the guard grumbled to his companion, 'It's past time for a shift change. Let's leave this one for the next crew. It will serve them right for being late.' His companion laughed in agreement as they walked away through the dimly lit shaft."

Pausing, the old man looked puzzled, as if some new vision was revealed by his words. "I continued to work even after the guards left. I had become an animal, uncaring and unresponsive to everything except that which affected me personally...my humanness lived only in my dreams." His once powerful shoulders shook as he buried his face in his hands. A choking cough shattered the garden silence.

"It was the chain binding me to the dead weaver that caught my attention. In the dim light, I saw my boyhood friend, dead eyes open, his hand clutching the chain. My first reaction was to yank the chain free lest the guards think I was being distracted from my work. I looked around frantically. I jerked on the chain, but the weaver's death grip held. I panicked. Once again I looked for the guards.

"Not only were there no guards, but no other slaves were nearby. I was alone. Like a beast numbed by routine, I stood staring at the slender vein I'd been working all day. I started to pick at it. My dream, my refuge, would not return. Suddenly the clear desert air of my dream stagnated into the foul soup of the mines. I retched. Reaching the end of human spirit I lay down next to the stiffening body. I felt the warm stickiness of his life against my face.

"Slowly, like the oozing of the weaver's blood, a thought formed in my mind. My ennui lifted slightly like a gap in a curtain that lets the dawn play against your lids. Suddenly the drape of my despair was flung back... hope glared like the sun.

"Quickly I smeared the weaver's blood against my throat and across my face. Lifting his desiccated body, I laid it across mine as booted footsteps approached. I commanded my racing heart to be still."

The man from Tab was breathing hard. Sweat beaded his brow. I reached out to ease his pain. "There is no need to go on," I said to comfort him. Although I wanted desperately to hear the rest of the story, I was afraid these dreadful memories were sapping his fragile strength.

"After all I've told you," he said with a sneer, "do you believe my memory can do any more damage to me than what has already been done?"

"Some memories are better left undisturbed," I said weakly.

"Not these," he growled with surprising strength in his voice as he resumed his frightful tale.

"When the guards discovered our bodies, slaves were fetched to carry them to the charnel pile. At the entrance to the shaft I was flung down on the ground in front of the metal worker's forge. The blacksmith lifted me by my hair. I felt the cool metal of the anvil against my throat, then the sudden strike of the hammer as he drove the rivet from my collar. I winced but did not flinch. I willed my body to remain limp. I slid from the anvil, my face slamming into the ground. I held my breath...a breath would surely disturb the dust that filled my nose.

"At the extreme of my ability to hold in my air a slave lifted me onto his shoulder. The suddenness of the motion caused me to exhale loudly. I felt a slight hesitation in the slave's grip. I fainted.

"Struggling to avoid waking, awareness came slowly...my eyes were caked with the weaver's blood. The smell of death filled my nose and the cold, stiff flesh of the dead embraced me. Alone, my heart beat among the discarded wretches of the mines of Effrifria. For two days, slipping in and out of consciousness, I lay undisturbed among the decaying bodies. On the third night, I awoke to the smell of smoke. I heard the guards as they instructed slaves with torches. The pyre was lit. The snapping of burning logs drowned out the voices. Smoke seeped into my nose like the approach of a storm; I felt the heat creep closer. The smell of burning hair and flesh sickened me. I wanted to flee but could not move, held in the embrace of the dead.

"I felt the body beneath me begin to soften. Fat crackled, feeding the flames. The flames swept upward as the human floor under me collapsed. Freed from beneath, I rolled into the maw of searing heat, swimming frantically in the flame, smoke, and bubbling flesh. Gasping for air, coughing, my hair burning, I burst from the pyre into the cold blackness of the night."

Rantel al Darem's story was so moving, I imagined I could smell the burning flesh and hear it pop and crackle like the skin of swine over the fire. Visions of my family smoldering in the Beyond assailed me.

"You look pale, Shepherd," he said.

Tears welled in my eyes. "It is the most horrible story I have ever heard."

His bony hand grasped my shoulder. "No matter, my friend, the worst is over."

"I can't imagine anything worse than that," I said, wiping my eyes on the back of my hand.

"Those still laboring in the mines have it much worse."

Neither of us touched the platter of fruit brought by a servant. The old man drank copiously from the pitcher of sweetened water.

"I'm growing tired," he said, though he plunged into the final days of his extraordinary tale.

"I did not stop when I escaped the flames. The lazy guards had already left for the comfort of their quarters. I stumbled into the desert away from the camp. I could hear the skin on my face snap in the cold air. Blindly I ran throughout the night. There was no moon. Dense, low-hanging clouds blocked out the starlight. The last thing I recall was lurching against a dead tree... one of its limbs rammed into my head, gouging out the unseeing eye from my face. The pain crushed me into darkness.

"When I woke I thought my skin was still on fire. Each time I tried to stand, I fainted. I was surprised to find I was still very near the mines. I must have run blindly in circles during my escape. Presumed dead, I knew no one would be looking for me, but the fear of accidental discovery overwhelmed me. Throughout the remainder of the day I pressed tightly against the old tree praying it would hide me from the watchful Effrifrians.

"When night fell, I traveled east in almost total darkness. Ahead I could hear the falls of Erite. With the rumbling falls guiding me I eventually came to the river. I plunged in, submerging myself in its purity. When the water touched my burns, I screamed in pain. Then I screamed in sadness. My screams turned to cries, my cries to laughter. I stood in the black night, my voice echoing off the cliffs of Erite, the last barrier between the netherworld of the cruel Effrifrians and my dream."

We sat listening to the trickling water in the pond. Hawker cries drifted over the garden like unbidden insects. The courageous man from Tab leaned against me as I helped him once again to the comfort of his pallet.

"Rest, old man," I said to him. "We can speak more tomorrow."

I felt him pull away from me so he could see my face. The eyeless socket seeped onto the scarred leather of his cheek. He looked at me with sadness more profound than death. His bony fingers dug into my arm as he whispered, "There is nothing more."

Two nights later Rantel al Darem died in my arms. I took the old man's body beyond the tent city and built a pyre from palm logs. Accompanied by a half moon dimmed by wispy clouds, I bid farewell to a man who had included me in his dreams. As the smoke of his life rose into the windless night, I vowed to fulfill his dying wish to be buried in Tab and make his dream mine.

❧

Six moons later I stood on the edge of what had been the prosperous village of Tab in the country of Bynethia.

Menacing clouds scudded across a leaden sky, their gloom echoing my feelings as I stared at the crumbled houses. Once sturdy stone dwellings, built with hope and love, moaned in sadness as the wind swept through the empty streets.

The thatched roofs of the houses and shops had been burned. The charred timbers lay askew, like fractured skeletons. Doors were ripped from their supports, curtains lovingly woven by the women of Tab flapped noisily in the breeze. Feral dogs darted from doorways, snarling at my intrusion. Bones, bleached by the sun and scattered by the dogs, littered the streets.

Closing my eyes, I pictured what it must have been like on that morning almost two cycles of the seasons ago. The village awakening, the sounds of old people hacking, women chattering as they went to the well, babies fussing, cocks blaring their greeting to a new day. How unsuspecting it must have been.

In my saddlebag was the urn with all that was left of a life in this village. I wandered the forlorn streets until I found al Darem's house. It was easily identified by the remnants of the stone forge that once fronted the cottage. The forge was smashed and all the tools of his trade stolen. The building faced what once was a handsome village square ringed with sturdy stone shops. The well, located in the center of the square, was now fouled with the corpses of the unwanted, the old, the infirm, and the unlucky.

It had taken me almost six moons to reach Tab, normally a journey of only eight days from Swanrab. After cremating the old man's withered remains, I had intended to slip quietly into Bynethia and fulfill my promise to him.

I entered Bynethia with the mistaken belief I was leaving the "Avenger of the Twan and Shepherd of Hamood" at the border. Indeed, I traveled dressed as a simple trader—my captain's scabbard and other ceremonial finery packed on a baggage camel. Setting aside the inherent sadness of my mission, I delighted in the solitude and freedom of aloneness.

The border between Hamood and Bynethia is unmistakable. The lush fields of Hamood abruptly end at the low, scabrous hills of Bynethia. Imperceptibly, the hills rise to a plateau, which after many days' ride slopes to the Sea of Oxyeon.

I made a solitary camp just a day's ride west of Hamood. The stony, barren ground reminded me of the Beyond. A large fire of dried dung and camel weed crackled joyfully, sending showers of sparks toward the distant stars. Lying on my back, reveling in the solitude of the moment, I drifted off to sleep.

As dawn breached the horizon, I threw off my robe and rubbed the sleep from my eyes. I stretched my muscles, stiff from the long ride.

Suddenly I sensed someone watching me. Jumping to my feet, sword in hand, I spun around expecting to be attacked. It took me a moment to understand that I was, indeed, surrounded…not by enemies, but supplicants.

"Who are you?" I shouted to the circle of kneeling strangers. "What do you want?"

In the distance, I could see several richly caparisoned horses idly grazing with the she-beast and my baggage camel. The elegant men kneeling around my camp remained silent.

"Who is your leader?" I demanded, frustrated by this ridiculous display.

A voice behind me said, "Prophet of Hamood, we apologize for startling you."

I spun around. One of the kneelers bowed, his forehead touching the ground.

"First of all, I'm not a prophet, and yes, you did startle me. Who are you and what's this about?"

The man slowly raised his head. His braided beard was bejeweled with tiny rubies glinting in the morning light. His wide-set black eyes were shaded by a heavy brow and broad forehead. The man on his right leaned over and whispered to him.

With a hint of doubt in his melodious voice, he spoke, "We seek the son of the ancient Hamoodian god of the stone."

"Well, I'm afraid you've made a mistake," I said with a slight bow. "I am but a shepherd on a mission of mercy for a deceased friend."

At hearing this, several of the kneeling men started to rise. "Shepherd, indeed," I heard one man grumble.

I kept my eyes focused on the leader. He stared at me with amusement and a hint of confusion on his face. When he spoke, those who had risen immediately found their knees again.

"Shepherd, you say," he mused. "Where is your flock?"

"I am from Hamrabi on the western border of Hamood. My flock is there. As I said, I came to this land to fulfill a promise to a dead friend from the village of Tab."

The mention of Tab sent a lightning bolt of fear through the supplicants. Many eyes narrowed, hands inched toward daggers. The leader rose and walked toward me. "Tab is gone. The only survivors are slaves in Effrifria. Our spies in Swanrab say you are the prophet of Hamood, but now I'm not so sure." His eyes darkened as he drew near.

A voice to my left whispered, "Perhaps he's an Effrifrian spy?"

Memories of my painful experience in Bensheer flooded my mind. Boldly stepping toward the leader I said, "Before one of us makes a mistake we will regret, perhaps you should tell me who you are?"

Now face to face, the leader's eyes searched my steady gaze. "You do not speak like a shepherd. Indeed, most shepherds would fall to their knees begging for mercy at the approach of Radiuus, king of Radule."

Bowing deeply I replied, "Your Majesty, exalted king of Radule, I bring you greetings from the king of Hamood. I am Ayuba, avenger of the twan, honorary captain of the guard, and shepherd of Hamood."

The tyrant's pupils expanded at the mention of the leader of the most powerful country in the world.

Radiuus was one of several petty chiefs—or, as they preferred to be called, "kings"—ruling the disparate tribes of Bynethia. An absolute monarch, he was unaccustomed to being addressed directly. It was only by aligning myself with his powerful neighbor that I could give him pause to reflect on his actions. The royal retinue gathered around me.

"Since when does the king of Hamood send a shepherd to my country without a seal or advanced warning?" he said, looking me up and down.

"The king has given me leave to pass freely throughout his lands. He is unaware of my visit to Bynethia, but as a captain in his guard I am authorized to act in his name. I may indeed appear a simple trader, but if you will allow me to open my pack I can offer the proof you desire."

Once the king and party examined the scabbard of the twan's guard, their deference returned. Politely but firmly, King Radiuus insisted I accompany him and his entourage.

Riding with the nobles of Radule through the scrub-covered hills, I saw many of the mines and salt beds that were the principal source of Radule's wealth. The seat of Radiuus's power was a beautiful stone village in a valley surrounded by great boulders—the most natural fortification imaginable. The king's home, which he called his palace, was a stout stone structure surrounded by verdant gardens in the center of Radule. Vines of roses and bougainvillea softened the palace walls.

Dismounting, I was ushered to an open area tiled with slabs of limestone, bordered with carefully trimmed citrus trees. Spread out on carpets was an elegant feast. Having eaten nothing all day, my stomach growled at the sight of the lavish spread.

Lady Radiil, the king's wife, and the palace chamberlain, an ancient man called Blyer, joined us. Without ceremony or discussion, we eagerly attacked the silver platters of cold meats, fruit, and honeyed cakes. Delicate young girls circulated among the diners, filling wine cups and replenishing depleted platters. Tiny songbirds and plump doves cooed and warbled in the fragrant trees.

Once we were sated, servants brought bowls of scented water and towels for each diner. With a loud belch, the king turned to me saying, "Ayuba, *shepherd* of Hamood, if your story is as good as your appetite, I expect we will be thoroughly entertained this afternoon."

It was clear I was somewhat of a mystery to the king and the assembled nobles. They had heard from their spies that I was the prophet of Hamood. Their religious fervor had caused them to prostrate themselves before me, only to have their faith dashed by someone claiming to be a simple shepherd...yet enigmatically, a shepherd who also claimed to be an honored member of the powerful house of Hamood. Opting for caution, they treated me with respect, knowing full well they could have their way with me should I be revealed as an imposter.

The sun slipped behind the trees. The courtyard lay in shade. I decided to tell my entire saga to Radiuus and his court, knowing it would be repeated throughout Bynethia, carried on the tongues of nobles, traders, and the ever-present servants.

Lanterns were hung from the trees. The sky darkened and cicadas began to call as I reached the end of my tale and my encounter with the metal worker, Rantel al Darem.

"Darem is alive?" the chamberlain Blyer asked excitedly as others whispered hopefully to each other.

"You knew him?" I asked incredulously.

"Of course," responded the frail old chamberlain. "He was the foremost metal worker in Radule. He made the very dishes on which we dined, the king's armor, the hinges on the palace door, and many other works of art in Radule. Please…is he alive?"

Blyer's innocent remarks about the man whose ashes rested in my pack affected me so intensely I could not speak. The light he shed on the half-burned cripple shone so brightly that everything al Darem told me was confirmed in that instant. Blyer's simple comment swept away the shadows lingering in my own mind as to what my role in the life of the dreamer Darem would be. The one-eyed escapee was known and respected by the king and nobles of Radule. The capital city was much closer to the path taken by Darem as he fled Effrifria than Swanrab. Bypassing the certain succor of his countrymen, his energy flagging, he had hobbled on following his dream.

I understood now what al Darem wanted to say as he died in my arms. His dream had not ended; it was now my dream. Like the fog lifting from a valley, I could see the landscape of my future with the clarity of a spring sun.

"Ayuba, are you well?" asked Lady Radiil.

"Yes, yes, I'm fine."

At that moment, my voice sounded different. It was not the voice of who I had been…but of who I would become. It was an adult voice. A purposeful voice, one that could not, would not, be stilled. A voice heard in a dream. A voice flowing from a vision spawned in a mind so pure not even the most unimaginable horror could dim its luster. It was the voice of al Darem's vision…and my destiny.

I stood now, slowly walking among the expectant diners. "Before I tell you of al Darem, I have two questions."

The king spoke impatiently, "Out with it, Ayuba, what is it you want to know?"

"Has anyone survived an Effrifrian raid on one of your villages?" I asked quietly.

The response was instant and needed no discussion. No one had ever lived to tell what happened after capture.

"As you have never spoken with a survivor, tell me what you think happens to those who are captured in these raids," I requested, looking at the king.

The king nodded to Blyer the chamberlain to speak on behalf of those assembled.

"Ayuba, you are new to our lands and unfamiliar with our customs. So before I answer your question, I must briefly speak of our history."

"Please do, Ancient One."

The advisor to the king took a sip of wine and then, in a surprisingly strong voice, began, "I was born in the time of Radiuus the First, great-grandfather of our current and most exalted sovereign," he said, bowing respectfully to the king. "I have been an advisor to the last two rulers of Radule. It is from this perspective I speak. Bynethia has changed little in all that time.

Indeed, our songs and scrolls indicate that Bynethia has, since the time of awareness, been this loose assembly of relatively weak tribes confined by the sea, the sand, and two powerful neighbors."

"Allow me," I interrupted. "I mean no disrespect to the king," I said, nodding in his direction, "but if the tribes of Bynethia are weak and the land so rich, why have your neighbors not devoured it entirely rather than simply taking an occasional bite as they did at Tab?"

"Ah, my young friend, you go directly to the very soul of our existence. The river Leb holds at bay the great swamps of our southern border. The gentle waters of the Oxyeon lap our eastern shore. We, of course, are blessed to have the powerful but reasonable Hamoodians to the west. As you can attest, they are as strong as the sea and as stable as the earth. It is indeed Bynethia's great fortune that the Hamoodians seek hegemony over none but their own."

There was a murmur of agreement from those gathered in the courtyard. Stars were beginning to peek from the sky, dimmed by a great orange moon lumbering over the horizon.

"And to the north?" I prodded.

"Ah, the north," the genteel old scholar said sadly. "The bane of our existence— Effrifria. They fear only the power of Hamood. The evil King Sognet would, as you say, swallow Bynethia whole if it were not for Hamood. The despicable ruler knows Hamood could not accept being surrounded by its archenemy. He also knows that, although strong, Effrifria could not survive a war with Hamood."

None of this was new to me. Many times while riding throughout Hamood, Dalnt and I discussed the delicate dance between these two powerful countries.

"But surely," I persisted, "if all the tribes of Bynethia worked in consort, it could secure its own borders?"

"We have tried," injected the king with a hint of irritation in his voice, "but each time we agree to join forces, suspicions harbored from centuries of bickering and conflicts tear apart the fabric of our pact. Every tribe blames the other for its failures and soon we all retreat to our own kingdoms and pray the next raid will fall on the other."

Blyer continued, "You see, Ayuba, Effrifrians are very clever. They do not raid often and never in the same place twice. We do not know why or how they select which village to destroy. The time between raids is often substantial, and as with all humans, the sadness and fear that follow in the wake of an attack dissipates with time, as does the resolve to prevent another. Those who are spared breathe a sigh of relief and tell one another their village gods are too strong for this evil wind from the north."

"Until the next time," I said quietly.

"Indeed, Shepherd, until the next time," the old man muttered tiredly.

"Now Ayuba, tell us of al Darem," the king demanded.

"In due time, my lord, but first answer my question. What do you think happens to the men and women who disappear in the clutches of your neighbor?"

The king glared at me, his patience wearing thin.

Lady Radiil, sensing the king's anger, spoke, "If I may, my lord?"

The king grumbled his ascent.

"We know not the fate of our brothers and sisters. Because the people of Bynethia are peaceful and capable, with many useful skills, we speculate they are made slaves in the households of Effrifrian nobles, and..."

She hesitated, "Perhaps the women are married off to warriors or used to raise their children...but of course it could be much worse."

"Worse how?" I asked gently.

The king spoke. "It has often been said that the men may be made to work the fields or carry supplies for the Effrifrian army and the women turned into prostitutes."

The moon now overhead cast a warm glow over the courtyard. No one spoke, each lost in his own vision of what lay beyond the edge of his knowledge.

"Your Highness, please have a servant fetch my saddle pack, and while we wait, I will tell you the story of al Darem and others of your kin and subjects who have disappeared from your lands."

The heart is a fragile thing. To protect it from the unknown, men often shield it with fantasies and hopes. A gossamer tapestry woven from their own experience; their illusions comfortably enslaving them in a life of denial. The truth when revealed is often so painful that the most carefully crafted defense is unable to withstand its power.

The hopeful myths of Radule fell in shattered tears as I told them the saga of the burned and weary dreamer who accosted me in a date grove on the edge of Swanrab. Even the cicadas were silent when I finished. Men held their heads, keening back and forth. Sobs and wailing filled the courtyard.

I took the urn containing al Darem's ashes from my pack. "This is all that remains of a man who once walked among you. We are all born to die, and it could be said that your friend died an honorable death. But the others, the fathers and wives and sisters who have died for generations and who, as we speak, are being slung onto a refuse pile on the edge of your kingdom—who will honor them?"

"Enough, Ayuba," sobbed the king. "Do not shame us further," he pleaded.

"I came to bury a friend, not to shame or sadden you. You are the creators of your distress. I am but a messenger; the carrier of the dream that freed this man whose life I honor. Tonight, as you lie thinking of the horror and brutality of the lives of those plucked from your land, ask yourself this question. When al Darem, friend and honored member of your kingdom, escaped the mines, burned, starving, half blind, begging for food just a short distance from where we sit, why did he not scratch at your door? Why did he not tug at the hem of your gown as you passed through the market and say, *It is I, your friend the metal worker, please help me.* Answer this question and you will become a part of his dream."

❧

After my encounter with the House of Radiuus I traveled throughout Bynethia visiting the six principal tribes. The response by each was similar upon hearing the story of al Darem. Each had lost tribe members to the Effrifrians and each constructed elaborate excuses to lessen the pain of their inability to deal with these infrequent but devastating tragedies. As in Radule, I challenged them to become a part of the old man's dream. The nobles sought me out and begged me to lead them against the Effrifrians. I did not commit, but I promised to meet them one moon past the summer solstice in Tab.

Night was falling as I led the she-beast and my pack animal out of Tab. I could not sleep in the sorrowful bones of a place where such horror rode on the winds. I found a once beautiful but untended orchard a short walk from the village. A small stream trickled from a spring. I hobbled the animals and let them graze among the trees.

I unpacked my finest robe emblazoned with my honorary captain's rank in gold thread. I polished my scabbard and bow. Stripping naked, I bathed in the stream. Plaiting my freshly oiled hair, I wove silver rings in each braid. Tomorrow as promised, one moon beyond the solstice, the nobles of Bynethia would behold the Avenger of the Twan.

⟡

At dawn, the Bynethian royals gathered at the eastern approach to the devastated village. I rose early and rode into Tab. The great mother camel sensed the importance of the occasion. She was adorned with her finest saddle, a silver bridle with brilliant scallions of yellow Bynethian wool hanging from her harness. My inlaid quiver hung from her right haunch and Father's beautifully tooled spear case on her left.

As the sun crept above the horizon, I rode to meet the assembled lords. At my request, the royals approached on foot leaving their mounts tended by grooms. The great dromedary and I rose from the devastated village with the sun, its rays glittering off the gold embroidery of my gown and the polished tips of my spears.

The vision of the Avenger of the Twan had a disturbing affect on the assembled nobles. They whispered among themselves as though beholding a ghost. I rode slowly toward them. These men were despots accustomed to absolute control of their dominions. They ruled with cunning and force. It would not be easy bending them to my will.

Stopping in front of the assembled kings I sat without speaking. The silence bore down on them like a great and fearsome weight. Slowly I shifted my gaze from one prince to the other, holding each one's stare until, faltering, they looked away.

"I have met with each of you," I began. "I have dined with you and heard your histories. For six moons, I have lived among you as a shepherd. Today I come as avenger of the twan, hero of the Gleb, protector of Bensheer, and official of the House of Hamood."

Although they had seen my scabbard and knew its rank, until now it had only been an abstract symbol. Now they saw the man behind the symbol and felt the overwhelming power of the House of Hamood vested in me. Eyes that were skeptical turned sincere. Arrogant smirks faded and fear sweat adorned brows. Once again I engaged the stare of each man.

"When told the story of al Darem, each of you in your sadness and shame pledged to meet me on this day. Who among you has previously visited this village of the dead? Who among you has come to Tab to pay your respects to your citizens who, on a sunny morning much like today, were slain or enslaved because of your cowardice and cupidity?"

There was only the soft moaning of the morning breeze, seeking its way through the ruins.

"Remove your headgear, lay aside your weapons, and walk with me through this hallowed place. Come not as despots, but as men. Come as fathers, sons, and brothers. Set aside your greediness and treachery. Listen not to your cunning advisors, but to the screams and cries of the people who agreed to be ruled and protected by you."

The she-beast couched at my touch. Dismounting I turned and walked into Tab. The sound of helmets and swords dropping on the ground assured me the chastened royals followed. I led them slowly through the twisted lanes. Ravens squawked and dogs snarled at our approach. The kings of Bynethia, unarmed and unadorned, walked in silence.

Presently we came to the village square with its foul well and al Darem's cottage. His urn was resting on the block where his forge once stood; where he had often made plate and plow for many of the assembled.

I had not looked at the group since entering the village. Turning now, I was encouraged to see tears of sorrow glistening on every cheek. How diminished these powerful men looked without the trappings of rank.

"You now stand in this place at the same time of day it was struck, and like these peaceful people, you are unarmed. Can you hear the children crying for their breakfast...the cocks crowing? Can you see young maidens at the well fetching water?"

It was an uncomfortable experience for these men who were normally shielded from the daily lives of their subjects.

"Close your eyes and smell the cooking fires," I whispered.

Trivaly, the chief of Oxyeon, started to moan, eyes closed, swaying gently.

"Do you hear a dog barking in the distance? Now another? Can you hear the distant sound of hooves? The first scream, maybe a child speared for sport while tending his father's goats? Now the thudding of hooves close by? These simple people whom you call your subjects...families who for generations have paid taxes to you, shared their meager profits with you...awakening on a morning like all others under your care with a false sense of security. They carried no arms, posted no guards because they felt safe as your subjects. All the dreams of these people shattered by the sound of hoof beats...blown away on an evil wind that entered your kingdom through a door you left ajar."

"Stop, stop, I implore you!" It was Radiuus, tears streaking his cheeks.

"But Your Highness," I said, innocently, "it is only a story."

"No, no, it is more," cried Exuba, king of the tribe Leedad. Sitting in the blood dust of Tab, the powerful king cried out, "It is a mirror of our shame."

I felt no sympathy for these tyrants who bled their subjects and broke the bonds of fidelity with those they swore to protect. Tears would not hold back my anger.

"Shame is what you see," I shouted. "You'll get no pity from me...this is your legacy. Look at these scattered bones. You killed these people, just as surely as the Effrifrians."

"No, no, Ayuba, you go too far," cried Trivaly.

Seething now, I countered sarcastically, "Oh, dear prince, I have only begun. I heap shame on you, your fathers before you, and theirs before them. Shame on your silent pact with evil. Shame on your willingness to sacrifice innocent people for the safety of your treasure."

My breath grew short, tears running down my cheeks. I walked toward Trivaly sitting on the ground with his head in his hands; I grabbed his brocade gown and lifted him to his feet. His eyes grew large and fearful.

The others backed away. My rage knew no bounds as I dragged the sniveling prince to the well.

"Can you smell that?" I screamed. Gagging, he tried to pull away. I pushed his head over the edge of the putrid shaft. Whispering in his ear, "This is the smell of your cowardice."

Releasing Trivaly, I turned my back on the humbled moguls trying desperately to control my anger. The rage inside me slowly abated. My legs felt weak. I dared not press the kings further. They were at the nadir of their shame. I picked up al Darem's urn sitting on the forge and held it aloft.

"The reason your friend al Darem, although on the verge of death, did not seek you out was because he knew you would turn away from him. He knew what you know now...your power is an illusion!"

The sun shone brightly on the dejected leaders of Bynethia. Some stood, heads down in self-disgust. Others sat on the dusty square, eyes fixed on the vision of brutality I had painted in their minds.

Stripping these men of their regal symbols while employing the trappings of Hamood, their ultimate protector, had humbled these men whose lives were filled with pride and arrogance. To carry out the plan fomenting in my mind for the past few weeks, I needed their unflinching support. I then proceeded to offer them the one thing they wanted more than all the treasure and comfort their positions demanded—I offered them their dignity.

"Rulers of Bynethia," I said softly, "before this moment you were blind. But now you see. Before today you lived in a fantasy of presumed power when all along you have done the bidding of Effrifria by turning your back to the pain of your subjects. Today, after breathing the foulness of your failures as men, are you ready to redeem yourselves?"

Heads snapped up. Confusion and hope struggled in the eyes of the petty chieftains. Bledla al Rand, ruler of the Bynots, spoke first.

"Bynethia takes its name from the tribe of Bynot. Until today, I fancied myself a great chieftain whose deeds would be woven into the enduring songs of our people. It is this vision of eternity that has sustained me since birth. You have ripped the shroud of deceit from my eyes. I am humbled by the scorn of your rebuke and I will do whatever you ask, spend all that I have, shed my blood, sacrifice my all, to die an honorable king, deserving of the sonnets of my people."

Al Rand was the youngest and most physically imposing of the royals. His large, handsome head, festooned with ebony curls, sat atop the powerful body of a warrior. With submission in his eyes, he knelt in front of me. Drawing my sword, I drew blood from his hand. I rubbed his blood on my finger and dipped it in the ashes of Rantel al Darem.

"Bledla al Rand, sovereign of Bynot," I said, looking into his tearful eyes, "do you pledge your life and your treasure to the defeat of the Effrifrians? Do you honor my leadership in this struggle? Swear now on the blood of your future, mingled with the ashes of your past shame."

"I swear my allegiance to the defeat of our enemies and fealty to the shepherd of Hamood."

Taking the mixture of blood and ashes, I smeared a line from the king's forehead across his left eye onto his cheek, symbolizing the loss of the old man's eye as he escaped from the putrid flames of burning flesh.

Nervous grooms rushed forward with the mounts, ready to help the lords buckle on their swords, only to be stayed by their masters. Slowly they walked their separate ways, unadorned and unarmed, radiating a strength and humility never before seen in Bynethia.

The men who walked out of Tab were different than the kings who entered. They were somber but hopeful, each in turn having taken the pledge.

(9)

CHICAGO (2004 CE)

A week following the final episode of *Ayuba,* Bryan's phone rang at three a.m.

"Bryan?" Gudabi's voice echoed over the satellite connection.

Instantly awake, Bryan said, "Dr. Gudabi, what's wrong?"

"Sorry, I don't mean to alarm you. I just want to give you time to prepare. I think you will be very busy today." There was a chuckle in the curator's voice.

How odd, thought Bryan, *I don't think I've ever seen Gudabi smile and here he is calling me at three a.m. chuckling.*

"Okay, Dr. Gudabi, I give up. What will keep me busy today?"

"I think it's best for you to turn on CNN...after all, a picture is worth many words, no?" With that the line went dead.

Finding his robe, Bryan made his way into the living room. A floor-to-ceiling glass wall looked out over the city from his thirty-sixth-floor condo. The night lights cast an eerie glow over the room. Sitting on a suede sofa, Bryan clicked the top button on the universal remote. Track-mounted antique Egyptian wooden doors quietly slid apart revealing a flat screen TV. He clicked through to CNN.

Bryan was almost asleep by the time the endless commercials, sports, and weather had run their course. After another promo touting the speed and accuracy of CNN he sat up when the announcer said, "The news media

247

are often criticized by the administration and others for focusing on the violence and strife in Iraq. Christiane Amanpour is standing by live in Baghdad with a breaking story of bravery and compassion."

"That's right, Terry," said the haggard-looking reporter. "This may be the strangest story we've ever brought you from this war-torn country. This is not only a strange story but may be a turning point."

The camera slowly pulled back, following the reporter's gaze down a street filled with children, most in school uniforms. The children were standing absolutely still—there was not a sound. The camera slowly panned from one child to the next revealing boys and girls of all ages.

The only common feature was a wide black line drawn from forehead to cheek over the left eye. Whispering now, as though her voice might shatter the trancelike state of the children, Christiane continued, "No one claims to know who's behind this non-violent display. Whether Sunni or Shia inspired, it is nationwide. We've had reports from Mosul, Falugia, and Basra of similar demonstrations. Let's go to Tom Kincaid in Basra."

"Yes, that's correct, Christiane," Tom said over a slow panning shot of several thousand children filling the main square. "These children began entering the square about an hour ago. As the sidewalks filled to capacity they spilled into the street and eventually blocked all traffic on this busy thoroughfare. It's truly remarkable. In more than forty years of reporting I've never seen anything like it."

Bryan, shaking, stabbed at the keypad on the phone. "Mom, wake up Alex and turn on CNN!"

"What's the—"

"Mom, trust me, get Alex and turn on the TV."

Bryan heard his mother drop the phone on the nightstand. Faintly in the background he could hear her calling Alex's name. After a minute Alex came on the line.

"Bryan, what's the mat—oh my god," she whispered, staring in disbelief at the screen. It was filled with close-up shots of the solemn-faced children with the mark of al Darem. "Bryan, what does it mean?"

"I don't know. It looks like—" Bryan stopped when Christiane Amanpour came back on the screen.

"I've been told by our interpreter, whose child is evidently one of these silent demonstrators, that she believes the line drawn on the children's faces is from the Scroll of Ayuba. The final episode aired last week here in Iraq. In that ancient story the line is adopted as a symbol of courage and determination." CNN split the screen between Baghdad and Basra. "This must have been coordinated by someone," Christiane said. "It's inconceivable this nationwide protest, if indeed that's what it is, was conceived and executed by children!"

She had no sooner finished expressing her disbelief when, like water on sand, the children evaporated down the warren of side streets away from the prying eye of CNN.

Bryan flipped to Al Jazeera. They were also showing a tape of the demonstrators. In the background played an audio from the last episode of Ayuba taking pledges from the kings of Bynethia.

I swear my allegiance to the defeat of our enemies and fealty to the shepherd of Hamood." Taking the mixture of blood and ashes I smeared a line from the king's forehead across his left eye onto his cheek, symbolizing the loss of the old man's eye as he escaped from the putrid flames of burning flesh.

"Are you on Al Jazeera?" Alex asked.

"Yes...they obviously have no doubt about what the children are up to."

"This is unbelievable," Bryan heard his mother say in the background. The call-waiting signal on Bryan's phone interrupted.

"Alex, I've got Farrell calling...I'm going to get dressed and go to the institute."

As he rang off he heard Alex say, "I'm coming too!"

⁂

There was a mixture of pride and confusion about the ancient scroll among members of the mosque. For the most part, the Iraqis felt a sense of identity with the story. As one member said to Amin, "Because Iraq is a creation of the western allies after the war we have no sense of history. Even though we are at the site of the world's oldest civilizations, they were well documented before Iraq was born. Ayuba, however...well, this is ours. It belongs to us—not the Turks or Assyrians or a thousand other rulers of Babylon. Ayuba is our discovery."

Many were confused by the mixed signals from imams across the world. The more radical preached that Ayuba was a story created by the CIA and others to energize and coalesce Iraqis around a secular issue, distracting them from the true faith.

There was, however, no confusion among the small group of men meeting weekly after prayers in the Chicago mosque. Amin was invited to join them. The hafiz often led the discussions as the five men sitting cross-legged on the floor shared a meal. The group consisted of two men from Pakistan, one from Saudi Arabia, and the hafiz.

At first Amin was uncomfortable as much of the conversation seemed directed at him. All the others had fought with the mujahadeen in Afghanistan and as such were honored as holy warriors. Amin suspected the older man from Pakistan was, or had been involved with, the Taliban. He frequently voiced a deep hatred toward what he deemed the licentiousness of American culture and women. The hafiz made no secret of his attendance at an al Qaeda training camp in the tribal area of Pakistan following the collapse of the Taliban.

For several weeks, Amin maintained a healthy skepticism about the vitriol accompanying the weekly dinner meeting. A voice within questioned whether or not these men, despite their devotion, were losers in life. He knew this was western thinking but nevertheless could not bring himself to totally embrace their views.

The night following the news of the children's demonstration in Iraq, the hafiz assembled the group in the tiny office under the stairs.

"It is good that we have an honored guest tonight. It is especially appropriate in light of the travesty taking place in Iraq. Many of you doubted me when I warned that Ayuba was a creation of George Bush and the CIA to lure the faithful from the true path," he said, pointedly staring at Amin. "Yesterday Iraqi children disobeyed their teachers, their spiritual leaders, and their parents. Tomorrow they will be singing the U.S. national anthem!" The hafiz was almost shouting, a thin film of saliva gathered at the corners of his mouth.

Abdullah, the visitor, nodded piously in support. He looked as though he had endured many hardships. His skin was tight against his sunken cheeks and tiny blue and red veins like lines on a map seeped down his large nose, spreading over the delta of his cheeks. His eyes, recessed in dark sockets, looked frightened. His hands were gnarled and deeply cracked and he was missing two fingers on his right hand. He wore the flat pakol hat favored by many mujahadeen, with a worn chapan coat covering baggy pants.

Amin sensed the respect the others held for the visitor. Even the hafiz's normally arrogant eyes softened when he looked at Abdullah. Without preamble the weathered man began to speak in a soft, almost painful, rasp.

"When the infidels had us trapped on Tora Bora…"

Everyone in the room sat up at the mention of this defining moment during the recent Afghan war. Bin Laden's escape from certain death by the Americans was the stuff of legend. Like the Long March by the communists in China, extremists throughout the Muslim world idolized those who lived through Tora Bora.

"…We were committed to fight to the death. We developed the cave network on the mountain to hide from the Russians and their airplanes, but the Americans brought new weapons…bombs that could find their way into the caves, seeking out those who hid within."

Mustapha, a Pakistani, asked, "How many fighters did you have?"

"Maybe two hundred fifty to three hundred…Saudis, Yemenis, Chechens, Pakistanis, Egyptians. We were all al Qaeda…all committed to Allah. We rolled grenades and boulders down the slope at the Afghan traitors on the American payroll.

"The night before, what we believed would be our last day, we prayed for the destruction of our enemies. There was no fear; we were prepared to be martyrs. I was with Bin Laden and thirty others when one of our most valiant fighters, Ismail al Rahim, scrambled into our hiding place."

Amin gasped.

"Yes," the man said, looking into Amin's eyes, "your father was with us on the mountain."

Amin didn't know what to say. He knew his father died in Afghanistan but was unaware he was al Qaeda. Mustapha handed Amin a cup of tea. It was cold in the drafty office. Amin held the tea in his cupped hands shivering—from the cold or this sudden news about his father he could not tell.

"Your father," continued the old warrior, "begged Sheik bin Laden to take his small band, the leadership of the movement, and flee toward Pakistan. Many valleys run from Tora Bora into the tribal area. It would be impossible, your father argued, for our enemies to cover them all. At first bin Laden refused, welcoming martyrdom. He would stand and fight alongside his soldiers. For hours your father persisted and one by one he convinced Alzaharri and the others they were needed to keep al Qaeda alive. Just before azhan, bin Laden agreed. He embraced your father. Kneeling, we all prayed."

The room was silent. No one looked at Abdullah, embarrassed to gaze upon a legend.

"My father...can you tell me what happened?"

"He died on Tora Bora along with the other martyrs," Abdullah replied without emotion. "They fought with all they had...bullets, rockets, stones. But in the end American airpower was too fierce. They held out long enough for the rest of us to escape. May they be blessed in the presence of the Prophet (peace be upon him)."

(10)

I left Tab shortly after meeting with the kings, camping for a month on the edge of the cedar forest grac-
ing the northern border of Bynethia. Although it was
high summer, the nights in the forest of Erite were cool
and refreshing. I located my camp in a small meadow
surrounded by the giant trees. The fragrance of burning cedar logs filled the air. Two plump grouse roasted
over the fire. Tomorrow the advanced delegations from
throughout Bynethia would arrive and, with them, the
end of solitude.

The whispering of the breeze through the boughs
accompanied the deep but distant roar of the falls of
Erite. I first learned of the falls when al Darem told me
their sound guided him to the river Ben as he stumbled
away from his imprisonment. Just half a moon cycle
ago, on my journey to Tab to meet the assembled rulers,
I first visited the cliffs of Erite and the falls to look down
on the mines of Effrifria. As I waited for the grouse to
cook I thought about the idea my first visit had spawned.

Never before had I seen such a powerful force as
the Ben plunging over the towering precipice of Erite.
Steep cliffs cut by the raging torrent framed this violent
spectacle. Through the mist, I could see the dreadful
mines far below hard on the banks of the distant shore.
Gazing upon this scene of tragic beauty, a brief glimpse
of the Hammer of Hamleed crossed my mind. I pushed
it away as one would a gnat, but like a gnat, the picture of the great bridge came again. A picture of Tab

255

followed but quickly dissolved into a vision of the massive stonework I had seen at a temple in Leedad.

Where do ideas come from? What force lies within us gathering bits and pieces of our experiences, our dreams, our past like a cook making soup, adding disparate ingredients to the pot? Marun was right... the harvesting of knowledge is man's most important role.

I was disheartened by the weakness of the tribes. Even if I could get them to agree to fight as one, their power would be as a candle compared to the sun of their enemy. I had called the meeting at Tab, now just a few days away, without a clear idea of its outcome. If I succeeded in gaining their allegiance...where would I lead them? To death...or victory?

Resting on the edge of the canyon the image of the Hammer once again flashed through my mind. Closing my eyes I pushed away my tiredness and doubt, giving free rein to the pestering dream. The vision of the Hammer, the temple at Leedad, and the wasted village of Tab flowed uninterrupted across the lids of my shuttered eyes.

Slowly, these disparate images coalesced into an image so clear and so simple it caused me to laugh out loud. Opening my eyes, I saw before me a vast lake filling the canyon. A giant dam held the water back, the river spilling over the top down the falls to Effrifria.

Agitated with joy, I ran back and forth along the rim, calculating how, and if, such a dam could be constructed. If released, the lake would flood the mines of Effrifria forever. Sognet's power came from the mines. Its wealth was used to pay his troops and buy off his enemies. Without the mines he would still be a vile monster, but one whose claws were dulled and bite defanged.

Threatening destruction of the jewel of his empire should stay his evil hand.

That night I slept peacefully beneath the forest canopy, confident that if I could win the fealty of the nobles, the Effrifrians would be defeated.

∾‿✕‿◌

I knew from al Darem that Sognet inspected the mines annually on the vernal equinox. It was important that the project be finished by that date—less than a year away.

Without revealing my plans, the kings of Bynethia were confused when I commanded them to send not warriors but craftsmen. This advance group represented the best carpenters, stonemasons, metal workers, weavers, and farmers from all the tribes.

These capable men, without artifice, immediately embraced my plan. I was relieved as they discussed the practical needs of the project, never questioning its possibility.

After several days of climbing over the cliffs and surveying the terrain, a meeting was called. Seated around a roaring fire under a sky raging with stars, the steady men of Bynethia told me of their findings.

A once giant of a man (although now diminished by age) named Polter spoke, "Ayuba, as you rightly surmised, it is possible to dam the Ben at the falls of Erite." My heart skipped a beat. "But," he continued, "it will not be easy and will require much manpower if we are to meet the date you have set." The somber builders of Bynethia nodded in agreement.

"It is good news you bring, Master Builder," I said, smiling. "I have sworn blood pledges from each of your sovereigns to supply all you need. But please," I begged, "tell me how you will build the dam."

Late into the night, these remarkable craftsmen explained how the dam would be constructed.

The following day, the representatives of the tribes sat before me to receive their instructions. The men of Leedad and Radule were instructed to return within the next moon's cycle, each with three hundred stonemasons and miners. These tribes excelled in the art of creating stone structures, as evidenced by the great temple at Leedad and the mines of Radule.

The ship builders of Oxyeon were called upon for two hundred woodworkers with chisels, saws, and augurs, plus one hundred metal workers with bellows and forges.

From Bynot, the call would be for 150 axe-men with their great double-sided bronze axes, and thirty ox teams with harnesses and fodder.

From the heart of Bynethia, the kingdom of Drulem was bidden to provide eighty weavers and cordage makers, along with a substantial amount of Bynethian wool.

Finally Bladoole, the breadbasket of Bynethia, would supply food, cooks, and kitchens to feed the workers.

As each delegation received their instructions, they knelt before me and pledged their lives to the project we named Al Darem's Dam. Once again I mixed the blood of each supplicant with the old man's ashes. On each man's chest I smeared a circle symbolizing the newfound unity of Bynethia. Determination and steadfastness radiated from the eyes of these estimable men, swearing fealty to the shepherd of Hamood and the dream of the metal worker from Tab.

During the intervening moon cycle, I rode to Swanrab to meet the twan's widow. Sitting in the garden where al Darem died in my arms, I told her of all that had happened since my departure and asked her to relay everything to the king, Barnlo, and Twan Dalnt in the strictest of confidence. In addition, I gave her a secret message for Dalnt. Hamood would play a small but vital role in subduing Effrifria.

Returning to the dam site just as the tree fellers of Bynot arrived, I was delighted at the determination and enthusiasm of these powerful axe wielders. Stout fellows smelling of pitch, hands calloused, their muscular arms stained with sap and scars, they had spent their lives among the great cedars. They wore the traditional woodman's vest of coarse wool, breechclouts, and sturdy rawhide sandals. Their ox teams sported intricately carved yokes and rugged harnesses.

Soon great clouds of dust rose to the south as the men and baggage trains from the rest of Bynethia appeared on the horizon.

Workers were divided into messes of ten men, each mess consisting of a mixture of men from each tribe. Even if the kings of Bynethia could not work together, I was determined to see to it the people of this country got to know and trust each other. There was much grumbling among the workers at this prospect, but it was only the first of many hardships they would endure.

I will not detail the endless days and nights of drudgery and danger the stalwart men of Bynethia endured building al Darem's Dam. Although there were daily injuries and frequent deaths, the workers' commitment to the project was undaunted. Their valorous behavior renewed my faith in the purity of the common man. They soon adjusted to living among strangers from other tribes and competitions arose between messes.

Resting around the evening fire, they competed to see who had the best singers, storytellers, and dancers.

It was during one of these evenings that a robust old cook from Bladoole spoke. His face pocked with scars from the sparks of cooking fires and smelling of garlic, he asked, "Ayuba, you have spoken, much to our delight, about many things. We have learned of courage and dreams. You have convinced us that only the present exists and the importance of the journey we share…" He paused, licking his substantial lips. "Of all we've learned from you, what shall we hold most dear?"

Stalling for time I asked, "Are you asking what joins these homilies together? What word, what saying, encompasses all we've discussed?"

The cook and others nodded in agreement. It was the faces of these men with their openness and good cheer despite the daily danger and separation from all they held dear that gave me the answer to this simple yet profound question.

"We cannot control many things in our lives," I began hesitantly, my tongue just a heartbeat behind the developing answer in my mind. "We do, however, have mastery over one thing; indeed, it is the one-stringed lute of our life's song and has mastery over all we have discussed. It determines if we embrace our dreams and value our present moments. All men have this powerful force—kings and cobblers alike. You men of Bynethia, by the cheerful expenditure of your energy on this great task have shown your mastery of it. This one stringed instrument upon which the success or failure of your life is played is called…attitude."

A moody orb like a bronze pendant hung low in the sky, casting long tree shadows over the camp. I could tell by the looks on the expectant faces that my answer was unsatisfactory. A voice from the edge of the fire's light called out, "Is that all there is? What about faith and the gods? Aren't they more important?" Many heads nodded in agreement.

Master Builder Polter asked, "Surely, Ayuba, it's more complicated than that?"

I laughed. "Dear friends, why do you seek complication and confusion where there is none? In your villages, indeed among your friends and family, are there not those who are devout and others who are less so? Perhaps there are even non-believers among you. Could it not be said that those who closely follow the tenets of faith have one attitude, while non-believers simply have another? When a non-believer becomes a believer, do we not say he has changed his attitude?"

In all my conversations with the craftsmen of Bynethia, I was careful not to talk about religion, not wanting to confuse my role as the shepherd of Hamood, storyteller and warrior, with the religion of those who came to hear me. Already there were those who whispered I was a prophet of their gods.

The Bladoolian cook, somewhat confused, said, "But aren't our attitudes controlled by the gods?"

"Men of Bynethia, we sit on the edge of a great forest. Our shared toil has made us brothers, regardless of origin. I am not among you to dispute or confirm your beliefs or your faith. When we came together, many of you had never met people outside your own tribe or clan. Yet in a few short moons you have set aside centuries of prejudice, fear, and suspicion. I suggest this miracle was performed by each of you in your hearts, regardless of what god you worship. Did our shared hardship soften the differences between your gods as it has between us?

"Whether it was a god who played upon your lute or it was you, the end result is the same. What do you think determines your attitude? I ask you, who controls your thoughts? Are you responsible for what you think or are your gods? It is an unanswerable question. If you believe gods control your every action, then pray not for wealth and safety, but for a clear vision. It is the vision within that controls your attitude and your attitude controls your destiny."

❧⚷☙

The forest floor, carpeted with flowers and sweet clover, heralded the arrival of summer. All through the fall, winter, and spring, the men toiled from sunrise to sunset. It was clear the dam would be completed on time.

It had taken almost six moons to complete the reshaping of the gap through which the river passed. Now, instead of a jagged gouge, the river flowed through rectangular stone abutments four cubits thick and thirty cubits high. A large log that would eventually be used to hoist the barrier logs spanned the opening and rested on the very tops of the newly made side walls. At the base of each wall, secure in the retaining cleft and protruding above the river, was a log weighted by stones. These temporary support beams were designed to hold the dam wall above the raging torrent. We could not lessen the flow of the river during construction without alarming the Effrifrians.

Each support log was attached to a stout rope as thick as a man's arm. At great peril, workers strung the heavy wet ropes through the raging water and down the face of the cliff. Perched on a small, slippery outcropping just beneath and to the side of the opening, the weavers of Drulem wove the two support ropes into a massive cable. The cable was then wound around a large boulder sitting on the slippery ledge.

Once the dam wall was complete and resting above the river on its support logs, the boulder would be levered off the cliff, and hopefully its great weight would dislodge the supports, allowing the dam wall to slide down the stone channels and block the river.

Two valiant weavers were lost during this difficult phase of construction, swept to their deaths by the unrelenting Ben. With each death, with each crushed leg or broken arm, my resolve weakened—doubt was my constant companion. Would these lives simply be added to the list of those who had already died at the hands of the hated Effrifrians? Would the dam be Ayuba's folly, resting above the river, a monument to foolish pride? Would the blood, sweat, and labor of these courageous men of Bynethia be for naught?

Two days before the equinox, Twan Dalnt, the kings of Bynethia, and a large contingent of Hamoodian guards arrived at the camp. All work on the dam was halted as the men shouted and danced in celebration.

Dalnt leapt from his mount to embrace me. I could not hold back my tears. The noisy crowd cheered as we hugged, slapping each other on the back. The men of Bynethia knew why the twan and kings had come. It was part of the plan they had relished in their dreams.

A bullock and several sheep were slain and spitted. Music came from many lutes and drums as the dam builders celebrated the successful arrival of the final important piece of the plan. Anticipation throbbed throughout the camp. Each mess adopted a Hamoodian soldier, sharing their meager wealth and abundant joy.

The kings, properly honored, were awed at the harmony and brotherhood between their subjects.

As the final glow of the sun seeped away in the west and a cool evening breeze sang through the great cedars, a huge fire was built. Sated with hope and food, the camp grew silent as I rose to speak.

"Twan Dalnt and kings of Bynethia, in the spirit of Rantel al Darem, the builders of the dam welcome you!" A thousand voices cheered wildly at the mention of the man who had inspired our venture.

"Honored guests, you have arrived at a most propitious time, for tomorrow we lay the capstone of our efforts. Kings of Bynethia," I continued, "your subjects have honored you with their valor and struggle. More importantly, they have demonstrated that the tribes of Bynethia can work together, finding harmony and joy in shared effort."

Men in various messes slapped each other on the back in confirmation of their friendship. The kings looked nervous at this display of harmony. Slowly they became aware that here in the forests of Erite a change beyond their control had taken place. A change they would have to adapt to if they expected to retain their power.

"Twan Dalnt," I said, taking him by the arm, "as the supreme military leader of Hamood and trusted friend of the people of Bynethia, we welcome you and your escort." The men hooted and cheered their greetings. The soldiers adopted by the messes were pummeled with joy by the calloused hands of their new compatriots.

Dalnt raised his hands to calm the crowd. His black braided hair shimmered in the firelight. "Valiant men of Bynethia," he started, "I must admit when I first heard of your plan I was skeptical."

The men laughed. A giant tree feller from Bynot shouted out, "You were not alone!"

"Nevertheless, when the shepherd of Hamood makes a request it cannot be ignored, even by the king of Hamood," he said, bowing toward me with a broad smile on his rugged face.

With this, the throng rose to their feet and began to shout, "Ayuba, Ayuba!"

Dalnt continued, "Hamood's role in your great venture was really quite simple. We were asked to gather up a couple of rodents and deliver them here under this moon."

Raucous laughter rose from the crowd anticipating what was coming. Dalnt gestured to guards waiting at the fringe of the camp.

The crowd parted as an armed escort marched through, leading two shackled but defiant Effrifrian warriors. The men jeered and hooted at the captives. The muscular warriors snarled, rattling their chains and beating their chests defiantly.

Dalnt quieted the crowd by raising his hands. Turning to me he said, "Ayuba, shepherd of Hamood, at your request we are delivering these two savages. Guard them closely for they are more than simple soldiers."

The guards forced the captives to kneel. "This one," said Dalnt, pointing to the larger of the two, "is a captain of the elite Border Corps. He is called Seg Begnet and is, I believe, cousin to King Sognet."

The arrogant prisoner, his muscles shining with sweat, tipped back his head and shouted, "Hail Sognet Kin—" His speech was abruptly interrupted by one of his guards, who yanked the chain around his neck. The men jeered and laughed at the captive's distress.

"And this fine fellow," Dalnt continued, "is called Digulnd who, we have recently learned, was formerly in charge of security at the mines of Erite."

A violent roar rose from the crowd. For a moment I thought they might dispatch these hated enemies before we could put them to their planned use. Digulnd refrained from any response.

"It may interest you to know," resumed Dalnt once the shouting and anger subsided, "these men were captured just east of Hamrabi by Aroon al Sumer, protector of the western border of Hamood and father of Ayuba.

"Your father and I laid a trap near the village upon learning that Sognet demanded revenge for the warriors we killed at the Gleb almost four cycles of the seasons ago. Along with your brothers, Frion and Pitoon, and a squad of guards, we intercepted this vengeful band, slaying all but these two."

With a broad smile, Dalnt concluded, "So it is, Shepherd, that I bring you greetings from your family who prosper in all ways, except in their yearning for your presence and..." he said, pointing to the captives, "their gift of these two conquered but untamed devils."

∽⊘⌣

At dawn, the captives were led to the dam site. Their continued insolence was tempered by what they saw.

After the stone walls with their u-shaped channels were complete, Polter had a stout wooden bridge built across the river adjacent to the new stonework, the floor of the bridge barely clearing the river.

During construction of the stone bearing walls, teams of loggers had identified trees that met Polter's specifications. Each tree measured three cubits in diameter over a span of twenty-five cubits. Trees were felled and hauled to the staging area on the edge of the gorge just above the bridge. To achieve the constancy of breadth, teams of adz men, shipwrights from Oxyeon, carefully smoothed the opposing edges of the great logs until perfectly flat. The end of each log was squared to the exact dimensions of the channels in the stone abutments.

Today was the laying of the final span. There were now ten of the huge logs resting on the frail supports just above the surface of the river. Each log fit snugly against the smooth surface of the next. The two logs closest to the surface and soon to rest on the river's floor were notched on the upstream side and braced on the downstream side.

I took the Effrifrians to the edge of the cliffs explaining that to breach the dam, all we needed to do was knock away the brace, and the bottom logs, weakened by the notch, would fail and release the massive lake—flooding the treasure of Effrifria.

Digulnd stared for a long time over the edge toward the mines as though imagining what would happen should we breach the dam. Turning to me he sneered, "You are but a camel herder. How can you be certain this contraption you have spent so much energy building will work?"

Insolent as it was, it was a question I had to address if I expected these thugs to play their role. Digulnd's dark eyes, radiating the corruption of Sognet, stared at me demanding an answer.

Dalnt, his face crimson with anger, spoke before I could answer. "Do you know who you're talking to? This man is the hero of the Gleb. Do you remember why you were sent to raid Hamrabi? It is because of this man who tracked down your thieving brothers and slew them at the oasis."

I saw the pupils in Digulnd's eyes dilate upon recognition of my role at the Gleb.

His anger unabated, Dalnt continued, "Unlike you who fought like women, Ayuba stood firm, slaying the last of your compatriots as he tried to run like a scared sheep to escape the carnage of the Gleb."

Startled but uncowed, the captives exchanged a flicker of doubt.

"Your question deserves an answer," I said, looking directly at Digulnd. I drew a deep breath. "We actually don't know if this *contraption* will work…"

I let this unexpected response hang in the air. Dalnt looked at me out of the corner of his eye, confused that I had not justified the certainty of our plan. Seg started to sneer, but I cut him off by finishing the sentence, "… But neither do you. It is for Sognet to decide if he will risk the wealth of the mines to discover if the threat is real. Look closely, for it will be up to you to convey to the king all that you have seen here."

I walked the arrogant captives along the edge of the valley, away from the dam where we came to a post with a piece of cloth tied around it.

"This," I said, "is the farthest point of the lake created by the dam. Look behind you to where the dam will rest and see how vast the lake will be." The captives looked as directed, cautiously glancing at each other.

❧

The final log slid down the muddy raceway onto the bridge. As with the previous logs now resting in place, tough camel hair ropes were attached and then strung over the hoisting log. The heavy cables were strung up the steep banks and attached to a dozen oxen on each side of the gorge. Bellowing, the powerful beasts hoisted the great weight to the top of the cleft in the stone.

The entire camp gathered on the banks to watch the capping of the dam. Cheering wildly, the guide boys atop the side walls danced and waved their arms. The kings of Bynethia, sitting on their brightly adorned mounts, joined in the merriment. Rams horns blew and cymbals jangled. Here was proof that Bynethians could join together, setting aside individual faiths and peculiarities, to achieve a common goal. Bynots hugged Radulees. Alidades danced with the boat builders of Oxyeon. The weavers of Drulem would always be weavers and the farmers of Bladoole farmers, but now they were also brothers.

The Effrifrians glanced at each other with doubt in their eyes. Raised from birth on the bitter milk of violence and hate, they had never seen the will of free men expressed with joy and harmony. I hoped the power of unity would seep beyond the walls of their hate and soften their stony hearts. More importantly, I wanted them to plant a seed of doubt in Sognet's mind, staying his violent hand long enough to consider the consequences of his actions.

While the dam was braced, I met with Dalnt to bid him farewell. "Dear friend," he pleaded, "let us stay and support you. Bynethia has no warriors comparable to my guard. Let us escort you."

Embracing this man who, more than any other, had tutored and supported me, I said, "Brother, there is no more valiant or honorable companion I would wish at my side, but the task ahead is for Bynethia, not Hamood. If we are successful, it will build a fire in the heart of Bynethia that will burn forever. Nothing must be permitted to lessen its light. When the story of al Darem is sung throughout eternity it must be sung by Bynethians, about Bynethians. Should we fail and fall under Sognet's wrath, we shall fall as Bynethians. Go now, my friend, your task is done."

The royals were charged with the rebuilding of Tab. Once the masons finished the dam walls, I dispatched them to Tab where for a month they worked to reconstruct the shattered village. Each king sent maidens from their domain to prepare lodgings for the soon to be free prisoners. The soft touch and gentle kindness of these young women would do more to revive the damaged souls and bodies of the tortured men than any unguent.

When the royals objected to the expense of rebuilding Tab before we were certain of a positive response from Sognet, I berated them saying, "There are no half dreams. Without the village in our dreams, the dam will fail. Your dreams are your future…they must be endless. See through the eye in your heart an unbroken path, for if the path ends so must Bynethia."

The nobles renewed their vows to me and al Darem in front of the combined camp. They pledged to maintain the harmony they witnessed between their subjects. They left with much fanfare, each tribe dancing and singing honors to their lords as they rode away.

I led the two Effrifrians to the edge of the gorge overlooking the dam as the sun set. It was time for the final act of this great play we had staged for so many moons. I wanted to confront Sognet just as he discovered the river had stopped flowing. Plugging the Ben at night would allow me time to descend the cliffs of Erite and arrive at the mines at daybreak.

A single torch lit the great rock lashed all about with the stout cables woven by the men from Drulem. Like ghosts, men with sturdy levers gathered in the mists around the boulder. Barefooted, stripped to their breechclouts, they struggled to find purchase for their poles. The torch flickered in a confusion of colors, reflecting through the mist.

Our efforts came down to this single moment—a few brave men on a slippery outcropping, trying to lever a boulder as large as a house from a perch on which it had rested since time began. Each man had volunteered for this, the most arduous and dangerous task conceived by Polter.

The captives sneered and laughed as the sound of breaking poles rose from the ledge. Stouter levers were passed down. Shouts of "HEAVE!" drifted up to where we stood. Prayers to the many gods of Bynethia tumbled from the lips of the expectant builders lining the banks of the gorge.

"HEAVE!" Crack went the poles. More poles were passed down. All was quiet. They shifted from one side of the ledge to the other. Polter, his gown soaked from the spray, directed the placement of the levers. Short, pointed posts were passed down to the men on the ledge.

"HEAVE!" went the cry. I saw the great rock tip slightly. The pointed posts were wedged into the gap created by the pole men's efforts.

"HEAVE!" Again the rock tipped slightly and the pointed posts wedged deeper. The men rested, gasping for air, their bodies exhausted.

"HEAVE!" went the cry. The great rock stirred toward the abyss. Quickly the men shoved their levers deeper and with the last of their strength shouted, "HEAVE!"

The boulder shuddered. Its great weight, now unstoppable, plunged into the void.

A thousand hearts stood silent. Not a breath was exhaled. Would the boulder simply snap the ropes that bound it and hurtle into the pond at the base of the falls? Or would the log supports weighted by the huge dam refuse to budge and the boulder hang dejectedly in the cold, untamed waters of the Ben?

Within a dozen heartbeats, there was the sharp sound of splintering wood as the supports snapped. The great log wall slid down its stone guides with a resounding thud. Water splashed high into the air. The river swirled and lunged at the barrier, confused and frustrated by its confinement. Men cheered all along the canyon rim. The pole men were lifted from the ledge, tears of joy and exhaustion streaming down their cheeks.

I could not tarry to celebrate. I needed to reach the mines by daybreak. With only a small guard, I led the captives across the bridge, now rapidly disappearing under the rising waters.

A short way upstream, a goat path wound its way down a steep cliff to Effrifria. Barely passable in daylight, it was a harrowing experience by torchlight. Following the trail of a long dead goat, we groped and stumbled through most of the moonless night. I had sent the she-beast ahead while it was still light and now wondered if she had survived the perilous descent.

In the deepest part of the night, we stepped onto Effrifrian soil. We were greeted by the small group of nervous Bynethians who had brought the she-beast.

They'd been in hiding since their arrival the previous afternoon. The men were delighted to hear the dam worked as planned, restraining their joy lest any Effrifrians were near.

We rested until just before first light. The advance party would return using the steep goat trail, destroying it as they climbed to render it unusable.

Dressing in my red leather tunic with my polished scabbard and sword cinched at the waist, I threw my black robe over my shoulders. My faithful she-beast had weathered the perilous descent unscathed. Freshly brushed, she was festooned in her finest gear...yellow tassels, polished saddle, and quivers of spears and arrows. She was a formidable sight.

The advance party had also brought a pure white goat. In all the known lands a white goat preceding an enemy indicated the approaching party came to parley. Although I did not expect Sognet to honor this ancient symbol of war, I hoped it would at least give him pause to hear my story.

The shackles were removed from the captives' legs and the leather collars around their necks were attached to a lead chain. Their hands were cuffed in front of them. Bidding farewell to the Bynethians, I led the prisoners toward the river.

As the sun breached the horizon, we reached the Ben. I wanted to laugh when the empty river bottom came into view. Water remained in only scattered pools along the river's course. The rising sun glittered off the wet, sandy bottom. Countless fish floundered in desperation. Cranes and other birds were feasting on the unexpected repast.

Leading my small party onto the damp but firm sand, I headed away from Bynethia and into Effrifria.

When we turned a bend in the river, the mines came into view. My stomach churned and my heart raced. I closed my eyes, driving the doubt from my mind. I cast a picture on my lids of the prisoners fleeing the mines. For the thousandth time, I saw victory...Sognet bowing to my command.

The sound of charging horses jarred my eyes open. Six Effrifrian warriors were bearing down on us. Their horses tossed their heads, snorting, eyes flaring wide and violent...water and sand leaping from pounding hooves. Halting the prisoners and the she-beast, I quickly notched an arrow into my bow. The sun rising behind us cast the attackers in sharp relief as they reined in their mounts just beyond arrow range.

Panting and shaking their heads, the horses were confused by the sudden halt of their charge. Two of the horsemen had strung their bows. The others unsheathed their swords. I aimed my stare at the lead rider. The sun, like a great orange eye, was now halfway above the horizon and directly over the silent falls. The lead horseman broke the silence.

"If you expect to live beyond the rising sun, you better have a good reason for being here," he growled. I jerked lightly on the prisoners' chain, indicating they should respond.

"Frent, you fool," Seg responded harshly, "put away your sword and take us to the king before this camel shepherd chokes me to death."

"It's Seg and Digulnd," one of the warriors whispered to the man named Frent.

"I thought you were dead," grumbled Frent sarcastically. "Doesn't look to me like you're in much of a position to give orders. What's happened to our river?" he demanded.

"The same thing that's going to happen to you, you son of a sheep, if you don't quit posturing and immediately take us to Sognet!" Seg shouted.

The horsemen whispered heatedly to each other.

"Very well," grumbled Frent, "the white goat will protect you...for now."

Three of the warriors rode past us to guard the rear as we followed Frent and the others toward the mines.

King Sognet and a large retinue stood on the banks of the Ben. Smaller in stature than I envisioned, the king, his head unshaven, hair braided in multiple strands with coral shells dangling at the end of each glistening braid, glared first at Frent, then at Seg. Finally his gaze focused on me.

His muscular arms were adorned with massive gold bands. He wore a silver vest inlaid with lapis. His stout legs were bare except for soft leather boots hugging his ample calves. A young woman wearing a breechclout and silver sandals stood behind the king holding a sunshade to shield her master. Burly guards, their shaven heads shining above their furrowed brows and hateful eyes, flanked him.

Frent and the other warriors dismounted and knelt. Seg and Digulnd strained at their tether, prostrating themselves in the wet sand. The king listened intently to Frent. From my perch on the she-beast I could see, beyond the entourage, the slaves plodding in and out of the mines.

"Release my men!" the king commanded, in a high-pitched, slightly feminine voice that belied his sturdy frame. He stared at me, expecting instant obedience.

"In due time," I responded, casually.

His sycophants, angered by my lack of respect, drew their weapons, expecting the king to order my death. With the slightest motion of his hand, he quieted them.

275

"That white goat will only protect you for as long as my patience will allow," he sneered. "Release those sniveling cowards who have failed me so I can deal with them before I deal with you."

Digulnd and Seg buried their faces deeper in the sand.

I let the silence between us build, staring beyond the shore at the mines. I could see the oily smoke from the smoldering cadavers on the charnel ground. The sweet, sickly smell of burning flesh tainted the air. Presently I let my gaze fall on the king. Unaccustomed to anything but instant gratification, I sensed his anger.

"I will release them and restore your river when you have released my men."

The king's guards stamped their spear butts on the ground, shouting, "Kill! Kill!" It was a tribute to Sognet's power that, with a gesture so slight that it was almost imperceptible, he was able to rein in these men who had been raised from birth to kill at the slightest provocation.

Without taking his eyes from mine, Sognet soothed their disappointment. "Time enough for killing, you hungry dogs. After all, the sun is barely up. Perhaps we'll have these traitors and this shepherd on that scruffy camel for breakfast." The king's guards laughed, stamping their spears. "But for now, let's find out why Seg and Digulnd have brought this ugly camel to our camp."

Seg started to speak...I pulled his collar tight.

"You will hear from my captives when I give them permission to speak," I said softly but firmly, my gaze locking onto Sognet's scornful stare. "As for my mount," I paused, reaching forward to pat the she-beast on the neck, "she possesses all the qualities you lack." My stare bore into the heart of Sognet's anger. "She is honorable, kind, brave, and steadfast." Sognet started to speak, but I cut him off. "And she can stand in the sun all day without a woman to protect her."

A massive guard standing next to Sognet, his dark face festooned with tattoos, his head completely shaved, could not stand the abuse I was heaping on his master any longer. With a great bellowing scream he broke from the ranks. Raising his spear, he charged down the bank, aiming his deadly weapon at me. I let him come two leaps closer and then raised my bow.

Sighting down the arrow's shaft I saw the attacker's eyes widen when, through his anger, he saw his own death whistling toward his throat. His momentum carried him closer. His spear landed on the sand with a soft thud; his eyes grew wide as he groped at the arrow buried in his neck. Blood spurted from the wound and from his nose and mouth. His energy spent, he dropped to his knees in front of Seg and toppled onto the wet sand.

Sognet's raised hand restrained his other guards. "You see what happens to those who do not follow orders?" he sneered, pointing at the fallen warrior thrashing like a dying fish in the remnants of the Ben. Turning to me, he spat, "I may like a sun shade, but at least I don't have to be protected by a goat." The troops shouted and laughed at his rejoinder. "Before I unleash these hungry dogs, amuse us by telling us who you are and what you want," he snarled.

While the king was talking, I notched another arrow into my bow. Nodding toward the corpse, its blood staining the sand, I said, "It was not the goat who killed this brute and it will not be the goat who severs your throat should any more of your puppies fail to heed their master."

277

Sognet's eyes grew large. It occurred to me that this might have been the first time in his life he had been directly threatened. I continued, not giving him time to respond.

"My name is Ayuba. Shepherd of Hamood, hero of the Gleb, avenger of the twan, protector of Bynethia, and master of the Ben."

"Very impressive," scoffed Sognet caustically. "I've heard of you; a goat herder from the Beyond! I have just one title," he said threateningly, "king!"

Father's voice whispered in my ear, *You have dreamed of this instant and you have been victorious.*

"KING!" he shouted again, as though I may not have heard him. The bloodthirsty warriors took up the chant, "KING, KING, KING!" Without removing his glare from my gaze, he silenced the thugs.

"With a flick of my finger I can destroy you and all the groveling tribes of Bynethia," he growled menacingly. I grinned back at him.

"What limited powers you possess for a king," I laughed. "Even a simple goat herder from the Beyond can wipe out your wealth and power with less effort. All I have to do is fail to return to my camp and you and all you value will sink like a stone."

The guards stood silent, uncertain of the threat or of the action expected of them; the debate now beyond their bloodlust abilities. Sognet took in a deep breath and started to respond. Once again I stilled his reply.

"I will return when the sun is directly overhead. I expect to meet four men on the opposite side of the riverbed from where you now stand. Digulnd has their names."

Dropping the chain that bound the captives, I continued, "Think clearly on what these men have to tell you. There is no devious way for you to avoid this threat. For once, be wise instead of cruel. Know that all problems cannot be solved by might and cunning."

I pulled the she-beast's head around and, as stately as possible, plodded toward the now dry falls of Erite.

I was strangely calm riding down the riverbed away from the mines. I had done all I could. If the king called my bluff, a wall of water would wipe out the mines and the long-suffering slaves. No doubt Sognet would survive, as would his elite guards. He would lose his wealth, but his vengeance would destroy Bynethia. It was a terrible gamble.

The she-beast grazed on the rich green grass along the river's bank as I walked along its shore. The smell of exposed riverweeds and dead fish tainted the air. Black flies buzzed and swarmed on the decaying vegetation.

I thought about my confrontation with Sognet. Should I have remained and explained the danger of the dam instead of leaving it up to Seg and Digulnd? No, leaving was the right choice. A single miscue and the king might have reacted violently without considering the ramifications of his actions.

"Always leave your opponent a way out," Barnlo once told me. "Without a choice, there is nothing to lose."

As the sun reached its zenith, I released the white goat—she had served her purpose. Either Sognet would acquiesce or he would be waiting for me with overpowering force. All the effort of the peoples of Bynethia—the toil, danger, pain, and death—came down to this moment.

Mounting, I thought of Rantel al Darem. He had immersed himself in the Ben after fleeing the charnel fire. Once again, the Ben would salve his wounded heart and all the hearts of those still alive in these mines of madness. By sunset, the slaves would be free or released from their bondage by the sweet embrace of death.

Breaching the bend in the river, my hands shook and my heart raced. There was no one standing on the bank nearest the mines, but as the far bank came more into view, tears welled in my eyes and a sob escaped my throat. Three men stood on the far shore.

I urged my great beast forward. Sensing my eagerness, she broke into a trot. Drawing closer I slowed her pace, careful not to startle the men who stood staring dumbly at the mines on the far side of the empty riverbed.

Stopping several paces away I dismounted. The emaciated creatures, their blistered shoulders slumping forward, arms hanging like withered vines, showed no awareness of my arrival.

They were naked. Dried feces coated their legs. Raw, bleeding bands of skin around their necks indicated where just moments before their shackles had been hammered free. They gave no notice to the black flies blanketing the festering whip wounds on their backs. I wanted to run to them and take them in my arms, to cleanse their wounds and succor them. I checked these impulses. These were, according to Rantel al Darem, the strongest slaves in the mines. The men most capable of leading the others to freedom.

Slowly I approached these shadows of humanity. Choking back my sadness, I stood before them. Their eyes were barely visible behind curtains of limp, greasy hair.

"I have come to take you home," I said softly. No response. Eyes covered with a dull sheen. "Your friend,

Rantel al Darem, the master of the forge of Tab, has sent me for you." No response.

I fetched my water bag. Carefully approaching, I offered it to them, saying, "Please, drink. I am here to help you." I saw one man's eyes widen imperceptibly, but he did not reach for the bag.

I felt defeated. Were their spirits beyond my reach? How could I scale the walls of fear they had created to shield their souls from the inhumanity of the Effrifrians?

With a pain so intense it felt like a dagger plunging into my heart, I yelled at the slaves as though their master. "Sit down!" I commanded.

They responded immediately. A cloud of flies hovered over them as they lowered their bony haunches onto the sand. Removing my robe, I soaked the hem in water and began washing their wounds. Speaking to them as one would to a child I said, "Phlen, Radii, Sang, and Clint are the names Rantel al Darem gave me when he sent me here to free you. Can you remember these men hiding in your hearts? Can you call to them? They need not be afraid. They are safe now."

Kneeling in front of the smallest of the three, I pushed his hair off his face. His unblinking eyes swam in pools of tears. I gently washed away the grime from his gaunt face. When finished, I kissed him softly on his forehead. He blinked, a river of tears flowing across his emaciated cheeks.

"You are safe," I whispered. "Search your heart for the man you once were." I took his calloused hand in mine. I felt him squeeze it hesitantly. "You are free and soon you will be well, but I need you to shed your fear to help the others."

More than kindness or the balm of touch, it was the call to that most human trait of all—nobleness—that fanned the lingering spark of humanity in the soul of this wretched animal. His lips shivering from lack of use, his tongue probing, moistening the scabby skin, his voice, like the sound of straw, escaped from the cage of his mouth, "I am Clint."

Sobs broke from my breast. I gathered him in my arms, our tears mingling on his bony chest.

One by one, the men hiding in the shadows of their souls clawed their way toward the light of humanity. Each struggled to shed the brutality that had outwardly turned them into beasts of burden. They drank from my water bag. I fed them small portions of dates and figs. Gradually their features of dumbness became animated with small gestures.

When I learned from Clint that Phlen had died just days before, a Hamoodian soldiers' song came to mind, "To die in battle is a tribute, to be the last killed, a tragedy."

The sound of hammers driving out the collar rivets of the other prisoners drifted down from the mines. Although I could not see where the prisoners were assembled, I could sense their confusion and fear. One false move on either side could panic Sognet or the prisoners into a desperate act that would kill us all. I prayed that the captives would stay docile while they were herded past the sweating blacksmiths.

It was vital to get the other prisoners away from this evil place before the mercurial king changed his mind. I knew I could not hope to single-handedly care for all the prisoners once freed. The difficulty awakening Clint, Radii, and Sang was proof of that. I needed these men to escort the others and verify that all prisoners had been released.

A commotion on the far side of the river startled the three men. "Stay calm," I said, "it is the other men being set free."

I heard the sound of a whip crack as a guard herded the ghost-like apparitions toward the river. Grabbing my bow, I sent an arrow plunging into the sneering guard's shoulder as he raised his whip. He cried out as he fell writhing to the ground. The prisoners stood perfectly still, void of any sense of self-determination.

Clint was the first to respond. He hobbled as fast as his tortured legs would allow toward the stalled column, followed by Radii and Sang. They moved through the men, gently urging them toward the riverbed.

Over two hundred prisoners stumbled toward freedom. Seg and Digulnd had done well; the king, although brutal, understood the mines were more important than the captives.

Due to the brutal policies of Sognet, all the prisoners could walk; those too lame or crippled had been slain. Twelve mules burdened with food followed the cadaverous band of humans.

The female slave who had sheltered Sognet followed the last prisoner. The sun sparkled off her silver sandals. Her oiled hair and body radiated power and lust. She approached, dropping a large leather sack at my feet.

Looking directly into my eyes, her chin held high, breasts jutting from her muscular frame, she said, "Sognet, ruler of Effrifria, has met your terms. As instructed, he will deliver five chests of gold on the equinox each year to the people of Bynethia. Now...he wants his river back." Her beautiful eyes radiated cruelty and hate.

"Tell Sognet *my* river will return by morning." The woman grunted in acknowledgment, turning toward the far shore.

"Oh, and one thing more..." She turned, glaring at me.

"Remind your king that should even a simple Effrifrian goat herder violate Bynethia's borders, or if his annual tribute is so much as a sunrise late, I will destroy the source of his wealth."

"I will tell him," she said, her eyes growing wide. Her change in demeanor from arrogance to fear puzzled me as I watched her climb up the far bank.

Other than the freed men and mules stumbling down the river, there was not another person in sight. Turning to mount the she-beast, my foot struck the bag at my feet. When I picked it up, the heads of Seg and Digulnd tumbled out. Their tongues had been cut out. Their bloodless skin looked dull against the glistening sand. I looked at the far bank where the woman stood staring at me.

It would take three days to reach the pass leading from Effrifria to the plain of Bynethia. The weary men mindlessly trudged along the empty streambed in silence. I walked among them, speaking softly. Although Clint, Radii, and Sang had been awakened from their nightmare, the habit of nothingness was not easily broken. They too often plodded ahead in a stupor unless encouraged by me to help their comrades. The damp sand of the riverbed soothed sore and blistered feet.

Well after the moon rose on the first night, I called a halt on the south side of the river. Radii, Sang, and Clint moved among the men with water skins. Although I had demanded fresh fruit and bread from Sognet, he had supplied the meanest victuals. The bread was mealy and dry, the fruit fit only for swine; however, the skeletal shapes eagerly consumed Sognet's putrid fare. Without complaint, these men, whose spirits had been pummeled and shredded, slept on the hardscrabble shore of the Ben.

The sound of trickling water awakened me. A small but growing stream sought its way down the center of the sandy riverbed. I marveled at the accuracy of Polter's calculation. I pictured Sognet standing on the shore as the river slowly filled the channel in front of the mines. Any doubts he harbored about releasing the slaves should be washed away by the timely reappearance of the Ben.

At mid-morning, our trail descended to a sandy beach. The river was now wide and shallow. I halted the march. Employing the painful ruse I used on Clint, I mounted the she-beast and in a loud, menacing voice demanded that the ox-men look at me.

In unison, the assembly turned. With heads covered in lank, dirty hair, eyes barely visible, they awaited their orders. More gently now I said, "Listen to me with your hearts—you are free men. You will never again work in the mines. Find the voices you have silenced for so long. Remember the names your mothers gave you. The nightmare of Effrifria is over, and soon we will be in Bynethia where food and rest await you."

I saw a few men sneak furtive glances at each other, but the herd remained docile and unresponsive. I continued, "We are on the banks of the river Ben. It is shallow and safe. I want you all to walk into the water." No one moved. "Now!" I commanded.

I shall always cherish the Ben. It supplied the power to check Sognet's evil and now it soothed the bodies of men who had forgotten what it was to be human. As they shed the filth of their bowels caked on their bodies, they uncovered their souls. As they scrubbed away the crust of their captivity, I heard the first human sound any of them had made since their release...a soft sob that was quickly snuffed out as though it was a dangerous intruder.

Sang, his voice weak and unsure, cried out, "What this man says is true, you are free. You will not be killed if you speak."

The Ben swept away the filth. The foamy ooze slid down the river like a dirty snake. Pink skin, covered with sores, replaced the smelly shrouds on frail legs. Several men began to weep. A voice near the middle of the group whispered, "Is it true?"

Many found their voices in the refreshing waters... but not all. Men who had labored and slept together without speaking exchanged names. Lessons learned by the deaths of others were hard to dispel. As we regained the bank, some looked directly at me for the first time. Fear still dulled their eyes and uncertainty their step, but heads were higher and backs less hunched.

The following day, I was surprised to see a fast-moving group of riders approaching from the direction of Bynethia. I halted our caravan and walked out to meet them. Joy overwhelmed my heart when I saw it was the kings of Bynethia and their guards.

Without encouragement or direction, they dismounted and immediately moved among the startled band, speaking gently while walking through the frightened miners. Many of the escapees could not yet speak, but others broke down and cried at the mention of their shattered homes. Royal hands, oiled and groomed daily by servants, reached out and touched the scabrous skin of their long-lost subjects.

The kings' guards dismounted their steeds. Gathering the weakest, they helped them onto soft saddles. Even the royals relinquished their beautifully groomed stallions to the poorest of their subjects.

On the morning of the next day as we approached Tab, hundreds of well-wishers streamed out to meet us. Stonemasons rebuilding the village picked up faltering men and carried them. Maidens moved among the weary ghosts, stroking them and singing softly, tears dampening their gowns. Weavers from Drulem covered the scarred and withered shoulders of the miners with soft tunics woven from Bynethian wool. The smell of roasting meats and rich soups wafted from the village.

As we crested the last hill, the village came into view. Moving away from the gathering I sat on a large stone. The tension of the last year welled up inside of me. Tears of joy streamed down my cheeks.

Tab was gone. The once shattered stone huts had been rebuilt, fresh reeds covering the roofs. The pathways, formerly littered with bones, were swept and paved with flat stones. Brightly colored curtains caressed the windows. Stout doors stood open, welcoming the lost men of Bynethia. A large stella by the side of the path leading into the village proclaimed its new name...Al Darem!

❧✕☙

The hope and confidence generated by the removal of the Effrifrian threat opened the eyes and hearts of the rulers of Bynethia. More importantly, all faiths and customs were now tolerated. The dam workers were the seeds of this change. The stories they shared around village fires shed a new and more tolerant light on the shadows of ancient prejudices. Trade increased between the tribes, as did cultural competition and visitations. The people of the clans became the citizens of a country.

Within a decade the fractured land healed itself. The rulers shared power in a grand council. Each king rotated as supreme ruler for two cycles of seasons, then relinquished the mostly ceremonial role to another.

The annual tribute from Effrifria was doubled when Hamood, freed from manning its border with Bynethia, volunteered an equal stipend. The newfound wealth was used to build a gleaming capital city called, much to my embarrassment, Ayubia. It is located in the fertile heart of the country between the Ben and Leb rivers.

Most of the freed prisoners recovered from their trepidations although a few were never able to regain their spirit. These mute ghosts of men are cared for and honored by their tribes.

Al Darem became a major trading center. Annually it celebrates the country's only national festival. On this occasion, the once small village becomes an island in a sea of colorful tents as Bynethians from throughout the land flock to the festivities. Competitions between tribes are fierce in sports, singing, and dancing. Indeed, it is at this grand party where intertribal disputes are often settled through sport instead of war. The climax of this great celebration is the reenactment of the prisoners' march to freedom. Only those who actually participated in the original event or their descendants are allowed to participate.

Unified Bynethia is not without problems. Melding the disparate tribes into a country presented many difficulties. Now called the "Father of Bynethia," I have spent over thirty cycles of the seasons as the arbiter of these disputes. I travel constantly, meeting with and speaking to the people and rulers of the fledgling nation. Joyfully, I do not travel alone.

Shortly after freeing the miners, a delegation from Hamood arrived to escort their captives home. Unannounced, Jute and Neeno entered my tent. Their delight at our reunion was obvious. I was unaware how my heart had longed for the gentle touch of love.

In their delightful girlish way, they informed me that when they requested permission to come to me, the king of Hamood readily agreed. Nervously they explained this was not a visit—they had come to stay with me as my wives.

Pulling at my gown, giggling and laughing, they announced that they had another surprise. They insisted on blindfolding me. Stumbling and laughing at their joy, they led me to the grove where I camped the first time I visited Tab.

Regaining my sight, I stood in a commodious tent. Beautiful carpets covered the ground strewn with luxurious cushions. Jute and Neeno, with the lightness of air, danced through the tent and my heart. The tent and furnishings were a gift from the king and the grateful people of Hamood.

Once again the girls had me close my eyes. I could not conceive of another surprise exceeding what I'd received so far. The three of us stumbled through the tent flap.

Opening my eyes I was delighted to see Lasheed, Joklee, and Fairtee, my faithful Bensheerie escorts. What joy to be reunited with friends and lovers!

Bowing low with exaggerated formality, Lasheed proclaimed, "When we heard the king of Hamood was assembling a dowry for these two maidens, we volunteered to become your servants." He paused, a mischievous grin on his face. "Plus we hear the girls of Bynethia are not only pretty, but at your command!"

Now thirty cycles later, traveling throughout Bynethia, we are a small tribe unto ourselves. My wives have blessed me with twenty-six children who in turn have produced thirty-seven grandchildren. In addition, the Bensheeries have been ensnared by lovely Bynethian maids and among them have more than seventy offspring.

Breeding and trading camels supports our boisterous family. Our herd of five hundred animals makes up the finest breeding stock in the world. Caravaners from throughout the region seek us out when replenishing their stock. Lasheed has put his fine wit and craftiness to good use as our chief trader.

❧❧

Three moons past the winter solstice, thirty cycles following the creation of Ayubia...the she-beast died.

In a meadow removed from the herd, I held her great shaggy head in my lap, the warmth of her body shielding me for the final time from the cold night air. Brilliant stars and a weak moon wept light from the dark sky. Her lids fluttered as I softly sang a Hamrabian dream song about her nurturing me during my captivity with the reed gatherers.

I reminded her that Father named me for her. I whispered the song of her valor when she rescued us on the Shale Sea. As she drew her last breath, I stroked her cheeks and sang of how she led the charge at the battle of the Gleb and sheltered me from the violence of the worley. She shared the journey that was my life, and I shared hers. I wept throughout the night clinging to her lifeless body. There was no one to share my sadness. My valiant friend could no longer lick my tears as she had so often done in the past.

Does the sky recall those it has sheltered? Does the breeze seek those it has caressed? Would the sand she trod long for her touch? If for a moment I thought the stones over which she climbed would recall her deeds... I would be content to simply let her go. I could not trust that her loyalty, strength, and courage would linger in the memory of the land. I intended to honor the great beast so her life would not be forgotten as long as mine was remembered.

With the sun breaching the horizon I recalled the fable of Griefere, replacing my grief with memories of joy and gratitude. I banned everyone from where the great beast lay. I asked Lasheed to secure a huge bronze kettle from a nearby village along with several loads of dried camel dung and a large crock of female camel urine.

Stripping to my breechclout I proceeded to skin the animal that had sheltered and protected me since childhood. Scores of vultures circled overhead, their shadows caressing the naked corpse. As I peeled back the tough hide, the bloody flesh was instantly covered with the ever-present desert flies. These angry pests swarmed over my bloodstained hands and arms, attacking the tears on my cheeks and fussing their way into my nose and mouth.

As the moon lumbered through a full cycle, I worked on the hide, cutting it into strips then drying them in the sun. Once dried, I scraped off the hair. Placing a water-filled cauldron over a large dung fire I fed the long, stiff strips into the boiling water. With each step in this lengthy and painful process I honored the beauty of her remarkable spirit.

Camped well away from the tribe, I spent many days in the shade of a small camp tent separating the skins. After drying them again they were as brittle and delicate as dried flowers. Filling the cauldron with female camel urine I slowly passed the sheets through the rising steam. With each pass they grew softer and more pliable. Each one took half a day to complete. When finished, I rinsed them in clear water and let them dry in the shade. The sheets, now as thin as a grape skin, were soft, pliable, and almost indestructible.

I began writing the history of my life and the creation of modern Bynethia at the urging of my family and the citizens of that country. The royals begged me as the father of the country to commit it to writing.

I know not how you came to possess this scroll, much less where in time you may be. I wrote these words following the death of my faithful companion. Just as we complemented and cared for each other while she lived, so too do we support each other's history. I hold her memory in my heart...she holds the story of our life on her hide.

The death of the she-beast was a fitting end to the story of the adventures we shared; however, in my early seventies, something so profound happened that I am compelled to rewrite the ending of this lengthy history. This last and greatest adventure I experienced without the comfort and protection of the great beast now residing in this scroll and in the fiber of the birds soaring over the lands she once trod.

At the advanced age of 105, Polter, architect of the dam, died. Leaving the herd and most of our family at our encampment near Steedtar, Jute, Neeno, the Bensheeries, and I swiftly traveled to Leedad for the funeral festivities. Veterans of the great project at the falls of Erite and many of the rescued slaves descended on the capital of Leedad to offer their respect.

His life was proclaimed with many fine speeches, songs, and poems. As was the custom in Leedad, the king held a magnificent banquet. Bonfires and torches lighted the streets. The air was filled with music as tribal orchestras from throughout Bynethia competed for the attention of the mourners.

I scarcely noticed when an old crone slipped a small leather scroll into my hand as I was passing through the throng. It was common for family members of the freed slaves, as well as other admiring citizens, to give me small tokens of their appreciation and esteem. Confined by the crush of admirers, I lost sight of the old woman before I could thank her. Without much thought, I passed the scroll to Fairtoo, whose job it was to care for these tokens until there was time to appreciate them properly.

Polter's funeral lasted three days. We stayed two more days to attend to the assembled royals. So it was that half a moon passed from the night I received the scroll until I opened it in our camp at Steedtar.

Lamps lit the tent. The sides were rolled up and a soft breeze cast flickering images on its ceiling. Jute and Neeno were attending the birth of our first great-grandchild nearby.

Fairtoo brought me the basket of gifts received in Leedad. I always enjoy receiving these heartfelt tributes. I laughed as I read that a man named Trudlee, a tree feller from Bynot who worked on the dam, had the good fortune to acquire an albino camel. In honor of the she-beast he named it Ayuba. There was a small clay statue of me mounted on a camel from the widow of a freed slave. A very fine obsidian knife wrapped in sheepskin came from an unknown admirer. My heart was light as I picked the scroll from the remaining gifts in the basket. Holding it aloft in the light I unrolled it.

I sprang from my cushion. My chest constricted. Spreading the scroll closer to the light, I saw not the glyphs common in the known world, but the ancient runes I'd only seen once before—carved above the archway leading to the Stone of Hamood. Slowly I unwound the scroll covered with the perfectly formed but undecipherable characters on a parchment finer than anything I'd ever seen. Running my fingers over the delicate surface, I tried to remember who'd given me the scroll.

At the end of the scroll, the neat rows of symbols were replaced by perfectly drawn images of the sun followed by several moons in phase. The strange drawings culminated in a full moon rising over what appeared to be an island. Beneath the moon was a drawing of a camel led by a man. My sight having grown dim with age forced me to move the lamp closer. I closed my left eye and stretched the skin over my right to bring the scroll into sharper focus.

What could this mean? Was it simply the author ornamenting the scroll or was it a message? My hands were shaking. I felt warm, although the soft breeze was cool. My mouth was dry. I poured a cup of wine to calm my agitated spirit. I spread the scroll on the carpet, weighting it with several clay lamps. I walked around it hoping that seeing it fully unrolled would reveal its secrets. Oh, how I wished for Barnlo, the only man who could possibly decipher the writing. Unfortunately my dear friend and mentor died shortly after the struggle with Effrifria.

Neeno entered the tent to tell me of the arrival of our first great-grandson. I embraced her with joy.

"What's this?" she asked, motioning toward the scroll. Unable to read, she knelt looking at the pictures, ignoring the glyphs. "Well," she said matter of factly, "whatever it says, it is obviously meant for you."

Startled, I said, "How can you be sure?"

"Look at the boy leading the camel...camel boy... Ayuba," she said, tracing her fingers across the finely drawn image.

Kneeling down, squinting with my right eye, I said, "How can you be so sure it's a boy?"

"If you could see more clearly you would know it's a boy. Wait a minute," she said as she fetched my travel pack lying by our pallet. I continued to try to focus my eye. She returned, holding the polished crystal lens I had been given in Hamrabi before departing for Bensheer.

"This might help."

The magnified image leapt into view. It was a boy leading the camel...what's more it was a boy who looked very much as I once did.

"Now can you see?" Neeno asked.

"Yes, yes, it is a boy. But what does it mean?" I whispered. A thin sheen of sweat covered my hands.

Using the glass, I looked closely at each image. With the help of the lens, I noticed a fine vertical line bisecting each sun. The line moved closer and closer to the middle of the orb with each drawing. The final sun was perfectly divided, with the left half of the orb slightly shaded while the right side remained clear.

Images of the moon starting with a quarter were directly below the split sun, ending with the full moon rising from the sea with a strange island below. I looked closely at the island. The shore on one end was indistinct. What appeared to be a beach ran along the other. Palm trees studded the clear end, rising above some sort of buildings...houses?

"What do you make of this?" I said, handing the glass to Neeno. She squatted over the scroll studying the island for some time.

"It appears to be an island, but like none I've ever seen."

I rubbed my eyes. "Islands, islands. Where are there islands?" I barely heard Neeno say she was leaving to help Jute and our granddaughter.

I thought of the few islands I knew. There were several small ones in the river Leb where it flowed by the great marshes of the southern border, but they were tiny and covered with reeds, not trees. I had seen islands off the shore of Bynot in the Oxyeon, but they too were barren, except for some old piers where fishermen once lived. Bynot?

Suddenly I remembered that my granddaughter's husband was a Bynotian. Following in Neeno's wake, I raced from the tent. Approaching the birthing tent, I found Hamrite, my grandson-in-law, pacing back and forth listening to my great-grandson wailing inside.

"Oh, Grandfather," he smiled, embracing me, "have you heard? It's a boy!"

"Yes," I said somewhat distractedly while pounding him on the back, "congratulations!"

Just then Jute stuck her head from the tent. "You two can come in now," she beckoned.

"In a moment," I said, taking Hamrite by the arm and pulling him toward my tent.

"But Grandfather…my son!" he shouted, trying to loosen my grip.

"Please," I said plaintively, "you will see him for the rest of your life. I only need a moment of your time."

"Ayuba!" shouted Jute.

"Be patient, woman," I said gruffly, "we'll be back soon." Sensing my distress, Jute ducked back inside and Hamrite ceased his resistance.

Scooping up the scroll, winding it on its spindles so only the island pictograph was visible, I handed it to Hamrite. "Do you recognize this island?"

Hesitantly he took the scroll, holding it up to a lamp. Although his look told me he thought I'd drunk too much wine, he studied the picture closely.

"Yes, Grandfather, I recognize it. It's the sacred island of Gleer," he said confidently, turning for the door. "Now can I see my son?"

"In a moment. First tell me where it is located."

Sensing my desperation, he turned back toward me. "Surely you have heard of the evil island located about a half-day's ride from Bynot?" he asked, surprised at my ignorance.

"Yes, yes, of course I've heard of the evil island. I just didn't know its name. Gleer, you say?"

"Yes, Grandfather," he said, once again turning to leave.

"Hamrite, please, just a moment more," I pleaded. "How can you be so sure it's Gleer?"

Turning away from the door he said, "Grandfather…I lived all of my life within a short walk of the beach facing Gleer. I've fished the waters around the island countless times. Annually during the Festival of the Righteous, all believers gather in the moonlight and wade out toward the island without stepping on its shore and cast stones at the evil spirits living there." Picking up the scroll, he held it for me to see. "Look, Grandfather, see these buildings on the west end of the island?"

"Yes," I said, looking closely at the finely drawn images.

"These are the ruins of the temple Gleer from which the island gets its name. In the songs of the Bynotians, this was once the center of our faith. It was also a famous observatory when Bynot led the world in astronomy and mathematics. The priests of Gleer were among the most knowledgeable men on earth. Because Bynot is dependent on the Oxyeon for its livelihood and sustenance, annually the priests held a festival to pray for an abundant harvest and to ask the gods to bless the fishermen."

"Yes, yes, I know of this feast. It is held even today. But none of this explains the island's evil reputation," I said, anxious to hurry him along with his story.

"According to the songs of our history, the day following the last feast held on Gleer, everyone who participated died. They died horrible deaths—it is said their tongues were distended, faces blue with veins ruptured by horrible gagging and vomiting."

"Hmmm..." I interrupted. "Sounds like fish poisoning?"

"Yes, Grandfather, that is probably what happened; easy for us to understand today, but myths are hard to dispel once enveloped in the hearts of a people as you have so often said. The deaths were followed by a long period of hardship. Tides abundant in fishes and plants turned red for much of the year. Winds unknown before destroyed many boats. Bynot became weak and isolated from other tribes. It became a pariah.

"In desperation the priests determined the suffering and hardship was caused by evil spirits seeking a place to live. They purified Gleer, burning the ancient compound and everything in it. They even burned their clothes, shaved their heads, and burned their shorn locks. Naked, bald, and destitute they waded through the shallow waters, cursing the island as they fled. Myth or fact, it makes no difference; no one in Bynot will ever set foot on the island of Gleer. All curse it. When Bynots are angry with other tribes, they pray they will go to Gleer. Such is the fear of this small island. Now, Grandfather," Hamrite said, handing me the scroll, "meaning no disrespect, I am going to see my son."

In the early morning, Jute and Neeno returned. With patience and understanding they urged me to put aside the mystery and sleep. Still baffled by the meaning of the scroll and by the urgency I felt to decipher it, I joined them on our pallet. As dawn broke, I awoke from a restless, dream-haunted sleep. Creeping from beneath the covers, careful not to wake my exhausted wives, I gathered up the scroll and took it outside, examining it in the pure morning light.

I ignored the ancient glyphs, focusing instead on the beautifully drawn images. Whether from the brief rest or the morning light, the message of the scroll became instantly clear to me.

My heart raced as I translated each image. The orbs with their dissecting lines represented the phases of the sun approaching the spring equinox. It was clear...the last orb, bisected in equal parts with one-half shaded, represented the date on which night and day are of equal length; a day worshipped by many as the beginning of a new year.

My breathing became labored. Polter's funeral was held on the equinox! I recalled the funeral priests equating his death with this auspicious event. I closed my eyes, trying to calculate how much time had passed since the ceremony.

Beneath the split sun was a full moon followed by a progression of waning and waxing moons, culminating in another full moon. Beneath the new moon was the island of Gleer with the camel and boy below. The message was unmistakable...the vagueness I felt earlier disappeared.

I was being summoned to the island of Gleer on the night of the first moon following the equinox. But who could be beckoning me? Who other than Barnlo could read and write in the ancient runes?

A soft, westerly zephyr accompanied the full sun as it edged over the horizon toward a cloudless sky. I felt the excitement and energy of youth coursing through me. A voice in my head whispered, "Hurry to Gleer."

I ran through the camp yelling for Lasheed. Faces fogged with sleep popped from tents.

"What's wrong?"

"Lasheed!" I shouted, ignoring their pleas. Lasheed sprang from his tent, sword in hand, expecting thieves or some other danger.

Breathing hard, I cried, "Pack two camels, we ride immediately for Bynot."

Lowering his sword, Lasheed shot me a perplexed look. "You've awakened the entire camp! Why are you shouting and running around naked?"

Embarrassed, I realized how foolish I must look, having forgotten I left my tent without dressing. Undeterred, I repeated, "I've no time to explain. Make haste, you and I must leave for Bynot before the sun reaches its zenith." Without further comment I retraced my steps, apologizing to the startled sleepers as I hurried to my tent.

We had less than half of a moon to traverse the entire length of Bynethia, a journey that would normally take a complete moon cycle. Unconvinced by my interpretation of the scroll, Lasheed grumbled and complained most of the way.

Stating that our efforts were in vain, he called our journey an old man's fantasy. His constant bickering caused me to doubt my interpretation of the scroll. If someone wanted to meet me, why not simply come to my camp? Or write the message using characters common to all? Lasheed believed the scroll was simply an artifact the old woman found, and unable to read it, she had passed it on to me as a gift.

We arrived on the shore of Oxyeon the night before the new moon. Exhausted, we made camp in an untended date grove within sight of the evil island. Weary but unable to sleep, I stood on the shore watching the moon slowly disappear into the light of day. Lasheed's snoring interrupted the soft sounds of the sea lapping at my feet.

The island looked deserted. No smoke rose from the ruins now clearly visible in the morning light. We spent the day resting and sleeping, waiting for the new moon to replace the sun.

As the fresh orb began to rise over Bynethia like a beacon, it illuminated the foreshore of Gleer. Lasheed made one last plea to accompany me.

"Look at you, the strength and vigor of your youth are gone. Your hair and beard are gray. Your tunic, once bursting under the strain of your shoulders, now stretches to contain your paunch. Your eyes, once glittering with light, have grown dim. How do you expect to protect yourself from whatever may be lurking on that dreadful island?"

"For this entire journey, you have scoffed and belittled my interpretation of the scroll and now you're afraid for my safety?" I chided him, removing my sword and scabbard.

"I'm not worried about some evil spirit attacking you. I am concerned that without me you might wander off. Who knows where you'd be if it wasn't for my protection over all this time," he pestered. "Look at you, you've removed your sword and bow! How will you protect yourself?"

"Ah, dear friend. If this is but an old man's fantasy, what need will I have for weapons?"

"If you won't protect yourself at least let me follow you in case there are robbers or wild beasts on the island. Besides..." he sputtered, "you can't swim!"

Hoisting my robe onto my shoulders to keep it dry, I stepped into the languid sea. "Lasheed, dear friend, do not follow me. If I have not returned or signaled you by the time the sun is fully above the mountains of Erite, you may come in search of me."

His reasoning defeated, muttering about the sanity of age, he turned to tend the camels.

The distance to the island was but a couple of hundred cubits. The water sparkled in the moon's glow. I could feel the gentle pull of the receding tide against my legs. One thing Lasheed was right about, I did not know how to swim; it was a skill rarely required in the deserts of the Beyond. But the turquoise color of the waters separating the shore from the island indicated an easily traversed shallowness.

302

Unconcerned, I waded into the breach between the shore of Bynot and the evil island of Gleer. Midway, the sea floor abruptly fell away where the encircling tide had gouged a channel. Suddenly I was in water up to my chest. The tide's gentle pull against my calves became stronger as the bay sought release into the sea. Lifting my foot I found myself pushed diagonally. Fear rose in my gorge, my legs moving more quickly as they tried desperately to gain purchase on the far side of the channel.

Still holding my robe over my head to keep it dry, my hands were useless. The water lapped against my chin. With each lunge, I bounced off the bottom trying to push myself toward the island only to drift parallel to the beach. I wanted to cry out for Lasheed. Desperately my feet searched for the sand. With my next step I sank beneath the water. Flailing with my arms I let go of my robe. Heavy now, my wet gown pressed all about me like a shroud. The more I struggled, the more entangled I became. I tried calling out…water flooded my mouth. I gagged as it filled my lungs.

My mind raced. Could this be how it ends? After so many dangers, so many adventures—defeated by the Sea of Oxyeon? Panic engulfed me as I struggled against the sea. My arms and legs wearied. How quickly it happened. I felt my strength flowing out with the tide. I could see the moon…a vague spirit through the clear water. Small bubbles drifted from my nose, rising toward the light. I quit struggling, becoming one with the flotsam headed for the sea.

So quick…so quick, my last thought before slipping into darkness.

The oarlock dug into my gut as I was dragged half-way into the boat. I retched, the sea flowing from my nose. Gagging, I gasped for air. My legs, entangled in my robe, floated alongside the boat. I felt a hand press against my back thrusting the sea from my lungs, another gently lifting my head, clearing my hair from my eyes and nose. My feet scraped against the sand. I wanted to laugh but sobbed instead as I sucked the night into my chest. I fainted.

My entire family was there. We were seated in the date grove just west of our house in Hamrabi. The exquisite carpet from the great hall of Hamood was spread on the sand, piled high with steaming meats and succulent fruits. Father was talking; I could hear his deep, rich voice, but could not understand his words. I began to cry. Extending my arms to embrace my family, they remained beyond my reach. I cried out for Lasheed to help me...the baby at Mother's teat smiled and gurgled. Father was standing now; it sounded like he was singing. Everyone was looking at me, smiling.

"Ayuba?" I heard Father call my name.

"Father, Father," I called.

A voice richer and deeper than Father's called to me. "Wake up, Ayuba. You are safe."

The incongruous sound of water lapping against the shore filtered into the scene of the family feast. I felt a hand gently brush sand from my forehead. Again the pleasant but unfamiliar voice called my name.

"Ayuba, open your eyes."

I did not heed the voice, not wanting to open my eyes for fear of once again losing my family. A gentle slap on my cheek jarred me awake. The voice, now smiling... "That's better. Come now, wake up, we've little time."

My eyes, crusted with salt and tears, tried to focus. I could see the moon now at its zenith, partially blocked by the head of a man leaning over me. The head spoke.

"Ayuba." The voice was rich with an unfamiliar accent.

"Who are you?"

"My name would mean nothing to you. The Hamoodians call me… *Great Guide* or *Shepherd*."

I started to say *me too* when suddenly the import of what he said filtered through my confused brain. Was I still dreaming? My heart racing, I struggled to sit up. Grasping my shoulders, the man helped me. I rubbed the crust from my eyes.

Kneeling before me was a man twice the size of an ordinary human. Blue eyes peered from beneath an elegant brow. A thick beard, veined with silver, framed his friendly face.

"*The* guide?" I finally managed to whisper.

His eyes crinkled as his finely chiseled lips drew wide, exposing perfectly white teeth. "Yes, *the* guide," he said, chuckling. "And I presume you are the fabled Ayuba?"

I shivered uncontrollably. The man stood.

"Regrettably, your robe got away from me as I carried you ashore. You've had quite a shock. This will help." Removing his robe, he wrapped it around me. Dressed now only in a breechclout, I could fully comprehend his size.

"Are…are you a god?" I stuttered.

Once again laughter exploded, fracturing the soft night air. "It is always the first question I get when traveling outside my own country. It's one of the reasons I keep out of sight." He moved gracefully gathering an armload of dried fronds for a fire. His entire body was finely chiseled, belying what I presumed to be his great age.

"Is that a yes or no?" I asked sheepishly.

Dropping the pile of fronds next to me he said, "No, Ayuba, I am human like you. Somewhat different, but the same, if you know what I mean."

"You mean, bigger?"

"Obviously," he said, snapping the tough fronds into smaller pieces with his bare hands. "But also more advanced in other ways. Ayuba, the night is half gone. Due to your unfortunate accident, we've little time and much to discuss."

Without preamble he began to speak as the warmth of the fire and his robe chased the cold from my ancient bones. The politeness and formality of his speech comforted me as much or more than the fire.

"I come from a land on the far side of the world. You know, I presume, the world is round like a ball?" he asked hopefully.

"Yes, Barnlo demonstrated this to me. He also showed me how the earth circles the sun rather than being circled by the sun, as most believe."

"Ah, Barnlo...advanced beyond most others. What treasures he discovered for Hamood," he mused appreciatively. "So then," he continued in an obvious hurry, "you understand when I say my country lies almost opposite Bynethia. A vast island, it produces all that is needed to support an advanced civilization. The ground is fertile, the weather complacent, and the sea abundant. We have populated this land, unmolested, through almost three cycles of the stars." He paused, letting this incredible claim sink in.

"Do you understand what that means in terms of season cycles?" he asked, staring at me across the flickering fire.

"No."

"Short-lived civilizations track time by the sun or seasons. It is effective and easily accomplished using the solstices and equinoxes as markers. I suspect even people in the Beyond understand sun cycles."

The mention of the Beyond gave me the opening to ask the question foremost in my mind. "Yes, even the clans of the Beyond follow the phases of the sun. According to the legend of Hamood, you have been to the Beyond, so why do you ask such a question?"

Rising, the giant let out a great laugh. "Your question makes me realize I've left out important details you'll need to grasp what I'm about to burden you with."

Throwing more fronds on the fire, the guide's great body looked even more like a god when viewed through the shower of sparks rising into the clear night sky.

"Where to begin..." he said, stretching his magnificent arms to the sky as if seeking guidance from the heavens.

"Why not start with the Stone of Hamood?" I suggested cautiously.

"The Stone of Hamood. Yes, that will do. What is it you want to know?"

Without hesitation I asked the question I had struggled with since Barnlo read the inscription over the door leading to the stone...*Who knows this stone is the shepherd of our dreams.*

"Why did you create the stone and how did you know I would become the shepherd of Hamood?" My heart raced as I looked at the one person in the world who could, at last, explain the strange journey of my life.

Gathering his thoughts, the great man stared at the fire. There was an aura of kindness and understanding about him. He thought for a long time before answering.

"As I said, my civilization has existed in an unbroken line for over sixty thousand cycles of the seasons...that's almost three star cycles." He paused to let this unbelievable span take root in my mind.

"Sixty thousand cycles!" I exclaimed.

"Yes," he continued, "a vast span of time."

"But...Barnlo claims the oldest civilization known to man has only existed for..." I quickly calculated, "three thousand cycles, at most."

"As with most things, Barnlo was correct. All civilizations in existence today are only that old in memory. That is...all except ours."

"But how can that be?" I asked, still wrestling with the incredible time span.

"Ayuba, I know that much of what I'm about to tell you will be beyond the boundary of your understanding. I'm asking you to open your mind and accept these truths without discussion as we've much to cover before the dawn calls me away."

I accepted his gentle rebuke, vowing to hold my comments until he'd finished. The flames of the fire slipped into embers as the moon transited the sky.

"Due to the fortunate location of my homeland, our civilization survived three great cataclysms that, over this great span of time, destroyed all others. After each shattering event, few people survived in the devastated lands. These became the seeds of future tribes. The memory of Hamood is but a fraction of their existence. The civilizations of today have their roots in the ashes of the last destruction that took place over twelve millennia ago. As survivors, our evolution has been undisturbed. If the peoples of Hamood had the luxury of unbroken time, they too would be as advanced in health and science as are we."

I could not help but interrupt. "As the sole surviving civilization, why didn't you expand beyond your kingdom?"

"A good question. As our society advanced unimpeded, we kept detailed celestial records. Our scientists studied the movement of the stars and their affect on the earth. Over a vast amount of time, we determined great cycles of destruction were inevitable and, outside of our homeland, not survivable. After each of the first two devastations, we watched the slow, painful rebuilding of civilizations. After the last destruction, we sent guides into the world to hasten the recovery process. It was one of these missionaries who helped the wandering Hamoodians in what you call the Beyond."

Fully recovered now from the shock of my watery ordeal, I set aside the guide's robe. The night was warm. A sense of awe enveloped me as the soft, strong voice of this compassionate being spoke of ancient times from which my life and countless others evolved.

"Are you the one who carved the stone?"

"No," he chuckled, "we are advanced, but not that advanced. I am but a couple of hundred cycles old. I know of the Hamoodian guide only from records left by previous guides."

I was both saddened and relieved to learn that this man, though advanced, was mortal like me. Somehow it made everything he spoke of more believable and understandable.

"I apologize for interrupting, but please, I need to know...why?" I stuttered. "Why, if the guide was so advanced, did he not do more to help the Hamoodians and what purpose does the stone serve?"

"Let me answer your question with a question. If, when you lived in the Beyond, a creature appeared and

309

told you of religion, agriculture, and medicine, how would your clan have responded?"

I thought for a moment. "With fear and disbelief."

"From vast experience we understood the only way to implant lasting knowledge in the minds of primitive peoples is through the creation of myths. The carving of the stone was but a simple trick to impress the tribe of Hamood. Their fear and awe of its creation became imbedded in their infant culture, giving them hope. The devotion and unbelievable effort they made to drag its great weight across impassable barriers created a history for a people without a past. It taught them to work together. The lesson the guide delivered was that shared experience, effort, and sacrifice are the cornerstones of civilization."

"You make it sound so simple," I said doubtfully.

"It is both simple and unbelievably complicated." His voice had taken on a sadness I'd not sensed before. "You of all people should know this."

"Why do you say that?"

"Did you not create a history for Bynethia where it had none? Did you not show the tribes how to work together on the dam?"

I could not refute what he said. Unknowingly I had created the legend upon which the civilization of Bynethia rested.

"Barnlo told me the inscription over the door leading to the stone came from the 'Great Guide.' If that's true," I paused, afraid of what the answer to my question might be, "how did he foresee my becoming the shepherd of Hamood?" There, I'd said it...I felt a sigh of relief escaping from my chest.

"This too, my friend, is both complex and simple. The simple answer is that he did not know or, for that matter, care if you or anyone else appeared to claim the title. The fact that someone might appear who was in some mysterious way connected to the guide was enough to give the people of Hamood faith in the future. It gave them confidence that if they followed the tenets laid down in the wastes of the Beyond, the 'Great Guide' would return as prophesied."

"A simple trick?" I exclaimed, feeling the flush of anger across my cheeks.

"No, far from it. The guide was simply laying the foundation for some future guide. Fortunately you appeared and assumed that role. You cannot deny that you know the stone and that you now walk in the shadow of the 'Great Guide,'" he said, paraphrasing the legend.

"I was afraid when told I was the person referred to in the legend," I whispered.

"It was only by chance you knew of the stone. You had yet to dream the dreams of the guide. When you began to see yourself as the shepherd, you became what you dreamed. Those dreams became the dreams of others, and soon the wispy threads of dreams became the reality of the ancient prophecy."

I could not deny what this remarkable man said; it was the core of my teaching. How I came to possess this knowledge will always be a mystery to me, but there was no denying my dreams had become those of a nation, and that nation was real.

There was a hint of light in the eastern sky. The man, as though in response to a silent message sent on the breeze, spoke with urgency.

"We must leap from the past to the future, for it is the future that has brought us together. What I'm about to tell you will place a profound burden upon you. A burden you cannot share with any other—one you alone must carry." The giant's rich voice faltered. Its timbre changed to a painful whisper.

"Within the next decade, another calamity will strike the earth, and all that we know will be destroyed. A great flood will cover most of the world as mountains of ice melt and reform and the seas are rent with destructive winds. This inundation will be greater than the three that have come before. Even our island redoubt will break away and drift into a mountain of ice." Tears filled the sad pools of his eyes as he paused to see my reaction.

"How can you be sure?" I said doubtfully, my stomach churning desperately.

"We predicted the last great calamity within one hundred cycles of its occurrence. Our astronomers are certain of their prediction," he said hopelessly. "We have known this for several centuries but have remained silent. There is no escaping what will come. If some good could have been gained by warning others, we would have sent guides throughout the world to prepare it for survival. Alas, ignorance for once is kinder than knowledge."

Agitated by this devastating prediction from a being I could not doubt, I stood, rubbing my eyes, trying to force away the vision of my family being washed into the abyss. I could hear their cries and their muffled sobbing as they sank beneath the rising sea.

"What about a boat!" I exclaimed in desperation.

"Dear friend, do you not think a civilization as advanced as ours, one that has sailed to every corner of the globe, has not considered all possible ways to survive? You must clear your heart and mind and accept that the world as we know it will be destroyed. Use the remaining time to prepare for the one thing you can do..."

"I don't want to know this!" I cried. "Why are you telling me this? Why not also leave me in ignorance?"

"Why indeed," he said, taking me by the shoulders. "When we determined that the coming devastation would eliminate all but a few of humankind, we decided to create a message a future civilization might read and know that we existed and that we were advanced, like them. Hopefully this message will warn that life, even for the most advanced, is finite and fragile."

Unable to shake the confusion from my mind, I responded glumly, "And how do you propose to do that?"

"Many days north of Bynethia on a great plain, beyond the impassable swamps of your border, we are creating a star map in stone. The map, guarded by a giant stone lion, points to our present time in the cycle of the stars. Should a future civilization become as advanced as ours, they will know we existed and when we disappeared."

Still angry and confused, I spat out, "So what, if all we know is destroyed? Is this arrogance on your part? Some sort of celestial chest thumping to show off? How do you know anyone will ever understand it, if indeed anyone survives what you say is coming?"

Saddened by my rebuke, the giant picked up his robe, shaking the sand from it. The sun was close to breaching the horizon.

"I understand your fear and anger, Ayuba. The stone mountain map is a warning to future peoples that when the stars regain the position of our demise another calamity may ensue. It is not from pride that we make such effort...but from compassion."

The word "compassion" swept away my anger. I felt ashamed of my harsh response. I took his great hand in mine.

"Please don't leave," I pleaded. "I have so many questions."

"I cannot tarry. A ship awaits beyond the offing," he said, gently holding my hand and leading me toward his small boat.

"But I still don't understand why you have burdened me with this knowledge?"

Laying his robe in the boat he turned toward me. The sun reflected from his intelligent eyes. He radiated a peace that washed over me like a soothing balm.

"Your life has been a dream beyond all dreams. Preserve your dream, Ayuba."

"But how?" I cried.

"I came not to tell you how, but to tell you why. In my land there is a fable about the wisest man in the world. It was claimed he knew the answers to all questions. His advice was sought on any important matter. As with all peoples, however, some in the village resented the old man. Two boys decided to create a question to which there was no correct answer. They called all the villagers together and approached the wise old man sitting under a tree.

"'Old man,' one of the boys shouted loudly.

"'Yes,' said the old fellow.

"'Cupped in my hands I have a small bird.' The boys smirked at each other in anticipation of victory. 'Tell me…is the bird alive or dead?'

"If the man answered dead, the boy would release the bird for all to see. If the man answered alive, the boy would crush the bird before opening his hands. No matter how the old man responded, his reputation would be tarnished. The crowd grew quiet as the old man sat thinking.

"Finally the old man said, 'It is in your hands.'"

The "Great Guide" looked deep into my eyes. "Find the song that lives in your dream. Protect it for those who follow." Turning he pushed his boat away from the shore. The sun crept over the edge of the earth as he raised the sail.

Confusion, fear, and awe attended me as I stood on the shore looking out over the sea, watching the sun swallow the small vessel.

I know not who reads this scroll. You exist in a future beyond the calamity predicted by the "Great Guide." How much of Bynethia survived, I cannot know. I have protected the song of my existence as best I could without revealing to the people of Bynethia the tragedy to come. Tomorrow I will secrete this scroll behind the last panel to be installed in the monument honoring the founding of our country. There will be great joy among the citizens.

I have set aside the crushing weight of sadness thrust upon me by the messenger from beyond the curve of the earth, replacing it with the joy of the present. For as I alone know, among all of the peoples of the world… the present is all there is.

To you, dear reader, I say…I have dreamed of you as my pen finishes its journey across the skin of the great beast who saved and nourished me. Dreams are indestructible. My dream is now…in your hands.

Ayuba
Shepherd of Hamood
Father of Bynethia
Master of the Ben
Avenger of the Twan

In the Shadow of Babylon

Hero of the Gleb
Protector of Bensheer
Son of the Beyond

The lion greets the dawn
when day equals night
heralding winter

CHICAGO (2005 CE)

When Alex entered the kitchen pouring her first cup of coffee, Salawa, sitting at the nook, said, "My, don't you look sporty."

It was unusual to see Alex dressed before breakfast. Usually she and Salawa enjoyed a cup of coffee together while still in their robes. Her raven hair in a ponytail stuck out through a black ball cap, and the black jogging pants, red tank-top, and white nylon windbreaker made it clear Alex had other plans for this Saturday morning.

"I'm not sure 'sporty' is a word, but it will do," laughed Alex, sliding into the banquette. "Actually your lovely son is picking me up to go jogging along the lake."

"Oh," said Salawa. "I didn't know he was back from Washington."

"He got in yesterday afternoon. Poor thing was exhausted. Hopefully a good night's rest and some exercise will help him recover."

"I suspect a day alone with you might prove more refreshing than sleep or exercise," Bryan's mother said, smiling over the rim of her cup. The doorbell rang.

"Who could that be at...uhh...nine thirty?" asked Alex, sliding out of the booth.

"Sit...sit...enjoy your coffee. Alana is here, she'll get it. I'll bet it's the FedEx man with the proofs from the Kennedy performance. Dr. Watson promised to send them just as soon as they were available."

～✗～

The hafiz has been right so far, thought Amin, walking up the long brick walkway to Mrs. Feroz's front door. Earlier when the old man stepped in front of the FedEx truck smiling and waving a FedEx package, the driver immediately pulled over to accept the delivery.

"He'll stop because of greed," he'd told Amin.

The hafiz, wearing a ball cap, sweatshirt, and jeans walked to the sliding door on the curbside, the truck shielding him from passing cars. When the driver slid the door open, the old man thrust the gun at his forehead and shot him. The sound of bone and blood against the back wall of the van was louder than the soft "plop" of the silenced 9mm Beretta.

Dressed in his stolen FedEx uniform, Amin climbed into the truck as the hafiz slid the curbside door shut and turned back to the van. The driver lay across a pile of packages. Amin felt sick as he put the truck in gear, turned on the signal, and pulled away from the curb. The smell of blood mixed with the stench from the driver's bowels now seeping through his pants reminded Amin of a slaughterhouse he had visited in Pakistan to learn about thabiha halaal, the approved Muslim way to slaughter animals. *Halaal...that's what it is, a halaal killing. Stop it...* he shouted in his mind. He wanted to laugh but knew it was panic, not humor, gripping him.

Reaching for the bell Amin thought how easy it had been. The way the blond-haired man with the floppy mustache at the Fox Glen guardhouse had smiled and waved him through the fancy iron gates. The old hafiz had been right about everything. Indeed he had figured out the subterfuge of the Ayuba fable long before most of the brothers. The president showing up at the Kennedy Center gala proved what the old scholar had said all along—Ayuba was an evil trick to distract the weak from the true faith.

Amin, his confidence growing, knew it would be easy to kill the two whores inside. Like his father, he was now al Qaeda and hoped soon to become a martyr.

Salawa's part-time housekeeper for twenty years opened the door. She smiled at Amin, holding out her hand for the package. The end of the FedEx box exploded, the bullet ripping through Alana's chest as Amin whispered the traditional blessing used before slaughtering animals...*Bismillah, Allah Akbar*...God is the Greatest.

Stepping over the dead woman, he entered the house.

꘡ꞈꞈ꘡

The thought of spending the entire day with Alex was invigorating. The public presentation of Ayuba was done. Alex's translation work was finished, and much of the supervision and interaction Bryan was involved with had ended on the glorious night at the Kennedy.

Steering his Escalade onto the off ramp at Waterman Avenue he was minutes away from what he thought of as "the rest of his life." He chuckled at the drama that implied.

Since the night he'd almost kissed Alex he'd been dreaming of this day. Although unspoken, he knew she felt the same by the way she leaned into him when walking or held his gaze a microsecond longer than necessary. *Lovers language,* he thought, smiling as the transponder in his car automatically activated the gate at Fox Glen.

Pulling in next to the FedEx van he shut off the engine and stepped from the car, careful not to let his door hit the side of the truck. As he edged between the vehicles he noticed a sickening smell. Glancing through the truck's open window he saw the driver's head lying on a pile of packages in a puddle of congealing blood. Instinctively he reached for the door handle then stopped...there was nothing he could do.

His heart racing, he had trouble thinking. Taking a deep breath he closed his eyes. *This must be the driver... where's the person who...* Crouching, he moved quickly toward the house while dialing 911 on his cell phone. Whispering, he said, "Contact the security detail at Fox Glen. There's been a murder at the Feroz house."

Shutting off the phone so the 911 dispatcher could not call him back, he slipped the phone into his pocket as he rounded the walkway. The front door was open.

Moving fast to the wall adjacent to the door, Bryan slipped off his shoes. He peered around the edge of the door. Alana, eyes wide open, lay spread-eagled in a pool of blood. Her skirt was bunched around her waist, her brown thighs bulging over the tops of her support hose.

A muffled voice came from the kitchen. Stepping over the dead woman, Bryan moved quietly through the living room into the dining room. Flattening himself against the wall, he could see most of the kitchen reflected in the glass covering a painting on the opposite wall. A man was standing facing the breakfast area.

Suddenly the man started yelling in Arabic, "Look at you whores! Two Arabic women who have sullied our religion and our culture!"

Bryan heard his mother's unmistakable voice. "Please, don—"

"Shut up, you old slut."

320

Bryan heard the unmistakable sound of a foot being driven into flesh. A soft, almost sucking sound. Grabbing a large crystal bowl sitting on the table with his right hand and scooping up a chair with his left, Bryan turned toward the kitchen door.

He heard the man cry out, "*Bismillah, Allah Ak—*"

Stepping into the kitchen, Bryan flung the heavy bowl toward the windows on the far side of the room. The skinny young man in the FedEx uniform was aiming a pistol toward the women on the floor. As soon as the bowl was airborne, Bryan charged across the room holding the chair sideways, the seat in front of his chest, the legs toward the man.

When the bowl smashed the window, the boy instinctively turned and fired at the noise. Catching a glimpse of Bryan, he spun away from the window, firing at point blank range. The bullet smashed into the padded seat of the chair as Bryan lunged. He later recalled, with some amazement, the voice of Bob Ryan, his high school football coach...*block through your target, not at it, otherwise you'll bounce off.*

The brace between the chair legs caught the man under his chin, slamming into his throat. Legs pumping, Bryan pushed him back toward the broken window. The gun discharged again then went spinning toward the refrigerator.

Out of the corner of his eye Bryan saw his mother on her knees, her face against the floor, her robe over her head. Alex was struggling to get between the man and Salawa.

When the man hit the sill of the shattered window, Bryan kept churning his legs, thrusting the chair frame against his neck, grinding it into the shards of broken glass until he felt the man go limp.

The student movement, bearing the symbolic stripe over the left eye, had grown substantially. From silent demonstrations that captured the imagination of the world, the students' new technique was to appear on the scene after any act of violence, giving comfort and sympathy to survivors and loved ones of the victims. With great solemnity they moved among the shattered, embracing and praying with them.

Media reporters were surprised how the students almost always arrived at the tragic scenes before them. The students became known as "Dreamers" because of their silence and because of Ayuba's faith in the power of dreams. None had ever granted an interview, content that their actions spoke for them.

Two months after the last airing of *Ayuba*, a suicide bomber blew himself up on a busy Baghdad street, killing twelve men standing in line to buy lottery tickets for an air conditioner. In minutes the Dreamers began arriving. Within half an hour the street was filled with the silent demonstrators, many with tears smearing the black slash on their cheeks.

With the news media present, a second bomber set off his deadly device. The few cameras not destroyed by the powerful explosion captured the gruesome scene as the dismembered bodies of the Dreamers tumbled like dolls smashing into one another…a wave of flesh, bone, and blood.

Western television networks refused to show the gruesome footage, but Al Jazeera and other Middle Eastern news outlets took a different view.

"We are not here to edit reality," said the president of Al Jazeera when criticized by an American news executive.

The morning after what became known as the Lottery Massacre, the square that once housed the famous statue of Saddam Hussein began to fill with demonstrators. News outlets spread the word and soon images of the giant square were beamed throughout the world. The now familiar sober faces of the children with the black eye stripe were accompanied by grown women—the mothers, sisters, and friends of the children who, with their quiet bravery, had shown the world they would no longer remain silent in the face of terror disguised as religion.

Some of the mullahs interviewed on local radio stations condemned the women for violating their pledge to honor their husbands. Advocates of women's rights made the case that women had been silent too long and it was only fitting mothers should support their children.

❧

In the first class lounge at O'Hare Airport, Bryan and Alex watched the remarkable events unfold.

"It's the first time I've been glad a plane was late," whispered Bryan.

Fully recovered from the horror of the attack at Fox Glen three months earlier, the two were on their way to the Sorbonne in Paris to lecture on the significance of the Ayubian discovery.

"Me too," said Alex, squeezing Bryan's hand. "Do you think this could be the tipping point?"

"God, I hope so...these poor people have suffered so much."

The Fox News camera in Baghdad slowly pulled back from the close-up shot trying to encompass the extent of the gathering, but the range of its lens proved inadequate.

"We have brought you many horrible scenes from Baghdad over the years," the announcer said, "but this … uh…this tribute to the one hundred twenty-seven children and twelve adults killed yesterday in the Lottery Massacre is beyond anything we've seen before. It was only a few weeks ago, when stimulated by the ancient 'Song of Ayuba,' these children began staging silent protests all over Iraq. The black line they paint across their left eye, as most people now know, is called Al Darem's Horror and represents the escaped slaves' dedication and courage. Most people believed, as did this reporter, that the terrorists would never attack children…not because they're incapable of such horror, but because the backlash might turn the vast silent majority of Muslims against them. Of course, the slaughter yesterday proves the terrorists are simply that…terrorists."

"Look at all the women," Alex said.

"Yeah…I wonder where the men are?" Bryan said with some disgust.

More than half the crowd was women, their hijabs clearly identifiable among the uncovered heads of the children.

"There's some sort of demonstration over on the eastern side of the square. Amal, can you pan over there?" said the Fox reporter. The camera zoomed in on a line of burka-clad women carrying what appeared to be a long pole. The crowd of demonstrators parted to let them pass.

"I can't tell what it is they're carrying," said the reporter, "but whatever it is, the women carrying it are

324

either very devout—as are most who wear the burka, the gown you see covering every part of their face and body—or they don't want to be identified with whatever it is they're about to do."

"What is it?" Alex asked, leaning toward the screen.

"It looks like some sort of sign or poster," ventured a gray-haired women sitting next to Bryan and Alex in the lounge.

"Ladies and gentlemen, it's probably difficult for you to understand how silent it is here. This is the quietest demonstration I've ever seen. There are no chants, cat-calls, speeches. Just the sound of thousands...weeping."

"Okay, here goes," said Bryan as the women stopped in the center of the square. Countless hands reached out to tilt the pole upright. As it was raised it became apparent it was wrapped in cloth.

"It appears to be a banner," the announcer said once the pole was erect.

The upright pole was balanced by several women. Children, grasping ropes leading from the top and bottom edges of the cloth, began to unfurl the giant scroll.

As the Arabic characters came into view, Alex began to cry. Putting his arm over her shoulder, Bryan remarked, "My god, that's incredible."

The gray-haired lady asked, "What does it say?"

Smiling through her tears, Alex said, "It's in our hands."

End

Made in the USA
Charleston, SC
09 August 2012